ALSO BY BRIGID KEMMERER

DEST
TH
DA

DESTROY THE DAY

BRIGID KEMMERER

BLOOMSBURY

NEW YORK LONDON OXFORD NEW DELHI SYDNEY

BLOOMSBURY YA
Bloomsbury Publishing Inc., part of Bloomsbury Publishing Plc
1385 Broadway, New York, NY 10018

BLOOMSBURY and the Diana logo are trademarks of Bloomsbury Publishing Plc

First published in the United States of America in January 2024
by Bloomsbury YA

Text copyright © 2024 by Brigid Kemmerer
Map by Virginia Allyn

Bloomsbury books may be purchased for business or promotional use.
For information on bulk purchases please contact Macmillan Corporate and
Premium Sales Department at specialmarkets@macmillan.com

Library of Congress Cataloging-in-Publication Data
available upon request
ISBN 978-1-5476-1323-6 (hardcover) • ISBN 978-1-5476-1324-3 (e-book)
ISBN 978-1-5476-1556-8 (exclusive edition A) • ISBN 978-1-5476-1531-5 (exclusive edition B)

Book design by Jeanette Levy
Typeset by Westchester Publishing Services
Printed and bound in the U.S.A.
2 4 6 8 10 9 7 5 3 1

To find out more about our authors and books visit
www.bloomsbury.com and sign up for our newsletters.

For my boys

who love each other so very, very much

KINGDOMS OF OSTRIARY

KAISA

ESTAR

FAIRDE

ROSHAN

SILVESSE

THE POLITICAL LEADERS OF KANDALA

NAME	ROLE	SECTOR
King Harristan	King	Royal
Prince Corrick	King's Justice	Royal
Barnard Montague (Deceased)	Consul	Trader's Landing*
Allisander Sallister	Consul	Moonlight Plains
Leander Craft (Deceased)	Consul	Steel City
Jonas Beeching	Consul	Artis
Lissa Marpetta	Consul	Emberridge
Roydan Pelham	Consul	The Sorrowlands
Arella Cherry	Consul	Sunkeep
Jasper Gold	Consul	Mosswell

*Sometimes called "Traitor's Landing" after the former king and queen were assassinated by Consul Montague, leaving Harristan and his younger brother, Corrick, in power.

THE REBELS

NAME	ROLE
Tessa	Apothecary*
Karri	Apothecary
Lochlan	Metalworker

*Now working in service to the king

WANTED FOR TREASON

NAME	ROLE
King Harristan	King
Quint Rifield	Palace Master
Adam Saeth	Royal Guard
Benjamin Thorin	Royal Guard

THE CURE

In Kandala, the only known cure for the fever sickness is an elixir created from dried Moonflower petals, a plant native only to two sectors: Moonlight Plains and Emberridge. King Harristan and Prince Corrick tightly control the supply to ensure fair market dealings and distributions, and to prevent smuggling and thievery.

DESTROY
THE
DAY

CHAPTER ONE

Corrick

I've lost track of the days.

I should've kept track. Prisoners in the Hold used to scratch lines into the walls, though they rarely got more than five.

This feels like more than that.

A lot more.

The first burst of sunlight peeks between the trees that I can see from the bars of our cell. It's not really a *cell* at all, more of a cave set deep in the woods of whatever island we're on. We're a good distance from wherever the pirates live, because unless they come to us, we never hear them: no talking, no shouting, no sounds of life at all. The cave runs deep underground, until the light disappears and we can hear water, but the walls go too narrow, leaving us with no exit that way. Bars block the entrance, fixed and mortared into the stone. Lochlan and I spent our early days testing every bar, every joint, every hinge. But despite the salty sea air and the rainstorms that drive us back below cover, the bars and mortar stand strong.

A well-constructed prison.

When I was locked in the Hold in Kandala, it felt like poetic justice.

It shouldn't feel like it now, but it does.

Footsteps crunch through the underbrush somewhere among the trees, but I don't sit up. This will be our breakfast.

I've stopped caring. I roll over and face the cave wall, pulling farther into the shadows.

The crunching stops, followed by a slide of metal against stone.

"Food, boys," a woman calls. It's Lina, one of Oren Crane's people. She whistles a few short notes, like we're caged dogs. "Come eat now."

I ignore her. I ignore all of them.

Lochlan doesn't say anything either. I wonder if he's asleep.

I don't care.

"Oren will be back soon," she says. "You'd best be ready. He'll have a plan for you, Wes. You want to keep that pretty head on your shoulders, you're going to do what he says."

Wes. The name tugs at me, reminding me of nights in the Wilds with Tessa. Her quiet smile, her quick hands, her gentle manner. Her intelligence. Her *bravery.* I fell in love with her by moonlight.

My heart clenches. I have to shove these thoughts away.

I can't be Weston Lark here. Wes was warm and kind and rarely had a harsh word for anyone.

If Weston Lark were real, he'd probably be dead already.

Weston Lark *was* dead already. I thought Tessa would never forgive me for it.

And now I'm sure she thinks I'm dead for a second time. Or is this the third? I've lost track.

I might as well be. I close my eyes.

Eventually, Lina gives up on our silence. Her feet crunch through the undergrowth again, and we're alone.

The scent of the food doesn't take long to reach me. Some kind of meat, and what smells like fresh-baked bread. They only feed us twice a day, so I should be starving, but I'm not. I stopped caring about food *days* ago. Birds chirp somewhere out in the trees, waking in the sunlight, but I burrow more deeply under my sparse blanket, pulling my jacket tightly against myself.

Not *my* jacket. *Harristan's* jacket.

I'll never see my brother again.

I try to shove this thought away too, but I'm not quick enough. My throat tightens and my eyes go hot. I hold my breath so I don't make a sound.

Maybe I'll hold it long enough that I'll suffocate and die.

"Hey."

Lochlan's voice. I ignore him, too.

"You need to eat," he calls.

A tear rolls out of my eye, making a path across my cheek.

I bite the side of my tongue until the pain chases away my emotion, and then I duck my face into the blanket and swipe the tear off.

The last time I cried, I was in a cell, too. I was on my knees, facing my brother.

"You didn't eat anything yesterday," Lochlan is saying. "Wes—you *need* to eat."

Wes. I hate that he calls me that. He started doing it when we washed up onshore, so the pirates wouldn't know I was the prince, but the name reminds me too much of everything I've lost.

I have to duck my face into the blanket again.

"Hey." His voice is closer, right behind me. "Get up."

I don't want to get up. My throat is still tight and my eyes are hot and I want him to go away.

Lochlan pokes me in the shoulder. "*Get up.* Eat."

I grit my teeth. "Leave me alone."

"No." He pokes me again. "Stop wallowing and get up."

"I'm not wallowing."

I am absolutely wallowing.

This time he tugs at my shoulder. "Stop being a baby," he says. "Get up, Wes."

"Stop calling me that."

"Fine." His voice drops, and it sounds like he's crouching behind me, leaning in. "Get up, *Corrick*."

My given name sounds like an insult. "*Go away.*"

"No." He smacks me on the back of the head, *hard*.

It's so startling that I whip around, throwing the blanket back. I inhale to snap at him, but he's ready for it. He claps me on the ear like I'm a child, sending me sprawling a little. "That's right," he taunts. "*Move*, Cory."

That does it. I growl and launch myself at him with enough force that he goes skidding into the dirt. I try to swing a fist, but he dodges most of my blows, and we roll, grappling for purchase, snarling with anger.

But he's right that I haven't been eating, and he's able to pin me to the ground a lot more easily than I'd like. He straddles my waist and puts an arm across my neck until it's hard to breathe, and he's bearing down on one arm so I can't swing at him anymore.

I have the pleasure of seeing blood on his lip, though. I strain against his hold and wonder if he'll break my neck.

He glares down at me, panting. "Lord, you fight like a wildcat. Are you ready to eat now?"

"Get off me," I grind out. Blood is bitter on my tongue.

"Breakfast?"

"Go to hell, Lochlan."

He leans close. His black hair hangs into his eyes, lank and filthy from our days locked in this cell. I'm sure I'm no better. "So this is all it would've taken to break the King's Justice?" he says. "A few days in a cage?"

I spit blood at him. "Eat shit."

"Well, that's not very princely." He reaches for something, and I try to take advantage of his moment of distraction to wrench free, but he's too quick. Lochlan grabs a fistful of my hair and twists it tight.

It's so sharp and unexpectedly painful that it pulls a yelp from my throat. I grab hold of his wrist, but his grip on my hair is too tight and I just hurt myself. "What the hell is *wrong* with—"

"Here." He holds a biscuit in front of my face. "Eat it and I'll let you go."

I stare at him like he's crazy.

He gives my hair another wrench. "*Eat*, you idiot!"

"Fine!" I bite into the biscuit and tear a piece free.

Lochlan looks at me like he's waiting to make sure I chew, so I do, glaring at him petulantly the whole time. It's not the *most* humiliating thing I've ever done, but it likely ranks among the top five.

"Good," he says. He finally lets go of my hair and climbs off me.

I launch myself at him again *immediately*.

This time he ends up with a scrape down the side of his face, and he'll probably have a black eye by nightfall. Unfortunately, so will I. This struggle ends with me facedown and inhaling dirt, his knee in my back, his hand twisting my hair again.

He finds the biscuit where it fell, blows dirt off the edge, and holds it in front of my face. "Ready for more?"

I inhale to tell him something even less princely, but it's like the first bite of biscuit woke my stomach. I actually am hungry now.

"Let me up," I grind out. "I'll eat."

I expect him to force-feed me each bite anyway, but to my surprise, he lets me go. I gingerly rearrange my limbs until I'm sitting cross-legged, and I swipe the biscuit from his hand. I tear another piece free and chew, and suddenly it's all I can do to keep from shoving the whole thing in my mouth.

"Slow," Lochlan says. "It won't do either of us any good if you throw it all up."

"Shut up." I don't look at him. I shove hair back from my face and try to ignore the ache in my scalp from where he yanked.

But I force myself to take small bites, because he's right.

The sun has risen further, bright through the trees. It makes my head ache. I want to curl up in the corner again.

Lochlan rises to his knees, and I tense, ready for him to attack me again, but he just holds out a small steel cup of water. "You need to drink, too," he says.

I don't take it. "What do you care?"

"If you make me hold you down and pour it down your throat, we'll end up wasting half."

I glare back at him—but he's likely serious, so I take the cup, then take a sip.

I follow it with a longer swallow, because he was right about the water, too. By the time I set down the cup, I'm looking for the rest of the food that Lina brought.

There are boiled eggs and roasted chicken legs and salted potatoes that have been cooked so long that the skin has gone crispy, the insides soft. Surprisingly good food for prisoners, but I suspect this is just whatever is left over from the food that Oren Crane's people prepare for themselves. I didn't get a *good* look at them in the darkness of that first night, but there were only ten of them on the beach, and it probably would've been more work to prepare us something less filling.

Lochlan sits across from me, eating his own. "And you were going to turn this down," he says, mildly chiding.

I keep my eyes on my food. I still haven't really looked at him. My pride is smarting from the way he pinned me to the ground and shoved a biscuit in my face. "You should've left me alone, and you could've had twice as much."

"I'm not watching you kill yourself."

That draws my gaze up. He's not looking at me either. His eyes are shadowed, his heavily freckled skin more tanned from our days on the *Dawn Chaser*. His sleeves are rolled back, revealing a dozen burn scars along his forearms, likely earned from working in the forges in Steel City. I broke his left wrist weeks ago, but he's long since lost the bandage he was wearing on the ship. It can't be fully healed yet, but it's not like we're getting any medical attention in this cell.

And he sure didn't have any trouble fighting me to the ground.

I scowl and look back at my food.

"When we were desperate for medicine," Lochlan says quietly, "we had rules drilled into us. For . . . for when we were caught."

There's a note in his voice that draws my attention up again.

He tears a piece of chicken from the bone with his teeth. He's still not looking at me. "The most important one was to never stop eating. If food's put in front of you, you eat it. If water's there, you drink it. Wasting food only spites yourself. Being weak only helps your captors." He pauses, and his voice is grave. "If you're breathing, you're alive. If you're alive, there's still hope. Don't undo it on your own."

I stare at him.

He shrugs a little. "I should've made you eat yesterday. I forgot that a spoiled prince in the palace wouldn't have learned that lesson."

I should bristle, but I don't. He's right. I didn't learn that lesson.

I learned different ones.

I narrow my eyes at him. "You're a funny one to lecture me about hope, Lochlan."

He tears another piece. "Well, I made it out of the Hold," he says slowly. "Then I made it off your stage, and that was with a hood over my head and a crossbow jabbed in my back." He shrugs. "I made it out of the Circle, when I thought your brother was going to have the army kill us all. And then I made it off that stupid ship." He looks up, his eyes a little fierce. "Still breathing."

I take a breath and tear a piece of my own chicken. I suppose he's got me there.

Still breathing.

Silence falls between us, and I don't like it. I'm rattled now, agitated. I don't know if it's the food or the fight, but I've woken up, and there's nowhere to go.

"What were the other rules?" I say.

"Always have fake names ready to offer, if you're questioned. If you're running from the night patrol, grab a wheelbarrow and walk. No one stops someone with a wheelbarrow." He hesitates, and his eyes hold mine. "If you get close to the prince, use whatever you can to hurt him."

I drain my cup and pour more from the water skin. "Do you want to pull my hair again?" I say flatly.

"A little."

"What, are you six years old?" I demand. "Who fights like that?"

"It worked, didn't it?"

I scowl. He grins darkly and tears another piece of chicken.

My thoughts are turning clearer. The food really is helping. I feel less like crying and more like *doing* something. Unfortunately, we're still locked in a cell.

I have no idea how to get us out of here. Harristan won't know we're missing for *weeks*. Rian, formerly Captain Blakemore, and currently the king of Ostriary, likely thinks we're dead—if he cares at all. I don't know what Oren Crane will do with me, but he's not in power here. Even if I tell him who I really am, I don't think he'd trust me. And I don't think offering steel from Kandala would give him leverage. Not yet, anyway.

Then again, these pirates left us alive, so they must see *some* advantage to keeping us here.

Oren will be back soon. He'll have a plan for you, Wes.

I don't know what that plan could be. On the first night, I tried to fight Oren Crane. I tried to kill him. I tried to run.

He laughed in my face. Then he locked us in here.

I look at Lochlan again. He's the worst person I could be trapped with. I can name a hundred others who would be more convenient than a man who spends every hour of his life *hating* me.

Then again, he cut me loose on the ship when Rian had me tied to the mast. And he was smart enough to give me a false name in front of Oren Crane. I might be in a cell, but as far as the pirates are concerned, I'm just a servant. A potential source of information, nothing more.

A prince of Kandala would be a source of leverage. Against Harristan for sure—and potentially against Rian, too, considering what he needs. A political prisoner. Whatever the pirates do to Weston Lark, it's not going to be half as bad as what they could do with Prince Corrick—and I have Lochlan to thank for that.

I strip the last piece of chicken from the bone.

Lochlan made me eat, too.

I'm not watching you kill yourself.

No, it's more than that. I study him, trying to figure out his angle.

He peers at me from under a fall of hair. "Why are you looking at me like that?" he says.

"I'm trying to figure out why you care if I live or die."

He shrugs and says nothing.

"I was tied to a mast on the ship. You could've killed me and all your problems would've been over."

He spreads his hands, gesturing around the cell. "Really? You think so?"

Well, no. Maybe not. I sigh and turn my attention back to the food.

But then my hands go still. Lochlan once figured out that Prince Corrick and Weston Lark were the same person, and he was savvy enough to find my workshop in the Wilds. He trapped me and Tessa, then led a mob to attack me. And as much as I hate him, Lochlan was also smart enough to lead rebels into the Royal Sector and imprison the consuls. That took strategy and planning.

He also spoke up for me on the ship, when I worried things were going to unravel with Rian. Things could have gone very poorly, and he saw a chance to help defuse the tension.

I remember sitting around a table in the palace during one of the few meetings between the rebels and the consuls that resulted from the attempt at revolution. Consul Sallister was speaking with nothing but disdain, while Lochlan was sitting there seething. On the ship, Lochlan confronted me about the way Sallister committed far more egregious crimes than Lochlan ever had, but the consul faced no penalties at all—just because he was a man of wealth and power. There was more to it than that, but at its base level, there was truth to it.

Everyone sat at that table and treated Lochlan like an uneducated fool. He was belligerent and angry, but now, looking back, I can't really blame him.

He wasn't a fool, though. We were, for underestimating him.

I can't imagine he wants me for an ally, but maybe he sees no other choice.

"We need to get back to Kandala," I say quietly. "But if we get out of this cage, I'm going for Tessa first. I'm not going back without her."

"Me too. Karri would never forgive me if I left her here."

Oh. He keeps surprising me.

"Rocco as well," I add. *If he survived.* But I don't say that. I hope he survived. I hope Tessa isn't alone.

Lochlan studies me anyway. "He was badly injured."

I frown, remembering the stab wound in my guardsman's waist. "If they die . . ." My voice trails off, and I feel a clenching in my belly. Rian was responsible for all of this. I think of all his lies, the way he judged *me* for my crimes, while ignoring his own. I think of the way he stood on his ship and told me that the people in Kandala weren't sick from a fever at all, but that they were being poisoned somehow. Rage surges in my belly, hot and sudden. "I'm going to kill Rian."

"Good. I'll help. But go back to the part about us getting out of here." Lochlan glances at the bars. "Lina said Oren would be back soon, so we don't know how much time we have."

"If Oren is coming back," I say, "it might be our only chance out of this cage. We need to make a plan."

"Well, we have no weapons, and we're clearly outnumbered. What else do you have in mind, *Weston Lark*?"

For an instant, my chest tightens. There's so much at stake, and panic threatens to overwhelm me. But I think of Harristan and Kandala, of everything that's gone wrong. Of every promise I've ever made to Tessa. Of wanting to do better. To *be* better. Of everyone and everything I might never see again. Of everyone I've failed—including the man in front of me.

I've had to play a thousand roles to help my brother hold Kandala together. I can play one more.

I take a breath. *Still breathing.*

"His daughter, Bella, was on that ship," I say. "So he's going to hate Rian as much as we do. We'll need to think of something to offer him. Something that will grant us a little freedom."

Lochlan's eyes light with surprise, and then he smiles a little dangerously, a little ruefully. "I've been waiting for you to wake up."

I don't smile back. "Maybe you should've picked a fight days ago."

"Welcome back, Your Highness."

CHAPTER TWO

Tessa

In any other situation, an isolated house on the beach might be paradise.

As it is, I can't wait to leave. Unfortunately, I have nowhere to go.

Worse, I have no *way* to go.

At first, Rian tried to convince me to stay in his palace. He made a lot of promises about how it would be safer, how he could ensure my comfort, how I would be given space to grieve my losses.

I told him I would find a way to slit his throat in his sleep if he didn't find us somewhere else. I've heard enough empty promises, and I've been betrayed by too many men. I've seen enough death and destruction to last a dozen lifetimes.

So now Rocco and I share a large house on the east side of the island. No, *Erik* and I. I still haven't gotten used to calling him by his first name—though he hasn't really stopped calling me *Miss Tessa* either. We're both a little raw, a little empty. Every time I look at him, I think of Corrick being blown off the deck of the ship, and my throat swells. I think of Kilbourne being killed in the hallway, or Lochlan being lost at sea.

Honestly, once the *Dawn Chaser* docked, Rian could have spared himself the trouble. I didn't need a house at all. There was a part of me that wanted to walk straight into the ocean and never look back.

But I can't. I need to figure out a way to return to Kandala.

I need to tell the king what happened to his brother.

I need to tell Karri what happened to Lochlan.

And I can't leave Erik either. He still has a healing knife wound in his side. I've been treating it every day with turmeric and tallow root, but it still looks a bit infected.

So I wake every morning, and I force myself out of bed, even though every fiber of my being wants me to hide in the darkness forever.

But at least Rian leaves us alone.

The house is far larger than we need, with four wide bedrooms, a sprawling sitting room, and even a well-outfitted kitchen with two ovens. A house built for a big family, clearly. One of the bedrooms even has two sets of bunkbeds, with whimsical creatures painted on the walls, and a few forgotten toys left under a bed. A children's room. It makes me wonder what happened to them, because the house was dusty and locked up when Rian first showed us to the door. I've heard there's electricity on some of the islands, but not in this part of Fairde. I don't mind, though. Electricity is a luxury I never grew accustomed to, even when I was living in the palace in Kandala's Royal Sector.

The house has a small stable, a paddock, a chicken coop, and a rabbit hutch—though they're all empty. No livestock. Rian offered to have horses and chickens brought, which I declined—though Erik later told me I should have accepted, because we don't know how large the island is, and we don't know when we might have a need or opportunity to travel. We don't know how easy food will be to come by.

I scowled at that, because it's smart. I can't let my grief-stricken anger make me stupid.

We're near the water, too, with a long stretch of beach behind the house, and a small dock that has two aged rowboats tied up. On the second day, Rian arrived with men to outfit the house with furniture and clothes and as much food as they could carry, and this time I held my tongue. He also brought any of our trunks from the *Dawn Chaser* that survived the journey. I sat outside in the sand and watched the waves roll up the beach while they unloaded the goods. The whole time, I imagined holding Rian under the water until he drowned.

I sat, tense, waiting for him to come find me anyway, but he didn't. Later, Erik told me that Rian said he would give me space until I was ready to talk about whatever else I might need.

He can't give me what I need.

I *need* to reverse time. I *need* Corrick back. Sometimes I remember his voice so clearly it's like he's beside me, and the memory is so painful that I think my chest is caving in.

Please, my love.

In the cavernous house, I don't sleep well. Every time I close my eyes, I'm haunted by dreams of Corrick being blown off the ship, his body torn apart by a cannonball. Worse are the dreams where I see him treading water in the dark, waiting for the ship to turn back—but of course we don't. In those dreams he screams my name until he slips under the water and drowns.

In the mornings, I sit on the beach. Fog usually hovers over the water at dawn, but once it clears, two other islands of Ostriary appear in the distance, along with the faint outlines of the bridges that Rian needs Kandala's steel to rebuild.

I spend a lot of time staring at the water, waiting.

I'm not sure what I'm waiting for. It's not like Corrick is coming back from the dead.

I can't help staring out at the waves, though, as if he'll do exactly that. Like I could sit here long enough and he'll come strolling up the sand one day, an apparition appearing out of the fog. *Lord, Tessa. Mind your mettle.*

Sometimes my waking thoughts are worse than my nightmares. I can't breathe through the pain when I think like this.

By the time I wake on the ninth day, we haven't seen a soul in at least a week, and it seems that Rian really is going to give me the space he promised. That's good, because I don't know how I'm ever going to face him again. At the same time, I know I'm eventually going to need him to get us back to Kandala.

I don't want to see him. I'm not ready.

But Erik must be done with living like a ghost, because he finds me trailing my fingers in the cool sand at sunrise, and when I look up, I see he's got fishing nets over one broad shoulder.

"Come on." His voice is rough and quiet from disuse, because we don't say much to each other. He's just as trapped by grief and loss and uncertainty as I am. "Let's see how much life the rowboats have in them."

I peer up at him in the sunlight. "I don't think you should be rowing yet."

"Well." He squints out at the pier. "Maybe I'll just see what kind of shape they're in then." He gives me a nod, hoists the nets higher on his shoulder, then strides off.

Something in his voice tells me he's going out on a rowboat whether I like it or not. I imagine him getting fatigued out in the middle of the ocean while the oars slip into the water. Then I'd really be alone.

I shove myself to my bare feet, brushing sand off my trousers. "At least let me take a look at your wound first."

He looks at me over his shoulder. "It looks better this morning. Hardly aches at all."

"Hmm." I don't believe that for a *minute.*

"I need to move, Miss Tessa."

That makes me frown.

He looks back again. His brown eyes skip over my face and down my form. "You need to move, too."

I don't know how to say that I don't want to leave the sand in case Corrick comes looking for me. It feels pathetic to even *think* it. Corrick is never coming back.

I swallow the lump in my throat and follow him out onto the dock.

Both rowboats are covered with broadcloth tarps, though one is worn and threadbare. The second is larger, and the tarp is sun-bleached, the ropes tethering it to the dock looking like they might fall apart if we dare to touch them. Erik wordlessly starts untying the threadbare one, so I move to the other.

The knots are dry-rotted, so they don't untie at all. They literally fall apart in my fingers.

I grimace and look at Erik. "Sorry."

"Don't be. These have been tethered here forever. It's a lucky thing they're still floating. We'll have to ask Rian for more broadcloth."

"*You* can ask him."

He nods. "I will." Then he jerks back the threadbare tarp, and enough dust flies up that we both cough.

Erik winces and grabs his side after he does.

He sees me looking and drops his hand, but there's still a pained look in his expression. *Hardly aches at all*, my foot.

But he looks between the boats and says, "This one looks solid. Just old. But no oars. How's yours?"

That spurs me into motion, and I jerk the sun-bleached tarp free. Less dust, but a dozen spiders scatter in the sudden sunlight, and I shriek and drop the tarp in the water, scrambling back on the dock.

Erik smiles, but just a little—then he stares down into the boat and does a double take. "Oh! A sailboat. Look. Yours has a mast."

I look, and he's right. There are four small benches across the boat, but in the very center is a hole set into a plank at the bottom, and laid along the benches sits a beam that must be designed to set upright as a mast, plus a shorter one that must serve as a boom.

"No sail, though," I say.

"I'll check in the shed where I found the nets, but if there isn't one, I'll ask Rian for one of those, too," he says.

I'll ask Rian. I clench my jaw.

Erik looks at me. "Let's move the beam onto the dock. We can row for now. I think I see some oars."

The wood is heavier than I expect, but we manage. I force myself to ignore the bloom of sweat on Erik's forehead once we're done. He tosses the nets into the hull, then steps down into the boat himself.

He looks a bit pale, so I don't follow him. "You *really* shouldn't be rowing," I say.

"I won't," he says. "I'll get us out from the dock, and then you can row."

"I—" I let out a breath. That isn't what I meant. But again, I think of him passing out a mile away from shore, leaving me with no way to rescue him. "I don't really know how to row."

"I'll show you."

I chew at my lip doubtfully, and I glance out at the water.

"You asked me to teach you how to fight, Miss Tessa." His voice is gentle, but firm. "I can't teach you how to fight if you can barely pick yourself up off the beach."

My face threatens to crumple. I asked him that when I was racked with grief, when Corrick had first disappeared into the darkening waves, when I thought nothing could ever cause me more pain, and I wanted to know the best way to lash out against it.

Just now, I want to go back to the beach and curl up in the sand.

I have to put a hand against my face. The tears swell before I can stop them, and I try to sniff them back. I'm barely successful.

Erik puts out a hand. "Come on. Maybe we can catch something good and have a better dinner than salted beef and cheese."

I swipe at my cheeks. "I'm an apothecary, not a cook. I don't know how to gut fish."

"So we'll learn how to row *and* gut fish."

It should make me smile, but it doesn't.

Then Erik says, "It's been over a week now. If I leave you here, Rian might show up to check on us, and you'd have to talk to him on your own."

Well, that does the trick. I practically *leap* into the boat. It rocks a bit from the force of my movement, and Erik smiles. He points to the rope tethering the boat to the dock. "Unwind that from the cleat, and I'll push us off."

When I do, he uses an oar to shove us away from the dock, then drops to sit on a bench across from me. The oars settle into two gaps along the rail of the boat, and I see that they have tiny notches cut into the wood to prevent them from slipping into the water. Maybe I didn't need to worry after all.

I reach for the oars, but Erik shakes his head. "I'll get us out. Watch."

He dips the oars in the water and pulls rhythmically, lifting and folding with each stroke as if he's been rowing boats all his life. He explains each movement as he does it, showing me how to keep my body upright, to use the current. He's not moving fast, but each pull is strong, and the small boat cuts through the water with ease, and within a minute, we're far from the dock. A breeze cools my cheeks, drying the tears, and I take a deep breath.

"Do you want me to take over?" I say.

"Not yet."

I think of what he said before. *I need to move.*

"Don't be *too* stubborn," I say.

He smiles. "Yes, Miss Tessa."

"How do you know about boats and fishing?" I say.

"I grew up in Sunkeep," he says as he rows. "Most of my family are sailors. My brother and his wife sail the trade route between Sunkeep and Steel City, and I often join them whenever I have a long enough leave. That's partly why—" He breaks off sharply, studying me.

I can't read his expression. "Why what?" I finally say.

"I'm not sure how much to say." He sighs, aggrieved, and looks out at the water himself. "Maybe it doesn't make any difference."

I turn that around in my head, because I can't figure it out. Maybe I've been sitting on the beach for too long. "How much to say about what?"

He gives me a look. "The king's business."

"Oh."

Erik nods. "*Oh.*"

He rows on in silence for a little while, and I realize for the first time that Erik must have a *lot* of secrets. He was part of King Harristan's personal guard. He was by the king's side all the time, overhearing all manner of conversations.

That's a little intriguing, and I tilt my head and look at him. "What's the worst secret you've ever had to keep?"

He smiles furtively. "I don't recall."

"Liar. Did you ever have to keep secrets from Corrick?"

As soon as I ask the question, I think it's foolish. Corrick was the King's Justice. Anything having to do with Kandala was his business. I can't imagine Harristan using his guards to keep secrets from his brother.

But Erik nods. "Sometimes," he says.

"*Really.*"

He grunts. "Well, the prince kept some secrets himself, I think." He gives me a more pointed look this time.

I suppose that's true. Corrick hid his identity so well as Weston Lark that I had a hard time believing it when the prince tried to reveal the truth.

But at least this line of conversation has given me a bit of distraction. "Can you tell me *anything* interesting?"

He looks out at the water, considering, then sighs. "Most everything I know is boring, Miss Tessa. Truly. The consuls never wanted to speak with His Majesty on anything very exciting. Most of them just liked to hear themselves talk. You were *there* for the exciting parts."

I frown. The sad thing is that's probably true.

"Here, I'll give you this much," he says, and he drops his voice just a little, as if we're not a good distance from the shore, with no audience except the sea and sky. "Captain Blakemore—well, *Rian*—refused to have sailors aboard the *Dawn Chaser*. Do you remember?"

I nod. "He said he didn't want to lead navigators to Ostriary. He didn't want to teach anyone how to get through Chaos Isle, because he was worried about leading a military force here."

"Yes. But the king wanted Prince Corrick to have someone competent on board, someone who could sail the ship just in case . . . in case it was necessary. I have experience at sea, so I volunteered. Kilbourne did too. That's why I chose him. He'd done summer work on the docks in Artis as a boy."

Someone who could sail the ship just in case.

As I consider the words, I remember Rian preparing to kill Erik, the morning everything fell apart on his ship. *He's a sailor,* he said. *Proof that Prince Corrick didn't honor our agreement.* I didn't really think about what that meant then, but I do now, and it chases away some of the intrigue.

I swallow thickly, remembering how I practically begged Corrick to get on that ship. I listened to Rian's stories of having acres of Moonflower, of the way he wanted to help his people, and I fell for every lie.

But apparently no one else did.

"So you never trusted Rian," I say quietly.

"No."

He says it so simply, while a bonfire of rage burns in my chest every time I think of Rian.

Maybe that's why Erik can ask for things like tarps and sails, while I'm content to envision holding the captain under the waves while he slowly drowns.

Erik keeps rowing, and I stare out at the water. Sunlight glistens on the surface, and it really is peaceful. Off to our left, the shore is an empty stretch of sand, as if our house is the only one on the whole island. When the *Dawn Chaser* was arriving to Fairde, I could see Rian's palace from the water, but it must be on the other side, because it's out of sight from here.

Good.

I listen to Erik's breathing, waiting to hear any sign of strain, but he's been talking like we're still standing on the dock. He's nearly twice my size, with muscles to spare, so I shouldn't be surprised, but I don't want him to regret this later.

I keep my eyes on the water and say, "Poor Kilbourne's wife won't even know what happened to him." My throat threatens to tighten again, and I swallow. The guardsman was so excited to have a baby. He wanted to buy his wife a house. "Sara, right?"

He nods. "We'll find a way back. I'll tell her."

I realize that Erik might have someone missing him just as much, and I've been so wrapped up in my own grief that I haven't even asked him. "What about you? Do you have a sweetheart waiting for you at home?"

He startles at that, then smiles just a little. "No. The pay is good in the palace guard, but the hours can be long. Duties are unpredictable, especially in service to the king. Secrets to be kept, lies to be told. The risk is high, especially in the last year. I've seen just as many marriages end as I've seen start. Not the best way to begin a life with someone."

I start to say that Kilbourne made it work—but maybe this is exactly the risk that Erik is talking about.

Erik shrugs. "Someone else is always a priority. I feel like that would just be a disappointment to a wife."

"Well, that sounds lonely."

His smile turns a bit wolfish. "I never said I was *lonely*."

I gasp in surprise, then scoop up a handful of water and splash it at him. "*Erik*."

He laughs—which makes me laugh.

But as soon as I hear the sound of my laughter, I choke it off, folding my hands against my belly.

Laughing feels like a betrayal. I don't know why, but it does.

I don't realize I'm holding my breath until I begin to see stars.

Wood brushes my fingertips. "Your turn."

I let out my breath in a rush, and it almost comes out like a sob. "What?"

Erik's face fills my vision, and he's pressing the oar handles against my knuckles. "Now, Miss Tessa. Let's trade. You row."

"Oh. Oh—all right." I grab hold, and we switch seats. Tears might be rolling down my cheeks, but I struggle to lift the oars out of the water the way he showed me. I'm clumsy and we slow dramatically, but the boat moves a *little*.

"I won't be as fast as you were," I say.

"It doesn't matter."

"Are you in pain?"

He glances away from the water to say, "No. But you were."

Well, that does it. I let go of the oars and press my hands to my face, because the tears are relentless. The sorrow and grief swell in me until I can't contain them any longer.

The boat rocks as Erik shifts to sit beside me on the little bench. After a moment he puts an arm around my shoulders. It's very kind, and very brotherly—but also a little awkward and stiff, especially when he actually pats me on the arm.

It's so unexpected that it chases some of the emotion away. I swipe at my face and look at him. "Sorry."

Erik pats me on the shoulder again, then sheepishly says, "No, *I'm* sorry. I never know what to do with tears."

I giggle and swipe at my face again. "I'm surprised you didn't say *there, there.*"

He smiles and shifts back to his own bench, then nods down at the oars, hanging from the notches that kept them hooked to the boat. "Row. You'll feel better. Like I said, you need to move."

I nod and take hold. My throat is threatening to close up again, so I force myself to talk. My voice is a little breathy, but I try to tease. "You never had to comfort all those girls who made sure you weren't *lonely*?"

A light sparks in his eye, and he teases right back. "Maybe I never gave any of them a reason to cry."

He would *never* be this forward in the palace. I feel like it's revealing a whole side to the guardsman I never knew. "How old are you?" I say.

"Twenty-eight. How old are you?"

"Eighteen."

He whistles through his teeth, then leans out to look over the side at the water. "I knew you were young, but not that young. Let's go out a little farther and I'll see if we can drag the nets a bit."

"Well, Corrick was only nineteen." My voice threatens to break, so I lean into the oars and pull harder. Erik was right. I *did* need to move.

"I know." He shakes his head and frowns. "Some days I'd forget, but he *was* young. So is the king, honestly. Their family legacy seems destined to be nothing but tragedy."

The good humor has slipped out of his voice, too, but his tone burns with an ember of fury.

"You're angry," I say in surprise.

He nods, then tosses the nets over the side with enough force that it seems to emphasize his anger—and then he winces and presses a hand to his side, breathing through his teeth. "When we return to Kandala," he says, "I will have to report to His Majesty that our suspicions were correct, that Captain Blakemore was not to be trusted, and that I failed to keep Prince Corrick safe. It shouldn't have happened that way, Miss Tessa. He didn't deserve to lose his brother, too."

I imagine Harristan learning of Corrick's death, and tears threaten to swell again. Erik looks at me sharply. "This is why I'm no good with tears," he says. "I'd rather get angry."

I remember how he was on the deck of the ship, chasing Rian away from me after Corrick and Lochlan had slipped beneath the waves, gone. I was sitting on the planks crying, but Erik was ready to throw Rian overboard if he came near me.

That was the night I asked him to teach me to fight.

I can't teach you how to fight if you can barely pick yourself up off the beach.

I dig deep for that same anger, biting my tongue until I taste blood, leaning into the oars, breathing hard.

"Good girl," says Erik.

"You said *when*," I say between strokes. "You think we'll be able to get back?"

"I don't know." He hesitates, studying me for a moment before leaning over again to check the nets. "But I do think you'll need to be the one to figure out a way to talk to Rian."

I almost drop the oars. "What?" I demand. "Why?"

"Because I don't think he lied about everything. Ostriary truly does need steel. He wasn't trying to kidnap Prince Corrick. I believe he was trying to do the right thing for his people, just like you were trying to do the right thing for Kandala. So I think his regret is genuine. That's why he's trying so hard to make amends with *you*." He tugs at the netting. "Eventually, that regret is going to wear thin—if it hasn't already. He'll have to admit that he failed, or those pirates will come after him again, or his people are going to figure out that he couldn't keep his promises— *something*. Once any of that happens, you will have absolutely no leverage over him."

I keep pulling at the oars, considering this.

I hate Rian. I *hate* him. I don't want to talk to him.

But if he's the king of Ostriary, he might be our best—our *only*—way out of here.

I look at Erik and remember what the king used to say when he needed his guards to help formulate a plan. "Advise." I hesitate. "Please."

"Well, Rian came to Kandala to negotiate with the king. He couldn't have been sure who he was going to bring back—if anyone at all." He shrugs a little. "He still needs steel. If I know anything of royalty, right now he's scrambling, stalling, *hiding*."

"Lying."

"Absolutely. Maybe you could lie a little yourself. Convince him that you knew secrets from Prince Corrick that could be advantageous to Ostriary. Bargain for passage back to Kandala."

That makes me falter. "He wouldn't believe it. I'm not a good liar."

Erik considers that, pulling at the nets, dragging them back over the side while he thinks. "Look! We'll have more than enough. I'll have to throw half of this back." He dumps two dozen fish in the hull of our little boat, and they all start flopping everywhere. He immediately starts tossing some back over the side, but his breathing has gone a bit ragged.

I let go of the oars and help. "You should rest."

"I'm fine. Let's keep six. Give me the oars. I'll turn us around." As he does, I look off to the island. We're a good distance from shore, and the beach has been mostly deserted, but for the first time, I spot another dock. A woman stands near the end, watching us. A small child is by her side.

I raise my hand to wave, but she doesn't wave back. We're too far to make out her expression.

Erik is rowing again, heading us back the way we came. "She's probably wary," he says. "Rian said these shores used to be attacked by Oren Crane's people."

"Oh," I say quietly. I hadn't thought about that.

"I'm sure that's why our house was empty."

I hadn't thought about that either. In all my anger at Rian, I forgot that Ostriary faced its own tragedies.

Erik is right. I'm sure Rian's regret is genuine.

But he was still a liar. He did a lot of terrible things to get what he wanted. Corrick is dead, and he has to know Harristan won't forgive him for that. If he needs steel for Ostriary, he might do something even worse to get it.

That gives me an idea. "Maybe I don't have to lie at all."

Erik looks back at me, pulling hard on the oars so we cut smoothly through the water. "Oh?"

"He still needs steel. He let Corrick die, so he must be worried that Harristan is going to set Ostriary on fire when he finds out."

"I'll help light the match."

"Me too. But neither country can sustain a war. Rian knows Harristan listened to me about the Moonflower. I think he'd believe that Harristan would listen to me again. Like you said, no one knew who Rian was bringing back, because he didn't know himself." Rage is burning in my gut. Erik is right. Anger is so much more powerful. "I don't need to lie about anything at all. Maybe I just need to convince him that I'm the only one who can help him get what he wants."

CHAPTER THREE

Harristan

When I was a boy, sneaking into the Wilds was an adventure. I'd have my brother by my side, and we'd lose ourselves among the people, spending coins and eating sweets and pretending to be Sullivan and Wes, just two boys who could escape the trappings and rigid rules of palace life for a little while. At the end of the night, we could always sneak back into the Royal Sector, climbing a rope into my chambers or following a tunnel into the empty palace kitchens. We never had to worry about a hot meal or a warm bed or a pair of boots that fit.

In retrospect, I'm ashamed to think that we were playing at being poor, though we never had to live it.

Now, I'm living it.

Some things, I've learned to ignore. The first time I was confronted with a straw mattress, I thought I'd never sleep again, but now I hardly notice. The autumn wind whistles through loose shutters and cracked windows at night, but I've been taught to stoke the fire and tie the curtains tight to keep the warmth in. My clothes are all borrowed or donated, and nothing fits *well*, but everything keeps me warm, so they'll do. I still have the boots I originally took from the palace, which should last me a while. The worst are the insects and rodents that seem to be everywhere. That might be the hardest thing to bite my tongue about—but I do.

Food doesn't seem scarce, which keeps taking me by surprise. So many of the people here are thinner than they should be. I've been sharing a small two-room house with Quint and my two guards, Thorin and Saeth, but meals have been delivered twice a day. On the seventh day, when dinner is delivered, it's two entire roasted chickens, a full loaf of bread, a steel bowl full of salted root vegetables, and another bowl full of fruit.

I stare at all the food, and then at the woman delivering it. Her name is Alice, and at first I thought she was young, because she's nearly a foot shorter than I am, but I've learned that she's closer to my age. Her voice always shakes a bit when she talks to me. I'm pretty sure it's less because of *me*, and more the fact that Thorin or Saeth usually loom at my side.

Tonight, it's Thorin. My guards don't wear their palace livery anymore, but they've kept their weapons, and there's no undoing years of training and discipline. They're wary of everyone in the Wilds. It's nearly impossible for them to look harmless. Between the two of them, Thorin always looks a bit more severe, too. When Alice eases the tray onto the table, she gives me a quick, crooked curtsy, then edges immediately toward the door. "W-we hope that will be enough for you."

"More than plenty," I say, because it's enough for *six* people, and Saeth is out walking a patrol. He won't be back for hours, and he won't go hungry either. I've heard my guards are offered food and drink at every campfire they pass. "Thank you, Alice."

She nods and slips back through the door.

I move to shove the letters I was writing into a pile, but Quint reaches across the table to put a hand down to keep them in place. "Finish first," he says.

The command takes me by surprise. My eyes flick up and meet his. I wait for him to falter, to hesitate, to *defer*—the way he would in the palace.

He doesn't. "If you please," he adds. "Karri is waiting with the runners. It will be dark soon."

I sigh tightly, because I'm hungry—but he's right. I reach for the kohl pencil I've been using.

"Go ahead and eat, Thorin," I say pointedly. "One of us should."

"I can wait."

I put the pencil back to the paper, and I fight to keep a childish scowl off my face. My focus should be on the three consuls we aim to reach, to see if I have any allies left among the elites. I have to be very careful not to give away any information about where I am hidden, because I could put *everyone* here at risk—though I have to share enough so the letter will be believed.

But instead, my thoughts are on Quint and these tiny moments of . . . well, not quite defiance. He's never rude or disrespectful.

Boldness, maybe. Audacity?

Because this isn't the first time. It's not even the second. Or the fourth.

What's odd is that I can't decide if I'm bothered. The question of it keeps tugging at me. I don't *really* mind. At least, I don't think so. Or maybe I do, but it's like the straw mattress and the rats. Maybe I'm learning to ignore it. My staff of hundreds has been reduced to a staff of *three*, and their loyalty feels dangerously precarious. Any of them could walk out of here and claim a hefty reward for my capture, so I'm not going to take a stand over writing letters.

Especially when Quint is right. Karri and the runners *are* waiting.

I just . . . I want to stall a *little*. The longer we wait, the greater the chance that Corrick could return. I wouldn't have to face all of this alone.

As soon as I have the thought, I realize how very selfish it is. How *cowardly*. I force it out of my head, and I start writing again.

Tessa's friend Karri is taking runners to deliver letters to the homes of Jasper Gold, Jonas Beeching, and Roydan Pelham, a very calculated attempt to see which consuls might *not* be conspiring against the throne. I'm hesitant to send away one of the few people I trust here in the Wilds, but I trust the consuls so little that I have to risk it. I'm most doubtful about Roydan Pelham. He's been working with Arella Cherry, who I saw working with Christopher Huxley, the captain of the palace guard, and Laurel Pepperleaf, whose father is slated to take over the richest sector in Kandala. If they're all working together, it could go very poorly for me, especially if Allisander Sallister comes to power.

But Roydan was always kind to me, especially after my parents were assassinated. He was the only consul who didn't seem to volley for power or try to have my crown ripped right off my head. So my letter to him focuses on his loyalty, how he has always seemed to care for me and Corrick, on how much we have appreciated his kindness toward us. I talk about his care for his sector, when several other consuls have done nothing for the people of Kandala. I ask if he's willing to put the people first one more time, as I am.

I mean the words genuinely, but I'm also hoping they'll prove to be strategic if he shares this letter with Arella or anyone else.

I hope they make it clear that *I* am willing to stand with the people, no matter what the cost.

I finish the letter and sign it. I don't have my seal, but I write my initials inside the curls of a few letters in the way I do to prevent forgeries. It's not as perfect as it would be with a fountain pen, but it's the best I can do. Karri is set to take the letters to three different sectors, to use the back roads and hidden courier trails farthest from each destination to help prevent discovery.

But it means *days* will pass before we know if any of the consuls are on our side. Possibly weeks.

As soon as I finish my final flourish, Quint all but snatches the paper up from under my hand, folding it crisply to match the others. "I'll take these to Karri." He's through the door before I can say anything at all.

I stare after him for a moment, then set down my pencil and run a hand over the back of my neck. I haven't touched the food, so Thorin is still waiting.

All the guards go by their last name when they're on duty, and until a few weeks ago, I couldn't have identified many of them by their first name. Outside of their ability to do their jobs, I didn't know much about any of them at all. But here, "on duty" seems to have become an endless assignment. I try not to address them so officially when they should be enjoying moments of freedom.

"Sit, Ben," I say. "Eat."

He sits, and as we pull food from the platter, he offhandedly says, "I thought Master Quint was ready to rap your knuckles."

I glance up in surprise, because I hadn't realized it was apparent to anyone but me.

Thorin sees my expression and frowns. "Forgive me. I shouldn't have—"

"No," I say. "I honestly thought the same."

He flicks his eyes at the ceiling. "I shouldn't be surprised that he would figure out a way to stage a revolution through *paperwork*."

That startles a laugh out of me, which makes him smile—but then my laughter turns into a coughing fit that's so strong I have to press my forearm to my mouth so no one outside the house will hear.

Thorin's smile vanishes, and he's staring at me with concern. After a solid minute passes with no relief, he pours a cup of water, too. He looks like he's ready to go for the door, but I glare at him between coughs, and he freezes.

I've spent days trying to hide this, but it's getting harder. Once I can breathe, I take a gulp of water, then inhale slowly until I'm sure I won't cough again. "Eat," I say. "I'm fine."

But I'm not, and he knows it.

There's so little medicine here. I get a dose every few days, but it's nothing compared to what I was receiving in the palace. Sometimes at night I hide under my blankets and cough into my pillow so they won't know how bad it is. Thorin and Saeth have begun working with the men and women who want to train to stand against the consuls, and I should join them, but I simply don't think my lungs could manage it—and I can't afford to reveal any weakness to these people.

Thorin is still staring.

"*I'm fine*," I snap. "Sit down. Eat."

"Yes, Your Majesty." He drops into his chair at once. "Forgive me."

That's not better.

I sigh and run my hands over my face, pressing my fingers into my eyes. I don't really know how to do this. In the palace, there are rules and protocol and . . . and *order*. Thorin joked about Quint organizing a revolution through paperwork, but at least the Palace Master is organizing it somehow. Thorin and Saeth are walking patrols and working with the people. Karri is delivering letters to see if we have any allies at all. As for me . . . I'm grasping at straws. Useless.

I can just imagine Corrick's reaction if he were here now. *Lord, Harristan. Is writing letters the best you can do? You might as well just turn yourself in.*

My brother is going to return from Ostriary and find the kingdom in shambles.

Well, more than it usually is.

I finally lower my hands. Thorin is eating, but only because I ordered him to do it. His eyes are locked on the plate, any sense of good humor completely gone.

He's got to be exhausted. I know I am.

We can't keep operating like this. I can't just wait on the consuls. I need to take action for my people *here*. I need to *do* something.

"If you could think of other guards to approach," I say carefully, "who do you think would be most likely to join us?"

His hands freeze on his food, and he looks up. "There were thirty of us in your personal guard. Rocco and Kilbourne went to Ostriary. Saeth and I are with you. That still leaves twenty-six. They might have been reassigned, or they could have been discharged from the guard entirely—but I'm still worried Captain Huxley would have thrown them in the Hold after it became known that we helped you escape. If they convinced others we were conspiring with you against the kingdom, he might have been able to justify it."

If my guards are in the Hold, they may as well be on the moon. I'd have no way to reach them. I might have a small army of rebels waiting outside this tiny house, but they don't fully trust me to lead them. Not yet. And while rebels bombed the Hold once before, it wasn't without loss—on either side. I can't justify that type of attack. Not just for more guards.

But maybe we don't have to. I work it through while I pick at my chicken. "Huxley has no proof that any of you were conspiring with me—because there was no conspiracy to speak of. They've spread rumors among the people, but that's harder to do with men who surround me every day. But implicating my *entire* personal guard implicates Huxley himself. He's the guard captain. He couldn't just throw twenty-six guards in the Hold without causing a bit of outrage—if not an outright scandal on top of the one they already have."

Thorin considers this, then nods. "That's true. It would destroy morale, too. If Huxley threw that many guards in the Hold, I can name a dozen people who'd quit on the spot. Tensions have already been high since the first attack on the sector. Most of us had started to close ranks anyway, and not just among your personal guard."

Most of us had started to close ranks anyway. Before Rocco left with Corrick, he warned me about Huxley, how many of the guards had started to suspect that there was more going on with the guard captain than just a taste for salacious gossip. I inwardly flinch, thinking about how much insurrection was happening right under my nose.

I wish I had people I could send into the Royal Sector, but it's just too dangerous. Even Karri's small apartment was searched, because she was known to be helping the rebels *and* me. Another reason it's wise for her to be the one to visit other sectors now.

"The entire palace staff is surely still scrambling," I say. "I rather doubt Huxley and Arella and whoever else they're working with expected me to disappear in the middle of the night. The consuls might have seized the opportunity to take control during my sudden absence, but they couldn't have been ready for it. Any control they have is still very precarious. Especially since Quint disappeared with me."

Quint, who's currently organizing this revolution with paperwork.

Thorin rolled his eyes, but Quint was also the one who, three days ago, suggested that we should start submitting reports to the palace of various "sightings" of the king in other sectors, forcing the night patrol to waste resources chasing down false leads.

I glance at the door. He's been gone for too long.

"Huxley isn't trustworthy, but he's not stupid," Thorin is saying. "No one was closer to you than we were."

It draws my attention back. "I don't know if he would keep them in the palace, or if he would feel safer giving them leave."

"It's a risk to keep them in the palace," Thorin says. "I don't know that Huxley fully trusted *us* at the end either."

That's promising. "How many do you know well enough to know where they live?"

"Between me and Saeth? Not everyone, but a lot." He winces. "A few live in the Royal Sector. That's a risk. We would be recognized."

I hold his gaze and lean in. "How many do you think would join us here?"

"All of them."

He says this so readily and with so much assuredness that it nearly hits me like a blow.

My chest clenches, and I have to sit back. "Surely not *all* of them."

"From your personal guard? Yes. All of them."

I swallow, and my throat is tight. I don't know why the loyalty takes me by surprise, but it does. I barely knew their first names. There were so few people in the palace that I trusted, and most of them sailed away on a ship to Ostriary.

"Well," I say, and my voice is rough.

And then I don't know what else to say.

The kingdom is falling apart. I don't *deserve* that kind of loyalty.

"Advise," I say, because I have to say *something*.

"Bringing everyone at once would be foolhardy," he says. "We don't know what's happened in the last week, and we don't want to risk discovery. Perhaps we could start with two or three. If Huxley doesn't have them in the palace, I'm certain he has some of them being watched, so we can't go for those we were close with. I'd personally go for Dart and Granger right now, but that's exactly what Huxley would expect." He looks at the ceiling, thinking. "We could try Reed and Sommer. They're newer to your guard, but they've never run afoul of Huxley. They're young, too. No wives or children to miss them."

I jerk my head up. *Wives and children.* I've been so worried about my own brother that I haven't spared a moment to consider that my guards might be missing someone. "You're not married, Thorin," I say, then realize I'm not entirely sure. "Are you?"

"No." He hesitates, and there's a weight to it now.

"But you have family you're missing? Tell me. Please."

"No. Not me." He pauses again. "Saeth is married. He has a son and daughter."

And we've been stuck here in the Wilds for more than a week. He disappeared from his family without so much as a word.

Lord, I'm a terrible king.

"He never said anything," I say quietly.

"No, Your Majesty," says Thorin. "He wouldn't."

I feel that same clenching in my chest that I did when Thorin said all my guards would join us here. "Did Saeth live in the Royal Sector?"

"No. Mosswell. Right by the border with Artis, on the eastern side of the Royal Sector."

I don't spend a tremendous amount of time outside the Royal Sector, but I estimate that to be less than two hours from where we are, by carriage or horseback. "Do you know his wife?"

"Leah? A little."

"When Saeth returns from patrol, tell him to come speak with me."

Thorin frowns. "He won't like that I told you. But you should know he's been sick with worry."

And he has been, I realize. Saeth has been as dutiful as Thorin, but over the last few days, he's been tense and restless. I assumed it was the same agitation we've all been feeling, but now I see it's more than that.

I should have noticed.

Voices echo outside, and I assume Quint is returning, but the conversation suddenly turns loud.

Very loud.

From outside the door, Quint says, "If you will wait just a *moment*, I will ask the king—"

Something heavy hits the door hard. "We're going to *tell* the king. Get him out here."

Thorin is on his feet in front of me, a dagger already drawn.

"No," I say. "Put it away." If I've learned anything during my time in the Wilds, weapons do very little to defuse a situation.

Outside, Quint says, "You will not—"

Something heavy hits the door again. "Get out of the *way!*" a man yells.

Thorin looks at me. The dagger is still in his hand.

"Put it away," I say again. Then I stride for the door.

My guard swears under his breath, sheaths the dagger, and moves to beat me to the door. "Your Majesty, *please.*"

I ignore him, grab the door handle, and swing it wide.

Quint's frame blocks the doorway. His back is to me, and he's facing more than twenty men in the darkness. Four have drawn close, stepping up onto the tiny porch that sits along the front of the house we share. Some have torches, the firelight flickering eerily across their faces.

Some have axes. Some have hammers.

Well then.

I put a hand on Quint's arm. "Step aside," I say quietly. "I'll talk to them."

At my side, Thorin is practically seething.

I glance at him and murmur, "Are you going to fight off two dozen men by yourself?"

Without waiting for an answer, I step onto the porch myself and look at the people gathered there. "I'm here. Tell me what you mean to tell me."

There's a slight ripple of shock, as if they didn't expect me to come out. Maybe they thought I would run. Maybe they thought they'd have to drag me out.

One of the men on the porch recovers first. I think his name is

Francis. He jabs his ax at me. "Lochlan would've attacked the palace already. It's been over a week. We told Karri that we're all risking ourselves to protect you, while it seems like you're just hiding here, eating all our food."

"Lochlan *would* have attacked the palace already," I say. I remember Karri assuring me that Lochlan had a rebel army ready to fight back, but I didn't realize that it was only an *army* in the loosest sense of the word. There are few real weapons here. Very little real training. "He'd be dead for trying."

"We did all right the first time," shouts another man. "We should have killed *all* the consuls."

"You 'did all right' because I didn't want to kill my people," I say. "I was willing to listen to your demands, as I am right now. I promise that Consul Sallister and the others do not care. If you march on the Royal Sector now, the army will shoot to kill."

Some of the men glance at one another. Thorin steps out onto the porch and stands behind me.

"How much longer is this going to take?" Francis demands. "Quint said you were sending *letters*." He jabs the ax at me again.

Thorin reaches out and snatches it right out of his hand.

Francis surges forward, and Thorin moves to block me. It's more aggressive than it needs to be, and I suspect he's going to shove him right off the porch. Some of the others shift and jostle, but I put up a hand before it turns into a fight.

"*Enough*," I say evenly. "Stay civil. You asked to talk to me. Talk."

"We're *done* talking," Francis snaps. "We're here and we're ready and we're done waiting." His hands have formed fists, and he glances between me and Thorin.

And then I realize that the raised voices and torches have

drawn more of a crowd. We suddenly have more than thirty people surrounding the porch. More than forty. There are women and children.

Then I see young Violet near the edge of the crowd. She's only thirteen. She shouldn't be here.

I take a slow breath. This was always the problem: the rebels wanted action, they wanted medicine, they wanted things to happen *immediately*.

The problem is that anything that happens fast generally doesn't *last*.

"I sent letters," I say carefully, "because it's important to know if any of the consuls will still support me. They rule the sectors. If they are *all* standing against me, we will have a larger fight on our hands. Before, you had funds and explosives from the Benefactors. Now, you have none of that. We need more people on our side. It does us no good to capture the Royal Sector if Jasper Gold sends more soldiers to take it right back."

"They've stopped giving us the medicine you promised," Francis says. "You said you were going to help. You said you were going to lead us. This isn't leading. This is *hiding*. How do we know they aren't telling the truth? That you weren't really poisoning us all?" He leans in. "Maybe we should just take the reward and be done with it."

"He's not poisoning us!" Violet calls. She runs forward like she's going to confront these men herself. "He's trying! He's trying to help."

"*Violet*," I begin—but that's as far as I get before I start coughing again.

When this happens in the palace, I can usually control it, and when I can't, Quint is rather skilled at distracting whoever is nearby, drawing them to another room or engaging them in conversation. But in the palace I was receiving medicine—a *lot* of medicine—and the coughing was never this strong or this frequent. It never happened when I was quite literally on display in front of this many people.

I want to turn away, but there's nowhere to go. Every time I inhale, my lungs don't want to work. Every time I cough, it hurts—and it feels like it goes on *forever*. When I get to the point where I feel like I'm drowning, my eyes begin to water, and I wonder if *this* will be the time I don't recover.

I've pressed a forearm to my mouth, but there's a part of me that's beginning to wish the earth would open up and swallow me whole. Maybe Thorin could give Francis back the ax so he could end this misery. This torment. This humiliation.

Just when my coughing slows, a hand takes hold of my arm, and I think it's Thorin or Quint, ushering me back into the small house. But then Francis says, "Here, King. Sit."

My vision has already gone a bit spotty, and my breathing feels thin, so I obey. I sit down a little too hard, and my body reflexively moves to press my forehead into my knees.

Francis catches my shoulder. "No," he says. "Sit up. Open up your chest."

His voice is gruff, but not unkind. Again, I obey, but in a way, it's worse. My coughing has slowed, but air whistles into my lungs, and now I can see that no one from the crowd has dispersed. If anything, there are more people.

They're all staring. I can feel the weight of their concern, like a hundred held breaths. I wonder if they all thought I might die right here.

Francis is sitting on the step beside me, and he says, "Maybe tell your guard not to put a knife in my back if I touch you again."

His voice is mild, and I can't tell if he's entirely serious, but I can just imagine how Thorin is reacting to this chain of events. This man was just shouting at me with an ax in hand. Thorin probably does have a weapon drawn.

"Thorin," I say, and my voice is barely a rasp between my shallow pants. "Don't."

Francis must be satisfied with that, because without hesitation, he reaches over and puts a hand against my forehead. He does it so casually that I'm not sure how to react. I don't know what I expected him to do, but . . . it wasn't that.

His palm is dry and cool, and he smells faintly of a farm, some combination of hay and livestock. He's an older man, probably twice my age, in stained overalls and worn boots. I wonder if he has children among the gathered crowd, too.

"No fever," he says. He sits back.

"No. I don't—" I break off and take a wheezing breath. "I don't often have the fever anymore."

He goes still at those words, and for a moment, I don't realize what I've said, and then he says, "*Often? Anymore?* Are you sick a lot?"

The people gathered seem to lean in, as if they want to hear the answer.

I've hidden this for so long that I don't know what to say.

I think of Tessa standing before me. *You could be loved. Even if your people are sick.*

I don't want to be a sick king. It feels like weakness. I remember the mockery when I was a boy. No one would say it to my face, but

I would still hear it. Corrick got into more than one scrape trying to defend me.

I loved him for it, but I hated it, too.

Quint speaks from behind me, and his voice is low. "Prince Corrick and Tessa took off their masks. It may be time to let them see you, too, Your Majesty."

I didn't want to run from their axes and hammers, but I want to run from *this*.

My breathing is finally steady, so I say, "I've been sick since I was a child. Since before the fever sickness even started. The Moonflower elixir helps, but it never goes away." I hesitate. "If I've been hiding anything, I've been hiding that." I look out at the others. My voice is so rough now that I can't shout, but I try. "If you want proof that I'm not poisoning you, I have no better than that. If I was, I was poisoning myself, too."

A low murmur takes up in the crowd as word spreads.

I look back at Francis. "I know you want action," I say quietly. "I know you all want to attack the Royal Sector. But we need to be strategic. If I can determine some allies within the sector, I'll be able to get more information, and potentially stoke some dissent. But if you storm the sector now, they *will* kill you. You have no leverage. Worse, it might trigger raids on the Wilds. We can run from the night patrol, but the army has longbows and skilled trackers. Armored men on horseback. I know you think I'm just writing letters, but I promise you, a letter can have more impact than a weapon. We won't have many opportunities to take the sector. I am begging you to not waste our chance."

Francis stares at me, and the few men at his back who heard all my words whisper among themselves.

I consider what he said about the food, and I feel guilty when I realize they've probably been giving us far more than we need. So I add, "I also don't want to take from my people. If you need the house back, I will sleep in the woods with my guards. If we are taking too much food, I insist that you give us less. I do not want more than our fair share. That was never my intent in coming here. I truly do want to help all of you." I glance at the others. "Sometimes helping takes time."

Francis grunts and looks away. "I'm not going to make the king sleep in the woods."

"You came at your king with an ax," Thorin says.

Francis draws himself up, and I think that one remark is going to spark another fight, but then he lets out a breath and runs a hand over the back of his neck and looks a bit sheepish. "I was just going to break down the door." He jerks his head at Quint. "*He* wouldn't let us talk to you."

My heart pounds a little to consider how close we came to that type of interaction. "Well," I say evenly, "in the future I urge you to *knock*, because I am willing to hear from you if you have concerns." I glance out at the crowd of people who've gathered, many of whom have pressed closer to listen. "That goes for all of you. If you come to me peacefully, I will speak to any of you." I look up at Quint. "Make sure the others know. Anyone, at any time. Day or night."

He stares back at me like I'm a bit crazy, but he draws his little book out of his jacket pocket and makes a note. "Yes, Your Majesty."

I turn back to Francis. "Are you and the others willing to wait?"

"Yes." But he doesn't look happy about it.

I consider what Thorin said about the younger guards, about Saeth's family. If they're going to try to reach anyone, I can't send them alone. They're only two men, and the risk is too great.

Francis is right. I did say I was going to lead them. Maybe I need to start.

I look at the gathered people clutching their axes and hammers. "It might not be time to attack the sector," I say, "but there are things to be done, if you all are ready for action."

Francis nods. "We are."

"Good. Come back tomorrow night."

CHAPTER FOUR

Corrick

By the time the pirates come for us, Lochlan and I have some semblance of a plan. It's rough, but well suited, because it won't require a lot of lying.

I hate everything about it.

Six pirates stand outside our cage, including Lina. Four men and two women. They're all armed, most with daggers and knives or crossbows, though one man has a sword. When they open the cage door, I expect them to charge in, to separate us and bind our hands, but they don't.

The biggest one just nods at the doorway. His name is Mouse, and we've seen him before. It has to be a nickname, because he's massive. He's not overly *tall*, just packed with so much muscle that I think he could give Rocco a run for his money. He's even bigger than Sablo, a man Rian had on the *Dawn Chaser*. Mouse probably could have ripped the cage door right off its hinges.

On the night we were captured, when I tried to run, Mouse

caught me by the ankle and held me upside down like I was a rag doll.

"Let's go," Mouse says, and his voice is very rough, very quiet. He's always remarkably soft-spoken for his size. "Oren is ready for you."

"Both of us?" says Lochlan.

Mouse nods. "Both of you."

We uncurl from the ground and move to follow.

The pirates give us no warnings, and so many weapons hang within reach. With our hands unbound, we could go for daggers and fight back right now. We're still in the woods, and there's no one nearby to hear and assist. Two against six isn't *so* terrible. Mouse would be the biggest challenge. One of the men with a crossbow has it hanging along his back. Lina and the other woman are laughing behind us, distracted.

Lochlan glances at me, and I know he's thinking the same thing.

But it's too obvious. Too easy.

It feels like a test.

This wasn't a part of our plan. I give a tiny shake of my head, hoping he doesn't decide to attack them anyway. I sense that pulling Mouse's hair would not end well.

Lochlan turns his eyes forward. We keep walking.

It's hotter here than it would be in most of Kandala. More humid, too, reminding me of the summertime climate in Sunkeep, the southernmost sector—though we're into autumn now. Once we break out of the trees, the sun truly beats down on us, and sweat immediately blooms under my tunic, the glare making me throw up an arm to cover my eyes. But then my boots crunch on gravel instead of the mossy softness of the woods, and I blink and look down.

We're on a road. In the distance to my left, the road leads down a hill to the sudden appearance of squat buildings and homes and structures that seem to go on forever, people and horses and wagons milling about—a small town, or even a city. Straight ahead of me is a wide swath of long grass that stretches on for at least a mile, where it appears to drop off into the ocean. I see nothing beyond but glittering water, sparkling in the sun, a few small boats bobbing with the current.

For some reason, I'd assumed we were on a remote island with the pirates. Someplace hidden and nearly deserted. The city is a few miles off, but this is very much . . . not deserted.

That could be promising. If we could escape, it would be a lot easier to hide in a city.

"Which island is this?" I say to Lina and Mouse.

"Silvesse," Mouse says. He points out at the water. "That way's south, so you can't see the others from this side."

I can see the sun, which tells me which way we're facing, but he's politely answering my question instead of knocking my head in, so I give him a nod and say, "Thank you, Mouse."

Lina jabs him with her elbow and rolls her eyes. "They know which way is south, idiot."

He frowns. "I'm not an idiot."

One of the other men, the one with the sword, says, "Both of you, knock it off." But his voice is tired, like minor bickering between Lina and Mouse is a common occurrence that no one wants to deal with. "Just walk."

We walk, but now Lina is muttering insults at Mouse, while his mouth is silently curled in a frown.

Maybe their distraction isn't a trap at all. Maybe it's genuine.

Lochlan must sense it too, because he glances at me again.

It's so tempting. If there were only four of them, I might chance it. If they had no crossbows, I'd *definitely* chance it. But it doesn't matter if we can face all of them hand to hand when it only takes one of them to shoot us.

I keep my eyes on the road and give a little shake of my head again.

Lochlan clenches his jaw. He doesn't like it—but he obeys.

Well, there's a surprise. Perhaps I can still be a *little* princely.

I hope we're walking all the way to the city, just because I'm intrigued by the potential, even if the thought of walking for miles in this heat is a little wearying. But we only walk parallel to the ocean for a short time before we turn off the road and head into the trees again.

Behind us, Lina and Mouse have fallen silent, though I've now heard her call him a dozen different insults and it's a contemptuous kind of silence. I glance back at Mouse and wonder if he'll answer more questions. "How far do we have to go?"

"Not far." He points vaguely, then peers back at me. "If you're too tired to walk, they'll make me carry you."

I shake my head quickly. "I can walk."

But I think about how he phrased that. *They'll make me.* Mouse might be the biggest man here, but he doesn't have the most power.

I think about Lina's steady stream of insults, the way he said nothing.

Maybe he doesn't have *any* power.

"I thought Oren might be in the city," I say.

A woman behind me snorts, and I glance over my shoulder. She's older, close to forty, with heavily scarred arms and closely shorn hair. "Redstone's got eyes around every corner. You'll never find Oren in the city."

Redstone. The name tugs at my memories, and it takes me a moment to realize they're talking about Rian. The whole time he was pretending to be Captain Blakemore, he was really Galen Redstone, the king of Ostriary.

"So he hides in the woods?" says Lochlan.

"Oh, he isn't *hiding.*" The man with the sword shakes his head and glares at the older woman. "Oren's got his own people around every corner, too, Esther."

"Oh, shut it, Ian."

This time *they* start bickering, arguing over who has the most spies in the city. I don't mind, though. It's very telling. These pirates aren't unified—and it's interesting to hear Rian discussed in this way.

While they ramble at each other, Lochlan gives me another significant glance. I don't even look at him. I'm worried about the other two, the men who haven't said a word.

Eventually we head downhill, and the going is so steep that my boots catch on roots and underbrush and I have to grab at tree trunks to keep my balance. There's no path at all, and I don't know what signified that this was the direction to go. I can't imagine that Mouse would have carried us all this way. I look up at his broad shoulders and figure he probably could have.

When the ground flattens, it goes soft, sand shifting among the underbrush. I hear water just before the trees open up, and then we're in the sun again, standing on the beach, facing west now. This appears to be a small cove, with a rowboat pulled up onshore, a larger ship bobbing in the waves out in the ocean. I wonder if it's anchored there.

Then Ian says, "Push the rowboat out. You two can row."

I don't know how to do much with a boat, but the pirates are staring at me and Lochlan expectantly, so we brace our hands on the wood.

Lochlan glances at me with my hands on the rail and keeps his voice very quiet as he says, "No. Go low. It'll be hard to move it at first."

I put my hands against the hull, then my shoulder, and we throw our weight into it. The boat barely moves an inch, but it shifts in the sand.

"Maybe this is a bad time to mention this," I whisper, "but I don't know how to row."

"I figured," he grunts. "Just sit behind me and watch."

Once the boat moves away from the sand, we're clearly expected to stay with it, and my boots fill with water immediately. Amazing. Lochlan grabs hold of the rail and hoists himself over, and I hear a little whimper as he does so.

I forgot about his arm.

I say nothing. It won't do any good for the pirates to know.

It's harder to get into the boat than I expect, but once we're in, the others join us, and I take hold of the oars behind Lochlan. Once I figure out the rhythm, it's not *hard*, but it's hot, and I'm not practiced at this. It's clear that they've made us row so we can't cause trouble. I remember Rian telling us that Oren would hide in coves among the islands, and I wonder if he's on this waiting ship. I consider the way Ian talked about Redstone's *eyes* in the city and wonder if Oren is rarely on land at all. Rian once said that Oren had lost favor here in Ostriary, that the people were tired and just wanted to rebuild after years at war. They were counting on Rian to get to Kandala and negotiate for steel.

I guess that's not happening anytime soon.

I blink in the glare and look past Lochlan's shoulder at the ship in the distance. I wonder if this is the ship that shot us off the deck of the *Dawn Chaser.*

I'm trying my best to keep up with Lochlan's smooth strokes through the water, but I've never done this before. It's obvious that my inexperience is evident when Lina puts a hand on my shoulder and says, "Not much of a sailor, are you, Wes?"

I grit my teeth and pull hard on the oars. "I have other skills."

I didn't mean for it to sound coy or taunting, but some of the pirates whistle. Lina laughs from behind me, and then her breath is hot on my neck, her body pressed against my spine. "Is that so?" she purrs, her fingers tracing up the outside of my arm. "I can't wait to hear."

The oars go still in my hands, and for an instant I consider shoving one right back at her. It would take almost no effort. I could put it right through her throat.

Because *this* is a game I won't play.

But Lochlan looks over his shoulder. "Fair warning: he's not talking about those kind of skills."

I don't know what she hears in his voice, whether it's cool practicality or just plain honesty, but the heat of her body disappears from my back.

I say nothing and start rowing again.

It doesn't take long to reach the ship, and once we're there, we have to climb a rope ladder. I watch Lochlan favor his arm all the way up, and I worry that the pirates might notice, so I try to go more slowly, so a distance forms between me and him.

Lina is behind me, and she smacks my ankle. "*Move,*" she snaps. No purring now.

"I have rope burns from before," I say, which is true, though they've mostly healed. "I'm going as fast as I can."

Eventually, we reach the top. We climb over the rail, and one of the nameless men jabs me with a crossbow and tells me to stand with Lochlan.

I was already doing that, but I scowl and move closer.

But then a man *tsks*, and a voice says, "Here now, have they not been well behaved?"

There, standing nearly six and a half feet tall, with a jagged scar on his face and another two dozen men surrounding him on the deck, is Oren Crane.

"They've been respectable," Mouse says in his rough-soft voice. "They gave us no trouble."

"Ugh, quit being so earnest," says Lina. She moves close to me and bumps me with her hip, but now it's not coy so much as aggressive. "We could have had a bit of fun."

"I'm not having fun," I say.

"Me either," says Lochlan.

"You've been well cared for," says Oren. His eyebrows go up and it pulls at the scar. "You claim you're not having fun?"

I look straight at him. That first night, I was half drowned, but I got him off his feet and put a knife against his chest. I remember the flare of surprise in his eyes, the quick burst of panic. He's not used to people taking him by surprise, and it was obvious. The other pirates dragged me off him, but for a bare second, I had the upper hand, and we both know it.

It makes me want to grab a knife or seize a crossbow or *something* that would demonstrate the weaknesses in the people he has working for him. To poke holes in his confidence. In *theirs*. It makes me want to show him I can take the upper hand if I want it.

But I wouldn't be able to keep it. Not against this many people.

And as much as I hate it, we're going to need Oren Crane.

"We've been locked in a cage for more than a week," I say. "I'm sorry to report it wasn't entertaining."

"I know you have," he says. "I can smell you from here. But you'll have to forgive me. I've been busy. That prick still has my daughter."

For a second, I have no idea what he's talking about.

Then my thoughts catch up, and I'm glad I have years of experience at court politics, because I'm able to keep any hint of surprise off my face.

Oren Crane still believes that Bella, his daughter, is alive.

Instead of at the bottom of the ocean, or in the belly of some whale, or wherever bodies go when they fall off a ship—or when they're *blown* off a ship, as the case may be. She disappeared when two brigantines from Kandala attacked the *Dawn Chaser* with cannons.

Rian—"that prick"—was keeping Bella prisoner as leverage against this man.

And now he thinks Rian is *still* keeping her prisoner. My thoughts race as I consider how to play this. Lochlan and I hadn't considered Bella being alive in our strategizing.

But if we're going to be disparaging against Rian, I'm all in.

"That *prick* killed my prince," I say. "If you were busy going after *him*, you shouldn't have locked us in a cage. We would've helped you."

He bursts out laughing. "I should have brought the prince's young servant along? Would you have served tea? Buttoned jackets?" He rubs at his throat. "Now that you mention it, I could use a shave."

I smile. "By all means, bring me a blade."

"Careful," Lochlan says under his breath.

But I don't need to be careful now. This isn't like the moment when I refused to eat, where Lochlan's lessons in the Wilds probably did save my life. Now it's time for *my* lessons. I've been dealing with men like Oren Crane my entire life: older and powerful and full of disdain, because they always think they know best. It makes them careless and sloppy, because they're unwilling to look beyond what they want—but they have too much power to realize just how much of a mess they're making of everything.

It's probably the very reason Rian took the throne, while this man is hiding here on this ship, thinking he has a chance at getting it back.

And now I'm going to have to deal with him.

"I wasn't that kind of servant," I say.

"Lochlan mentioned that Weston here has other *skills*," Lina says. She presses close to me again, but her voice has turned mocking. "What did you do for your prince, servant boy?" Some of the sailors whistle, so she smiles, encouraged. Her voice drops to a whisper as she traces a finger over my lips suggestively, then moves to stroke a hand down my chest. "What did he like you to do for him?"

I grab hold of her wrist, spinning her around so quickly that I hear muscles tear—or bones crack. She cries out, but I jerk her back against my chest, gripping her throat with enough force that I could break her neck.

But I don't.

Half a dozen crossbows are pointed at me, but none have fired yet. Most of the men on the deck are staring at me in shock.

I look at Oren Crane. "I killed people."

Lina is trying to struggle against me, and little whimpered

gasps are coming out of her throat. I definitely hurt *something*. I have years of experience with prisoners in the Hold who actually tried to kill me, so I don't yield an inch. Her pulse pounds fast and hard against my hand, and she's fighting to inhale.

Beside me, Lochlan is having no trouble. His breaths are coming quickly, like he's unsure of the path we've decided to follow.

I want to kick him. *This was your idea!* I want to shout.

And it was. He sat in the grit of the cage and almost goaded me about it.

It should be no trouble to convince them you did vile things for the prince, he said. *You don't even have to pretend to be vicious.*

He's right. I don't.

I have to shove aside thoughts of Tessa when I'm like this. She's a weight in my heart that I feel every time it beats, but she hates this part of me.

If being vicious means a chance to rescue her, I'll do it. If it means a chance to get back to Kandala and my brother, I'll do it.

Oren is staring at me. The others are staring between the two of us.

"So the rumors about Kandala's royal family are true," he says appraisingly.

I'm not *entirely* sure what that means, but I remember what Rian used to think of Kandala, and none of it was good. "The prince had ways to make sure order was maintained," I say.

"Prove it," he says.

Lina squeals and tries to throw me off, but my grip is too tight.

The men around me are absolutely silent. Mouse is wringing his hands. "Mr. Crane," he says softly.

"Death can't be undone," I say.

"I know," says Oren. "Do it."

My thoughts ice over, my vision turning dark. I don't want to do this.

As usual, fate doesn't care what I want.

Thoughts of Tessa sneak into my head anyway, a memory of the day she found me in the Hold, soaked in blood after I'd been forced to execute two prisoners. I have to choke back a whimper. *Please, my love. Forgive me.*

I've done it before. I can do it again.

I don't *want* to do it again.

But my grip on Lina tightens.

"No," says Lochlan. "We don't work for you. What's the pay?"

I freeze. Lina's breathing is so thin it's barely a whistle. She's almost limp against me, hardly struggling now.

No one has come to her rescue. None of them are willing to stand against Oren Crane.

"The *pay*?" Oren says incredulously.

"Yeah," says Lochlan. "The *pay*. The prince paid a lot. You gave us a week in a cell. Wes isn't your errand boy. If you don't like Lina, pay up, or kill her yourself."

Oren looks like Lochlan just told him to eat a handful of sand. "You're my *prisoners!*" he seethes. "I am not *paying you to—*"

"Fair enough." I let Lina go. She drops like a rock, crumpling to the deck, gasping for air. I can hear her rage with every inhale. Her arm is hanging crookedly against the deck. I think I've dislocated her shoulder.

The glances between us and Oren have redoubled.

"I don't work for free." I glance at Lochlan. "He doesn't either."

Oren's face is turning red. "I could *kill you—*"

"Go ahead," I say. "That's better than going back to that cell. Either way, you're wasting time. You want your daughter back, and you want Redstone off the throne. We want him *dead*. We want to go back to Kandala. We could be helping each other."

Lina roars in sudden rage and launches herself at my legs, but I kick her back, then drop to a knee and pin her to the deck by her throat.

She spits at me. I think she'd take a swing at me, too, but her arm won't work.

I glare down at her. "Touch me again," I say, "and he won't have to pay me a *cent*."

Whatever she sees in my expression must be chilling, because fear lights in her eyes, and she goes still.

"Why should I trust either of you?" Oren says. "It doesn't seem like the pet henchman of a nefarious prince would make a very trustworthy ally." He sniffs and looks disdainfully at Lochlan. "And I honestly don't know why I need to bother with a deckhand."

"A deckhand." Lochlan looks at me. "He thinks I'm a deckhand."

I let go of Lina and straighten. This is the harder part of our plan to sell, but we're halfway there. I keep my expression bored and look back at Oren. "You already know he's more than just a deckhand, or you wouldn't have locked him in the cell with me."

I have no idea whether that's true, but this kind of false praise works well at court. It makes him sound intelligent, calculating. He's not going to deny *that*.

"Then what are *your* skills?" Oren says to Lochlan. His voice turns suggestive, just like Lina's was. "What did *you* do for the prince?"

Eyes flick to me before shifting back to Lochlan. No one whistles or jeers this time.

"I didn't do anything for the prince," Lochlan says. "I was a spy for the king."

Complete silence. Any hint of mockery is gone from Oren's expression. He's regarding us steadily.

I'm mentally throwing daggers at Lochlan, warning him not to say another word.

Here's one of my lessons, I said to him when we were planning. *The more people talk, the more it tells me they're lying. Lies require convincing. When people are telling the truth, it's simple.*

He snorted at me. *Did you learn that from interrogating prisoners?*

When I said yes, he wasn't happy.

But the lesson must have stuck, because he keeps his mouth shut.

"So the royal family of Kandala really can't be trusted," Oren finally says.

"They can be trusted to maintain their own interests," I say. "By whatever means necessary."

Oren takes a few steps closer, evaluating us both. "Fine. There's a man in central Silvesse named Ford Cheeke. He monitors the shipping logs in and out of the main harbor. He's well guarded, because the harbor is full of sailors loyal to Redstone. Cheeke also has a secret way to pass messages to Redstone's people on Fairde, but we haven't been able to figure it out."

"And you want us to figure it out," says Lochlan.

"Yes. And I want you to bring me his head by daybreak tomorrow."

Beside me, I can hear Lochlan swallow, so I say, "How much?"

At my feet, Lina growls, "I should have poisoned your food."

"You're right. You should have." I keep my eyes on Oren. "*How much?*"

"One hundred silvers."

Someone on the deck swears, and I think I hear a whistle from someone else.

"Half now," I say.

He bursts out laughing. "You can have *ten* now, just because I know you need to clean yourselves up. The rest when you come back."

I glance around at the men and women on deck. "And I want six of your people if Cheeke is so well guarded."

"No," says Oren. "Just you two. I'm not having Redstone come after *me* when this goes poorly. If you're lying, I have eyes in Silvesse, too, so I'll get you back eventually." He pauses, and a light sparks in his eye. "If you're not lying, a spy and a killer should find this task to be fairly easy."

I have no idea how we're going to find a man we've never met in a city we've never seen, especially in less than a day. But it's ten silvers and a little bit of freedom.

It's more than we had an hour ago.

Still breathing.

I glance at Lochlan, then back at Oren. "Give us the silver. You're on."

CHAPTER FIVE

Corrick

The streets of Silvesse are hot, and the air smells like fish no matter where we go. By the time Lochlan and I find our way into the thick of the city, the sun is high overhead, and sweat has collected under my clothes. I've snuck through the Wilds of Kandala in the dead of night as an outlaw, but I'm somewhat shocked to realize that I've never really walked through a city as a commoner. In Kandala, as Prince Corrick, I'd be backed by guards, and people would yield a path without being asked. Here, the roads are crowded, and sea-worn sailors and sweat-stained laborers must not be too foreign. No one gives us a passing glance. I can almost forget who I am.

Thieves might be common here, so I've tucked my five silvers into an inner pocket of my jacket, right up against my heart. I have no idea what Lochlan did with his. There was a part of me that expected him to take his coins and bolt the very instant we were out of sight of the pirates.

But he hasn't left my side.

He hasn't said a word either, which is probably smart, though we're going to have to talk at some point. But I'd forgotten that our Kandalan accent is going to paint us as outsiders the instant we open our mouths. The Ostrian accent is different, with round vowels, and I'm not sure I could imitate it without practice. I can't even imagine what type of story we could tell to explain it away.

Then again, maybe it doesn't matter if people question our accents. We just need to find one man and kill him.

The thought makes my heart trip and stall over and over again. Can I kill a man who's never done anything to me? To anyone I know? Lina worked for Oren, and she was helping to keep us prisoner. My skin still crawls from where she touched me. I didn't want to kill her, but I almost did it. I *would* have done it if Lochlan hadn't stopped me. But it was a means to escape. A step toward rescuing Tessa. A step toward *home*.

Ford Cheeke is a complete stranger.

Oren is the one demanding it. Is this simply another means to escape?

This is worse than when I was acting as King's Justice, when no good options lay in front of me, but I had to choose what would cause the least harm—even if that meant someone had to die. As King's Justice, I *had* to maintain order, because when the sickness wasn't killing people, they were killing one another over access to medicine.

But in this case, I'm not protecting a kingdom. I'm protecting myself.

I hate the path of these thoughts. Maybe I'm the one who should take the coins and run.

Lochlan grabs hold of my sleeve and gives it a tug. "Come on," he says, his voice low. "We can't just walk all day."

I blink and look up, startled to discover that he's dragging me into a clothier's shop. I've never been inside one of those either. When we need apparel in the palace, Quint sends a summons, and tailors and seamstresses and fabric merchants come to *us*. Once we cross the threshold, the odors of fish and sweat remain in the street, replaced by fresher scents: cotton and linen and what appears to be a small fragrant candle burning on a low table. A middle-aged man and a woman are sitting together, both stitching fabrics while they talk in low tones.

When they look at us, they fall silent. The man's eyebrows go up. The woman frowns.

I didn't realize we looked *that* bad.

The man recovers first, and he stands. "Ah . . . gentlemen," he says. "How can we help?"

"We need some clothes," Lochlan says.

"If you please," I add, because clearly his early lessons didn't include *manners*.

The man and woman exchange glances.

I have no idea whether that's about our appearance or if our accents took them by surprise, but I step toward a rack where a linen tunic is hanging, and the woman swoops out of her chair before I can touch it. "Please, sir, allow me. I'll find something to fit. We wouldn't want you to . . . ah, trouble yourself." Then she whisks the tunic away.

"Perhaps a recommendation for a place where we could rent a room to wash up as well," I say.

Lochlan looks at me and hisses under his breath. "Just how much money do you think we have?"

"You can stay filthy if you like," I whisper back. I'm rarely cavalier, but we can't hide what we sound or look like, so I smile at the woman. "Forgive our appearance. We've fallen off a ship from Kandala, so we're not at our best. But we do have silver to pay."

The man starts, then coughs, then offers a choked laugh as if he can't decide whether I'm kidding. "Well. Yes. Of course. Right this way. I'm sure we can find you both something suitable."

While the man starts asking Lochlan about whether he prefers wool or broadcloth for his trousers, the woman shifts close and peers at me. "Are you serious about the ship from Kandala?" she says quietly.

She's staring at me earnestly, her lips slightly parted. I'm not sure what to make of it, but I want to figure it out.

"I am," I say.

She glances at Lochlan, who's telling the man that we'll take whatever is cheapest, and moves closer. "Your accents are real?"

"They are."

She swallows and glances at the door, then drops her voice further. "So Galen Redstone made it to Kandala. Was he able to negotiate for steel?"

Galen Redstone. My chest tightens at the mention of Rian's real name. I inhale to tell her no, that Galen Redstone is a lying, cheating scoundrel who should be lashed to the bottom of his own ship and run across a bed of rocks, and I'll do it myself after I break every bone in his body.

But then she swallows thickly and says, "Please. We're so desperate."

The emotion in her voice tugs at me. I've heard that kind of desperation before.

"Yes," I say. "He made it to Kandala."

She grabs hold of my hand, heedless of my appearance now. "You said you fell off a ship. Was it Crane? Did he attack? Was the king able to get past?"

The king. Even now, it's so hard to think of Rian in these terms.

Her fingers are pressing into my hand so tightly. "Please," she says. "If there's any news you can share . . ."

Across the room, Lochlan is staring at me. I can't read his expression, but no matter what I think of Rian, there's nothing to be lost in telling this woman the truth.

"He made it past," I say. "The ship was under fire from Crane's people, but your king was able to sail on."

She kisses her fingertips, then presses them over her heart. "Oh, such a relief. If he made it past Silvesse, then he should have been able to make it to Fairde." Her eyes lock on mine again. "If you're here, then he must have reached an agreement with the king of Kandala. We've been so worried. Everyone knows your King Lucas is callous and spiteful—"

I jerk back. "He was *not*," I say hotly. I've spent years hearing every possible insult hurled at myself and Harristan, but I wasn't ready to hear someone say that about my father.

Lochlan coughs. "*Wes.* It's all right. You know how rumors are."

Wes. I have to shake myself. And he's right. I do know how rumors are.

The woman is staring at me. "I'm sorry. I'm speaking of your king. We—we just know what damage he caused *here.*"

Supposedly my father didn't honor a trade agreement and sent ships to attack theirs. I didn't believe it when Rian first talked about it, but I forgot that people *here* would see Kandala as an aggressor.

I remember Rian standing at the helm, glaring at me, proclaiming that he hadn't lied about much of anything.

I can hate him, but maybe that was true.

I take a breath. "King Lucas is dead. His son, King Harristan, is in power now."

The man seems to have formed a pile of clothes for Lochlan, and he's approaching us with a pile for me, too. His voice is equally quiet. "It's a relief to hear that the king made it back. My brother lives on Iris, and they haven't been able to rebuild yet."

The woman nods. "All the lumber keeps getting diverted to Roshan and Estar, and I heard that half the freighter ships were damaged in the war." She squeezes my hand. "But you haven't said. Was Redstone able to come to terms with this King Harristan? He must have, if he brought people from Kandala back with him." But then she draws back, looking worried again. "I don't want to speak ill of your king, but can he be trusted?"

The question pricks at me. I stare at the shop owners, and I'm not sure what to say.

Your king is the one who can't be trusted. Harristan will never come to terms with him.

Galen Redstone is a dirty liar who approached us under false pretenses.

I'm going to find him and make him regret setting foot on Kandalan soil.

But it's hard to look into their desperate faces and even *think* those things. They really put their hope and faith into Rian.

Just like Tessa did.

I can't decide if they're *all* naive, or if Rian genuinely did want the best for these people, and he just went about everything the wrong way.

The most cynical part of my brain wants to believe the former, that he duped them all.

My heart is relentlessly insisting it's the latter.

I tell my heart to shut up.

"My brother has four children," says the man. "Iris has a lot of livestock, and Crane's people destroyed many of their buildings in the war. They get the worst of the summer storms. They're struggling without access to building materials. It would be a blessing to know that hope was on the horizon."

I glance at Lochlan, wondering if he'll have another quip to keep me in line, but he's studying me just as hard as they are, as if their emotion has caught hold of him, too. For all our differences, Lochlan was also desperate, also trying to do what he could to protect people. He wants to hear what I'm going to say.

Despite the warning a moment ago, he's not looking at Weston Lark right now. He's looking at Prince Corrick, as if he knows any words I say will have the weight of the Crown behind them.

Ugh. Fine.

I run a hand across the back of my neck, then offer the woman as much truth as I can. "I know the stories you've heard. I can't speak to the past. But King Harristan is a good man. He stands by his word, and he'll do whatever he can to help people in need."

The words are true, but they feel empty—like a vague promise. Something I'd say at court. But her eyes well, and she stands on her tiptoes to kiss me on the cheek. "Thank you," she whispers.

It shocks me still. No one has *ever* kissed Prince Corrick on the cheek. I don't even know if anyone's ever done it to Weston Lark.

"You'll have to be careful if you're intending to book passage to Fairde," the man is murmuring. He casts a glance at the doorway. "Oren Crane has people all over Silvesse. If you have silver you can get space on a boat, but if he learns there are survivors from Kandala onshore, he'll want to get a hold of you. I'll write down some names for who you can ask at the harbor." He heads back toward his table.

"We've already learned about Crane," says Lochlan.

"What about the bridges?" I say. "Is it possible to walk to Fairde?"

"No," says the man. "The bridges from Fairde were the first to be destroyed in the war. You can walk to Iris, but it would take a day at least, and it's a less populated island, so there aren't as many ships coming and going. You'd have a harder time finding passage."

The woman tugs at my hand and pulls me toward the front window. "Look," she says, pointing down the street toward a squat building with a blue door. "There's a boarding house there, not too expensive. I'm friends with Harlow, the girl who works the door. Tell her we sent you, and she'll set you up with some soaps and towels, and probably a meal, too."

"That's very kind of you," I say to her.

The man has wrapped up the clothes and tied them together with a bit of twine, and he slips a roll of leather under the knot. "I've added a shaving kit, too," he says, holding out the bundle.

Lochlan glances at it warily. "How much?"

The man shakes his head. "Nothing. For the kindness of your king."

Lochlan looks relieved, and he gives them a nod. "Thank you."

But I pull three silvers out of the pocket over my heart and press them into the woman's hand.

Her eyes go wide. "No! This is *far* too much, sir! This is—"

I press her fingers closed around the money. "Weston Lark," I say. "And these are for *your* kindness."

"Thank you," she whispers.

Lochlan is staring at me like I'm a bigger fool than he ever realized. Quite the shift after he was staring at me like the King's Justice.

I sigh and barely glance at him. "Did you get the names? Let's go."

Out in the street, the sun is just as hot as it was before. Lochlan folds up the slip of paper with the names and shoves it into his pocket.

"You could've just given her one silver," he says.

"I know."

"You're not Prince Corrick here. You don't have an endless supply of coins in your bedroom."

"For what it's worth, I never did."

"You have *no idea* how much it's going to cost to buy passage to Fairde."

"True, but even if we kept all ten," I say, "I rather doubt Oren gave us enough."

He says nothing to that. After a minute, he gives an aggravated sigh, digs a hand into his pocket, and thrusts a coin at me.

I shake my head.

"*Take it*," he snaps.

We're nearing the boarding house, and I wait for a break in the crowds in the street so we can cross. "No."

He leans close and growls, "I'm going to force-feed you this *coin* in a second—"

"Don't threaten me with a good time, Lochlan." I stop in front of the blue door and knock. I hate the curl of fear in my gut that's warning me that he's right, and I should've held on to the coins. "If you want to make it up to me so badly, just use it to pay for the room."

He inhales sharply to protest, but the girl opens the door, and Lochlan does exactly what I said.

—+—

We asked for a private room and we got one, but there's only one bed and one washroom, and a small table with two stools in the corner. We won't be here long, and there's no sense wasting a coin on a second room. The woman from the clothier's shop was right, and Harlow gave us a basket of towels and soaps when Lochlan handed over his silver. A small bowl of fruit and dried biscuits sits on the table, too, along with a pitcher of water. Once we're inside, Lochlan tosses the bundle of clothes onto the bed, and I tell him to take the washroom first. I expect him to argue about that, too, but he doesn't. He slips the shaving kit free from the bundle of clothes and disappears behind the door.

Then I'm alone.

Much like the moment we walked into the city, that's a bit jarring. I can't remember the last time I was alone. We spent so many days locked in the cave together. We didn't talk much at all, but until this very second, I didn't realize how weirdly *accustomed* I've grown to his company. I don't think I've ever spent so many hours in the presence of anyone, including my own brother.

I unbuckle my jacket and toss it on the bed, then sink into one of the chairs and run a hand over the back of my neck.

I should be making a plan, but I keep thinking about the man and woman in the shop. I wonder if everyone here is as desperate as everyone in Kandala, just in a different way.

Not like I can do anything about it.

And now I'm supposed to go kill someone I've never met.

Someone who might be just as desperate. Someone who's *helping* Rian help these people.

Tessa would hate everything about this.

I know, my love. I'm trying.

I have to choke back emotion before it can form. If Lochlan comes out here and finds me on the verge of tears, I'll perish on the spot. I wonder if Ford Cheeke is on the list of names. I should've asked Lochlan before he went into the washroom.

There's a flaw in the wood on the table, and I pick at it absently while I think. Again, I should be plotting, planning, strategizing, but instead I just keep seeing Tessa. I hope she's safe. For as much as I hate Rian, I don't think he would hurt her. I remember the way he sat across from her at dinner in the palace, mocking me and flirting with her all at the same time.

He's exactly the man Weston Lark would be, if he were real.

I swallow and it hurts. She thinks I'm dead. Rian might not harm her, but what I'm imagining him doing is a whole lot worse.

The washroom door opens sooner than I expect, and Lochlan emerges with his black hair damp and slicked back, his skin pink and scrubbed, his face freshly shaved—cleaner than I've ever seen him, and that includes the day he was invited to the palace to meet with the king. He has a towel wrapped around his waist, held in place with a clenched fist.

"Your turn," he says.

"All right." My thoughts are still tangled up with Tessa and Rian and nothing I want to imagine. Maybe I should just drown myself in the bathtub.

Lochlan tosses his old clothes onto the bed beside my jacket, then looks at the new bundle, still tied and bound with twine. His expression turns peeved, and he calls out to me before I close myself into the washroom. "You couldn't unwrap the clothes, you idiot?"

He's right. I probably should have done that. It would have been better than poking at an old wooden table and torturing myself.

"Unwrap them yourself." I close the door in his face.

The water is very hot, and the soaps smell like oranges, but I hold myself under the water for far longer than I probably should. I soak away the sweat and filth and aches of a week of sleeping on the ground, holding my breath until I can't bear it anymore. I barely recognize my face when I look in the small mirror over the washbasin. My skin is a shade darker, and I've earned a lot more freckles from my time in the sun. The pinkish-white scar over my eyebrow—courtesy of Lochlan's mob—is much more evident now. Brown stubble coats my jaw, too. I don't think I've ever gone this long without shaving. No one would mistake me for royalty now.

You're not Prince Corrick here.

It feels oddly rebellious. The shaving razor is in my hand, but I set it back down without using it. I tie my own towel in place and go to fetch my own clothes.

Lochlan is fully dressed, sitting in the same chair I abandoned. He's in an oatmeal-colored tunic and simple dark brown trousers that fit well enough. He doesn't even look over when I emerge.

I grab what's left of the clothes. "Was Ford Cheeke's name on the list of people they gave us?"

He hesitates, his eyes on the window, then shrugs. "I don't know."

I roll my eyes. I guess we can both be useless. I affect his tone from when he mocked me about the wrapped clothes. "You couldn't read the list, you idiot?"

"No, Your Highness." He finally looks at me, then takes an

apple from the bowl on the table. His eyes bore right into mine. "I couldn't."

I freeze. *Oh.*

An odd weight settles over the room as I realize the impact of what he's telling me. I know there are a lot of people in the poorer parts of the sectors who never learn to read, especially in the Wilds, but I've never been confronted with it before. It's never really seemed to *matter* before. I was only echoing his words about the clothes, but now mine seem arrogant and soaked in privilege.

You couldn't read the list, you idiot?

A flush has surely crawled up my neck, and I'm glad I'm clutching the new clothes against my chest, because it's likely that *all* of me is turning red. Despite everything I've done, I'm not usually cruel in this way. After all that's happened between me and Lochlan, I shouldn't care. A few words are the least of the injuries we've offered each other.

But a wash of shame has swelled in my gut anyway. "Lochlan," I say roughly. "I didn't—I didn't mean—"

"Whatever you're going to say, I don't want to listen to it from a naked King's Justice." He takes a bite of the apple. "Go put your clothes on."

That makes my flush deepen, but I'm grateful for the chance to hide in the washroom. I pull the clothes on, then lean back against the small table with the basin.

When Lochlan came to the palace to meet with me and Harristan, I remember his belligerence when he sat at the table, glaring at everyone. He kept snapping at Quint, which I found particularly annoying, because Quint isn't just a close friend, he's one of the most considerate men I know. It made me want to punch Lochlan in the face.

But just now, I consider *what* Lochlan was saying when he was being so surly.

What is he writing? he was demanding. *What are you doing?*

Quint was recording the details of the meeting so there would be a record of what was said. He turned the papers around for Lochlan to see, because . . . well, because he's Quint. I'm pretty sure he even offered to have a copy of his notes made right then and there.

But now I evaluate that moment differently. Quint could have been writing anything he wanted, and Lochlan wouldn't have been able to do anything about it. Later, during that same meeting, I wrote a small note to Tessa in my own folio. It was nothing, just a few words between me and her, but I wonder how that looked to Lochlan—that we could speak privately, of sorts, but he could not.

He already didn't trust us. He already thought we were trying to trick him out of the medicine we'd promised.

Without knowing, we likely made it worse.

I finally open the door. He's still sitting there, eating the apple, his eyes on the window. But the slip of paper from the shopkeeper is beside the fruit bowl now, still folded neatly.

I move to the table and stop there. "May I join you?"

He snorts a laugh, but not like anything is really funny. "We're not in the palace. You can do whatever you want. Did someone have to drill these manners into you?"

"Yes." I drop into the chair and take an orange from the bowl. "A governess with a switch."

That jerks his attention away from the window. "Really?"

I nod. "When you're not the heir, your primary job is to look pretty and not embarrass anyone." I peel the skin off the orange in pieces and let them fall to the table. I wonder if he wants to let the moment pass, to forget what I said. But he placed that note on the table, and it's obvious that I'm going to have to be the one to read it, to determine whether we should seek any of these people or if we should continue on our morbid path toward Ford Cheeke.

I don't want to let it go.

"Lochlan," I say. "Please. Forgive me. I didn't know—"

"Shut up."

I draw myself up. "Would you—"

"I told you to *shut up.*"

"At the very least, allow me to—"

"Lord, you are the *worst,*" he snaps. "Fine then. Apologize. Do it on your knees and *beg.*"

"I will do no such thing."

He takes another bite of the apple. "Then shut up."

I clench my jaw and snatch the piece of paper from beside the fruit bowl. If Oren Crane wanted me to kill Lochlan, I don't think I'd have any hesitation whatsoever.

I scan the list of names.

No Ford Cheeke.

"*Well?*" Lochlan prompts.

I'm tempted to toss it at him and say, *Read it yourself, asshole,* but I don't.

"His name isn't on here," I say. "I don't really know what that means. Oren said he worked for Rian, but maybe he's too high-ranking. Maybe the shopkeepers don't know him."

"But if he works for Rian, any of these people should *know* him."

I nod.

Lochlan finally looks at me steadily. "Are you really going to kill him?"

"I don't know."

His voice drops. "You were really going to kill Lina, though. I could see it in your face."

I have to look down. "I just want to find Tessa. I just want to go home." I pause. "I'll do whatever is necessary."

Lochlan reaches out and taps the paper. "We could try to find these people and see if it's possible to barter passage to Fairde. That's where Rian would be, right?"

"So he can take me prisoner and hold me for ransom against Harristan? No thank you. You heard those people in the shop. Rian is surely desperate right now—and surely surrounded by people. You and I can't take him on alone. We're going to need Oren and his pirates, at least for a little while."

Lochlan takes another bite of the apple and thinks about this for a minute.

While he does, I consider that it's entirely possible that he's realizing *he* could just kidnap me and hand me over to Rian himself. He overpowered me in the cave because I was starving and dehydrated, but that doesn't mean he couldn't do it again right now.

As if he has the same thought at the same moment, Lochlan stops chewing.

I go tense immediately, and I can't help the way my eyes flick to the window, to the hearth, seeking potential weapons and escape routes.

"Oh, relax," Lochlan says. "If I work against you now, I'd never escape a hanging in Kandala. I want to go home, too."

I glare at him. I hate that I was so transparent.

But then Lochlan says, "Are you sure you want to help Oren go after Rian?"

"I don't know what you mean."

"You gave that woman so much money. I know she got to you. She got to me, too. They trust Rian. Redstone. King Galen? Whatever. They *love* him. They put a lot of hope in him, and they did that for a reason."

"I know." I sigh. "On the *Dawn Chaser*, once we knew the truth, he kept insisting that he hadn't told many lies. After speaking to the tailors, I find myself thinking that perhaps Rian truly was working in earnest for his people. He simply went about it in the wrong way."

Lochlan shrugs and finishes the apple. "Sounds familiar, Weston Lark."

My eyes narrow. I cannot believe I'm trapped with him for a companion. "You're the worst, too, Lochlan."

He wipes his hands on his trousers like an absolute savage. "Quit stalling. You told Crane you were an assassin." His eyes are piercing. "Let's go find this man so you can do what you do so well."

CHAPTER SIX

Corrick

By the time darkness falls, Lochlan and I are down to our last two coins. We've paid to keep the room for the night, as we'll need a place to return to once we've taken care of Ford Cheeke. It also provides us with a meeting point if we get separated—though I'm beginning to reach a point where I *long* for separation from him.

We've also spent a bit of silver in a few taverns, trying to learn about the people here. As we discovered in the clothier's shop, the king is well loved, and it's impossible to hide our accents, so I don't bother trying. Everyone seems happy that their king has returned safely from Kandala, but everyone seems wary of Harristan and what the future might hold. The people really *are* distrustful of my father—and my grandfather, I learn in one tavern—which makes me wonder about the trade agreements that went wrong so many years ago. But Rian's influence is strong, and it's clear that they're ready to take a chance on Kandala if it means they can access steel to rebuild their bridges—especially since

Rian is back, and our presence is evidence that Kandala sent people with him. When we mention that we're seeking passage to Fairde, we're often given the same names to contact that we were given by the tailors.

One barkeep near the harbor slid our silver back across the bar before we could say a word. "Gossip already made it this far, and you boys should know Crane's people are in the back room. Run afoul of *them*, and they'll be selling your body parts back to Kandala in exchange for their precious steel. Come back after dark. They'll be gone by then. You need to find a new tavern for now."

We didn't have enough silvers for another tavern, so we walked loops through the streets, mapping the turns, learning the paths to the harbor, finding convenient places to hide if the need arises.

Well, that's what *I've* been doing. Lochlan hasn't said much, so he could be singing nursery rhymes in his head for all I know.

I should probably be figuring out how I'm going to kill some man I've never laid eyes on, but I don't want to think about that.

Instead, I'm thinking about what Lochlan said earlier.

You told Crane you were an assassin. Let's go find this man so you can do what you do so well.

The words are like a handful of thorns stuck to the inside of my clothing, and I can't escape them. They needle me at every turn. He acts like I was a heartless executioner. I know this is an image I spent years cultivating for myself, but I hate it. I hate that he sees me that way. I hate that *everyone* in Kandala sees me that way, and I can't even escape it on an island where no one knows who I am.

I shouldn't care. I *shouldn't*. It doesn't matter what Lochlan thinks of me. I've had hundreds of prisoners in the Hold spit their hatred right in my face.

But every single step pokes me with a reminder.

Once the sun eventually drifts behind the buildings, we come to a stop in a shadowed alley near the tavern.

"Should we go back inside?" Lochlan says. "Was he trying to tell us he could help us?"

"We're going to have to ask someone directly about Ford Cheeke," I say. "No one has mentioned his name yet, which is concerning. I wouldn't put it past Oren to trick us."

"Crane said he monitors shipping logs. It's also possible that Ford just doesn't sail *himself.*"

Yes. That is also possible. I chew at the inside of my cheek. The food from the boarding house seems like we ate it days ago, and hunger gnaws at my gut. I'm tired from walking all day, too. I hurt my ankle weeks ago when the rebels captured me and Tessa, and though I thought it was healed, it seems that a day of trudging along cobblestones brought more of a strain than I was ready for. At this point, I'm tempted to steal a boat and sail it to Fairde myself.

I just don't know how.

But is that an option? Have I been overcomplicating things?

I look at Lochlan. "If we stole a boat, could you sail it to Fairde?"

"I thought you were worried about Rian capturing you and holding you for ransom."

"I am. But if we stole a boat, we wouldn't have to worry about anyone warning him that we were coming."

He regards me silently for a long moment. "Do you remember how many sailors Rian had manning the *Dawn Chaser*?"

"Yes."

"Do you see that many people in the alley with us right now?"

"I'm not talking about a ship of that size," I snap. "Obviously."

His eyes flick toward the sky. "Well, it's nighttime, and if you wanted to be *this* reckless, it might have been a better idea this morning. I don't know what the sea is like between here and Fairde, and we'd have no warning of hazards in the dark. It's not like we can just—" He breaks off, then clears his throat emphatically. "I mean, it's not like *I* can just start rowing. I also don't know if it's five miles or fifty, since we don't have any maps." He rubs at his jaw. "Or more than one person who knows their way around a boat—"

"All right, *enough.*" I drop to a crouch and brace my forearms on my knees. I miss home so much that it *aches*, and I have to shove the feeling aside.

I've had to do terrible things before. I can do them again.

Tessa, I'm coming. Forgive me.

"I'm ready to be done," I say, straightening. "Let's go talk to the barkeep."

I expect Lochlan to fire back at me with another sharp comment, but he doesn't.

Now that it's nighttime, the tavern is packed with bodies, and the stench of sweat is overpowering. The sound is overwhelming, too, with musicians on a stand in the corner, the off-key whistle of a flute making my head ache. When someone starts pounding on a drum, I want to set myself on fire.

Lochlan leans in close. "Well, this seems like a good place to get some private information."

I scowl, but we push between bodies until we reach the bar. The barkeep from earlier isn't even here.

I sigh heavily.

The new barkeep is a young woman, not much older than Tessa, with waist-length blond hair and very pretty blue eyes. She spots us and makes her way over immediately.

"Ale?" she calls over the music. "Or something stronger?"

Lochlan inhales to decline, I'm sure, but it's been a long day and it promises to be an even longer night.

"Something stronger, if you please," I call back.

Lochlan snaps his mouth shut and stares at me, but the barkeep smiles when she hears my accent. "I think I've heard about you boys. Are you looking for sweet or sour—"

"Just strong." I slap a coin on the bar. "Whatever that will buy."

Her smile widens and she swipes the coin, then turns away to fetch a bottle.

Lochlan leans in close again. "Now you want to get drunk?"

I wish. "I doubt we have anywhere *near* enough money for that."

The barkeep reappears, slapping four small glasses on the bar in rapid succession. She pours from a green bottle wrapped in silver threads, but the liquid is completely clear.

While she pours, she looks at Lochlan and gives him a wink. "Anything for you, handsome?"

That takes him by surprise, because he startles, then smiles— which makes me realize I don't think I've *ever* seen Lochlan smile.

"He's not drinking all of that himself." Without hesitation, he snatches one of the glasses and tosses it back.

"By all means, help yourself," I say, annoyed. But I give the barkeep a nod. "Thank you."

"I'll be back when you're ready for more." She turns away toward another patron.

I lift one of the glasses and tap it against Lochlan's empty one. "Cheers, handsome." Then I toss it back as quickly as he did. The liquor tastes like nothing I've ever had and burns like fire. I'm simultaneously eager for the second one and already worried it's going to hit me like a brick.

I reach for it, but Lochlan takes both glasses and moves them out of reach. "No. One was a terrible idea. You don't need two."

"Those are mine," I growl.

He leans very close. "Quit stalling."

I set my jaw, but there's nothing to say. He's right. I am stalling. I've felt his judgment all day, but being confronted with this accusation makes me feel like a coward, too.

By morning, I have to prove my claims to Oren, or that cage will be the least of my worries. I can't let Rian get a hold of me, or he really will use me against Harristan. He kept Oren's daughter locked up on his ship; I have no doubt he'd do the same thing to me if it meant he could trade me for steel.

As usual, I've been backed into a corner, and the only way out is violence. It's not fair that an innocent man has to die because of it.

I reach into my pocket and pull out our last coin.

Lochlan snatches it right out of my hand. "No more drinking."

"That's not what I'm doing."

He glares at me and holds it up anyway, the piece of silver glinting in the night. The barkeep sees it *immediately* and begins to sashay in our direction.

"So you're getting some for yourself?" I say.

"No. I'm getting information."

I scoff and reach for one of the glasses he pushed away, and he smacks my wrist. By the time the barkeep is in front of us again, we're glaring at each other, and it's a miracle I haven't punched him in the face.

But the girl's smile is bright, and she's looking at Lochlan. "Ready for more?"

"No," he says curtly, and her smile falters. "We came here

because we've heard there's a man at the docks who can get a message to Galen Redstone. What do you know about that?"

The smile has completely fallen off her face, and she glances past us. I can't tell if she's worried about other patrons or if his gruff manner is about to chase her away. Likely both.

If Lochlan ever had to come to court, he'd probably end up in a dozen fistfights within an hour.

I clap him on the shoulder and give her a knowing look. "Forgive his rudeness," I say mildly. Then I beckon her closer and whisper loudly, "He can't hold his liquor."

She giggles. The smile is back.

While I'm leaning forward, I say, "We really do need to know how to send a message, though. If you had any information to share, I'd be rather grateful."

"You'd have to speak to the harbormaster about posting messages to Fairde." She tucks a lock of hair behind one ear and takes the coin from between Lochlan's fingers, but her eyes are on me now. "They lock up the docks at midnight, though, unless you have a license. The harbormaster tucks in well before then, so you might need to wait till morning. But if you head that way, the night watchman might let you talk to the bookkeeper. He'll sometimes post messages if the harbormaster is gone for the night."

"The bookkeeper," I say.

"Yes. He does the receipts and ledgers for the dock. His name is Cheeke." She pauses. "Just be careful. The docks are dangerous at night." She leans in so close that I can feel her breath against my cheek. "Crane's people are everywhere. They watch to see who goes to see Cheeke. If your message is very private, someone might take it off your hands first."

"Thank you," I say.

She kisses me on the cheek like the woman in the clothier's shop did. "My thanks go to Kandala," she says. "A lot of people don't trust your country, but if you and your king can find a way to help us rebuild, I know ours will be grateful."

That makes my heart give a twist. She turns away before I can say anything else.

Lochlan is staring at me.

"You scoff at manners," I say. "But they serve a purpose."

That makes him scowl. "Learn anything good?"

"I know what we need to do. Let's go."

When he turns away, I go to reach for one of the remaining glasses of liquor, but they're *both* empty.

So he took them for himself. What an ass. I glare at his back as we press our way out of the crowd.

—•—

After the heat and stench and clamor of the tavern, the night air feels like a cool balm against my skin. I'm tense and irritable after being chastised over drinking, and I'm practically stomping alongside Lochlan like a child.

He has no patience for it. "Are you going to tell me what she said or not?" he demands.

"She said Cheeke keeps ledgers at the dock. But she warned me that Crane has eyes all over the harbor, waiting to intercept."

We're passing a crowd of older men who are loudly arguing about a woman named Bertha, so Lochlan says nothing until we're well past.

When he does, he comes to the same conclusion I did: "So when we kill this man, there could be witnesses from both sides. Crane said Cheeke was well guarded."

I nod. "Very likely."

"So Crane did set us up."

"Probably." I shrug a little, because I'm not surprised. "Maybe he really does want Cheeke dead, and this is an easy way to get someone else to do it. If we're caught by Redstone's people, it looks bad for Kandala. There are already enough people here who think my father and my grandfather defaulted on their promises and worked shady deals. It wouldn't take much to spread rumors that my brother and I are just as underhanded—especially if I'm quite literally caught in the act."

"But if we get away with it, Crane's people will think we're trustworthy. We'll be aligned with the pirates."

We. If *we* get away with it. I snort derisively. Lochlan has made no secret of who he expects to do the killing here. I could have left him on the ship with Crane, and the outcome would've been no different.

But Lochlan is silent, working this through. "But enough people know you're here now. That you 'worked' for the prince. If *we're* aligned with the pirates, then *Kandala* will be seen as aligned with the pirates."

"I'm glad you've caught up," I say flatly. "As usual, I'm con-fronted with horrific options, yet I'll be judged for whichever choice I make. I hope you enjoyed the drinks. I rather wish you'd left me *one*."

He frowns. "I didn't drink those. We need a clear head for this."

"Then what did you do with them?"

"I poured them out so you wouldn't grab them when I turned my back."

Oh. Considering I was going to do exactly that, I don't know what to say.

He glances over. "What the hell is wrong with you? Are you limping?"

I look right back at him. "We've been walking all day. Some self-righteous rebel told a mob to beat me to death a while ago. My right ankle is starting to give me trouble."

"Oh, right. I know how you feel." He holds out his hand and flexes his joints gingerly. "Some stupid prince broke my wrist a few weeks before that."

"That is *nowhere* near the same and you know it."

"It's exactly the same."

He's so exhausting. I want to shove him into the wall. "I didn't assault you out of hand," I say sharply. "You were trying to kill Consul Sallister."

He glances at me, annoyed. "Would you keep your voice down?"

We're passing a pair of young women who give me a lingering look. Once they're gone, I turn my head to glare at him, and I fight to keep my voice low. "I am the King's Justice, Lochlan. I couldn't watch you attack a consul *right in front of me.*"

Now it's his turn to snort derisively. "You should have let me keep going."

"I did."

He looks at me in surprise.

I shrug and look back at the darkened streets. The scent of the harbor is getting closer. "I didn't know what he was doing to the people yet, but I've never liked him. I could have stopped you more quickly. I took my time."

Lochlan says nothing to that, and we keep walking in silence. Eventually the narrow roads spill into a brightly lit span of cobblestones that lead to the docks, and we stop near the corner of a building.

"The docks at Artis are usually deserted this late," Lochlan says. "I expected it to be the same."

"Me too," I say. But the docks here are bustling with activity. Lanterns are strung up along posts at regular intervals, and street vendors are selling fried fish and sugared rolls and roasted root vegetables. Workers are everywhere, sweeping cobblestones, gutting fish, mending nets and sails. I can't decide if all this activity is better or worse. Enough rumors have spread about our identity that I don't want to be overheard down here. Not when we're this close.

I scan the shadows along the docks until I come to a wide three-story building in the center. Most of the windows are dark, but three on the second level are flickering with candlelight, shadows moving within. On the street, four armed men in red-and-black livery are stationed near the door. A large faded sign is affixed to the top of the building:

SILVESSE HARBOR STATION
UPON DOCKING, ALL VESSELS
MUST DECLARE GOODS WITHIN.

I glance at Lochlan, who's followed my gaze, but his expression gives no indication of awareness. A twist in my gut reminds me that he can't read. I nod toward the building. "He'll be in there," I say to him. "That's the Harbor Station. The girl at the tavern said Cheeke does the receipts and ledgers, and that he works late into the night."

Lochlan whistles low through his teeth. "Only four armed guards on a crowded street?" He scoffs, the sarcasm heavy. "I thought this was going to be *complicated*."

"Oh, please. You took on the entire Royal Sector. Surely this is child's play for a revolutionary like yourself."

He gives me a look. "What else did the barkeep tell you?"

"She said that Cheeke accepts messages for secret passage, but Oren Crane has eyes all over the harbor, and sometimes those messages are intercepted before people can get through."

He looks back at the guards. "Do you think those men are on Crane's payroll?"

I think of the guards in the palace back in Kandala. Before we left, Rocco was worried about Captain Huxley working against the king. On the ship, Rian talked about my country being overrun by sedition and sabotage—but I wouldn't be surprised if it's similar here. He said the royal court was still shaky, and we're not even on the same island. "At least one of them, I'm sure," I say. "And they've probably already been warned to look out for us."

"So we can't walk right up and bribe them to let us past."

"*That* was going to be your plan?"

"Not very revolutionary, I admit. But at least I didn't drink the last of my silver."

I ignore him and study the building. There's a lot of light from the street, but the back is to the water and is likely pitch-black. Likely unguarded, too, because the building is set right along the dock.

"Lord, I wish I had a treble hook," I say.

"Why?"

"I'd swim to the back and scale the rear wall."

He looks at me like I said I could build a ladder to the clouds. "You can't row a boat, but you can do *that*?"

"Weston Lark never had cause to row a boat. I had *lots* of practice sneaking in and out of the Royal Sector." I study the building again. "Let's move down to the next alley. I want to see what's on the other side."

We do, weaving among the crowds of people, remaining silent so no one has a chance to pick up our accent. I try to see if anyone notices us, but there are just too many people, too many voices, too many eyes. When we stop at the next alley, we pull into the shadows more deeply.

"There's an escape ladder from the third floor," Lochlan says. "But it's tethered up."

He's right. But there are also several windows with decorative brick framework, especially close to the back, where it's darkest. "I can climb to it from the windows."

"Are you insane?"

"There are ledges around the frames. I can see from here."

"That's barely excess mortar, you idiot."

"I'm good at climbing, Lochlan. I'll untie the ladder for you."

"You said your ankle was bothering you."

I shrug. "Well, it'll bother me a good deal more if I have to fight four guards barehanded."

"But—"

"What do you care?" I demand. My heart is pounding, and a whip of wind comes off the water to rush through my hair. The shot of liquor from the tavern has fully hit me now, and this time *I* get right in his face. "Maybe I'll fall and break my neck and all your problems will be solved. You told me to quit stalling. Now it's your turn."

I don't wait for an answer. I step right out into the crowd.

I'm savvy about my path, so I don't make a beeline right for the building. I head east a bit, lingering, studying storefronts like a casual customer out for a stroll. I think Lochlan has followed me at a distance, but I can't entirely tell, and I don't really care. I keep going, zigzagging across the road until I'm a good distance away from the guards, and then I double back.

I go more slowly this time, watching the guards, watching the people, waiting to see if anyone is watching *me*. There was a woman who seemed to be lingering suspiciously, but she moved on a few minutes ago, and now I've lost her in the crowd. An older man was standing under an awning smoking a pipe, and his eyes met mine at one point, but he's gone now.

When I near the Harbor Station, I don't hesitate. I slip right into the shadows alongside the building and stop there.

And then I realize I've lost track of Lochlan, too.

It feels like forever since I was last hiding in the darkness, and it's weird to do it without Tessa beside me. I'd know her emotion without her having to say a word, whether she was feeling brave or frightened, angry or eager. I'd know the pattern of her breathing, the scent of her skin, the meaning of every indrawn breath or frown.

I'd give anything to have her here right now.

Though she would hate everything about this.

The night the rebels first attacked the Royal Sector, they first bombed the Hold. Tessa and I stood in the palace and watched the first explosions. Many of the prisoners were freed that night, but there were two who were too badly burned to make it out, and I remember Consul Sallister demanding that I execute them right then.

I'll see to it, I said.

Tessa cried out for me to stop, and I didn't say anything. I didn't look at her.

I just went and did it.

The captives wouldn't have survived the night. They were too badly burned, too badly injured. The execution was an act of mercy, really.

But in that moment, I didn't know that—and neither did she.

I promised her I would be better, and here I am, on a mission to do my worst. I heave a breath of heavy sea air.

Despite everything, I still wish she were at my side. Maybe she could help me figure a way out of this.

No such luck.

I look at the window ledges in the shadows, and I sigh when I realize Lochlan was right. The angle of the moonlight made the ledges look deeper than they are from across the alley, but from here I see that they *aren't* much better than excess mortar. Twenty feet above me, the escape ladder is tethered against the wall, so it's high enough that it'll hurt *spectacularly* if I fall before reaching it. There are three windows below that, but only the one closest to the front flickers with candlelight. I'm hopeful the highest windows aren't locked, but I'm rarely that lucky. Even so, the streets are crowded, and the sound of the water against the harbor wall is noisy. I can break one of the windows and hope the guards don't hear.

This is truly a piss-poor plan, but I don't have many better options. Maybe I shouldn't want Tessa here right now—because this is genuinely about to be the stupidest thing I've ever done.

I might as well get on with it.

My boots grip the ledges better than I expect, but my fingernails protest almost immediately. I try to ignore the near-constant twinge in my ankle, too. The sounds from the street are muffled back here, leaving my breathing loud enough to echo against the brick wall. I'm not afraid of heights, though, and I'm patient, letting my feet and fingers feel for purchase each time I shift my weight. I make it to the top of the first window and brace there for a moment, feeling a gust of wind come in off the water.

My fingers are screaming at me, but I only allow myself one breath, then force myself to keep climbing. If I stop moving, I'm a sitting duck. A target. If someone comes down this alley, I'm done for.

A memory from childhood comes to me: climbing trees in the orchard with Harristan, branches tugging at my clothes. We were racing to the top. My fingernails were full of tree bark, and I had no hope of beating him—he was a young man of fifteen while I was barely eleven. But he always let me think I had a *chance*, so I was scrambling to keep up when a branch gave way, and I fell.

Harristan caught me. He grabbed me by the arm, and it wrenched so hard that it was sore for a week, but he kept me from a broken ankle—or worse.

I remember his worried eyes, his panicked breathing as he pulled me back onto a sturdier branch. "Always check, Cory. *Always.*"

I've lost track of how many days it's been since we left Kandala. Since I last saw my brother. Another gust of wind stings my eyes, and I blink away the emotion.

If Harristan were here, he'd be up this wall in a heartbeat. Everyone saw him as the sickly heir when he was a child, and once he was king, I heard the whispers about weakness when he tried to hide his cough. When it came to sneaking and climbing though, Harristan was always like a cat.

He would *also* hate that I'm doing this. But he would understand why.

Forgive me, brother. I hope I'm not starting a war.

Then again, Rian was already angry that someone sent

brigantine ships after us. He said he considered *that* an act of war—right before he said he was going to hold me for ransom and use me against Harristan.

So this is probably fine.

I make it to the top of the second window just as a heavy gust sweeps off the water to blast against my face, and I have to shift my weight. I'm very high now, the tethered ladder just a few feet off to my left. I set my foot on the tiniest ledge of mortar, and my ankle gives a sharp twinge. I grunt, ignore it, and shift again, and the mortar gives way.

I fall.

My fingers dig in instinctively, but I don't have enough purchase to support my weight, and I scrape along the wall for a foot until something catches my ankle, stopping my descent. My opposite knee is pressed into the window ledge now, my fingers clinging to almost nothing, and I'm panting against the pitch-dark brick. Wind whips against me again. I've completely lost track of where I am on the wall, and I can't see anything to get my bearings.

Lochlan's voice floats up to me. "I've got you. Move your left hand five inches to the left. You can grab the windowsill."

I can't believe he was there. I had no idea he was following me. Regardless, my hand refuses to move. I'm terrified that my grip will give and I'll fall the rest of the way.

But then he says, "We can't hang here all day, Cory. I've barely got a grasp on this window myself."

I hate that he keeps using my brother's nickname for me. "Don't *call* me that," I grind out.

"If you don't like it, move your ass."

I grit my teeth and reach for the windowsill. Just as he said, it's five inches away. As soon as my fingers close on the ledge, I have a better grip, and I'm able to pull free from the hold he has on my ankle. My heart gives a lurch, but I dig my toes into the wall and pull myself higher again. This time I'm more careful, and I make it all the way to the ladder. I'd never admit it to Lochlan, but I'm very grateful he tossed the second drinks. I pull the release cable and it swings down hard, and I'm barely able to stop the wood from slamming into the bricks. But now I have rungs to grab on to, not slivers of mortar and stone in the darkness.

"There," I whisper-shout to Lochlan. "Can you reach it?"

He's barely more than a shadow, but he leaps, then grabs hold.

A moment later, we're on the landing beside the third-story window, the wind whipping hard now that we're so high. We're pressed against the wall, both breathing too heavily. He's clutching his bad wrist to his chest, his jaw tight. I wonder if that's the arm that grabbed hold of my leg to stop my slide down the wall.

"Thank you," I say.

He scoffs at my gratitude and turns for the window. "I'm not telling the king his brother is dead." He tugs at the sash. "This is locked. Know how to pick it?"

"I do, but I don't have tools."

He snorts derisively. "Of course you do. I like how the King's Justice is turning out to be more of a criminal than most of—"

I ignore him and kick a hole through the window.

Lochlan flinches back from the glass, then nods appraisingly. "That works, too." He glances at me, then leans out to look toward the street. "You'll be lucky if we don't draw the guards."

"We're too high up for that. You told me to move my ass. Move yours."

Inside the Harbor Station is warm and dark. The third floor

seems to be mostly storage, and we bump into everything in the darkness, hissing profanity when we trip and stumble. The candlelit rooms seemed to be on the second floor, so we're going to need to find a staircase at some point. I'd give anything for a lantern.

Then we hear a male voice, and Lochlan and I both freeze.

"No, Mr. Cheeke, I heard it, too. I'll take a look upstairs." Almost immediately, feet begin thumping up a set of wood steps. They must be close, and whoever it is sounds like they're sizable. Brave, too, if they're volunteering to take a look.

This could be a guard or a sailor, or even just a worker—but they're a threat.

Either way, it's someone who knows Cheeke.

Either way, the time has come.

Forgive me, Tessa.

We're going to have to act.

CHAPTER SEVEN

Corrick

Lochlan and I have tucked ourselves into the shadows, and while neither of us has a *weapon*, we've each put a hand on something sturdy enough to use as a club. Mine is a heavy wooden dowel about the length of my arm. The man's feet climb the steps heavily, lacking any stealth at all, so he's clearly not worried about scaring off thieves. We're ducked behind a large chest, so I can't see anything at all, but I can hear when his footsteps reach the landing. Lantern light suddenly flickers on the walls.

The man lets out an aggrieved sigh. "There's a draft up here," he calls down. "Someone left a window open. I bet some gulls got in."

"Can you get them out?" a woman's voice calls.

"I'm looking," the man calls back. "I know *someone* is going to be discharged for this tomorrow."

Lochlan looks at me. His eyes gleam in the darkness.

I wonder if he's thinking the same things I am.

There's this man, and now a woman, too. Plus Ford Cheeke himself. Four guards outside. He has a lantern, so he's going to discover the shattered window eventually—if he doesn't discover us first. Do we kill him, too?

The man is moving away from us now. He's wearing a white shirt with sleeves rolled back and pants held up with suspenders, and he's built like the kind of man who spends a lot of time sitting at a desk. I can't tell how old he is, but the top of his head is bald, and what's left around the sides looks gray. I don't want to sit here and stare at him much longer, because if he doubles back with that lantern, he's going to see us.

I turn to Lochlan. I point at him, then toward the stairs. I point at myself, then at the man. I hope my meaning is clear. *Go for the stairs. I'll take care of him.*

Lochlan nods and doesn't hesitate. Silently, he slips away from me, and I'm alone behind the chest. My heart pounds against my ribs, and I consider that for all the hours I've spent hiding in the darkness, I never did it with the intent to cause harm.

I hate that I'm doing it now.

I have to close my eyes and take a breath. *Please, Tessa. Forgive me.*

I slip out of my spot as silently as Lochlan did. The lantern light helps me avoid the obstacles that made us trip earlier. I creep along behind the man, who gives another sigh. He's muttering as he goes, and he sounds like the kind of person who rambles as he works. "I know it's hot during the day, but those men have *got* to remember to close up before they go. They were probably lingering with Penny again. Now where are those gulls?"

It reminds me a little of Quint, and I feel a pang of homesickness. I wish I could have brought him instead of Lochlan. Traipsing the streets of Silvesse with my best friend would've felt like a holiday, regardless of what Oren Crane wanted us to do.

Well, I'll never see Quint again if I don't handle things here. I steel my will and tighten my grip on the dowel, ready to knock him across the back of the head.

But the man turns around.

He jumps a mile when he spots me, and he drops the lantern. It cracks into the floor with a little tinkle of glass, but the flame doesn't go out. Now that I can see his face, I realize he's older than I thought. Fifty, maybe sixty. I'm prepared to fight, so I'm surprised when he falls back a few steps and gasps.

His eyes skip up and down my form, and he actually says, "You're not a gull."

"No," I say.

His eyes shoot behind me, where the draft is coming from, then flick toward the stairs. I see him put two and two together, and when he inhales sharply, I know he's going to shout for Mr. Cheeke and the woman we heard.

I don't give him the chance. I surge forward and punch him right in the face.

He drops like a *rock*. I stand there with my fist drawn back to hit him again, because I genuinely didn't expect to knock him out with one strike.

He's landed in a crumpled heap, and I drop to a crouch next to him. I'm a bit horrified at the thought that I might have killed him without meaning to.

But no, he's breathing and already moaning a little.

"I'm sorry," I say softly, and I mean it. "Please forgive me. This wasn't my intent."

His fingers are already shifting against the floorboards. No one ever stays knocked out for long.

Maybe it's because he reminds me so much of an older version of my best friend, but I don't think I can kill a doddering man who says things like *you're not a gull* to an intruder.

Well, he wasn't our target anyway. I reach for his suspenders, unbuttoning them as he feebly begins to try to fight me off.

"Stop," he gasps. "What—what are you doing—"

"Tying you up," I say. I pull the suspenders free and wrench one of his arms behind his back.

He cries out, and I wince at the sound.

"If you're not quiet," I say, "my only other option is to kill you, so I need you to shut up."

He goes silent at once.

That lasts for exactly three seconds—which again reminds me of Quint.

"Please don't hurt Penny," he says in a whispered rush. "Please—not in front of Ford. He's been through—he's seen—"

"I told you to be quiet," I snap. I jerk the suspenders in a knot around his wrists. "I'm not here for Penny."

"Yes. Yes. All right. But you—your accent—you're not—"

"I'm going to punch you again."

He clamps his mouth shut.

I move to tie his ankles.

He starts babbling immediately. "The bankers take the day's draw at dusk. There's no silver on the premises, sir."

"I'm not a thief."

"But—"

I yank the knot on his ankles so tightly that he cries out again, then cuts off the sound abruptly when I meet his eyes. I load my gaze with cruel promise, the way I'd look at prisoners in the Hold.

"I only have one thing to do," I say. "So you're either going to be quiet and let me do it, or I'm going to have to kill everyone in this building. Do you understand?"

His face goes white. But he clamps his mouth shut and he nods vigorously.

"Good." I look down and see the edge of a handkerchief sticking out of his pocket. I seize it and pull it free, then ball it up in front of his face. "Open up."

"Oh, you cannot be ser—"

I shove the handkerchief in his mouth, and he cuts off with a muffled gasp. He's glaring at me, but I clap him on the shoulder. "We'll be out of your way in no time."

Then I slip down the stairs to find Lochlan.

———

My "partner" is waiting in the shadows at the bottom of the stairs, and he grabs hold of my wrist without warning, dragging me into an alcove. I'm so keyed up that I nearly kill *him* with my dowel.

"It's just me, you idiot," he breathes in my ear as he drags me against the wall.

"Did you find Cheeke?" I whisper, because it's obvious the job isn't done yet. I hate myself for it, but there's a part of me that's disappointed that Lochlan didn't take care of this for me, that we could be done and get out of here.

"Yeah, I found him," Lochlan whispers. "I've only seen him and the girl. I'm waiting to see if there's anyone else, but I haven't heard anything." He peers at me in the darkness. "Did you take care of the man?"

"Yes."

Lochlan frowns a little and looks away, and I realize he thinks I killed him.

I set my jaw and peek out of the alcove down the hallway, where candlelight flickers from three different rooms. "Which one?"

"To the right."

"Has Edward come back down yet?" calls a female voice, and I duck back quickly. She's obviously in one of the rooms to the left. Her voice sounds a bit closer, and I wonder if she's stepped into the hallway. "Maybe I should go see if he needs help."

"I'm sure he'll be back in a minute," calls a man. His voice is kind, and he sounds like he's as old as the man I tied up upstairs. "Have you found the logs from Kaisa yet? I'd really like to get through these ledgers so you can get home."

"You know I don't mind staying to help." Her voice is muffled again, and lightly teasing. "*You* need to get home, old man."

"Ah, Penny, hush." He chuckles, his tone low and gentle.

They sound so friendly and kind that I want to climb back up those stairs, untie those suspenders from Edward, and throw myself out the broken window. I thought the first man was too much with his *sir* and *you're not a gull*, but I'm supposed to kill *this* one? I'm supposed to bring back *his* head? He sounds like the grandfathers in the Wilds who'd share warm stories about their childhoods while Tessa and I were bringing them medicine. They'd pat me on the cheek and call me a good boy and wink at me, asking if I was sweet on Tessa when she couldn't hear.

Just a little, I'd always say.

Lord, how she'd hate this.

I pull back into the shadows of the alcove, bracing my shoulders against the wall. My heart is pounding hard. I don't want to hurt anyone—but my thoughts are so tangled up, and I don't know how else to work with Oren Crane to find a way back to Tessa. There isn't going to be anyone else in Ostriary who's willing to stand against Rian—and I know what Rian will do if he gets his hands on me.

Lochlan looks at me, studying my face for a long minute.

"Do you have another idea?" he says.

"No," I grind out roughly.

"Do you know why I didn't kill your brother when we held the Circle?" he says.

The question comes out of nowhere, and I turn my head to look at him. "What?"

"When we held the Circle. In the middle of the Royal Sector. During the revolution—"

"No, I know when you mean. What are you talking about?"

He steps closer. "Do *you*, Cory, know why I didn't kill the *king*?"

"If you call me that again, I'm going to shove this dowel somewhere you won't like it." I glare at him. "If you'd killed the king, the army would have filled you with a hundred arrows before your finger left the trigger."

"Maybe, maybe not. There was a lot of smoke. A lot of cover. And I had a clean shot at least three times. The king had armor, but I had a crossbow. I could have got him in the face. Or the throat. Tessa, too."

I've gone completely still, frozen in place in the little alcove. I have to shake my thoughts loose and remind myself that he *didn't* kill my brother. That he didn't harm Tessa. My hand is tight on the dowel anyway.

Lochlan's eyes haven't left mine, and he laughs under his breath, but not like anything is really funny. "Exactly," he says. He leans in close. "I wasn't worried about the army. I'd seen you as Weston Lark, and I'd seen you as Prince Corrick. If I killed the king, I was afraid of what *you* would do."

I look away from him and shift to peer down the hallway. "I already know you think I'm a monster, Lochlan. It's the only reason we're here."

He grabs my shoulder and jerks me back into the alcove. "No," he growls, his voice low. "I actually kind of hate that you're *not* a monster." His eyes are very dark in the shadows. "But I know you can do terrible things when you have to."

I stare at him. It's the closest he's ever come to acknowledging that my actions are backed by something other than cruelty, and *I* actually kind of hate that he's said it in a way that won't let me enjoy it.

But he's not done. "I hate all of this," he says. "I don't want to be a part of Rian's stupid conflict either. But I want to go home as badly as you do. I wouldn't have followed you this far if I expected you to hesitate. The *King's Justice* wouldn't hesitate."

That shocks me still again. Lochlan is the last person in the world I ever expected to hear such a thing from. But maybe it's a reminder I need, because I take a deep breath and let a cool band of focus wrap around my thoughts. I've done terrible things to protect Kandala for years. I've supported my brother's reign for years. I can't be better for Tessa if I can't get us out of this mess.

I steel my spine, and then I tap Lochlan on the cheek, a little too hard to be friendly. "Love you, too. Now cover my back."

With that, I slip out of the alcove. Cheeke's room is first, and I cling to the wall, because shadows are shifting in the room where the woman is working. Cheeke is visible from the hallway, but he's not quite as old as he sounded. He's sitting at a desk, writing in a ledger by the light of several lanterns. He's slender, and doesn't seem overly tall, with thick gray hair. A pipe sits on the desk beside him, and I catch a whiff of tobacco smoke. He's facing the door, so there's no way I'm going to take him unawares. I'm going to have to run at him, and considering his build, he'll probably put up a fight. Based on the distance, he'll have time to pull a weapon, if he's got one.

But none of that is what's really caught my attention. His clothes are buttoned up nicely, his hair and beard finely trimmed, but a massive cluster of burn scars run from his ear to the back of his head and down the side of his neck. The scarring is profound, disappearing down the collar of his shirt.

While I'm staring, I notice the scars affect his hand, too. It looks like he's missing a finger or two.

And then I realize I've stared for one second too long, because the woman appears in the other doorway, carrying two books under one arm. She's saying, "I really do think I should check on Edward," but she breaks off with a shriek when she sees me.

"Penny!" the man shouts in alarm, and he shoves back from his desk.

"One of Crane's people got in here!" Penny cries. She's young and pretty and full of scars herself—and that's all I notice before she chucks a book right at my head.

Well, there goes my element of surprise. I knock the book out of the way and prepare to fend her off.

But Lochlan slips out of the darkness to seize her. "Get *him*!" he snaps at me, just as she cries out, trying to wrench herself free.

"Try not to hurt her," I tell him, and then I turn to face Cheeke.

I'm almost too late. The man tackles me with a knife in hand, and it nearly goes right into my gut. As it is, I knock his arm to the side with the dowel, but he slams into me anyway. We go tumbling into the hallway. My shoulders take the impact, but I use momentum to my advantage, and I roll Cheeke into the wall. I'm distantly aware of Lochlan struggling to keep a grip on the girl, and it sounds like she's trying to scream, but he's got a hand over her mouth. I get a hold of Cheeke's wrist and slam his hand against the floor. The knife clatters to the floor, and he grunts, trying to twist away from me.

"Penny!" he gasps.

Behind us, she squeals, and she must do *something*, because Lochlan yelps. Cheeke surges against my weight, but I have the upper hand now. I shift to kneel on his wrist, then pin his neck to the floor with the dowel. The blade hasn't gone too far, and I take hold of the hilt, putting the point right against his throat.

He's panting, wheezing from the pressure on his neck. It reminds me of the way Harristan breathes sometimes. I force the thought out of my head, because if I compare him to my brother, I'll never be able to do this.

The King's Justice wouldn't hesitate.

The blade is in my hand, but I can't move. My heart won't stop pounding.

This is nothing like what I ever had to do in Kandala. Maybe Harristan and I could have done *better*, but we were *trying*. We were trying to keep our people alive. We were doing the best we could in an impossible situation. When I did terrible things, I was enforcing laws to protect the people.

There's no justice in this. None at all.

Cheeke isn't even looking at me. His eyes are straining past me, at Lochlan and Penny, who don't seem to be struggling as much now. She's whimpering.

"Please," Cheeke gasps. "Please let her go. Don't hurt her anymore. Tell Crane I'll give him whatever he wants."

Penny squeals a little in Lochlan's grasp, and her voice is muffled, but she says, "Papa, *no*."

Now I understand the fondness in his tone when he spoke earlier. She's not an employee. They're not business partners. Ford Cheeke is her *father*.

It reminds me of Tessa. Tessa, whose own father was killed right in front of her. I watched it happen.

Tessa, who would hate every single part of what we're doing.

Tessa, who sat in front of me on the *Dawn Chaser* and lectured me about the way I turn every single person I meet into an adversary before I give them a chance to be an ally.

Much like I'm doing right now.

Lochlan grunts with strain again, but his voice is tight with something akin to sorrow. "I'll take her down the hall."

A cord pulls in my chest. He'll take her down the hall—so she doesn't have to see.

I stare into Ford Cheeke's face. His eyes blaze into mine. He doesn't look afraid, and he doesn't look furious.

He looks *beseeching*.

"Please," he gasps, and his voice has grown so soft it's barely a whisper. "Please just let her go. She's been through so much."

"Papa," she whimpers. Then she must fling her head back, because there's a cracking sound, and Lochlan swears—but he doesn't let her go. He begins wrenching her backward.

"Please," Ford says again. "I beg of you."

I try to steel myself against the words, but I can't. I'm so tired of listening to people beg me for mercy and never being able to grant it. My brother is the king. There should be another way. There should be a *better* way.

I hear Tessa's voice in my head.

You could have been kind, and you could have been gentle, and you could've explained.

She was talking about the night she snuck into the palace, when she woke up and discovered I was the terrifying Prince Corrick, not the warm outlaw Weston Lark she'd grown to love and trust.

And she was right.

"Stop," I grind out. "Lochlan, wait."

"It's her da," he says, his tone resigned. "She doesn't need to see this."

I look down at the man I'm pinning to the floor. "Are you Ford Cheeke?" I say, because I want to be absolutely sure.

He swallows hard against the dowel. The burn scars against his throat have an unusual pattern—not like someone who's been caught in a fire. Like someone who's been exposed to fire over and over again.

"Yes," he chokes out.

"Are you passing secret messages about Oren Crane to the king?" I say. "You have the means to get word to Galen Redstone?"

"What are you doing?" Lochlan hisses.

Ford looks back at me, and his expression shifts as he studies me. But that only lasts for a second before his eyes flick back to Penny. "My daughter—you have to let her go—"

"I'll let her go if you answer honestly."

"Don't tell them anything," Penny is saying behind Lochlan's hand. "It's a trap."

Then she must bite him because he yelps and jerks his hand away.

And then she starts screaming.

It's only for a second before Lochlan clamps his hand over her mouth again, then braces his back against the wall as she redoubles her struggles. He's practically panting from the effort to keep her still. "Either get it done, or we're going to have to run. The guards probably heard *that*." Now he sounds aggrieved.

I press the blade against Ford's neck. "I don't work for Crane," I say. "But I need to know if I'm speaking to someone who truly has the means to get word to Redstone. Tell me now."

He studies me again. "Your accent. You're from Kandala." Realization dawns. "Penny—Penny, *stop!*"

His daughter goes still.

I don't look away from Ford. "Yes. We are. Your turn."

He nods, then winces as his chin touches the cold steel of the blade. "Yes. I can get word to the king. Who are you?"

I take a deep breath and hope I'm not making a mistake here. I withdraw the blade, then the dowel. I sit back and let him go.

"I'm Prince Corrick," I say. "Younger brother to King Harristan of Kandala. We were separated from the *Dawn Chaser* on our journey to Ostriary and captured by Oren Crane."

Ford pushes himself to sitting, but at that, he goes still. His voice is very quiet. "I received word that the prince was killed."

"I'm very much alive." I glance at Lochlan, who's let Penny go. She's staring at me, too. I look back at her father. "Master Cheeke, forgive the violent intrusion, but we need your help."

CHAPTER EIGHT

Corrick

We end up in Ford Cheeke's office, standing around a long table. I think we're all still too tense to sit. The room is warm and smells faintly of tobacco smoke. Ford is clearly an organized man, because the room is neat as a pin, not a paper or book out of place. The bookcases that line the back wall of the room are so perfectly ordered that I'd be hesitant to remove a book. Even the ledgers and papers on his desk seem arranged with precision.

We had a brief moment of worry when two of the guards from out front *did* come to investigate Penny's scream. Ford urged us to hide in a storage closet, so Lochlan and I tucked ourselves into the space, leaving the door only slightly ajar so we could hear.

"We might have just trapped ourselves," Lochlan breathed at me. "You'd better hope he believes you."

"I'm not killing an innocent man just to get home," I whispered back.

But then I stood stock-still while sweat gathered in the small of my back, and I wondered if I'd made the biggest mistake of all. If Ford and Penny turned us over to the guards, there would've been no telling where we'd end up.

But we stood and listened as Penny told them she'd only screamed because a mouse had burst out of the closet. The guards had rolled their eyes and left.

Penny went to untie Edward, who's joined us in the office. Now the three of them are at one end of the table, staring at me and Lochlan a little warily.

Ford glances at his companions in a way that tells me there must have been private conversations during the time Lochlan and I were hiding in the closet. Then he clears his throat.

"If you wouldn't be opposed, Your Highness, before we get to your request, I would like to attempt to verify your identity."

"How are you going to do that?" demands Lochlan, and they all pull back a little.

Honestly. He's so *brusque*. If anyone needs a governess with a switch, it's him. I shoot him a glare, then lift a hand, placating. "It's fine. I understand their caution."

"Thank you," says Ford. "My report that said you were . . . ah, *dead*, also claimed that warships from Kandala followed the *Dawn Chaser* and attacked on the open sea. So we're a bit wary of a trick. After your rather violent entrance."

"Those brigantines sank," I say. "But again, I'll answer what questions you have."

Edward moves to the bookcase and puts a finger against his lips, surveying the contents. After a moment, he stoops to withdraw a slim volume from a low shelf. He flips it open and scans a page, then moves close to Penny. He's got quite a bruise on his jaw, and I refrain from wincing. He and Penny engage in a rushed whispered conversation, hastily flipping pages.

Lochlan leans close. "What are they going to do, quiz you on Kandalan history?"

I have no idea. I surely hope not. Would they have books on Kandalan history here? Would they be accurate?

Penny finally looks up. "What was your maternal grandmother's middle name?"

Well, that takes me by surprise. I blink, then think about it. "Ah . . . Annabel."

"Excellent!" says Edward, as if I'm a prize pupil and didn't knock him flat twenty minutes ago. He really does remind me of a much older Quint. "Your paternal great-grandfather. What was his fourth name?"

I honestly can't believe *this* is my quiz, but I'll take it. I mentally work backward through the family tree.

"Are you counting on your fingers?" Lochlan mutters.

"What's *your* paternal great-grandfather's fourth name?" I say under my breath. I look at the others. "Druvil."

Penny takes the book. "Ooh! Your great-great-grandmother had a *sister*, and she actually had six names, which is quite a lot, even for royalty—"

"I think that's enough," says Ford, and he gives his daughter a bit of a withering glance. He moves to the bookcase and selects an even larger book, and I wonder if I'm going to be forced to list the pets of my uncles or something—but Ford then reaches *behind* it. He must press a latch or turn a lever, because we all hear a *click*.

After a moment, he withdraws a folded slip of paper, and he unfolds it carefully. He glances at it, then back at me. "Name the individuals you brought on the ship with you—and what happened to them."

"Myself, Tessa Cade, and Lochlan Cresswell." I gesture at Lochlan. "In addition to three guards from Kandala: Erik Rocco, Liam Kilbourne, and Matthew Silas." I pause, and my voice turns grave. "Matthew Silas was lost at sea when the brigantines attacked. Liam Kilbourne was killed by the crew. Erik Rocco was injured in the fight. I don't know if he survived." I hesitate. "Tessa . . ." My voice trails off, and I frown. My heart is suddenly pounding, because until this moment, I hadn't considered that Ford Cheeke might be a source of information that might benefit *us* as well.

Tessa.

I glance at the letter, which I'm assuming came from Rian himself. My voice goes very quiet. "If you know this much about our journey, I'm very hopeful you have word of where she ended up."

Ford considers this, then glances at the others. "Put the book away, Penny." He slips the letter back into its hiding place, then gestures to the chairs. "Please. Sit."

We do.

Ford wastes no time. "Tessa Cade and Erik Rocco are both alive. They safely made it to Fairde."

A tightness in my chest seems to ease and tighten simultaneously. "So they're with your king."

"The letter didn't specify, but it would stand to reason that they are. I have a skiff departing at dawn tomorrow." He moves to his desk and pulls a slip of parchment from a drawer, followed by an ink pen. "I'll send word at once that you've survived—"

"No," I say.

He stops short and draws himself up. "*No?*"

"Your king lied about his identity and tricked me into

journeying to Ostriary. I have no interest in escaping one man's manipulation and being traded for another's."

All three of them exchange a glance. "Manipulation?" says Edward.

"Did Kandala not agree to barter for steel?" says Penny.

But Ford's gaze is more appraising. "Does this have anything to do with why you were ready to cut my throat upon arrival?"

"Quite a lot," Lochlan says dryly.

"The only reason we survived was because Oren Crane's people fished us out of the water," I say, and Penny gasps. Her hand goes to the burn scars at her neck.

"He's kept us prisoner until dawn yesterday," I say. "We convinced him to let us go temporarily. He believes Lochlan is a Kandalan spy and I am an assassin. He gave us a task to prove our roles, because he believes we want vengeance against Rian for letting Prince Corrick die. But he expects us back at dawn." I pause, studying Ford across the table. "And I'm not sure how he'll proceed once it becomes clear that we did not succeed."

He studies me right back, and his eyes are piercing. "So you've aligned yourself with Oren Crane?"

"I'm trying to stay alive until I can find a way to bring my people back to Kandala, Master Cheeke."

"What was your task?" says Edward.

Before I can answer, Ford does it for me. "To kill me."

I nod. "He believes you have a secret way to pass messages to your king."

Ford gives a little humorless laugh. "*Secret.* I suppose to a man like Oren, the matter of detail and precision might seem like a secret. Everything that passes through this harbor is weighed and measured and recorded in this office. Every letter, every parcel, every piece of freight. The sender, the receiver, the weight. I and my people are known for our accuracy, Your Highness." He gestures toward the hallway. "If you wanted to, you could find the details for a pallet of firewood shipped to Roshan ten years ago. Third room on the left, I believe."

"So there are no secret messages?" says Lochlan.

"None at all." Ford tugs at his jacket and spreads his hands. "But I am getting older. Perhaps I miss a few things here and there."

Fascinating.

I eye those scars along his skin, remembering the way he said his daughter had gone through enough. "Has Oren Crane tried to torture this information out of you in the past?" I say.

He nods. "His people have. Lina is particularly vicious." His eyes flick to his daughter, and she shudders.

"We've met Mouse, too," says Lochlan.

Ford shakes his head. "Mouse wasn't always that way. He used to work on the docks. Moving the heavy loads. A lot of dockworkers are on Crane's payroll, but Mouse refused to work for Crane once everyone started trying to rebuild. Crane sent Lina after him, and I heard she and her henchmen threw bricks at his head until he stopped moving—but it didn't kill him. It just broke his mind. When he eventually woke up, Lina convinced him that he worked for Crane all along."

I didn't think I could hate Lina any more.

"So there's truly no other details about sending secret messages you can share?" I say to him.

"No. I simply don't track certain missives."

That seems a little too deliberately vague, and I've spent too many hours questioning prisoners who spin the truth to avoid execution. I raise an eyebrow. "For certain *people*, surely."

Ford's eyes narrow. "You broke in here to kill me, and you haven't offered a clear indication as to whether you're working *with* or *against* the people of Ostriary." He folds his arms. "Kandala has quite the sour history with our country, so I believe I've said all I'm willing to say, Your Highness."

"If your king had been forthright," I say, "my motives would be crystal clear. Rian presented an opportunity to help Kandala in exchange for steel—and I boarded his ship with the intent to begin negotiations. Instead, he lied about his identity, killed my guards, and told me that someone is poisoning my country. I'm trapped here with no way home. I'll work with whomever grants me the best options." My voice turns sharp. "Right now, I rather doubt that's your king."

Lochlan leans toward me. "Not for nothing, but a few minutes ago, you did tell this guy you wanted his help."

His voice was quiet, but Penny adds, "After breaking in and scaring us half to death."

Edward nods. "Quite true. And while I'm glad to be alive, you do strike quite a blow, Your Highness."

Lord. I run my hands across my face and wish I could undo so much about the last few weeks.

Honestly, so much about the last few *years*.

"Ostriary spent a great deal of time at war," Ford says. "Many of the islands have only just begun to rebuild. You did say you wanted my help, but if you're going to align yourself with Oren Crane to tear it all down again, please tell me now."

I don't want adversaries, but it seems like that's all I'm good at making.

Harristan is really better at keeping things congenial. The night we first met Rian, I thought we were going to come to blows across the dinner table, but my brother kept cutting through the tension with quiet ease.

But memories of that moment help me stop and think.

"I don't want any part of your war," I say. "I've already seen evidence of what Crane has done. But he did indicate that he has eyes all over Silvesse. Is that true?"

"Yes," says Ford.

"Then I have no doubt his people have been trailing us all day. If I leave here without completing this *task*, they'll likely recapture us. They might be waiting outside right now."

Penny and Edward exchange a worried glance.

"So I need something else to give him," I say. "Something *better*."

"If my options are to benefit Crane or to face my own death, you don't want my help," says Ford. "You mean to blackmail me."

Edward leans toward Penny, and his voice is very soft, but I hear him. "It's no wonder Kandala's royal family has such a nefarious reputation."

I let out a breath. I suppose this does look like that. I need to *think*.

As much as I hate Lochlan, he was good at strategizing when we were trapped in the cage—and our plan did get us away from Crane, at least for a short time. He might be terse and lacking in manners, but he was also able to organize a revolution and lead rebels into the Royal Sector.

So I look at him. "If we walk out of here, Crane's people are going to be on top of us."

He gives a short nod. "Yeah."

"If *they* sneak us out of here, they're going to send us to Rian, and that's not better."

"You've said."

"Crane thinks Rian still has his daughter. Can we use that somehow?"

His eyebrows shoot up. "You're asking *me*?"

"Yes," I say. "I am."

His mouth quirks up like he wants to be flippant, but then his gaze sharpens, and he frowns a little. He looks at Ford. "Why hasn't Rian been able to get rid of Crane?"

"Too squirrelly. Too many allies." Ford pauses. "Again, they're all over Silvesse. On other islands, he doesn't have a stronghold, but here, he does—and his allies are *very* loyal."

I consider how he didn't even come on land to talk to me. I wonder if he's always on that ship. He certainly had a lot of people surrounding him. I wonder how many people Rian has. I doubt Ford will tell me.

Lochlan looks at me. "We could tell Crane that when we discovered the 'secret' messages, we learned where his daughter is being held—and we decided it wouldn't be prudent to kill Ford in case that tipped off Rian."

Ford looks alarmed. "But I have no idea where his daughter is being held. I don't want Crane coming after *me*—"

"His daughter isn't being held anywhere," I say. "She's dead."

My words drop like a rock.

"Oh," says Ford.

I look back at Lochlan. "But that's a good idea. It would also motivate him to sail to Fairde to rescue her—especially if we said Rian was hiding her."

Ford is glaring at me. "And how is this *not* leading an assault on our king?"

I glare right back at him. "Because you're going to send him a warning of exactly when and where this 'rescue' is taking place, and you're going to tell him that Prince Corrick of Kandala handed him his primary rival on a silver platter, and I expect restitution in the form of a return journey to my home country."

Ford turns this around in his head, and I'm sure he sees all the same places this can go wrong that I do. This plan is full of holes that I'm going to need to fill in later, but it's more than we had an hour ago.

"What if Crane doesn't believe you?" he says.

"Then I'm no worse off than I am right now." I glance around the table. "And you're all still alive."

"You're going to need to return here," Ford says. "If he believes you, this will take some arranging. I can't snap my fingers and instantly receive a response from our king. How will you convince Crane that you need to come *back*?"

That almost throws me. It's a good question, and my thoughts are spinning.

But then I have a solution, and once the idea comes to me, it's so obvious that it shouldn't have taken me any time at all.

"Don't worry." For the first time in what feels like weeks, I smile. "I have an idea."

━━━━

I was right. Crane's people jump us before we get far. We're dragged into an alley and shoved up against a wall.

I find myself glaring at Lina and Mouse. Lina's got her hands on her hips like she's the leader of this little pack, while Mouse stands off to the side like a wounded-yet-trained bear, waiting for orders.

Two of the men are pinning me against a brick wall, but Lina draws a dagger and puts it right against my throat. I feel the bite of the blade and then a trickle of blood, but she doesn't press any harder, and I refuse to flinch.

"I knew you'd fail," she says. "Give me one good reason I shouldn't kill you right now."

"The fact that you'll never forget that I could have killed you with my bare hands, but you need two people to hold me down while you do it with a knife."

She growls in rage, then spits right in my face.

"Well, that's horrific," I say, clenching my eyes closed. "I might have preferred the knife."

"I can do it with my bare hands," she says. Then she punches me right in the stomach.

My eyes are still closed, so I take the hit fully. It knocks the wind out of me. The only thing holding me upright is the grip these men have on my arms.

"If you beat him to death," Lochlan says, "then Crane won't get his daughter back."

She punches me again and I see stars. I'm choking on air.

"Fine," says Lochlan. He sounds bored. "I'll tell Crane it was your fault."

"Lina," says Mouse worriedly. "*Lina.*"

"They're lying."

I fight for air and barely succeed. "We're not," I gasp. "That's— that's why—"

"That's why we couldn't kill Ford Cheeke," Lochlan finishes for me. "He knows where Redstone is hiding Bella."

Lina has her fist drawn back, ready for another punch, but Mouse catches her arm. She's breathing hard and spitting mad, but Mouse isn't looking at her, he's looking at me.

"Is that true?" he says.

I nod. "Yes, Mouse," I wheeze. "It's true."

Lina tries to tug her arm free. "You let me go, Mouse, or I'm going to carve my name into your *back*."

He looks at her. "Stop hitting him, Lina. Oren needs to know first."

She glares at him, but one of the men pinning my arms to the bricks says, "He's right, Li. Oren needs to know."

She swears. "Fine. Bring them."

—+—

The ship is black in the moonlight, only a few lanterns hung from the masts. Now I have an ache in my gut to go along with my sore ankle. At least I was able to wipe Lina's spit from my eyes.

It's clear that Lina doesn't believe us when she announces our arrival to Oren and anyone on deck to listen.

"They didn't kill Cheeke," she says, sounding exasperated. "They didn't even have anything with them. They completely failed, and now they're making up a story about Bella so you don't hang them."

"What story?" says Oren.

"We broke in," I say. "We met Cheeke and his people." I pause and look around at the other sailors. "While Lina might like to leave people in a pile of broken bones, Lochlan and I find it's easier to get information with a little bit of sophistication and grace. What we discovered was too important, so we were returning to you for further orders."

I say "orders" deliberately, offering Oren Crane the power here. I see the flicker in his eyes as it registers.

"Ask your people," I continue. "We didn't even resist when they dragged us into the alley."

Oren studies me, looking for a lie.

But there isn't one.

Mouse offers, "They didn't fight, Mr. Crane. They asked us to bring them to you."

"You still haven't told me what you've learned about my daughter," says Oren.

I nod. "Ford has received letters from Redstone that indicated he still has Bella held captive."

That flicker in his eyes turns into a gleam. "Where?"

"In his palace. But he would obviously move her to a new location if he thought you were planning a rescue."

"Then how does that help me?" Oren demands.

"I could leak false information to Ford Cheeke," I say. "Tell him that you're planning a rescue—and find out where they're moving her. Then you could plan a *real* rescue that they're not expecting."

"Why would you help me?" says Oren.

"Why *wouldn't* I help you?" I say. "As I've said before, Galen Redstone killed my prince and tricked my king." It takes no effort to insert fury into my tone. "You think I can't wait to cut his throat, too? I'll do anything I can to help you. I'll even rescue her myself if you want—though I'm sure she'd rather see her father's face as her savior."

Those words hit their mark, too.

Lina practically explodes. "Why would Ford Cheeke tell you any of this?" she demands. "You broke in to kill him. This has to be a lie."

Oren turns his gaze back to me and Lochlan. Some of that spark in his eyes dims. "Indeed. Explain *that*, Weston Lark."

"Oh, that's not who I said I was," I say. "I told Mr. Cheeke that Weston Lark drowned in the attack."

Lochlan nods and claps me on the shoulder. "It was very tragic. I'm so sorry for your loss."

Oren is studying me now, and he looks like he can't decide whether to be angry or amused. "Then who does he think you are?"

"He believes I'm Prince Corrick of Kandala," I say. "And we desperately need his help to reach the king."

CHAPTER NINE

Tessa

Since we don't have horses or a carriage, we'll need to walk to Rian's palace. I only vaguely know the direction, because on the night we arrived on the barely functional *Dawn Chaser*, I didn't care where I was going. I just wanted it to be *away from Rian*.

Luckily, Erik paid closer attention. He says most of the roads seemed heavily traveled and well-marked, so it shouldn't be hard for us to find our way. It took about an hour by wagon, so he estimates it'll take twice that on foot. That almost makes me reconsider going at *all*, because I remember him wincing when he tossed the nets. I didn't want him to lose consciousness in the middle of the ocean, and I don't want him to collapse on the side of the road either.

When I tell him this, Erik sighs and finally allows me to redress his injury. I mix a new poultice in the kitchen while he peels the old one free. The wound doesn't look worse, but it doesn't look much better. I still don't think he should have been rowing or haul-ing nets, and I tell him so.

"I can walk, Miss Tessa."

I scowl, and I double wrap the bandage so it'll sit in place snugly. "For *four hours*?"

"I said *two*."

"Well, we'll have to walk back. I'm *not* staying there overnight."

He regards me evenly. "The longer we wait, the less leverage you'll have. And you should not go alone."

"Fine." I put away my things while he pulls down his shirt. "I'm ready to go whenever you are."

He frowns, then studies me more critically while he reaches to unlace his boots. "Perhaps you should arrange your hair. Do you have any pins? Maybe a dress, too."

I look at him like he's grown another head. "You want me to arrange my *hair*?"

"Regardless of your feelings, Rian is the king here. We *are* visit-ing his court."

Right. I somehow keep forgetting that.

"Well, I don't care." I set my jaw. "If Rian doesn't like my hair, he can go suck a—"

"There is more than one way to fight." Erik looks at me levelly, then yanks a boot free, and I try to ignore when he winces again. "I remember the day you came to face King Harristan. The way you challenged him about medicine, how he offered to have you meet with the royal physicians. Do you think he would have lis-tened as clearly if you'd arrived like this?"

That gives me pause. I do remember that. I was terrified of the king, but Erik is right. Harristan barely believed my theories as it was. He probably wouldn't have listened to a scared girl from the Wilds at *all* if I'd been dropped in front of him in my patched skirts with uncombed hair.

The clothes and makeup in the palace hadn't even been my choice. Not really. Quint had been the one to send me an attendant, to order that my closets be stocked with clothes, my dressing table filled with cosmetics. At the time, I found the silk and lace and powders and creams to be frivolous, but it wasn't. It was just another type of armor. I didn't realize it at the time, but Quint was sending me into battle, fully prepared.

And Quint would *never* let me go see Rian like this.

Quint. Telling him about Corrick will be as bad as telling the king. My chest tightens, and I have to force the emotion away again. "You're right," I say. My eyes skip over his trousers and tunic. He's pulling off the second boot, but more gingerly, and he doesn't wince this time. "Are you changing, too?"

"I am."

I nod. "All right. Let me go see what I have."

Despite the condition of Rian's ship, most of my finer things survived the journey, but I haven't bothered to unpack these trunks yet. I lay out my dresses across my bed, and all the silk and chiffon and velvet is pressed into creases from being folded in the trunk for so long. Since we're walking so far, I don't want to wear anything too elegant, but I locate a light muslin dress that isn't too wrinkled, with tiny blue flowers embroidered along the bodice and the hem. The short sleeves leave most of my arms bare, but it has a leather belt that works perfectly for holding one of the daggers I found among the weapons in the guards' chests. I've been sleeping with it under my pillow. It's not as decorative as the dagger Corrick once gave me, but the hilt is leather wrapped and gold-plated, stamped with the crest of Kandala.

It'll still stab someone, so I don't care how pretty it is. If I get the chance to stab Rian, I actually wouldn't mind a little rust.

A collection of hairpins is stashed among my things, and I brush out my hair to twist it into fresh plaits that I twirl artfully on the back of my head. There are cosmetics too, but I leave those in the trunk. Armor or not, I won't give Rian the satisfaction of thinking I care about his opinion of me.

I find some jewels as well, wrapped up in velvet pouches and nestled among the dresses. Nothing that was *mine*, as I've never owned anything so expensive, but again, Quint must have ensured that I would be prepared for all manner of events in the Ostrian courts.

Thank you, Quint.

I don't want to wear any of the jewels, but I consider that we don't have any money here, and we don't know who or what we'll encounter on the road, so we might have the need to trade for something. My life in the Wilds also makes me wary of thieves, so I can't be too ostentatious. I settle on some demure hairpins that have tiny blue stones at the ends, and a small bracelet made of gold and opals.

When I emerge from my room half an hour later, I'm startled to discover Erik rubbing a shine into his black boots. He hasn't just changed, but he's buttoned into his guard uniform, including all his weapons. He even has a crossbow slung over one shoulder, extra bolts in a narrow quiver along the outside of his thigh. After more than a week seeing him in his shirtsleeves, I'd forgotten he could look *quite* this imposing.

"You're going as a guard?" I say.

His eyebrows go up, and he straightens, tossing the rag into his trunk. "That's how I came. Did you expect otherwise?"

I have no idea. Maybe I should have figured. I really need to get it together. "So . . . farewell to Erik, then," I say. "Welcome back, Rocco."

He grins. "Either is really fine." He pauses, considering. "Though . . . perhaps in front of Rian, it might give you an edge of authority if you stuck with 'Rocco.' The prince would have." He looks me over, his gaze approving until he spots the dagger.

The smile vanishes, and he sighs. "Do you know how to use that?"

"I know where the pointy part goes."

"Fair enough. Draw it then. Show me."

Oh. I wasn't prepared for that. But I reach across my body and draw the dagger, jabbing it at him, trying to look fierce.

I wait for him to tease me, but he doesn't. He steps toward me and holds out a hand, gesturing for the weapon. "Point it down. If you're not experienced with it, you'll be stronger with a downward strike." I let him take the weapon, and he demonstrates. "See?"

I nod, and he points at the belt. "Let it hang from your opposite side so it's beside your hand. It'll be easier to draw this way."

He sounds so official, and I swallow, then twist the sheath until it's hanging on the opposite side of the buckle.

But once I'm done, he holds my gaze, and he doesn't return the dagger. "You can't kill him."

"I can look like I'm ready to." I hold out my hand.

"Fair enough." He hands me the weapon, and I take it, point down this time. I mimic his downward strike, and he's right. There is a lot more power to it.

He smiles. "See?"

I nod, then slam the dagger into the sheath. I already feel better.

He picks up a pack and tosses it over one shoulder. No wince at all this time. Maybe the new bandage is helping. "I've put together some supplies in case we get hungry." He rolls his eyes. "Or for when trouble finds us."

I hadn't considered getting into trouble. "Here." I hold out my hand, gesturing for the pack. "Let me add another set of bandaging supplies then. Just in case."

He sets it on the floor so I can add what I need. After I've tucked muslin and scissors and poultice supplies in among the other things, I buckle the bag closed and swing it onto *my* shoulders. The weight slams into my back, a lot heavier than I expected, and I have to sidestep to balance out the weight.

Erik gives me a *look*, but I stare right back at him. He sighs and reaches for the pack, but I take a step away as if he's going to yank it off my shoulders.

"I've got it," I say hotly. "You don't have to carry *everything*."

He raises an eyebrow. "May I adjust the straps so you don't fall over?"

"Hilarious." But I step forward again, and he tightens the straps, then buckles a length of leather at the base of my rib cage, securing it all in place.

Once he's done, he gives the strap a steady tug, back and forth. "See?"

The pack barely shifts on my back—but his tugging makes me sway in a silly way, and I realize he's teasing. He really is very brotherly.

I give him a sheepish smile. "*So* much better. Thank you."

"You're welcome."

Then we're off.

Much like when we set off in the boat, there's no one around. The air is warm, the trees humming with insects. Sweat blooms under the pack almost immediately, but I don't complain. The weight, the effort, it all makes me *feel* something. Erik was right earlier. I do need to move.

"It wouldn't be this warm in Kandala," I say.

"It would be in Sunkeep," he says. "We'll have to ask Rian for some maps. I want to know where we are in relation to the other islands."

Maps, I think, adding that to my list of things to ask for. *Check.*

"I know you don't want to betray the king," I say, "but is there anything you can tell me that might give me a *little* leverage over Rian? Anything that might help us negotiate a way to get back?"

"I can tell you everything I remember about what Rian told King Harristan and Prince Corrick about Ostriary. Again, I don't get the sense that he lied about very much at all. He claimed that decades ago, Ostriary and Kandala were engaged in the trade of steel and lumber, but that went sour, causing a rift between the countries." He frowns a little, thinking. "That would've been under the reign of King Harristan's grandfather, I believe. But six years ago, Kandala *must* have sent spies here, because Rian did have official documents from King Lucas naming the real Captain Blakemore as acting with the full authority of the king. The original Captain Blakemore was real—he just wasn't Rian."

I put a finger to my lips. "I remember on the night he arrived, Arella and Roydan came to talk to Corrick about discovering the names of unfamiliar cities among the shipping logs from Trader's

Landing. Those cities turned out to be the islands here. They said it wasn't just steel and lumber, but explosives, too."

"Yes. Between that and records from the docks in Artis, the king was able to confirm much of his story. It's the only reason we came at all. During his first meeting with the king and the prince, Rian said that Kandala attacked and destroyed Ostrian ships after a deal went sour. He said that views of Kandalan royalty were not favorable here in Ostriary—to the point that some people were wary of a new agreement. They'd seen the damage Kandala had caused, and they didn't trust our king. I believe Lieutenant Tagas was the one who spoke about it most earnestly. She said she was a girl at the time, and she watched the ships burn."

Unlike my feelings for Rian, I don't have much animosity toward his lieutenant. I remember Gwyn Tagas telling me about the way Rian sailed along the shores of the Ostrian islands, looking for survivors during their war. I imagine her telling Harristan about attacks on Ostrian ships, and I suspect she probably *was* very earnest.

I can also imagine it having a massive impact on the king. Many people in Kandala think Harristan is cold and distant, but he's not at all. He always seems to feel the plight of his people so acutely.

I look at Erik, and the striking blue and purple of his guard uniform helps to remind me that I need to start thinking of him as Rocco again. "I bet King Harristan didn't like the idea that Kandala might have been the aggressor," I say.

He glances back at me. "No. He didn't."

I chew on that for a while. My thoughts keep burning with rage against Rian, but I try to push some of that away, because it's not allowing me to think clearly.

And as soon as I tamp down some of that fire, I realize something else. "If everyone here thought Kandala was ruled by a vicious king who burned their ships and attacked their people over a bad trade agreement, Rian must have seen Harristan and Corrick as the enemy. No wonder he didn't want to risk leading warships back."

Rocco nods. "No wonder."

But now I've found a thread to chase—and I kind of hate where it leads me. "No wonder he lied about his identity *at all*." I make an aggravated sound. "No wonder he hated Corrick."

Rocco says nothing to that.

I heave a sigh. "But you're right. He must need steel very badly if he was willing to risk so much."

"I agree, so that might be all the leverage you need." Rocco looks up and around. "They have plenty of trees for lumber, but it's possible they have few mines for iron ore here. Nothing like Trader's Landing and Mosswell. They might need Kandalan steamships to transport it, too. Steel is heavy. I don't know what kind of naval fleet they have left after their war, but Rian wouldn't have sailed the *Dawn Chaser* if he had access to more impressive vessels—and his ship wouldn't have been able to manage much."

"Well, those brigantines that were chasing us *sank*."

"Yes, because they didn't know the waters through Chaos Isle. Rian did. Another reason I need his maps in case we can find a way home."

I peer up at him in the sunlight. "Why did you become a guardsman if your family was all sailors?"

He shrugs. "Same story you'll hear from a hundred other men, probably. I didn't want to do what my father kept telling me to do." He glances over, smiling a little fondly. "Josef—my brother—says that I'm a fool for defying our father just to follow someone *else's* orders. I tell him I'm actually brilliant because now I get paid for it."

That makes me smile. "How long have you been doing it?"

"Six years now? Almost seven. I didn't set out to join the palace guard in the beginning. I don't think it would have even occurred to me. Far too grand for a sailor out of Sunkeep. I wanted to become a patrolman, so I did that for a year or so."

Those words give me a jolt, and I nearly whip my head around. "You were a patrolman? In the night patrol?"

Rocco nods. "The guard captain doesn't take raw recruits right into the palace, so he scouts the night patrol when he needs new guards. Sometimes the army, too. My name was offered, so I applied, and here I am."

I'm staring at him.

"What?" he says.

"I just . . . I never thought about you being in the night patrol."

My voice sounds hollow, and I have to fix my eyes back on the path, listening to my booted feet crunch with every step. My heart keeps thrumming in my chest. The night patrol killed my parents. I've hated them ever since I watched it happen. I know Rocco couldn't have been involved, not if he was a patrolman that long ago. But still. This feels like discovering he used to kick puppies or steal from children.

I fold my arms against my abdomen and take a shallow breath. I hate that this is so jarring—and the worst part is that it *shouldn't* be. It shouldn't be jarring at all. Rocco was one of the king's personal guards, and I used to hate *them* just as much. He was probably on the dais during the failed execution that led to revolution.

Rocco has probably been there for a *lot* of executions.

Well, these thoughts are going nowhere good.

I have to unwind my emotion. He's also saved my life. Corrick's life. Harristan's life. Quint's life. He might be risking his *own* life to walk at my side on the way to Rian's palace. I doubt he strapped on all those weapons for show.

Rocco glances at me, and I can tell he's watching me work out thoughts in my head. He must know the night patrol killed my parents if he was there for my first conversation with King Harristan. An odd tension hums in the air between us. We walk for the longest time in silence.

Eventually, he speaks. "It couldn't have been me. I've been in the palace guard since—"

"No—I know that."

"It was just a job, Miss Tessa."

"The night patrol hurt people." I keep my eyes on the path. "It shouldn't be just a *job*."

"Smugglers hurt people, too."

"My parents never hurt anyone. *I* didn't hurt anyone." As I say the words, I remember the king's even tone when I challenged him this way.

It's the same to the night patrol.

Rocco screws up his face a little, considering what I've said, and I expect a similar response, but that's not what he says. "I know from your conversation with the king that you were an outlaw, but you weren't a smuggler. You were stealing medicine for the good of the people, right?"

"*Yes.*" I clench my hands on the straps of my pack.

"Well, most smugglers weren't doing that. They were stealing it for *money*. Money and power and control. It's rare that anyone was in the Hold for trying to steal medicine just to stay alive. Maybe some were, but most of them were *criminals*. *Not* kindhearted, *not* giving, *not* trying to save a life. Smugglers and thieves who'd cheat and steal, then extort desperate people. *Criminals*, Miss Tessa. Just because you had good intentions doesn't mean *everyone* does. You've met the king yourself, so you must know there would be a reason he set the penalties so high."

My jaw is tight, my eyes fixed ahead. I want to reject this out of turn, but I can't. I'm trying not to think of the multitude of scars on Corrick's body, the way he once said, *Sometimes I try to ask questions and they have other ideas.* I'm trying not to think of the rapists and murderers I've heard about in passing, the ones committed to the Hold for stealing medicine in the middle of heinous crimes.

And I remember the atrocities committed by the rebels themselves. I saw the bodies left strewn along the cobblestone streets of the Royal Sector, leaking blood and viscera on the night of the revolt. I watched Lochlan himself stand among the flames, ordering his rebels to shoot a consul while the king and I begged them to stop.

Rocco keeps going. "And not every patrolman is a brutal lout just waiting for the chance to take someone down either. I certainly wasn't. They're just people doing a job. Just men and women trying to put a roof over their heads like everyone else. If you're going to judge them, why not judge the guards who *protect* the shipments instead of handing Moonflower out to everyone they pass? *They're* just doing what they're paid for. Or what about the harvesters working the fields? They could be stuffing their pockets with Moonflower, handing out petals when they get home. But no, they're *also* doing their job, putting the petals where they belong, then going home to a hot meal. Is everyone supposed to risk their livelihoods? Their families?"

"Yes!" I snap. "That's exactly what my parents did!"

He stares right back at me and says nothing.

He doesn't have to. The message is clear.

My parents risked themselves—and they died.

I risked myself—and I was caught.

I take a deep breath and let it out. All these years and I still—*still!*—don't know if what they were doing was worth it. I don't even know if my years with Corrick as Wes and Tessa were worth it.

I'm trapped *here*. Corrick is dead. How many people did we really save? Did it matter, or did we just delay the inevitable?

"I just feel like people should do the right thing when they have the chance," I say quietly. Then I scowl and kick at the rocks. "Ugh. Corrick always used to tell me that's naive."

Rocco glances over again. "*Expecting* people to do the right thing is probably naive. Wanting them to isn't." He hesitates. "And what we think is *the right thing* can obviously change."

I look at him sharply. "No it can't."

"It can't?" he says. "You snuck into the palace to kill the king—and then you found yourself helping him." He gestures at the path ahead of us. "You're quite literally on a journey to negotiate on his behalf."

Well, that smacks me in the face.

"And I'd venture to guess," he continues, "that before the journey here, your ideas about *the right thing* might be a bit different from now, after learning the truth about Rian and everything he revealed."

That smacks me in the face twice as hard. I flush a little. "Ouch, Erik."

He glances over, then gives my pack straps a little back-and-forth tug again. "Besides, if you hated the night patrol so much, I can't *wait* to hear your opinion on palace guards."

His voice is gently teasing, trying to pull some of the sting out of the air.

It works. "Maybe a few of you are all right," I say.

"That's fair. Some of us are real bastards."

I giggle and cast a glance up at him in the sunlight. "And you're right. I didn't understand before. But I didn't have all the information."

"No one ever does. How could we? We all come from a different place. Sometimes I listen to the consuls blustering about something stupid, and it's hard to remember that they've never spent a single moment of their lives outside a palace or an estate. But it's not just them. When I started as a patrolman, I was in Sunkeep first, and there's so little crime. It was easy, so I thought that's what it was like everywhere. But then I was assigned to a new unit, farther north, through Trader's Landing. And you might not know this, but back then, before anyone was smuggling Moonflower, they were smuggling *explosives*."

I turn wide eyes his way. "Really?"

He nods. "For raiding the mines in Mosswell. I had been chasing down cutpurses and the occasional night burglar in Sunkeep, and suddenly I was grouped with patrols that were facing armed smugglers sitting on piles of bombs. The main roads were safe, but as soon as you took a wrong turn, you could be dead. I was young—it was intense." He shakes his head and whistles through his teeth. "I had no idea anything like that was even happening in Kandala. I've heard it's worse now since there hasn't been a consul there in years. I'm sure that's how rebels were able to smuggle explosives all the way to the Royal Sector."

I think of my parents slipping down darkened paths of Artis and through the Wilds to pass out medicine. Our biggest threat was always the night patrol. I've never been as far south as Sunkeep, but that's where Karri was from originally. I've been to Trader's Landing, but not since I was younger, fetching medicinal supplies with my parents. It seemed to be a bustling, lively sector, and even though my parents always warned me to stay close, I always assumed it was because of how crowded the roads were. I never considered being afraid of people smuggling something like *explosives.*

"Does the king know this?" I ask.

Rocco looks at me like I've asked how to breathe. "Of course."

So Corrick must have known it, too. I pair this with everything Rocco just said, and it all really does make me feel naive. Corrick must have tried to tell me in a million different ways, but somehow the lesson lands this time.

"How long were you there?" I say.

"Less than a year. That's where I was chosen to apply for the palace guard, so I went from Trader's Landing to the Royal Sector. I remember when I wrote to my parents to say I was taking a position as a guardsman, my mother wrote back and demanded that I ask the king why he kept changing the shipping levies at the ports. Of course I couldn't do that—but it wasn't until I stood beside the door through a thousand boring consul meetings that I learned how much negotiation went into those stupid shipping levies, because it wasn't like King Harristan was doing it on a whim." He glances down. "But that's what I mean about how we all come from a different place. We don't really know until we . . . *know.*"

"Did you ever tell your poor mother you just couldn't ask about shipping levies?" I tease.

"I told her I'd have to wait until I was in the king's personal guard to get that close, because I never thought I would. Now I never hear the end of it." He rolls his eyes. "One day she'll stop asking."

"Wait—you weren't in the king's guard the whole time?"

"Oh no. I was just a rank and file palace guard in the beginning. I wasn't chosen for King Harristan's personal guard until after his coronation." He pauses, and his tone turns grave. "None of us were. He had all of his father's personal guards dismissed, then selected his own from among those remaining."

The words fall into the air and land more heavily than I'm ready for. *Dismissed.*

Because Harristan and Corrick's parents were assassinated.

Rocco was right. Their lives are so touched by tragedy. All of Kandala seems shadowed by it.

He glances over again, and he seems to sense the need to change the subject. "What about you?" he says. "I know you were raised to be an apothecary. Did you grow up in the Wilds?"

"No," I say. "In Artis, really. Though we used to travel into—"

Rocco shoves me to the side of the path so forcefully that the weight of the pack nearly takes me down. I have to grab hold of a tree. Wood cracks somewhere nearby, but I barely hear it over the sound of my breathing. My nails dig into the tree trunk, and I realize Rocco is blocking me now, his crossbow drawn and aimed.

I duck a little to peer under his arm, but I don't see anything or anyone.

"What's happening?" I whisper.

"Don't move," he says. "She's behind that tree there." He gestures with the weapon a little.

I look, and then I spot the woman, most of her body hidden behind a wide tree. I don't have time to recognize much more than curly black hair, skirts that brush the ground, and a crossbow in her own hands.

She points it right at us and fires.

CHAPTER TEN

Tessa

The snap of the crossbow barely registers before Rocco shoves me again, pushing me behind a larger tree. This time, the weight of the pack *does* pull me to the ground.

He's returned fire, and now he's on one knee. He's calmly slipping two more bolts into place on the crossbow. "Slip the buckle at your waist," he says. "Lose the pack. Be ready to run."

My fingers fumble at the buckle. "Who is she? Why is she shooting at us?"

"No idea. Want to ask?"

A bolt from her crossbow hits the tree right above his head, and he swears under his breath.

He fires back, and the woman ducks back behind the tree. "You get off this island, Lina!" she shouts. "I thought we were done with the lot of you!"

Rocco lifts the crossbow to return fire again.

I grab hold of his arm. "Stop!" I hiss. "She thinks we're with the pirates."

"She's still trying to kill us." Another arrow hits the tree, skidding off the bark this time, and Rocco's eyes quickly flick my way. "See?"

"Wait!" I call out to the woman. "We're not here to hurt you!"

"I don't care why you're here!" she shouts. "You take Mouse and go back where you came from!"

Oh, how I would *love* to go back where I came from.

"We're from Kandala!" I call just as I slip one arm free of the straps. The woman's crossbow snaps again, and Rocco grabs my arm to jerk me sideways. This bolt goes right into our pack.

I stare at it breathlessly. That might have been my shoulder. Or my chest.

"Please!" I shout. "Please, we're not with Oren Crane's people! We came from Kandala to *help*—"

Another shot hits the dirt by my boots, and I yip.

"Maybe you should fire back," I whisper.

"I will. I don't have a lot of bolts. I'm letting her use up hers."

"I can hear you plotting," the woman calls. She fires again, and as soon as we hear the snap, Rocco is in motion, stepping out to shoot back.

The woman shrieks, her body jerking sideways. The crossbow clatters to the ground.

"Stay behind the tree," Rocco says sharply, and then he's striding across the distance, pointing his own.

The hell I will. I draw my dagger and follow him, but I keep a good distance behind. The woman is older than I am, probably in her midtwenties, with light brown skin and dark curly hair that's pulled back under a kerchief. She's on the ground, blood in a wide streak down her right arm, though it looks like a glancing blow. Her crossbow is six feet away, but she's glaring up at Rocco as he bears down on her, his weapon pointed the whole time.

"You're not Mouse," she says, seething.

"No," he says, kicking her crossbow out of reach.

The woman is panting, and she slaps a hand over the wound on her arm. "And you're not Lina," she gasps at me.

From somewhere behind her in the trees, a small voice starts shouting, "Mama? Mama!" Branches rustle, and out of nowhere, a young boy comes sprinting through the trees. He's six or seven years old, and the woman snaps her head around.

Something hard hits me in the arm, then the cheek, and I cry out in surprise, just as a rock hits Rocco in the temple and he swears.

The boy is running right for us, pelting *stones* at us.

"Stop!" the woman shouts, her panic clear. "Ellmo—get back!"

Rocco turns with the crossbow in his hands, and in a flash I'm remembering a different moment, when I was by Wes's side. I'm remembering a different young boy facing the night patrol. That night, I was almost too late.

This time, I'm too far away. Rocco's finger is already on the trigger.

I'm going to be too late.

"No!" I cry as I try to close the distance anyway. "Rocco, *please!*"

"*No!*" The woman's agonized cry mixes with mine to echo through the trees.

But Rocco hasn't fired. The little boy sees his mother on the ground, roars in rage, and flies at the guardsman. Rocco lowers the weapon and grabs hold of his shirt, catching him like an errant kitten.

The boy thrashes against his hold, beating at his arms with hands filled with stones. "You hurt my mother!"

The woman scrambles off the ground. "Let him go!" she gasps. Her face has paled, and blood now soaks the outside of her arm. She looks from the dagger in my hand to the crossbow in Rocco's, and a note of panic enters her voice. "You let him *go!*"

"Wait," I'm pleading. "Just—wait—" But my voice can barely compete with the boy's enraged wailing now.

The boy throws one final handful of rocks, and they bounce off Rocco's chest, then scatter wildly, rattling among the brush. The woman surges forward like she's going to tackle the guardsman, but he whips the crossbow up just in time, putting the point right against the base of her throat, and she freezes.

"Hey!" Rocco barks. "We aren't here to hurt you. So that's *enough!*"

His voice is so loud and so sharp that all three of us jump, and the sudden stunned silence is jolting. Even the little boy is staring with wide eyes, his breath shaking, lower lip trembling.

But Rocco glances my way. "Not you, Miss Tessa."

Oh. Oh, of course. I have to shake myself. "I know what you thought," I say to the woman. "But we aren't with Oren Crane's people."

"I saw you on the water," says the woman. Her eyes haven't left her son.

I nod quickly, realizing this must be the person we saw onshore, the woman with the little boy who didn't wave back. "We've been staying in a house half an hour's walk back that way." I gesture. "We came with Rian—" I have to break off and correct myself. "With *Galen*. Galen Redstone. Your king. We came from Kandala. We were walking to his palace."

She glances between me and her son, and she swallows tightly. "If you're being honest, then let him go."

I remember little Anya on the ship, the way she had scars from whatever Oren's people had done to her. I glance at Rocco and nod. "Erik," I say softly. "Let him go."

Rocco is bleeding from where one of the rocks hit him in the face. He lowers the crossbow, then pulls the boy a little closer, leaning down to speak. His voice is stern, but not unkind. "If I let you go, you're going to behave yourself, yeah?"

The boy swallows and nods, eyes still wide. Rocco's fist uncurls from his shirt, and he takes a step back.

The boy darts forward to punch him right in the crotch. "That's what you *get!*"

Rocco doubles over *immediately*. He grabs for the boy, but he's already scampered away.

"Ellmo!" the woman calls, but he's disappeared into the trees.

Rocco is still half crouched, making unintelligible sounds. "I should have seen that coming," he mutters.

"Are you all right?" I say.

"No. Yes. Ask me in five minutes."

"You deserve it for grabbing him that way!" the woman snaps. "Who scares a little boy like that?"

"Someone getting shot at," Rocco grunts. He heaves a breath and forces himself upright. "He's lucky I just scared him."

She takes a step closer to him and pokes him right in the chest. "It's a shame he didn't have a knife in his hand."

He inhales like he's going to spew venom, but I have no desire to see them start shooting at each other again, so I step forward and put a hand on Rocco's arm.

"I think we can all appreciate that this was a misunderstanding,"

I say. I look at the woman, whose skin seems to have paled further. "What's your name? I have supplies. I can treat your arm. There's a lot of blood. That needs stitching."

"Blood?" The woman blinks at me, then turns to look. "It just stings a little—"

Her voice breaks off as she sees all the blood, which has slowed, but now coats the back side of her arm and drips onto her skirts. The skin is torn down to her elbow, a bit of muscle showing.

"Oh," she says, quite simply. Then her skin slips from light brown to ashen gray, and her knees buckle.

I rush forward to catch her, but Rocco is quicker, and he looks aggrieved—but he eases her into his arms. Her head lolls to the side, falling against his neck.

He rolls his eyes and blows a tuft of her hair away from his face. "As I said, Miss Tessa. Trouble knew where to find us."

"I know," I sigh. "That's why I brought bandages. Come on."

<hr>

For as much blood as there is, the wound actually isn't very big, and I'm able to get four stitches in place before the woman starts to come around. She shot a bolt into our pack, but it didn't pierce anything essential. Rocco pulled it free, then reclaimed all of the bolts he shot, and now he stands over us, looking out into the trees.

"Come on, boy," he calls. His voice has lost most of its edge. "You don't have to be afraid."

Rustling sounds from among the trees, but Ellmo doesn't appear.

I tip some water from a canteen onto a twist of muslin and begin to wipe the worst of the blood from the woman's arm. "I'm glad you didn't shoot him," I say.

"I'm not going to shoot a child for throwing *rocks* at me, Miss Tessa." He looks out into the woods again. "Come on," he calls again. "Your mother will likely be worried if you aren't here when she wakes."

I wet another piece of muslin and hold it out to him. "Here. You have some blood on your forehead. How's your other wound?"

"It's fine," he says dismissively. But he takes the muslin and wipes at his face.

More leaves rustle, but Ellmo remains hidden.

"Maybe I should whistle for you like a dog," Rocco calls.

"Maybe I should whistle for *you* like a dog," the boy calls back, but he sounds closer than I expected.

I wet another fold of muslin and tap it against the woman's forehead. "What's your mother's name?" I call. "Do you want to come help me wake her up?"

This silence is a little more pointed, and after a minute, the boy pops out from behind a tree off to my right. "Her name is Olive, but everyone used to call her Livvy."

Used to? I think. But I pat the woman's face again with the damp muslin. "Olive?" I say. "Olive, wake up."

Her eyelids flutter. She lifts a hand to her head.

The boy comes a little closer, sneaking through the underbrush. "Mama?"

The woman's eyes open, snapping between me and Rocco at once. "Ellmo?" she says, trying to shove herself upright. "Where's Ellmo?"

"He's fine," I say. "Go slow."

She ignores me and sits up too fast—but as soon as she sees her son between the trees, she heaves a breath of relief. She looks down at her arm and then at me. "Thank you." She flexes her elbow, then winces. "I'm sorry I shot at you. When I saw the boat—I worried it was a scouting boat since you were on this side of the island. I thought Oren's people had found their way to Fairde again."

"I'm sorry," I say. "I should have thought. We didn't mean to scare you." I pause. "I'm Tessa Cade, and this is Erik Rocco. Like I said, we were on the ship from Kandala. Who are Lina and Mouse?"

"Some of Oren Crane's worst henchmen. She's vicious. I've seen her cut people apart. Mouse just does what he's told—and he's big enough to do a lot of bad things." She shudders. "I hadn't heard that Galen had returned, but we don't get many visitors out here. Ever since . . ." Her voice trails off, and she glances at her son. "Well, it's been a few years now. But we keep to ourselves."

Ever since. I want to ask what, but I can guess. Our empty house is proof that something terrible happened on this side of the island.

Ellmo has crept closer, and he's peering up at Rocco.

The guardsman is looking back at him. "How old are you? Five?"

"I'm *seven!*"

"Well, you're small for seven. You look like you're five."

"You look like the back end of a pig."

Olive scrambles to her feet. "Ellmo!"

Ellmo picks up a handful of pebbles and chucks them at the guardsman. To my absolute shock, Rocco picks up a small handful of his own and lightly flings them right back. Ellmo yelps in surprise and skitters away, which makes Olive glare at them both—but the boy bursts out laughing.

"Are *you* five?" I say to Rocco.

"He started it."

"So the answer is *yes* then?" I begin to pack away my supplies.

"We should go. We don't know how many other people are going to be waiting to shoot at us."

"You shouldn't have too much trouble once you reach the main road," Olive says. "And truly, I wouldn't have caused harm if I hadn't thought . . . well. You know."

I look back at her. "I know." I hesitate with my hand on the last of my supplies. I want to give her my jar of ointment, but it's my only one, and I might need it for Rocco's wound. "I really am sorry we frightened you. I don't know how late we'll be back, but if you come to our house tomorrow, I'd like to put some more salve on your stitches to prevent infection."

She looks startled by that. "Thank you, Tessa."

I tie up my pack and glance at her son, who's creeping forward again. "I think there are some toys that were left by the last children who were in the house, if you'd like to come, too."

His eyes widen, and he nods.

Rocco picks up my pack, and I slip my arms under the straps. It's just as heavy as it was before, but I'm better with the buckles now.

Olive catches my arm. "Wait."

I wait.

She studies me, her brown eyes searching my face. "If you came from Kandala with our king, why are you staying all the way out here? Why didn't you stay in the palace?"

I should have expected this question, but because I didn't, it summons emotion I'm not ready for. I think of Corrick and the lies and the way I want to hold Rian under the water. I have to swallow it all away.

"Because," I say, "there were . . . complications."

Her hand is still on my arm, and a pulse of shared understanding passes between us. I don't know if it's loss or fear or past betrayal, but I feel it, and I can see in her eyes that she feels it too.

"You don't trust him," she says.

I should lie—but as I told Rocco, I'm terrible at that.

"I know he's your king," I say. "And I know everyone here is remarkably loyal to him. I understand why. He's done amazing things for the people of Ostriary. I know Oren Crane was terrible, and the war was terrible, and that you all need steel so desperately." I have to take a deep breath. "But no. I'm sorry. I don't trust him. That's why we're out here."

Olive nods and lets go of my arm. "I'll let you be on your way then." She glances between us. "I'll see you both tomorrow."

I nod in return. "Tomorrow." I wave to her son. "Goodbye, Ellmo."

"Goodbye, Tessa," he calls. He throws a pebble at Rocco.

"I'm going to break all the toys before you get there," Rocco says.

"I'm going to break your face when I get there," the boy calls back.

I sigh. "Let's just go."

But we're a short distance off when Olive calls my name. "Tessa."

I look back, and her expression is very serious.

"Our king is very good at convincing people that the end justifies the means," she says.

I stare back at her. "He won't convince me."

"You spoke of loyalty," she says. "And you're right—a lot of people *are* loyal to him. Part of the problem is that he really does mean well—even if he ends up hurting someone to get what he wants. I thought you should know."

Her words kick me in the gut unintentionally, and I frown. "I already know."

That look passes between us again.

"I'm sorry," she finally says. She kisses her fingertips and touches them to her heart. "Be safe on your journey. We'll talk when you get back."

Then she takes her son's hand, and they head off into the trees.

—+—

Olive was right: we don't find any trouble on the main road. It's actually more crowded than I expected, with carts and horses and workers going in both directions. It's clear when we near the city, because trees fall away, and homes and shops suddenly line the road. I'm glad for all the distractions, because every step I take fills me with a different emotion.

Longing. I miss Corrick so very much.

Fury. I hate Rian for everything he did.

I still have no idea what I'm going to say to him. I don't want to be naive. I don't want to believe anything he says. Olive's parting words remind me that I'm not the only one who doesn't trust him.

The sun beats down, voices filling the air with the Ostrian accent. No one pays me much attention, but I can tell that people notice Rocco. Their eyes linger on the colors of his palace livery, on his weapons, on the insignia emblazoned on his sleeves.

I hear more than one person whisper the word *Kandala*, so it's clear they know our colors.

Then we pass a small food vendor where I hear a woman mutter, "Only one guard. She can't be a queen."

"Maybe an adviser?" someone else replies. "She looks very official."

"There's a crown on his sleeve. I suppose she could be a princess."

But then we're past and I can't catch any more gossip.

A *princess*. If our predicament weren't so perilous and sad, it would almost be enough to make me burst out laughing.

"I can't believe they think that," I say to Rocco once we're down the road a little bit, but when I look to my right, I realize he's not directly at my side, but just behind me.

Like . . . a guard.

"I can," he says. "You *are* someone official."

I don't feel like it. I feel like I'm faking it. As usual, the only time I ever felt like I was really *doing* something was when I was in the Wilds with a mask over my eyes.

The road is hilly, with several winding curves, but the closer we get to the city, the more I spot the signs of strife with the other islands. Some buildings have clearly been burned out and never repaired. Cracked windows are everywhere, while some are missing panes of glass entirely. Broken bricks and tiles have been swept up against buildings in various places, while others lie untouched in alleyways.

But the attempts to rebuild are obvious, too. Many buildings have been patched and repaired. New glass gleams in the windows, masons can be found laying bricks here and there, and bright tiles shine in front of the occasional shop. Some of the paint is so fresh I can smell it.

We haven't seen any sign of a palace yet, and I feel certain we should be seeing spires or turrets or *something* by now. Just when I'm about to ask Rocco if he's *sure* he remembers the way, the road curves sharply and we crest another hill—and there it is.

Rian's palace is down in a valley that forms a natural harbor for the sea, which explains why I haven't been able to see it until now. We'll have to walk downhill to get to it. Unlike the white palace of Kandala, this one is made of dark stone, with spires stretching into the sky, making the structure look black against the sunlight— though gleaming stained-glass windows glitter in yellow, orange, and red, a stunning contrast against the blue of the ocean. I remember Rian calling it the Palace of the Sun, and now I understand why.

I also remember him telling me that the surrounding citadel was in ruins, and I can see the evidence of that as well. We've been passing burned-out shops and homes, but what lies below us in the valley is far worse. There's rubble everywhere, and it's almost as if the air still holds a scent of cannon powder.

On the night we arrived, it was pitch-dark, but I didn't look at the palace anyway. I couldn't focus on our surroundings.

I had no idea it was this bad.

"This is terrible," I whisper.

"Yes, Miss Tessa."

I study the glistening water, then look over my shoulder at Rocco. "Where are the bridges? Aren't there supposed to be bridges?"

"Rian said the connections to Fairde were destroyed by cannon fire." He points. "I believe those structures are all that remain."

I look along the coastline until I see what he means, and there, near some empty docks, stands the beginning of a bridge, just as charred and crumpled as everything else.

Then I think of all we've seen so far of the rebuilding efforts. Plenty of bricks, plenty of wood. Lots of paint and tile.

But no steel.

And down there, in the citadel surrounding the palace, there's little motion at all. All of the crowds have been on the roads up here, away from the palace.

I frown. Like I told Olive, I don't trust Rian at all.

But I agree with Rocco. I don't think he lied either.

I sigh. "Let's keep going."

—+—

Despite what it looked like from above, when we reach the palace, there are guards—and a lot of them. After Rian's casual crew on the *Dawn Chaser*, I somewhat expect the guards to be ragtag and roughshod, similar to the rebel army that Lochlan was able to assemble in the Wilds. But these men and women are armed and liveried in red and black, and while their weapons and armor bear the marks of hard-fought battles, they look ready to fight some more.

There seem to be a hundred of them, too. None of them look friendly. I can feel every eye on us as we crunch across rubble-strewn cobblestones toward the palace. Much like when we were walking along the road, I know they recognize the colors of Rocco's uniform, and they probably know *exactly* who I am.

Until this moment, I hadn't really considered facing Rian as an adversary—which is a bit ridiculous, since I've been envisioning his death for days.

"This is a lot of guards," I whisper to Rocco. "Are you worried?"

"No sense in being worried," he says. "I can't fight them all. If they want us dead, we will be."

My heart kicks into double time. "Well, that's fun."

"You have something he wants, Miss Tessa."

Do I, though? I swallow my panic and swipe my hands on my skirts. My back feels damp under the pack. "What should I say to the guards?"

"I'll announce you when we reach the main gate."

When we draw close, the stained-glass windows glitter vibrantly, as if someone captured the fire of the sun inside the building. There's a small circle in front of the palace where carriages could wait, but none are here—a sharp contrast to the bustling activity at the palace in Kandala, where carriages and wagons are always coming and going, day or night.

A guard steps down from the gate to stop us, and his eyes flick over me, but I watch him size up Rocco. "State your business."

"I present Tessa Cade, adviser and apothecary to the king of Kandala," says Rocco. "Here to visit with King Galen Redstone, if he is receiving callers."

"I'll see if he is."

The guard turns away and gives an order to someone else. We're left to wait, the palace looming above us. If it's anything like Kandala, there will probably be attendants and footmen or someone like Quint who will fetch us, and we'll have to endure a sitting room, or tea, or an hour of pleasantries before Rian deigns to acknowledge our presence.

I consider how I wouldn't even look at him when he visited the house. The way I sat in the sand and gazed at the sea, leaving Rocco to deal with everything. Maybe Rian will make us stand out here in the sun for an hour, just to be spiteful.

We're closer to the water, and the scent of fish and salt water fills my nose. I stare out toward the distant harbor and wonder if we could have rowed our little boat here, how long that would have taken.

But as I stare, I recognize one of the ships tethered against the longest dock, because the damage to the sails and the hull is unmistakable.

The *Dawn Chaser*.

My stomach clenches. Even from here, I can see the gaping hole in the deck where a cannonball ripped through the wood, tearing Corrick away from me. Sending him and Lochlan into the water forever.

As soon as I recognize it, a gasp breaks free of my throat.

Oh, I can't do this. I can't. As much as I love Kandala, and as much as I want to do the right thing for everyone, the sorrow is too overwhelming. My knees are in danger of buckling. I press a hand to my abdomen, because my stomach clenches again.

But then my fingers brush that dagger, and the steel is cold against my fingertips.

Mind your mettle.

It's like Corrick's voice is there in my head, cool and stabilizing, and I hold my breath against all that emotion. My entire body is tense, my stomach rolling, but I force back the tears, and they obey.

"Tessa."

Rian speaks from behind me, his voice full of surprise. The fact that he came out himself is so startling that I whirl around. He's striking in the sunlight, his black hair and tan skin and broad shoulders making him as eye-catching as he was when I first met him as Captain Blakemore. After the signs of battle and all the guards, I expected to find arrogance in his eyes and pride in his stance. I really did expect to find an adversary, someone ready to fight with me.

But he *doesn't* look ready to fight, and I hate it. I hate that he looks as kind and thoughtful as he did on board his ship. I hate that he looks like he cares that I'm here, that he's *relieved* that I'm here. I hate that his eyes are full of concern and worry.

I hate that he looks like a man who is rather desperately trying his best to do the right thing in impossible circumstances.

And I hate that the instant I see him, I'm reminded that Corrick might have seemed like an adversary in the beginning—but he was doing *exactly* the same thing.

My face must be full of tumultuous emotion, because Rian frowns, then looks past me at the harbor to see what I was looking at. He must see the *Dawn Chaser* bobbing against the dock, because when his eyes snap back to mine, his expression softens with knowing concern, and he pulls open the gate. "Tessa. I've been so worried about you. Please—*please*. You must understand—"

"To be clear," I choke out, my voice shaking with a combination of tears and rage, "I will *never* understand."

Then I draw that dagger, and I lift my hand.

He's too quick, of course. He catches my wrist, deflecting my blow. It brings us closer, which isn't better. But he glances at the weapon, and then at my face.

I suck in a breath, intending to scream at him. To chastise him. To cry on him. I don't know. All I keep seeing is that damaged ship, the scorch marks on the sails, the memory of the cannonball smashing through the planks.

All I keep remembering is Corrick on the deck one moment, and gone from my life in the next.

Again.

I choke on a sob. My fingers have gone slick on the dagger, but I still have a tight grip.

"Let her go," Rocco says sharply.

Rian glances at him, and then at my white knuckles clutching the dagger. "I will if she drops the weapon."

I don't. May stomach is roiling, and I'm so angry. So sad. So full of burning rage at the man in front of me. But the guards have moved in closer, and I keep thinking of Rocco saying, *If they want us dead, we will be.*

"Tessa," Rian whispers. "Please. You don't want to do this. I know you don't."

It's the same thing I said to him when he was going to kill Rocco on board his ship.

I hate you, I think. But I can't even say that. I said it to Corrick so many times, and the words are too wrapped up in my grief. A grief so strong that it twists up my insides and wrings me out until I can't see straight.

I shouldn't have come here. I don't know how to do this.

I let go of the dagger, and it clatters to the stones at our feet. He lets me go.

It takes everything I have to keep my hands to myself, because I want to fly at him. I want to tear him to pieces. I know there are things we need, but I want to be away from here, because I don't know if I can stand to look at him for one more second.

I inhale to say that, but instead, I open my mouth and throw up on his feet.

CHAPTER ELEVEN

Tessa

I don't know what's more embarrassing: that I couldn't stab him, or that I threw up on him.

Either way, I've been given some time to figure it out, because Rian needs to change his clothes. Or at least his boots. We've been invited into the palace, left to wait in a grand room that was probably designed for hosting balls or parties or fancy galas. The ceiling stretches high above us, unlit chandeliers strung from glistening silver chains everywhere I look. The walls are all painted in stunning murals that span the width of the room, featuring landscapes that must display each of the islands of Ostriary. This must have been a stunning room at one time, but signs of war have crept in here, too: burn marks mar one of the windowsills, blades have slashed through one of the painted walls, and there are stains in some of the woodwork that I don't want to examine too closely. Even the furniture is surprisingly sparse, as if much of it has been removed. There are only a few low chairs and a table near the windows, though there are signs of fading on the parquet floor, indicating spots where rugs and furniture once sat.

Loss clings to this room as tightly as it clung to the harbor outside.

You must understand.

I don't want to understand.

But I think I do.

Two guards have followed us in, but they remain by the door. Rocco stays closer to me, but he takes a place by the wall, and I realize he's positioned himself so he can watch me while also see-ing most of the room—windows and all.

I want to ask if he's nervous, but I don't want the guards to hear me. It hasn't escaped my notice that his crossbow has a bolt loaded.

I'm probably supposed to leave him alone, to allow him to be an invisible guard the way the king or Corrick would, but I can't do that. When I shift close to Rocco, his eyes stay on the room.

"Throwing up on him probably wasn't the most elegant way to start things," I whisper.

He doesn't smile, but the skin around his eyes crinkles a little. "I guarantee it was unexpected."

"I'm too angry at him," I say. "I don't know if I can talk to him."

"Even if you can't convince him to return us to Kandala, it would be better to leave here alive, so please remind your anger that I can't fight off a hundred guards alone."

That's sobering. "They took my dagger."

He finally pulls his eyes off the room and looks at me. "Again, there is more than one way to fight, Miss Tessa."

I look back at him and nod.

Footsteps echo from the other side of the room, and I turn with my heart in my throat, expecting Rian. But it's not him—it's a woman carrying a tray of food, with a little girl skipping along beside her.

"Dabriel," I say in surprise, recognizing the cook from on board the *Dawn Chaser*. The little girl beside her is Anya, the daughter of Rian's first lieutenant, Gwyn Tagas.

Well, at least she *said* she was his first lieutenant. I have no idea if anyone was who they said they were.

But Dabriel gives me a brisk nod and sets the tray on the table. "Tessa," she says a bit gruffly. "I'm glad you returned so soon. One more day and I would've had to pay Tor."

"I . . ." I blink. "What?"

Little Anya grabs hold of my hand before I get an answer. "Miss Tessa," she says solemnly. "I know you were gone because you were very sad, but I'm glad you came back."

Without waiting for a response, she hugs me around the waist, her sleeves drawing back to reveal the scars along the brown skin of her arms.

"I *am* very sad," I whisper, but there's something so earnest in the way she's hugging me, and somehow it doesn't summon my tears.

"Me too," she says.

But then Dabriel says, "Tor didn't think you'd ever talk to him again. I bet him a week's pay you'd be here by tomorrow, and it looks like I was right."

She was gruff and no-nonsense on the ship, and it seems like that hasn't changed on land. "I'm . . . glad I could help," I say.

"I brought some coffee and warm bread," she says. "Real milk this time, no powder." She hesitates, then glances at my stomach. "But if you're in a different way and you'd like something else, let me know."

" 'In a different way'?" I echo.

She stares at me and flicks her eyes at my abdomen again.

Anya pulls back, then pats my belly. "Dabriel said that babies make you feel like you're seasick sometimes, so—"

"No!" I say quickly, and I practically shove the little girl's hand away from my belly. "No, I'm not pregnant."

Dabriel looks back at me, then arches an eyebrow. "There's no little princeling in there?"

"Absolutely not! We never—he never—" My cheeks must be on fire, and I clench my jaw. "*No. There is not.*"

"Then why did you vomit on Rian?"

"Because I *hate* him."

The words echo in the vastness of the room, the intensity of my emotion seeming to fill the space. Dabriel and Anya stare at me for a long moment as the last reverberations of my words fades.

Then Rian speaks from somewhere behind me. "Dabriel. Anya. Thank you for bringing some food. I'll speak with Miss Cade alone."

The heat on my cheeks stays right where it is—but my hands curl into fists. I can't turn to look at him. All my emotions are still colliding.

"Send word if you need anything else," Dabriel says. She gives me a nod, then turns to leave. Little Anya goes skipping after her.

But before she reaches the door, Anya stops and turns. "Don't hate him, Miss Tessa," she calls, followed by, "*I* don't hate you, Rian." But then Dabriel must shush her, because there's a muffled sound, followed by an echoing silence.

In it, I can hear every beat of my heart.

After a moment, I hear the shift of Rian's boots, too, as he comes around to face me. I don't want to meet his eyes, so I focus on his jaw, on his throat, on the stitched leather collar of his jacket.

"You should probably stay out of reach," I say.

"I'll take my chances," he says. "Come. Sit. Have some coffee." He pauses. "If you think you can stomach it."

That draws my gaze up. "Would you all stop?" I snap. "I am *not* pregnant."

"I didn't mean to imply you were. I was just being kind, Miss Cade." He pauses. "And possibly self-preserving. I do have a limited supply of boots."

I hate that he's being so mild. Every muscle in my body just wants to claw at him.

"Please," he says. "Come. Sit."

Fine. I'll sit.

He doesn't offer again. He just pours me a cup of coffee, then adds milk and sugar the way he did on the ship. The scent is heavenly, and I want to ask him to pour some for Rocco, too, but I remember what the guardsman said about my position. I don't want to weaken myself.

He sets the coffee in front of me, then serves me a slice of the bread, which looks to be crusted with cinnamon and sugar.

I don't touch either.

He serves himself some, then sits and takes a sip of coffee. "What do you think of Fairde?" he says, as if I'm here on a social call and there weren't deaths and betrayals between us.

Fine. I can play this game.

"It's very warm here," I say.

"Warmer than your Royal Sector, I'll agree." He takes another sip. "Did you have a pleasant journey?"

I think about Olive and the way she said she didn't trust him, but I keep that to myself. I'm not sure I want to lead with the fact that we were shot at. It doesn't seem smart to lead with vulnerabilities.

"Pleasant enough. It was a long walk." I consider what Rocco said about horses and how long it took to get here. "Last week you offered horses and livestock, and I declined, because we hadn't had time to consider." I smooth my hands on my skirts and fix my gaze on the collar of his jacket again. Speaking to King Harristan was always a bit terrifying because he was so *intense*. Rian is nothing like that, but I'm desperate to regain some footing after the way we arrived here. "I've had time for some reflection, so I'd like to request both to be delivered to the house as soon as possible."

His eyebrows go up. "Was this reflection on your part, Miss Cade?" His eyes flick to Rocco, standing quietly along the wall.

"Yes, after discussion with my guard," I say.

Those words land with a bit of weight, and Rian's eyes don't leave Rocco's position. After a moment, his gaze returns to me. "Your guard?"

Maybe I shouldn't be calling him *mine*, but I don't want to backpedal. "Yes."

Rian's expression turns a little more coolly assessing, and I wonder if he's going to ask what kind of person begins by trying to stab him, then starts asking for favors.

But he doesn't. "Very well," he says. "I can outfit you with two horses and a wagon to return, and enough silver to buy chickens and a goat when you pass back through town. Dabriel can give you the names of some vendors, or I can ask her to accompany you. Would that be sufficient?"

I hesitate, and it takes everything I have not to look at Rocco for confirmation. "Yes," I say again. "Thank you."

As soon as I say the words, I wish I hadn't. I don't want to thank him for anything.

I wait for him to demand something of *me*, but he doesn't. He simply nods. "You're welcome, Miss Cade."

Miss Cade. He keeps calling me that, though he called me Tessa before I tried to hit him.

But it makes me think of *his* name, and I study the line of his jaw because I still don't want to meet his eyes. "I don't know what to call you."

He frowns a little. "You can call me Rian, as before. Everyone does."

"Is it really your name?"

He nods. "I didn't lie on the ship. It *is* a nickname from childhood, a shortened form of my middle name. I didn't lie at dinner with King Harristan either. My father—the last king—had a complicated family tree, and there was no clear heir to the throne. I was named Galen after my mother's brother, and Redstone was her surname. I was a captain on a ship before I ever made a claim for the throne, so I'll never expect anyone to address me as royalty. It still takes me by surprise when people do it." He pauses for a long moment, then leans toward me. "I tried not to lie about much at all. Truly."

I keep my eyes locked on that spot on his collar, studying each individual thread. "You lied about *enough*."

He sits back in his chair. "I offered Prince Corrick the truth, before he died. I'd offer you the same, if you're ready to hear it."

Before he died. My heart gives a lurch, and I clench my hands in the fabric of my dress to keep from shuddering. I wish I still had the dagger. Maybe it's better that I don't.

Rian's voice softens. "But it doesn't need to be today." He leans forward again. "Please. I know you're grieving. I don't want to be your enemy."

"You killed him!" I shout, and for the first time, I really look at him. "Corrick, and Lochlan, and Kilbourne, and Silas—"

"No!" His voice is just as angry, and just as loud, and it shocks me still. "I *didn't.*"

The echo of our voices reverberates like a bell, and I can feel my fingernails nearly drawing blood from my palms.

"Your lies convinced us to get on that ship," I say, seething.

"Well, *his* lies put us in danger. *Again*, I told him to stay out of that room, but you took it upon yourself to break the lock. I told him that it would be a risk for ships to attempt to follow us, and brigantines were on the horizon by the third day. I told him—"

"You were keeping a girl *prisoner.*"

"Yes, so we would have leverage to get past Oren Crane safely. And because she was lost in the attack, we *didn't.*" His eyes, so much lighter than Corrick's, are so fierce. "I lost people, too, Tessa. *My* people died, too. Because of *his* lies. Because of *your* actions."

"Don't you see that the lies began with you?" I demand. "Don't you see that you set everyone up to fail?"

"Is that what you think? From Ostriary's point of view, the lies have *always* come from Kandala. You can't even deny it! Your entire country is a breeding ground for treason and insurrection. I said no sailors, and he brought a sailor. Hell, he brought one of the leaders of your *revolution* onto my ship. The citizens of your country are being poisoned by Moonflower, and you say *I* set everyone up to fail? Why is it all right for your prince to lie and cheat and steal to protect his people, but you hold me to a different standard? Your people might have been dying—well, so were *mine.*" He smacks the table so forcefully that it echoes.

I'm breathing so hard. Tears might be on my cheeks.

Rian takes a deep breath, then lets it out slowly. He presses his palms together in front of his face.

But then his gaze flicks up. "If he's your guard," he says roughly, sitting back in his chair, "call him off."

That makes me startle, and I turn my head to see that Rocco has moved away from the wall to stand at my shoulder.

"Rocco," I say, and my voice is just as rough and shaky as Rian's. "Stand down."

I have to force my fingers to unclench from my skirts. I hate that Rian is right about so much of what he said. Corrick was also to blame for a lot of what went wrong.

So am I.

But my apothecary brain has seized on one word in the middle of his lecture, because it's possibly the *only* word that would break through all my grief and rage and fear. I have to roll it around in my head to make sure he really said it, because out of everything, it's the one part that doesn't make sense.

"Wait." I sit up straight, then swipe the tears out of my eyes. "Did you say *poison*?"

CHAPTER TWELVE

Tessa

Much like Corrick's home in Kandala, the Palace of the Sun is vast, and it takes a while to walk from room to room. When Rian leads us to a wide, spiral staircase, sunlight beams in through the yellow-and-red stained-glass windows to create a vivid pattern on the walls. We're heading to his strategy room so we can look at maps and records, but my eyes keep falling on the signs of battle that must have happened right here. Little burn marks along the walls, nicks in the railings that must have come from a blade.

Rian sees me looking, and he says, "I didn't lie about the war either."

It's the first thing he's said since offering to explain about the poison, and his voice is quiet, mild, almost an apology after the way we were yelling at each other.

"I know," I say, making my voice match. "I saw the outside."

"A lot of people haven't returned to Tarrumor. You saw the

damage—they're afraid to rebuild in case Oren's people return to raze the citadel again. Easier to head into the hills."

"But you stayed," I say.

He nods. "I'd never convince them to return if I were hiding, too."

"What have you told them?" I ask.

We've reached the landing, and he looks at me in the buttery light from the windows here. "Told them?" he echoes.

"Your people," I say. "What have you told them about what happened with Kandala?"

"They've seen the ship. It's not seaworthy right now. It's clear we were attacked, and there's no secret the most likely offenders would be Oren and his pirates. I've said a few people from Kandala's contingent survived." He glances between me and Rocco, who's followed along with Rian's guards. "And here you are."

My heart thumps against my rib cage. I didn't intend to walk right into the reasons Rocco and I discussed coming here, but the opportunity has arisen, and I don't want to waste it.

There is more than one way to fight. I swallow and hope I don't throw up on him again. It doesn't help that I still want to stab him, too.

"On the ship, you were so worried about the promises you made to arrange for a trade for steel. Are you still?"

He glances over in a way that tells me he can see right through me. "Of course."

"Do you intend to return to Kandala to negotiate again?"

"I sense it'll be a bit harder if I return without the king's brother and two of his guards."

I take a slow breath to let those words land so I can speak evenly.

"To say nothing of the fact that you'd be returning as a king yourself, not a displaced emissary."

"You seem to be maneuvering toward a goal, Miss Cade, and you've made no secret of your feelings for me." He stops beside an open door, and I can hear the muffled sounds of a woman's voice somewhere deep within. "Ask for what you want. If we can come to terms, we will."

I somehow forgot that he was like this. Everyone at court in Kandala was always full of double-speak and hidden motives. Rian obviously hid some things, but he's always been direct.

"Fine," I say. "I want to go back to Kandala. If you need steel, you want to go back, too. You know King Harristan won't negotiate with you after what happened. You need me and Rocco to explain so you don't look like a complete villain."

"So I should return you to Kandala, under the pretense of *negotiation*, where you would claim to speak in my defense. An intriguing offer, but you just came at me with a dagger. I feel rather certain your king would hear that his brother was dead and shoot me on sight." He extends a hand toward the doorway. "After you."

I stare at him with my mouth open. "So . . . you're never going back? But you were so desperate for steel!"

"I was desperate. I *am* desperate. I didn't say I was never going back, but it was a tremendous risk for me to go once—and you see how it turned out. I don't know if I can attempt returning again so quickly."

I can't believe this. I'm defeated before we even started. "But—but if we went with you . . . we could explain—"

"*Explain?* Explain what? There is no explanation the king would hear that would work in my favor. And even if I believed *you* would speak in my defense, which I'm not sure I do, there is still the matter of your guard." Rian looks past me at Rocco.

Behind me, the guardsman is silent. "What does Rocco have to do with anything?" I demand.

"He's the only one to survive. His one charge is *dead*. He failed in his duty. Do you believe the king would turn a blind eye to that?"

I inhale sharply—but then I remember the story Rocco just told me during our walk. How Harristan dismissed all of his father's personal guardsmen after his parents were assassinated.

Rian's eyes haven't left Rocco. "I would expect *your guard* to say anything possible to keep himself in the king's good graces—and that certainly wouldn't paint me in a good light. No matter what you say about me, I feel rather certain that Rocco would tell a different story if it meant he might keep his head. It's no surprise he's dedicated himself to you. If he can bring at least one person back alive, it might be the only way he escapes an execution."

"King Harristan will not *execute* him," I snap.

Rian looks back at me, and his eyebrows go up. He gestures into the room again, where the voices have fallen silent. "Again, Miss Cade. After you."

I clench my jaw and walk into the room. I glance at Rocco, wondering if he's bothered by Rian's comments, but his expression is cool and unaffected. Guard eyes, the way he'd be if he were standing behind the king.

So I look back at the room—and I'm surprised to find Gwyn, Rian's first lieutenant, and Sablo, both from the ship. Sablo lost his tongue in an attack by Oren Crane, and he was rescued by Rian. Gwyn and her daughter were both attacked by Oren, too, and she bears the scars. They're both sitting beside a table that has a wide assortment of maps and books and instruments strewn all over.

Gwyn gives me a nod as if I've been coming here daily. "Tessa. Good to see you."

Sablo taps the table and gives me a nod as well.

"Hello," I say, because I don't know if it's good to see them yet.

"I see you already started arguing," says Gwyn. "I heard what happened out front."

She was always even more direct than Rian. My cheeks warm. "I'm glad gossip travels as quickly here as it did in Kandala," I say.

Rian slices through my embarrassment and says, "Miss Cade was curious about the Moonflower poison, and I wanted to show her what we know."

"You brought it to Kandala as a cure," I say. "How is it a poison at *all*?"

"If you boil the stems," says Gwyn. "It causes the fever and the cough. Too much, and it can be downright debilitating. That's how we kept Bella subdued for so long."

I look between them, trying to work this through. "But the petals are a cure. That's why you brought it."

"No," says Rian. "I truly only brought it for Bella. Making an elixir of the petals acts as an antidote for the poison." He pauses. "It was a lucky turn to discover you were all so desperate when I first docked at Port Karenin."

"None of this makes sense." I stare at him. "How would someone poison an entire country?"

"I don't know." He moves closer to the table. "Come look at the maps. I have a few thoughts."

My curiosity is overpowering my anger, and I join him beside the table—and a second later, it occurs to me that the guardsman shouldn't be excluded from this conversation.

"Rocco," I say. "Come look."

He steps away from the wall, and he stands on my opposite side. I wonder if that's deliberate.

He's been completely silent since Rian basically accused him of manipulating me against the king, and I'm sure *that's* deliberate.

I wish I could reach out and squeeze his hand to reassure him, but this feels more precarious than any second I spent in the Kandalan court.

I look at Rian instead. "Even if someone had the means, *why* would someone poison all of Kandala?"

"Perhaps because there's so much money to be made in curing it?"

My heart pounds when he says that. I don't want to think someone could be that heartless—but I'd be wrong. Consul Sallister was funding the rebels himself, raiding his own supply runs to drive up the cost of Moonflower petals. He practically funded the whole revolution—then supplied the rebels with faulty medicine so they got sicker.

"Well, there's still the matter of *how*," I say.

Rian taps the first map on the table. "These are the islands of Ostriary." He points to the center. "We're here, on Fairde. We were attacked by Crane's people *here*, just south of Silvesse. Kaisa is where the Moonflower grows." He points to the northernmost island. "That leaves Iris, the strip of land that you all believed was the whole of Ostriary, and Roshan and Estar." He drags another map closer, laying it alongside, and I realize it's a somewhat rudimentary map of Kandala. "Here. Kandala sits north, so Fairde actually lies about parallel to your southern sector, Sunkeep." He adjusts the maps a bit.

I study the two countries lying side by side. The sectors are very crudely marked, and I wonder how old this map is. Each sector has a name labeled under it, which I'm assuming are the consuls, but some of the names are unfamiliar. I'm about to ask how old this map is until I get to the Sorrowlands. Under that one is the name *Pelham.*

"Roydan Pelham," I say. I glance at Rocco. "He's the current consul for the Sorrowlands."

Rocco nods—but his eyes hold mine, and he says nothing else.

I don't know if he's telling me not to give away any more information—or if he just doesn't have any to give me.

But at my side, Rian nods, too. "These are old maps, so a lot of the consul names are out of date. I was surprised to hear this one at dinner, though." He taps the northern part of the map.

Pepperleaf.

"Laurel," I whisper. "Her father was a baron. But not a consul."

"Well, someone in her lineage was a consul in the past."

Rocco taps on Trader's Landing.

Montague.

I inhale sharply, but Rocco's finger brushes against my hand when he withdraws, and I swallow.

That was *definitely* a warning.

Rian's no fool. He looks at me. "What?"

"Montague died," I say, scrambling for something to say, because I have to say *something*. "King Harristan never replaced him." I pause. "It's been a bit of a scandal in Kandala for years."

He studies me as if he suspects I'm lying, but I'm not, and maybe he realizes that. "Why has it been a scandal?"

I'm frozen in place, staring at him. I'm such a terrible liar—and I'm so unprepared for a discussion about *this*. Barnard Montague was the consul who was behind the assassination of King Harristan and Prince Corrick's parents. He was never replaced because they were never able to determine a motive. I don't know if any of that information is good or bad to share with Rian.

I consider how the entire sector was always suspected of shady dealings—until the fever sickness grabbed everyone's attention. I frown a little, thinking of Rocco's job in the night patrol, how he talked about explosives being smuggled out of Trader's Landing. Trader's Landing was also involved in the shipping logs that Arella Cherry and Roydan Pelham were reviewing—the same ones that showed trade deals with Ostriary from long ago that went sour.

All of this has to be related somehow, but I don't know the key players in the palace well enough to piece it together.

Rian has clearly had enough of my silence. "Did it have anything to do with Montague poisoning King Harristan as a child?"

I nearly choke on my tongue. "*What?*"

"You said it was a scandal. According to *our* records, Montague is the one who used to barter for steel—and the one who first began demanding more silver. He said he had leverage on King Lucas. That the heir wouldn't survive. I've seen the letters to my father myself."

My mouth has gone dry. "That doesn't mean anything. King Harristan—he's always been sick—"

"Miss Tessa." Rocco's voice is soft at my side, but a tone of warning hides under the words.

Rian glances between him and me. His eyes narrow.

I don't say anything else—but my brain is spinning. *Could Harristan have been poisoned?* I don't know enough about this side of the Moonflower. I don't know enough about any of this.

I shake off all the things I *don't* know. But I can't deny basic facts. "Montague killed the king and queen. He was killed during the attack. That's why there was a scandal. But if he thought he had leverage, it didn't work. Harristan and Corrick clearly aren't getting more silver from Ostriary."

Maybe Rian can't deny that either. "And they're not benefitting from sales of the Moonflower?"

He asks this like a genuine question, which takes me by surprise. I have to remind myself of what Olive said, how he truly does mean well—but he also doesn't care who gets hurt when he thinks he's right. "No. They're not." It draws my attention back to the maps. "So let's say someone *is* poisoning all of Kandala somehow. Why did you show me the maps? What have you figured out already?"

"Nothing yet. But I showed you where Moonflower grows here." He points to Kaisa again. "Where does Moonflower grow in Kandala?"

I point to the northernmost sectors. Based on how he's positioned the maps, they sit farther north than Kaisa. "Here. Moonlight Plains and Emberridge. But how would they poison the entire country? They barely produce enough Moonflower to *treat* it."

Rian winces. "I'm not sure. But it doesn't take very much poison to cause an effect. Just a bit of boiled stem will cause the fever in an adult. A bit more will bring the coughing."

"And it has to be boiled?"

"Or soaked," Rian says. "Though that takes longer. Far quicker just to boil it."

I study the maps, remembering the way Corrick and I did the same thing in the palace. It was so late at night, and we went through books and records and pored over maps, talking about how Sunkeep fares the best with the fevers, but it has the lowest population in Kandala. He revealed that several people had theorized that Sunkeep's access to the ocean water might stave off the fever sickness, but it was determined that *every* sector has access to fresh water. It was a dead end.

"Could the 'medicine' be tainted?" Rian asks. "Could they be handing out vials of poison mixed in with the cure so no one would know what they're getting?"

I shake my head. "No. Moonflower is sold as petals. No one is given vials of elixir because it doesn't really last, and the elites are allowed to buy as much as they want."

Rian scoffs. "Of course they are."

I can't even disagree with his reaction.

"How much does it take?" I say. I look up at him. "You said you brought so much Moonflower to keep Bella subdued. Does the poison take repeated doses?"

He hesitates, and for the first time, a hint of shame flickers in his eyes. "Yes. And you have to be careful. Too much, and it can be debilitating. Too *long* and damage can be permanent."

I think about that, turning it around in my head. "But if people in Kandala were given access to an antidote, even infrequently, maybe we weren't curing the fever sickness. Maybe we were just holding back the poison, over and over again. Only the most vulnerable fell very sick and died."

Or those who didn't have access to medicine at all.

My eyes trace the lines of the rivers that neatly slice through Kandala on both sides again, the Queen's River in the east, and the Flaming River to the west. Rian said *boiled* or *soaked*. There'd be no way to hand out vials of poison to the entire population on a regular basis—but there must be hundreds of streams branching off each river, leading into towns and valleys that each have their own system of water mills, with pumps and wells and sewers all throughout each sector, even the Wilds. The Royal Sector, completely landlocked, even has running water provided by a complicated sewer system that diverts water directly from mills fed by the Queen's River.

The Queen's River, which starts at the northern tip of Kandala, just like the Flaming River.

The northern tip of Kandala, coincidentally home to the two sectors where the Moonflower grows.

Where the "cure" was discovered.

I stare at the map. Maybe every sector *doesn't* have access to fresh water.

"They're putting it in the water," I say in horror.

"In the *water*?" Rian says in surprise.

But Rocco leans close. "How, Miss Tessa? How would they do it?"

I have to shake my head. "I don't know. I don't know enough about water mills or wells or how any of that works." But now that I'm thinking about it, a lot of other things begin to fall into place. "But it would explain why Sunkeep doesn't have as many sick people. If the rivers are poisoned in Emberridge and Moonlight Plains, by the time water travels that far south, the poison is probably diluted. It would also explain why people who work at the river docks always seem to get the worst fever sickness."

I tap my finger against my chin. I'm on a roll now, and I can't stop. "It would *also* explain why it's so difficult to determine who gets sick and who doesn't. Some people might be drinking water from a rain barrel, some people might be drinking from a well, some people might be drinking water from a faucet. With the size of Kandala, the rain surely dilutes the poison from time to time, too, so there'd be no way to figure out a rhythm or pattern to who is getting the sickest either. And some people would be more vulnerable than others. Maybe the sea life can be affected, too. So people who eat fish would be influenced. Or what about livestock who've drunk the water? Would the poison be in their flesh?" I let out a breath. All of a sudden, I want my books. I need to get to the king. I need to warn someone. "This is too big! There's too much."

But then my eyes lock on Rian's, and I remember what he said about returning to Kandala.

I don't know if I can attempt returning again so quickly.

"We have to go back," I say. "We have to go back *now*. I have to tell the king."

Rian looks at me steadily. "And how will you get there? Swim?"

I inhale a breath of fire and move like I'm going to launch myself at him.

Chairs scrape against the floor, and the two guards who followed us step away from the wall, but Rian puts up a hand, and they all stop. I'm aware of Rocco right against my side.

"I can't," Rian says to me. "Not even if I wanted to. You saw the condition of the *Dawn Chaser*. The ship is going to take weeks to repair, if not a month—"

"I know you have other ships," I snap.

"I do. But you *also* know we were just engaged in a war, Miss Cade. A lot of the bridges have been destroyed, so any steamships I have are running cargo to rebuild. If I claim failure on this mission and then take a ship away from rebuilding, it's going to be a tough sell to my people. If I do that and leave now, Oren Crane will *absolutely* take over."

My fists are clenched at my sides.

People are dying, I want to scream.

But he knows that—and as much as I hate to admit it, people are at risk *here*, too. I saw the citadel.

I hate this. It's no better than it was in Kandala.

I wish we'd never come.

But if we'd never come, I never would have known about the poison. We would've kept trying to figure out a way to make better medicine, fighting our own war endlessly.

I unclench my fists and sigh.

"Fine," I say. "Then I'm going back to the house. I'll take the horses and cart you promised." I remember what Rocco said about our little boats and add, "Some sailcloth, too. And some maps, if we're to navigate Fairde on our own."

He could easily make a dig about how we wouldn't have to navigate anything alone if I weren't choosing to leave, but he doesn't. "I'll give you anything you need to make yourself comfortable, Miss Cade."

I somehow refrain from giving him a rude gesture, and instead, I turn for the door. "Goodbye, Gwyn," I say. "Goodbye, Sablo."

As I listen to their farewells behind me, I stomp down the stairs, feeling Rocco's presence at my back. Rian's footsteps are lighter behind him, and I'm sure there are guards following him, too. This all feels like such a failure. He hasn't promised to bring me back. I have no way to tell Harristan what happened to Corrick—or about what's truly happening in Kandala. I don't know how much time will need to pass before he'll launch a rescue mission, if he can even accomplish one.

Rocco and I could be stuck here . . . forever.

My chest tightens, and my breathing hitches for a moment. That's almost too overwhelming to comprehend.

There is more than one way to fight.

Well, I told Rocco I couldn't lie. I'm not an emissary, and Rian saw right through me immediately. I probably ruined any hope we had the very instant I drew that dagger and vomited on his toes. The only thing I know how to do is take care of people.

Is that something? I don't know. It never seems to make a difference.

I think of those people we passed when we rode through town. The ones who looked at Rocco's livery and wondered if I was someone important. I'm not. Even in Kandala, the only time I felt like I was making a difference was when I was working in the Wilds as an outlaw, with Weston Lark at my side.

When we get to the bottom of the stairs, I turn and look at Rian. "In addition to the horses and the cart and everything else, I'm going to need extra silver."

His eyebrows go up. "Oh, you are?"

"Yes. I worked as an apothecary in Kandala. I'd like to do the same here. If your people are rebuilding, they surely get sick and injured from time to time. I have my books and a few things I brought on the ship, but I'll need to buy supplies so I can be prepared. Once we have the wagon, Rocco and I will ride through your towns to determine what's needed."

Rian stares at me. His mouth opens like he wants to say something, but he's not sure what. I think I've truly surprised him.

"Stop looking at me like that," I say. "I'm certainly not going to sit in that house waiting around for some man to decide my fate. If I'm stuck here, I'm going to make myself useful."

He clamps his mouth shut. "Fine. I'll grant you whatever you need." He pauses, and his eyes narrow. "But if I hear that you're causing trouble among my people—"

"I'm not causing trouble." I take a step closer, looking him dead in the eye. "I've never caused trouble. You criticized Prince Corrick for manipulation and scheming at every turn, when you did exactly the same thing. And you know what the problem with that is? You think you're doing the right thing, but all you're really doing is turning everyone into your *enemy*. If you knew Moonflower was a poison, you had a chance to tell King Harristan when you were there. You could have saved lives *right then*. But you knew it was a way to lure Corrick onto that ship, so you didn't."

"I *didn't* because it was clear I was sitting with traitors and—"

"I'm done talking to you, Rian." I have to take a deep breath to steady myself. "All I've ever wanted to do is help people, and that's all I'm doing now."

"Truly." His eyes search mine, and I can tell he suspects me of lying.

But I'm not.

"Truly," I say. "So give me my silver, and I'll be on my way."

He hesitates, and for a breath of time, I think he's going to refuse. We'll have gained nothing at all.

But then Rian nods. "Consider it done."

CHAPTER THIRTEEN

Tessa

We prepare to leave the palace with more supplies than I expected. Rian provides a wagon loaded with rolls of muslin, sacks of grain, and bales of hay. There are two crates filled with jars of everything I can imagine, from dried herbs to pickled vegetables to cooking supplies. Not one but *three* rolls of sailcloth, as well as two new fishing nets and another set of oars. A leather folio has been tucked along the front seat of the wagon with a set of maps, too. Two small hatches near the front of the wagon will do for chickens once we pass back through town, along with a larger pen tied to the back for goats or even a calf, if we get that lucky. Rian gives me a small sack of silver once we're done inspecting everything, telling me to thread it through my dagger belt.

"This is it?" I say to him with a raised eyebrow, even though I can feel the weight of it, and I'm sure it's more than enough.

"No," he says, regardless. "The wagon has a false bottom under the hay bales, in case you encounter thieves. In it, you'll find a small chest with more."

Oh. Well, that's surprising. I'm still angry at him, so I don't want to offer him one single speck of gratitude—but if I'm an absolute shrew, there's a chance he'll never give me anything again. "I'll be sure to put it to good use," I say instead.

He's given us four horses as well: two in harness to pull the wagon, and two tethered behind. "All four are broke for riding," he tells me. "So you'll have spares in case any go lame."

I'd only *just* begun to learn to ride in Kandala with Corrick, but now doesn't seem the time to tell him that. I nod and refuse to look at him. "These are more than enough."

Then I climb into the wagon beside Rocco, and the guardsman takes up the reins.

Rian steps close to the wagon. "I'm not your enemy, Tessa."

That finally gets my attention, and I meet his eyes. "Your entire country is now my prison, Your Majesty. If I'm not your enemy, then find a way to send me home."

I turn my head to tell Rocco to go, but his career as the king's guard must have given him a talent for reading between the lines, because he snaps the whip and the horses trot forward, leaving the palace behind.

It's dusk, and I expect Rocco to talk about how horribly that went, but he says nothing—so *I* say nothing. My stomach is curling with guilt, because I feel like I've failed, and I'm worried he's thinking the same thing. The longer the silence continues, the more sure I am. So the wagon rattles along in silence for a while, until a few stars appear overhead and the citadel disappears behind us.

Eventually, we reach the villages at the top of the hill, and I'm glad we have the wagon, because it's steeper than it looked going down. The streets are still crowded, and food vendors are everywhere now, the scents making my mouth water at every turn. When we stop to buy chickens, there's a young man at a stall across the road selling small pockets of dough stuffed with meat and corn and cheese. He also has stoppered jugs of sugared tea.

"My sister hung the jugs down the well all day, miss," he tells me. Dark hair hangs in his eyes, but it's been chopped off at the neck. "So they're still cold."

I touch one of the glass jugs, and to my surprise, they *are* cold, speckled with condensation. "I'll take two," I say. "And four of the dough pockets."

He smiles and begins to wrap the food in wax paper. "Hungry, hmm?"

"It's not all for me." I gesture over my shoulder at where Rocco is latching several hens into the small hutches in the wagon.

The young man's eyes widen when he takes in Rocco's size, and then he grins. "Well, I should give you a *fifth* one for him, or I'll worry the chickens won't make it back to wherever you're going." He slips the food into a cloth satchel for me, then waves off my hand full of coins. "Keep your silver. No charge."

"Oh! That's very kind, but you don't have to do that. I can pay—"

"You're from Kandala. Rumor says your king has finally seen fit to help *us*, so I can help you."

I freeze in place, because I'm not sure what to say. I don't know if Kandala will be able to help these people at all.

But I also don't want to smack away his generosity. I give him a nod. "That's very kind. Thank you." I hesitate. "I'm Tessa Cade. The guardsman is Erik Rocco. We came on the ship from Kandala."

"I'm Henry." He's younger than I am, but not by much. He

tucks some of that hair behind an ear, and sharp brown eyes glance at Rocco again, then back at me. "A lot of us saw you pass through before. If you stop at the tavern, they're probably still laying bets on whether you're royalty."

That startles a laugh out of me, and I remember the gossiping women speculating over whether I was a princess. "No, I'm definitely not royalty."

Rocco climbs down from the wagon, and he must overhear us, because he says, "Miss Tessa is the king of Kandala's personal apothecary and adviser."

Henry's eyes sharpen further. "Is that so?"

My heart gives a little jolt, like Rocco is lying. I almost want to deny it—even though I suppose it's true. Rocco just makes it all sound so *official*, when I quite accidentally fell into the role.

But I nod, then shrug a little, because I don't want to put on airs. "I'll be coming through town again in the next few days to put together more supplies. I told your king I'll be available to his people while we're here, so if you know of anyone who's sick, or ailing, or needs—"

"Oh, there are plenty of people who are sick and ailing," Henry says. His eyebrows go up, and he glances at Rocco again. "The king of Kandala would share his *personal* apothecary?"

"I—ah, yes. He would." I honestly have no idea, but King Harristan isn't here, and it's not as if I can say he's a selfish lout who'd keep me all to himself. I consider Henry's comment about *plenty of people*. "Would you be able to let anyone know that if they need my services, we can come back here . . ." I think quickly, trying to remember the state of my apothecary kit back at the house, and how long it might take to put things together and make some salves and tonics. "Ah . . . the morning after tomorrow?" I look at Rocco for confirmation, since I'll need him to drive the wagon, and he nods. "It'll take a little time to put a full kit together, but I can make a few basic supplies to start with."

Henry nods. "My sister works in the courier's office, so she can spread the word."

"Good." I smile. "Thank you for the food."

He gives me a nod. "You're welcome, Tessa Cade." He smiles at Rocco. "And Erik Rocco."

Then we're off again.

We eat in silence, and the food is delicious, the sugared tea a relief after the heat of the day. The horses clop along at a walk, and the chickens cluck at our backs as the last of the light fades, leaving a sky full of stars twinkling overhead.

Rocco is the first to break the weird silence between us. "It's late, and Rian mentioned thieves, Miss Tessa," he says. "We could leave the goat for tomorrow."

I can't read anything from his voice. "Sure," I say. "We have enough to unload already."

"I could return on my own," he says.

I hesitate. "You don't want my help?" Though maybe that's a stupid question. I can't drive the wagon. And I doubt I know any more about goats than he does.

Maybe he just doesn't want my company after I wrecked our chance to get back to Kandala.

He glances over. "I didn't want you to feel you had to take time away from preparing your apothecary kit."

Oh. I stare out at the darkened path. "I'll probably need to get more supplies once I take stock of everything, so we can go together." I hesitate again. "If that's all right."

"Of course."

We're quiet again for a little while, until we both turn toward each other at the same time.

"I'm sorry—" I begin.

"Forgive me—" Rocco starts.

But we both break off, staring at each other.

Eventually, he has to look back at the road, and he adjusts the reins. "Why are you apologizing?"

"Because I couldn't do it," I say. "I couldn't convince him to take us back to Kandala." I frown and fold my arms against my stomach. "I just saw the ship in the harbor, and it reminded me of . . . everything."

"It's not your fault," he says. "*None of this* is your fault. It's not your responsibility to get us back. It's not even your responsibility to help Rian's people."

"I can't keep doing *nothing*," I say. "You were right before. I need to move." I look up at the stars and think back to when I was younger. I was so eager to help my father each day. He was always patient, even when I was very young, showing me every herb, every plant, every leaf, every petal. I learned how to make teas and elixirs and how to grind roots into dust, and how to weigh and level right down to the tiniest measurements. My father was careful and composed, so I learned to be careful and composed. With people, my mother was gentle and kind, so at her side, I learned to be gentle and kind. When the fever sickness began to spread, much changed— but not his patience and composure. Not her kindness. We were distributing stolen Moonflower, and I knew it was a risk. But they were willing to risk their lives to save others, so I was too.

I consider all my father's books and records and ledgers, some of which I have in my pack back at the house. All his research, and he never suspected poison. None of us did. Well, someone in

Kandala knew—and they were doing it deliberately. This is worse than simply making profits off the medicine. I keep waiting for this to hit me like a fresh round of loss, but maybe there's been too much. The sadness is already too thick, and there's no room for more.

"When my parents died," I say, "Wes was the only thing that kept me going. He was risking his life to help the people, so that's how I made it through each day. Knowing he'd be waiting for me in the workshop that night."

"Do you mean His Highness?"

I blink and realize I said *Wes*. In my memories, he's still Weston Lark. My throat goes tight, and I swallow thickly. "Yes."

"And you truly never knew he was the King's Justice?"

"No. Never." I wait for this line of conversation to summon my grief, but somehow my heart only feels fondness. Maybe because I already grieved Wes once, and this feels different. "Sometimes Wes and I would even talk about how terrible the king and his brother were."

"*Really.*"

I nod, remembering. "Though I suppose I was always the one to start *those* kinds of conversations. It's not like he could have argued with me about it. What would he have said?" I drop my voice and imitate Wes—*Corrick*. "'Lord, Tessa. King Harristan really isn't that bad once you get to know him.'"

Though now that I think about it, I remember some of our conversations.

I hate the king and his brother, I'd say. *I hate the things that they do.*

Wes would always agree with me without hesitation.

Corrick didn't hate his brother, but I know now that he hated his role.

Rocco glances over, and there's a bit of intrigue in his voice when he says, "How did the prince slip past the guards, night after night? Do you know?"

I look at him in surprise. "You *don't* know?"

"No. He couldn't have been climbing a rope from his chambers *every* night. There was a night on the ship when Liam and I were playing cards—"

"Wait. Liam?"

He grimaces. "Kilbourne."

I frown. Until now, I didn't know his first name. I feel like I should have. "Sorry. Continue."

"We spent the whole time trying to figure it out. Was he bribing a guard? Or a group of guards?" He shakes his head without waiting for an answer. "I can't imagine. There was too much turnover. He wouldn't have been able to keep it a secret for years."

I hold my breath for a moment. I don't want to give up Corrick's confidence—but at this point, maybe it doesn't matter.

"I don't know all of his paths in and out of the palace," I say softly, "but I know he had Quint."

Rocco goes still. "Ah." He considers that for a little while, then looks at me. "It doesn't explain how he got out of the palace without being seen, though. Master Quint wouldn't have been able to distract *all* the guards."

"He told me there are spy tunnels all over the Royal Sector. We used one of them when we escaped the attack. You remember. At the back of the palace gardens. Downhill from Stonehammer's Arch."

He frowns. "Those spy tunnels are caved in."

I shake my head. "Corrick said a lot of them are, but you can still slip through if you know how. He said he and the king used to use them all the time when they were younger." I mentally do the math and realize Rocco was probably a guardsman during the time Harristan was slipping out of the palace as a teenager, dragging a rebellious young Corrick behind him.

Rocco scowls, but he's also nodding like I've helped him solve a riddle. "No wonder the king was able to show up at the docks the night we left. None of us were expecting him there."

"That's right," I whisper. I'd forgotten that the king snuck into Prince Corrick's carriage.

Rocco nods. "They never travel together. It's too great a risk. And it certainly wasn't planned. None of His Majesty's personal guard were with them."

A sudden wave of emotion threatens to overwhelm me. That would have been the last time they saw each other. The brothers' closeness was something very special, very touching, that they always seemed to feel the need to hide. I'm glad Corrick and Harristan had those private moments, instead of whatever public farewell was required of them.

The night is growing darker, and I need to think of something else, or I'm going to start crying again. I fight for other thoughts, and I remember that we both began to apologize, but he never finished his.

"What—" My voice is breathy, and I sniff back the waiting tears. "What were you going to apologize for?" I ask Rocco.

He's quiet for a moment. "I pushed you to confront him. I didn't intend to cause you so much distress." He pauses. "I'm sorry."

"No, I needed to do it. I'm glad you pushed me." I roll my eyes. "I do wish I hadn't thrown up on him."

"Are you kidding? That was my favorite part."

That makes me giggle, and it's enough to chase any risk of tears away. But eventually, silence grows between us again, and I don't want sorrow to fill the space. "Was Rian right?" I say softly. "Are you worried about facing the king if we get back?"

He makes a frustrated sound. "*That* was Rian attempting to manipulate you. Or maybe he and his people really do suspect the worst of everyone from Kandala." His jaw tightens. "But I volunteered for this journey, so I'll see it through. I swore an oath to the king. In all those long hours I've stood guard over countless meetings, I've never once heard him *not* do right by his people."

I nod, remembering the first time I sat and faced King Harristan myself. I remember being surprised by the same thing. So many people in Kandala think he's horrible, but he isn't. Not at all. He truly cares, and he's trying to protect everyone the best way he can.

We hit a bump in the road, and Rocco makes a small sound of discomfort. He shifts on the bench next to me, pressing a hand to his side, then shifts again, before sighing and shaking out the reins, clucking to the horses to pick up the pace. I look over, and it's tough to tell in the moonlight, but his jaw is still tight.

"You're in pain," I say. "How long has it been bothering you?"

"I'm all right, Miss Tessa."

I don't believe him. He didn't even eat all of the food we bought. "Can I take the reins?"

He makes a face, then shakes his head. "A lot more can go wrong with horses than a rowboat. We don't have much farther."

I flatten my lips into a line, but I nod. I think of the way he was helping to load the wagon. "I wish you'd said something."

"I wasn't going to make you stay at his palace."

I frown and look back at the road, feeling guilty. I announced that this morning, how I didn't want to risk staying near Rian. "I would have," I say quietly. "You've been risking yourself to guard *me*. I might not know how to fight, but I'll do what I can to protect you, too."

As soon as I say it, the words seem silly. He doesn't need my protection. But he glances at me in the darkness, and he gives me a nod. "Thank you, Miss Tessa."

We trot on in the moonlight, and I recognize the woods when we get back to the path where we met Olive and Ellmo. I've been listening to Rocco's breathing for the last twenty minutes, and I'm trying to determine whether it sounds strained, when a smattering of rocks hits the side of the wagon, and a light bit of laughter rings through the trees.

Rocco draws back the reins and sighs as the horses come to a stop. "I don't have the patience for it now, boy. I might just shoot you this time."

I expect Ellmo to fire back with a saucy comment or scamper away through the trees, but he leaps up onto the wagon like he's been invited. "Mama and I have been watching for you. I ran ahead." His eyes are wide in the moonlight. "Look at all this *stuff*." He begins poking through the wagon, and the hens go wild with clucking.

Rocco twitches the reins, and the horses walk on. "I'm glad you're here," he says. "We need a five-year-old to help unload."

"I'm *seven*!"

"Is your mother nearby?" I ask him, just as I hear Olive call his name from the shadows ahead. Rocco draws the wagon to a stop again when we reach her.

She has a small lantern, and she holds it up toward the wagon.

She whistles low between her teeth at all of our wares. "I see our *king* sought to curry your favor, Tessa Cade."

I hear the tone in her voice when she says *king* and wonder if she means that as an insult. "No," I say. "He refused everything I asked for."

Her eyes widen. "Exactly what did you ask for?"

"Passage home."

She meets my gaze and holds it. "I see."

"Since he refused," I say, "I asked for supplies to set up an apothecary here. I won't sit around waiting for him to grant my wishes."

She blinks in surprise, much like Henry in the village. "You're going to set up an apothecary . . . *here*?"

"Yes. I heard there were people who might be sick or injured. Now we have a wagon, so I'll help if I can. I used to make rounds in Kandala, so I may as well do the same."

"The people might not trust your medicines," she says. "There's still a lot of worry after the way Kandala betrayed Ostriary."

"I know," I say. "But I can try."

She studies me again, and I can't make out much of her expression in the shadows beyond the lantern. Behind me, Ellmo is still digging through the supplies. "Mama, they have a jar of real *honey*. Can we take it?"

Rocco clears his throat. "Miss Olive, if you would be so kind as to take this little demon off our hands, I would be most appreciative. Either that, or come help. The day isn't growing any shorter."

Olive shakes herself. "Oh. Of course." To my surprise, she takes hold of the wagon railing, then pulls herself up to sit right beside him.

Both Rocco and I stare at her.

"I'm coming to help," she says.

Rocco shrugs and cracks the whip.

"And my child is not a demon," Olive adds, glaring at him.

From behind us, Ellmo growls like a wildcat. "I can be a demon."

"Trust me, I know," says Rocco.

After we reach the house, we busy ourselves with unloading the wagon, and there isn't time for more banter. I watch Rocco carefully, and although he's not moving as stiffly as I expected, I've still seen him wince a few times. When he's untethering one of the horses from the wagon, I peer at him in the darkness while Olive and Ellmo are carrying things into the house.

"Truly," I say to him quietly. "You should rest tomorrow. A goat can wait."

"We'll see."

I frown, but he smiles. "I need to move, Miss Tessa."

I put a hand on his arm. "I really meant what I said. I know you're guarding me, but we have to help each other."

He loses the smile, then nods. "I know."

"And if we get the chance to go before King Harristan again, I *will* tell him that you did everything possible to protect Prince Corrick. To protect all of Kandala. If he tried to punish you for failing in your duties . . ." I set my jaw. "I wouldn't let him."

Again, it feels silly to say it, because what can I do against the king? But Rocco's eyes soften. "Thank you, Miss Tessa. But I wouldn't be trying to get back so desperately if I were worried." The back door to the house creaks as Olive and Ellmo come out. Rocco looks back at me and clasps me fondly on the shoulder. "I know what people in Kandala think of the king, but after what I've heard in some of those meetings, it's the consuls who aren't to be trusted. I've been in King Harristan's personal guard for four years, and if I'm offered the chance, I'll give him forty more. He'll grieve the loss of his brother. He'll retaliate against Ostriary. But I don't believe he'll punish me. There's a reason we closed ranks when the revolution started. Like every other man in his personal guard, I trust the king."

His eyes are so dark in the shadows. I think of our conversation in the woods, how our thoughts can change as we learn new information. A few short months ago, I hated the king and his brother. I was wondering if I had the mettle to kill them both.

And now I'm on the other side, where a few short *weeks* ago, King Harristan slipped into my chambers and confided that he was worried about receiving the right dosage of medicine from the palace physicians while I was gone.

For the first time since we've arrived, a twinge of worry tugs at my heart. He's always the center of attention, always surrounded by guards, and always so lonely.

There are very few people I trust, he said to me. *Three of you are climbing aboard a ship tonight.*

My heart twists again. I hope he's all right.

"I trust him, too," I say softly.

"Good." Rocco nods. "Let's hope we make it back to Kandala to tell him."

CHAPTER FOURTEEN

Harristan

The first knock at the door comes at midnight, and it makes me immediately regret my promise of *any time.*

The small house is dark, the fire still burning in the tiny hearth, throwing shadows everywhere. It's so quiet that for a moment, I sit up in bed and wonder if I dreamed the sound of the knock.

But then the shadows shift and Thorin appears beside the door. He looks to me. "Your Majesty?"

I run a hand over my face, then nod. "Go ahead. Open the door. I did say *day or night.*"

"Wait!" Quint hisses from the other side of the room. "A moment, *please.*"

I think he must be in some state of undress, but he's not. Instead, he strides across the room, fetches *my* tunic from where I tossed it at the end of the bed, and holds it out to me.

I stare at him.

He doesn't falter. "I thought you might not want to greet your people shirtless," he says, and my eyes narrow.

Another knock sounds at the door, louder this time.

I snatch the tunic out of Quint's hand. "Go ahead," I say to Thorin again. As I pull the tunic over my head, I realize we're the only three in the dimly lit room. "Has Saeth not returned from patrol?"

"No," says Thorin, and in that one word, I can hear his concern. But then he opens the door.

I'm wondering if it will be another group of men with axes and hammers, but I'm surprised to find a middle-aged woman on the doorstep. Her graying hair is in a long braid hanging over her shoulder, and she's wringing her hands.

"I'm sorry," she says. "I know it's late—"

"It's fine," I say. "Come in."

Quint is already lighting the candles on the table, drawing the chairs back. The woman hesitates in the doorway, glancing from me to Thorin and then to Quint. Her handwringing turns to fingers gripping knuckles, and she appears ready to flee.

"I shouldn't be here," she says quickly. "My husband didn't want me to come. I—I had to wait for him to fall asleep. I—I'll just—" She backs through the door.

"Wait," I say, but she's already off the small porch. By the time I make it to the doorway, she's in the yard, scurrying into the darkness. "Please," I call. "Wait. I'll hear whatever you have to say."

She stops before she reaches the trees. "I heard that you granted amnesty to those who held the Royal Sector."

I step down off the porch, but as soon as my bare feet touch the dirt, she looks like she might bolt, so I just nod. "I did."

"I wasn't there. That night. I—I wasn't there."

I frown. I'm not sure what she's trying to tell me. "But you were a part of it?"

She takes another step closer to the trees, until she's almost invisible in the darkness. "I'm not admitting anything."

Talking to people in the Wilds is so very different from talking to people in the palace. In the Royal Sector, everyone always has a hidden agenda. Words are barbed like weapons, and every syllable is calculated. I'm generally good at sensing when the consuls are lying to me, to say nothing of the courtiers who simper at dinner every night. I have no hesitation in cutting through their nonsense. If I'm not decisive and sharp, it's seen as weakness. They circle me like sharks who sense blood in the water.

If I'm sharp with this woman, there's a good chance I'll never see her again, so I sit down on the step. "Are you worried I'll punish you if you were?" I say quietly. "Amnesty wasn't just for people who were there that night. I know you were all desperate. I said I wanted things to change, and I meant it. You can speak freely." I lean forward, then brace my forearms on my knees. "Besides, it may not be obvious, but I'm currently without a throne. Truly, you have nothing to fear."

She's silent for a while, considering that, but she eventually draws closer, pulling her shawl tightly around her shoulders. I glared at Quint when he offered me the tunic, but now I'm glad for it, because there's a chill in the night air. My bare feet are freezing against the ground, but I'm worried she'll bolt again if I stand up.

I gesture beside me. "Please. Sit."

She regards me for a moment, then eases forward to gingerly perch on the step beside me.

"What's your name?" I say.

"Annabeth, sir. King? Your Majesty." She frowns and tugs her shawl closer, then bites her lip. "I—I don't know what to call you. A lot of people have been calling you the Fox."

The Fox. Violet started that, when I was an outlaw leaving coins on steps and stumps and windowsills. Now that I'm living among them, I wonder if it's easier to think of me as someone separate from the king. As if I'm not the man who, in their eyes, simply lazed about the palace and allowed his brother to execute people for stealing medicine they needed to survive.

A lot of them used to call me Horrible Harristan, the way they called my brother Cruel Corrick.

Annabeth didn't show up with an ax, so she can honestly call me whatever she wants.

I glance over. "You don't have to be formal. Fox is fine."

A bit of light flares behind us, and I realize Quint is lighting the lanterns.

And in that light, I notice there are tears on Annabeth's cheeks.

"Please," I say. "You came here to talk to me. I'll listen."

She takes a slow breath, and her voice trembles. "I know the men are ready to charge the Royal Sector like they did before. But they wouldn't have been able to do it if we hadn't hit critical parts of the city. It was the women who figured out where to lay the explosives."

I'm glad I have a lifetime of experience at keeping any hint of emotion off my face, including every gruesome execution Corrick forced me to witness, so I don't even blink.

"How?" I say.

"My cousin is a day maid in the palace," she says quietly. "She snuck us some uniforms. Piece by piece. We made more. We've been able to slip inside."

I keep my breathing very slow and even, but my heart feels like a galloping horse. The people in the Wilds speak openly about revolution, but this is the first time someone has directly admitted their own specific role in what happened during the attack on the sector.

"Who is your cousin?" I say.

She says nothing. It's clear she still doesn't trust me. I'm shocked she offered this much. I know they don't have any explosives left. "The Benefactors" have stopped providing money and medicine, and I ordered that any shipments from Trader's Landing be thoroughly searched following the attacks. They're not getting any more.

"You had to be working with the guards," I say. "They know the maids. A stranger wouldn't have been able to sneak in, even with a uniform."

Though Tessa snuck in, I remember.

"No." Annabeth hesitates. "Though—"

A shadowed figure steps out of the trees, and her head snaps up in alarm. A boot scrapes on the porch behind me, and I realize Thorin has spotted the figure, too. I'm frozen in place, remembering the crowd who showed up with axes, but then enough light reveals Saeth. A bit of the tightness in my chest loosens. "It's all right," I say. "My other guard is just returning from patrol."

But Annabeth has been spooked, and she's already off the step and into the shadows. "I need to return before my husband realizes I'm gone."

"Please," I say. "At least tell me—"

But she's slipped into the trees.

"I can go after her," Thorin says quietly.

"No," I say. She barely trusted me enough to reveal this much. I'll wait and see if she comes back.

Saeth has drawn closer, and now I can see stains on his tunic, and a dark streak across one side of his face.

I'm on my feet in an instant. "Are you hurt?" I demand.

"No, Your Majesty." He grimaces. "Well. Not badly. The night patrol started searching homes a few miles south of here. I picked a fight to give them a different quarry. Then I had to wait for them to stop chasing *me*."

A few miles south. That's close. Possibly too close.

At my back, Quint says, "Were they searching for the king?"

"No, they were looking for smugglers." Saeth has moved close enough to the light that I can see bruising along his jaw now, and blood on his lip. He's not very old, probably not much more than thirty, but his eyes are shadowed and tired, and sweat threads his hair. "I led them into Steel City and through the merchants' quarter, then lost them somewhere after we crossed into Artis."

That's a lot of ground to cover, and my guards haven't been going out on horseback. We're hamstrung in so many ways. "On foot?" I say.

Saeth nods.

"Sit," I say, gesturing to the step. I glance behind me. "Quint, fetch him some—"

But when I look, Quint already has a cup of water, along with a damp rag. Saeth drops onto the step, his movement heavy with exhaustion, and he takes both. He runs the rag across the back of his neck, then drains the water without taking a breath.

I want to give him time to recover, but if the night patrol is searching for me, we don't have time. I ease onto the step beside him.

"Advise," I say quietly. "Do we need to move?"

He shakes his head. "No, Your Majesty. I lost them miles ago.

I doubled back through the creek half a dozen times to cover my tracks."

But still. That was very close. "If they came this way once, they'll do it again."

He nods, then wipes the rag against his cheek, wincing when it finds broken skin. "I don't remember the night patrol being that determined."

"Someone is paying them to be *more* determined." I imagine it's Allisander, or one of his barons. I keep thinking of Arella Cherry working with the head of the palace guard, though. I still don't know how or why they're tricking people into thinking I'm *poisoning* them. "They know I'm out here somewhere."

Saeth nods and looks out at the night, but he says nothing to that.

As always, there are so many people, so many angles, so many *worries* to consider. I have all of Kandala to think of, but when I'm sitting here in the dark, it's hard to cast my concerns beyond the people in front of me. Like Annabeth, who came to tell me about her means to sneak into the palace. Like Quint, who's whisked away Saeth's water cup to refill it without being asked.

Like the man at my side, who must have run for *miles* tonight, just to protect me.

All while worried about a family that he hasn't seen in more than a week.

When I was first crowned king after my parents' assassination, I had to choose my own personal guard. It would have been easy to use the same men my father had used. As the crown prince, I knew them all, and was familiar with each one of them.

But my mother and father had died on their watch, and in the days after it happened, I found I didn't trust *any* of them.

So I discharged them all.

When it came time to interview applicants to staff my *own* personal guard, however, I found it more challenging than I expected. It didn't help that I had years of hearing little remarks about my illnesses, little snickers about my frail health, little moments of mockery behind my back when I would pass. Comments that weren't quite soft enough for me to ignore—especially when they were coming from the hall guards themselves. Comments that would have been petty to address but sat under my skin for weeks.

I would sit across the table from each man and woman and try to remember if it was someone who'd mocked me behind my back, or if it was someone I could trust with my life. Until our parents were slaughtered right in front of us, we rarely faced any threats. But suddenly I was trying to discern which guards would truly risk their life to save mine, when a week before I was trying my best to *ignore* them.

But for some reason I'd remembered Saeth from when he'd been among the general guard. I don't remember what he said during his interview, and it probably didn't matter. When he sat down at the table, he'd looked familiar, and it only took me a second to remember why. He'd been a hall guard when I was younger, and some footmen were whispering when I passed. Saeth had snapped at them to stop.

He was one of the first guards I chose.

I should've known he had a family.

It's quiet and cold and dark, and I think Quint and Thorin have gone back in the house, so I say, "Ben told me about your wife and children. That you've been worried."

Saeth goes absolutely rigid, and his head whips around, but he doesn't look at me. He's looking for Thorin.

"He didn't betray you," I say.

"He shouldn't have said anything."

"Saeth. *Adam.* I asked him. I should've asked earlier."

He glares at the door, then gives an aggravated sigh and runs the rag over his neck again. "Leah knows the risks. She's a brave girl. She'll take care of them, Your Majesty. You shouldn't have to trouble yourself."

Every word of that sounds like he's trying to convince *himself.*

"If I could give you leave to return home," I say, "I would."

"I'd be arrested," he says. "I'm sure they're watching her."

"No doubt."

His throat jerks as he swallows, and his jaw is set, his eyes fixed on the trees. "I won't abandon Thorin either."

"I'm glad to hear it." I pause. "If we could manage it safely, would you be willing to bring them here?"

He goes still again.

"Thorin suggested approaching two of the younger members of my personal guard," I say. "Reed and Sommer. You know them?"

He nods. "Yes."

"Karri is gone, but it could be some time before we hear back from any of the consuls. We need more insight from inside the palace. From the Royal Sector. The men here are ready to fight, and it's time to make a small move. We have a plan. If the men can quietly bring Reed and Sommer without notice, I would ask them to bring your wife and children, too." I pause. "If you're willing. This is not without risk either."

Saeth hasn't moved. He's still staring out at the night. Eventually, he looks at me.

"You don't need to risk yourself for my family," he says.

"Why not? You're risking yourself for me."

He lets out a breath, then shakes his head. "I can't ask for this."

"You're not asking. I'm offering. Are you willing or not?"

"I'm willing," he says, and his voice is very quiet. "Thank you."

He shouldn't be thanking me. Not yet. I have no idea if any of my decisions are the right ones. So many *wrong* ones led me to this point.

But Saeth hasn't looked away, and I have to say something. I gesture toward the door. "You should rest. You've earned it."

"Thorin and I agreed we wouldn't leave you alone," he says.

"His Majesty is not alone," Quint says from behind me, and I turn my head to realize he never left the porch. He's seated against the wall, his little book open on his lap while he writes, a lantern beside him on the boards.

He turns a page and continues writing. "I can certainly shout for one of you if more trouble appears."

Saeth looks like he wants to object, but he really must be exhausted, because he says, "Yes, Master Quint," and then he disappears into the house as well.

It leaves me alone on the porch with the Palace Master.

Or . . . *whatever* Quint is, now that we're no longer welcome in the palace.

I rub a hand over the back of my neck and sigh, then shift so I'm leaning against the post that supports the roof. I'm tired, and I need to return to bed, too, but I'm also somewhat rattled. I don't know what Annabeth really wanted, but if she planted explosives, she could have knowledge that might be useful later. I don't know if we'll be able to retrieve more guards and Saeth's family—or if we'll all be in the Hold by this time tomorrow.

Or maybe the men who showed up to confront me won't think this plan is worth their time, and they'll kill me themselves.

All of these thoughts make me feel sour and prickly and nowhere near ready to sleep again. I look at Quint. "You don't have a family, too, do you?"

I mean for the question to be genuine, but somehow it sounds a bit argumentative. His eyes flick up from his little book. "Your Majesty, I lived in the palace."

He says this like it's obvious, and it *is*, and it makes me feel like an idiot.

I scowl and look out at the night. "I know. There could still be someone you're . . . missing."

"It's kind of you to ask. But no."

With that, he looks back at his book.

It feels dismissive. On the first day we had to flee the night patrol, Quint mentioned that Corrick asked him to look after me. It annoyed me then, and something about this moment, of the way Quint is remaining on the porch, reminds me of it.

Much like the way he put his hand down on the piece of paper, or the way he thrust a tunic at me before I answered the door.

Like I'm a child who needs minding, not the king of Kandala.

For some reason, that turns my mood even pricklier.

"What on earth are you writing?" I demand.

His eyes flick up again, and he closes the book. "I was making an accounting of what Annabeth said, in the event you query it later. Then your offer to Saeth as well, as you had not made your plans with Thorin known. I wanted to remember—"

"I didn't know I needed to consult with you," I say sharply.

"You don't, of course, but now I'm aware. Reed and Sommer are a decent choice. I see no reason to question their loyalty. I was also making note to discuss lodging with Beatrice, because if you intend to bring two more guards here, as well as Saeth's family, we will need more than a two-room house." A line appears between his eyebrows, and he flips the book open again. "On that note, I should also—"

I roll onto my knees and snatch the book right out of his hands. His pencil goes streaking across the page.

It's possibly the most childish thing I've ever done.

For the barest moment, a flare of challenge hangs in the air. I think he's going to snatch the book back, that we're going to tussle for it. It's a weird sense of anticipation, because I can't remember the last time I ever tussled with anyone for anything. Not even Corrick.

But then he must remember his place, even though I seem to have forgotten mine. He draws his legs up to sit cross-legged, and he straightens to sit upright against the wall. "Your Majesty?"

The light from the lantern flickers off his features, turning his red hair gold. He was always lax about shaving in the palace, and he's even more so now, leaving a dusting of red to coat his jaw.

I frown and sit back on my heels, then hold out the book. "Forgive me."

He takes it, but he doesn't look at it. "It's not private," he says. "You could have asked."

"Don't chastise me, Quint."

"I'm informing you. It's simply palace notes."

Much like the moment I thought we were going to fight over the book, this quibbling has a weirdly anticipatory feel to it. We would sometimes bicker in the palace, but Corrick would always interject.

"Are you *arguing* with me?" I demand.

His eyes glint in the light. "I fail to see how I could be."

I inhale sharply, but the door opens, and Thorin stands there. He looks down at me, and then at Quint—and then back to me. "Is all well?" he finally says.

And then I realize that I'm kneeling on the porch, glaring at Quint petulantly, and there's no way to undo it without drawing more attention to my position.

Thorin's expression doesn't give away a single hint of surprise or judgment, but I doubt it's escaped his notice.

"All is fine," I say evenly.

"The king simply wished to debate semantics," says Quint. He opens his little book and goes back to writing as if the last three minutes didn't happen.

Now I want to snatch the book back and hit him with it.

As soon as the thought occurs to me, I realize that none of my agitation is with Quint at all.

Thorin glances between the two of us again, then says, "Forgive me," and he closes the door.

I shift to sit against it, then draw my legs up to sit cross-legged too. Everything inside me is so jumbled up. I shouldn't be bickering with anyone, but I'm just so angry and sad and worried and a whole host of emotions I probably couldn't name.

I rub my hands over my face and sigh, then look out at the night. "Lord, I miss my brother."

"Yes, Your Majesty. I do, too."

I turn my head and look at him. Again, I'm a fool. Of course there's someone Quint is missing. He's probably as lonely as I am. He and Corrick were always close.

A part of me envied that, especially once I learned that my brother had Tessa as well. I never had anyone.

"Corrick would be better at all this," I say.

Quint laughs as if I've startled him. "No." Then he sobers, and his pencil goes still for a moment as he reconsiders. "Well."

I sigh. "Exactly."

"Prince Corrick is always quite good with details," he says. "And his experience in the Hold gives him an edge that you lack. I rather doubt Francis would have dared to come near him with an ax, of all things."

"I wasn't sure it was possible to feel worse, Quint. Thank you."

He resumes his writing. "Though it may be worth considering that Annabeth likely wouldn't have found the courage to speak to Prince Corrick at *all*."

I'm not sure what to say to that.

Eventually, he sets the pencil down, then begins flipping through the book, going back a few pages. He holds it open near the light so I can read. "Here. The day after you agreed to send them to Ostriary, you chose to send Lochlan instead of Laurel Pepperleaf, as a measure of goodwill for the people, as well as a means of protection, so he could not launch another revolution in Corrick's absence. You had me draft a letter to Baron Pepperleaf in appreciation for his daughter's offer to attend the journey, but insisting on declining for her protection."

I look at his brief notes to that effect, then back up at his face. "I remember."

He flips back a few pages. "On the day you suspected Corrick of conspiring with the rebels or the Benefactors, you sent the army into the Wilds to collect him." His hand runs down the page, then stops somewhere near the center. "Look. You specifically gave orders not to arrest the people. Corrick only. Tessa if she was with him. You did not want the army's presence in the Wilds to stoke revolution."

I frown. I don't understand why he's showing me this.

Quint keeps flipping. "Here. Jasper Gold wanted a special tax on trade routes through Mosswell, but he'd conspired with Sallister to make sure they both got a cut. When you approved it, you ensured the tax went to the benefit of the sector, not to line either of their pockets." He taps at the page. "I did enjoy the look on his face when he realized what you'd done."

This page is full of tightly packed notes. It must have been from a meeting with the consuls. Quint's handwriting is small and hard to read, full of shorthand. Messy too, because he was writing quickly. It takes me a moment to figure out that he refers to the consuls with their initials. AC for Arella Cherry, RP for Roydan Pelham, and so on. It looks like many of them protested the tax outright. I remember that meeting now, because Corrick had been the one to identify that the tax was somewhat justified, but I wanted to make sure the money was going where it was needed.

I take the book from Quint, because it's hard to read in the flickering lantern light.

He shifts a bit closer, then leans over to tap a finger over two words. "I rarely editorialize, but . . . well."

JG annoyed.

I smile, remembering. "Jasper Gold. He *was* annoyed."

"Yes. He asked me to have a porter call for a carriage the very instant the meeting was over." He pauses. "Prince Corrick never fails to take action in the moment, but you always look out for the entire kingdom. Do not doubt yourself. I don't know that he could calm and rally the people the way you have."

That makes me look up, and I realize that we're very close, almost tucked around the lantern, the book held between us. Quint's eyes are on the pages, and when he goes to turn another, his fingers brush mine.

It's a bare touch, brief and meaningless, but somehow it contains the force of a lightning strike. It's so startling that I nearly draw back. I have to swallow, to force myself still while he turns another page.

I don't know how he has the talent to annoy me to *no end*—and then sit beside me in the dark and offer encouragement so offhandedly.

Quint has worked in the palace for years, so we have a thousand moments between us. Maybe a million. Some have been absolutely interminable, like when he demands that I weigh in on the color selection of table linens, when I absolutely could not care less. But others have been downright intimate, from the time I dressed his wounds, to the time when he dressed *mine*. When Tessa's friend Karri stitched up my thigh after I'd been shot by the night patrol, he let me clutch his hand until I thought I might break his fingers.

My thoughts are scattering dangerously, and my cheeks feel warm. I need to remember myself. It was easy in the palace because I was surrounded by protocol. When I was younger, I could escape the Royal Sector and forget myself for a time, but once I was crowned king, I knew what was expected of me. I had rigid rules to follow, and deviating from them could mean disaster.

Here, I have nothing. I'm wearing patched broadcloth and wool, sitting outside in the middle of the night. It was bad enough when I snatched the book out of Quint's hands, when that spark of challenge hung in the air. I should go back inside before I do anything else.

I don't.

Quint continues turning pages as I watch. I'm not sure what he's looking for, but his notes go on *forever*. Several apply to meetings I was a part of, but most of the time, I have no idea what his scrawled shorthand is even about.

Linens - 24?

Geo - morning

Heath - discuss tea leaves

Pr Corr - interrupt dinner

I stop his turning and tap that one. "What was this?"

He leans close to read, and he has to think for a moment. "Prince Corrick was dining with Hugh Jansson."

Hugh Jansson is old and fond of telling stories that last for *ages* and are more boring than watching snails crawl through grass. He's the kind of man who talks with his mouth full and has a tendency to spit when he enunciates.

He's also one of the wealthiest barons of Emberridge, so everyone puts up with it.

I stare at Quint, fascinated. "Corrick asked you to *interrupt* him?"

He draws back. "Ah . . . yes, Your Majesty. Rather urgent matters requiring the King's Justice." His expression turns sly. "Of course it happened every single time, but surely the baron would understand the sheer demand for the prince's attention. Couldn't be helped, really."

I burst out laughing. "Brilliant. I should have employed you to interrupt *my* dinners."

"Gladly."

Now that I've discovered this, I take over, flipping through more quickly, looking for more. "What other secrets have you kept?"

"You know what secrets I've kept."

He's right, I do, but there's an intriguing note to his voice. I want to look up, but the book has flipped to the front, and it's just a list of dates that have clearly been added to over time. Some are widely spaced, by a span of weeks, while others are divided by only a matter of days. "What's this?"

"A list of dates."

There's a tone in his voice I can't quite parcel out. "I can see that. What does it mean?"

"It's nothing," he says. "Simple recordkeeping for my needs."

It doesn't quite feel like a lie, but I'm too practiced in the double-speak at court to know that it's definitely not the entire truth. I'm not sure why I care. I don't even know why a list of dates might *matter*.

I finally turn my head to look at him. He's very close, and like before, I can't decide if I'm annoyed or intrigued—or something else entirely. "Are we going to argue over semantics again, Quint?"

His eyes hold mine, gleaming in the flickering light. "If it pleases you."

My heart gives a little stutter. I have to look back at the page because I don't know what to do with it. I feel flushed and uncertain and off-balance, and I haven't felt like this since . . . I don't know when.

At my back, the door clicks, and I jump a mile.

Thorin stands over us. "I should take a post by the trees if you're going to remain outside, Your Majesty."

"No. It's late. I should retire." I sound like I've been eating sand, but my heart won't stop pounding. I drop the book beside the lantern and practically scramble up from where I was sitting. "Thank you for the debate, Master Quint."

"Yes, Your Majesty." His voice is so calm, so composed. There's no spark in the air, no blush on his cheeks, which makes me feel foolish. Like my heart got twisted up with my imagination.

Over Quint, of all people.

I need to stay focused. Too much is at risk here. I move to follow Thorin into the house.

But before the door falls closed, I notice Quint flip open the little book, just turning back the cover to that list of dates.

At the bottom, he adds one more.

CHAPTER FIFTEEN

Harristan

I'm wearing a cloak and sitting beside Thorin while we drive a wagon full of hay bales toward Mosswell. Saeth and half the men who volunteered for this mission are sitting on the bales behind us. Tucked between the bales are weapons: the guards' crossbows, half a dozen daggers, some axes, and one long bow that the rebels were able to steal from the night patrol weeks ago.

Weapons I hope we won't have to use.

It's earlier than I'd like, but Francis said that if we wanted to pretend to be a labor wagon returning workers from a day in the fields, we wouldn't be doing that too late. So we're going to strategically drop men along the way to stand as lookout while we first fetch Reed, then Sommer—and then hopefully Saeth's family. I was surprised that the rebels were willing to agree to this small mission—but they seemed surprised that I was willing to go *with* them, so maybe we're even.

But I couldn't have sat in that little house for hours, wondering about the outcome.

I couldn't ask them to risk their lives if I'm not willing to risk my own.

The wagon rattles along as a darkening gray sky spits rain down at us. The roads are crawling with citizens, but few people even glance our way. I'm tense under my cloak anyway. No one will recognize me as the king, but that doesn't mean we won't be stopped or questioned. It's unlikely, but not impossible. Saeth still has bruising along the side of his face and a split in his lip from his fight last night. To the night patrol, it would look suspicious.

I should be worrying about everything we're doing here. Once we approach Sommer and Reed, there's a high possibility their homes are being watched—if they're there at all. But if we succeed here, I'll need a better plan of what to do next. A successful mission *tonight* won't leave anyone content to sit idle. Victory breeds hope, and there's precious little of that. I need to nurture it, not squash it.

But I'm not pondering all that, because I can't stop thinking about that stupid list of dates in Quint's little book.

What could it be? Why wouldn't he tell me?

Instead of going back to sleep last night, I laid in bed and stared at the ceiling and wondered about it for an hour. If it were innocuous palace nonsense, like the dates when a tailor was to arrive or when the stationer requested a fresh supply of paper, there'd be no reason for him to keep from telling me. And *none* of those things would require adding a date to the list after our conversation.

Something to do with the revolt or the rebellion against the palace, then? My heart went cold when I considered that angle. But . . . I couldn't make that work in my head. Quint is part of the revolution now. He was in danger from it before. If he were working *against* me somehow, there'd be absolutely no advantage to staying by my side. He could hand me over to Allisander Sallister and be done with it.

Besides, I can't figure out why a list of dates with no other information would *matter*. What good is it? What could he possibly need it for?

Honestly, that's why I should stop thinking about it.

But I can't.

The night was so quiet, the light from the lantern spinning his red hair into gold.

Are we going to argue over semantics again, Quint?

If it pleases you.

He's infuriating. I'm glad he remained behind.

Alone.

A little spike of fear pokes at my heart. He stood in the doorway, blocking Francis and the other men when they came after me with axes and hammers. I have half a dozen of those men with me now, but there are plenty left to harass Quint if they were so inclined.

To say nothing of the patrolmen who fought with Saeth last night.

They were miles away. Saeth said he crossed the stream a dozen times. They won't be able to find his tracks or follow. Quint is safe. Surely.

He can sit in the house and write notes in his little book.

"Up here," one of the men says, jarring me from my reverie. "Let me down by the bakery."

Thorin nods and draws the horses to a slow walk, and the man leaps down from the wagon.

"Thank you kindly for the passage, gentlemen," the man calls, all part of the act. "I can make it home from here."

The others shout back to him cheerfully, but my tongue is tied up in knots. Beside me, Thorin clucks to the horses, and they trot on.

I glance at my guard. "They're all so calm," I say under my breath.

"They haven't done anything yet." He casts a look at me. "And no one wants them dead."

I suppose that's true.

Another two drop off the wagon by a bowyer's narrow shop: a young man named Nook, who can't be more than sixteen, and his father. Another man jumps down by a butcher's stall that has dogs lounging on the bricks out front. They'll all follow the wagon, but quietly. Secretly.

"You know the route?" I murmur to Thorin once most of the others have all dropped off the wagon. Now it's just me, my guards, and Francis.

Thorin nods. "I know this part of the sector."

I'm glad one of us does.

Rain falls harder, and the people on the street swear and try to duck under cover. I can't decide if that's better or worse. It'll be harder for the men to surreptitiously follow us, that's for sure.

A woman shouts out, "You there!"

I startle hard, but Thorin doesn't even turn his head. The horses don't slow.

"Just a washerwoman," Saeth says at our back, but he draws his hood forward. We're not close to his home yet—I don't think, anyway—but I wonder if he's worried about being recognized.

I don't have the mettle for this. My leg still aches from the arrow I took through the thigh over a week ago.

The washerwoman calls out again. "I said, *you there*. With the wagon!"

Thorin sighs. "Whoa," he says to the horses, drawing them to a stop.

"Are you crazy?" I whisper at him.

"It might look crazier to ignore her," Francis says from behind us.

"Be on your way!" Thorin says to the woman, making his tone bored. "I have to deliver this to the Royal Sector and get back before dark."

"I need some hay for my mules. Can I buy a few bales off you?"

"It's prime alfalfa," calls Saeth, his voice pitched lower. "Too rich for your mules."

I don't want to look down at her, but I need to relax into this role, or I will be the one who ends up ruining our plans. I spent years slipping out of the palace as a young man, and weeks doing it as the Fox. I can do it again.

She's drawn close to our vehicle, and there's less risk of her recognizing *me*, so I pull back my hood and peer at her in the rain. Mud has begun to collect between the cobblestones of the street, and her clothes are already sodden and clinging to her frame.

"These are already bought and paid for," I say, and then I cough hard before I can stop myself.

She moves a step closer, and her voice drops to a whisper that's hard to hear over the rain. "You're sick. I have Moonflower to trade."

That's unexpected, and my eyes snap to hers. Somewhere

behind me, Francis draws a sharp breath. I've hardly had a dose of medicine since leaving the palace, and I know doses run thin in the Wilds, so I haven't dared to ask for more. A part of me wants to toss her a few bales right now, the mission be damned.

It's only been a second, but the woman must sense an easy mark, because she moves even closer. "I have enough for three weeks. A month if you're careful."

A month! That would help a lot of people.

Francis shifts closer to me. I can sense his eagerness, too.

But a note in the woman's voice is tugging at my awareness, and I study her, trying to figure out what it is. When I was a boy in the Wilds, hiding in plain sight with Corrick, it was rare that someone could trick me, but it's been years and now I'm more used to the slick and polished manipulations of the consuls. My instincts are rusty and slow.

"I could meet you at the end of the row of shops," she adds. "There's a wheelbarrow there. No one would be the wiser."

My heart keeps thrumming in my chest, but the woman is peering up at me expectantly, waiting for an answer. She puts a hand against the rail of the wagon, as if she could hold it in place through sheer force of will. Thorin is a statue beside me, waiting for an order.

"It'll only take a minute," Francis whispers. "We don't need the hay."

The woman shrugs. "You need to decide soon, though. If you won't do it, I need to find someone who will."

If I don't do it, someone else will have a month's worth of Moonflower.

My throat tickles, and I think of the way I could barely catch my breath when Francis first confronted me.

Here, King. Sit.

Oh, how I wish Corrick would return.

The sky is darkening overhead, and she's right. I do need to decide soon.

But then the woman glances off to her left, and her eyes seem to lock on something. *Someone.*

When her gaze shifts back to me, in that moment, I *know.* Whatever this is . . . it's not a genuine offer. Maybe she's a lookout for the night patrol, hoping to trick someone into illegal dealings, or maybe she's with a group of common thieves who wanted her to slow the wagon so they could steal what we have.

Either way, I look down at her and say, "No. Again, this alfalfa is due for the Royal Sector." Then I snap at Thorin, "*Go.*"

He must hear the order in my tone, because he clucks to the horses, and the wagon lurches forward roughly enough that people in the road scatter and stare.

Francis grabs hold of my arm from behind. "It only would have taken a minute!" he growls, his tone low. "We don't really need this hay!"

"If Moonflower were worth the price of animal feed, Kandala wouldn't be in this mess."

"But she had enough for a *month*!"

"She was working with someone. It was a trap."

He glares at me in the rain. "You don't know that."

He's right. I don't know for sure. But I glare back at him. "If you want to try your luck with that woman, I'll toss you off the back with some hay bales, and you can give our regards to the night patrol when she turns you in for smuggling. There's a reason she targeted a wagon full of strangers. If she has a month's worth of Moonflower, she could be selling it in small doses, not trading it for alfalfa."

He blanches a little at that, then draws back.

I turn my head and look at Saeth. "She was with someone else. Stay sharp."

He nods, but *I'm* the one who needs to stay sharp. We press on, leaving the village behind. The sky grows darker, the rain pouring down to drench us fully. Francis has moved back in the wagon to sulk along the railing, but he hasn't said anything else about the woman or the Moonflower. I hope he's not going to be a problem.

"Do you still see the others?" I murmur to Saeth. "Are they following?"

"I've spotted some of them," he says.

"Do you think that woman was on to us?"

He shakes his head. "I don't see how she could have been."

And she's far behind us now. The others who've followed should have spotted her, and they would have sent up an alarm.

"We're close to Reed's house?" I say.

Thorin nods. "Another ten minutes."

It feels like an hour.

But eventually, the sky is pitch-black, and Saeth shoves a dagger through the wall of the wagon, making wood crack and splinter without causing any actual damage—though Thorin swears loudly and jerks the horses to a stop. Many of the houses out here are more widely spaced, with barns and small livestock pens, or large planted gardens. Some, however, are smaller and close together, with shared yards.

Saeth makes a show of jumping out of the wagon and examining the "broken" wagon wheel.

"Can it be fixed?" I say loudly.

"I'll need some tools," he says. "I don't have any with me." Saeth looks at Francis, then nods at one specific house. "Go see if anyone can help."

The rebel scowls and climbs down from the wagon.

This was our plan, but I'm suddenly wary. What if Reed is also suspicious? Francis is clearly still resentful after what happened in the town square. What if he says something to put us all at risk?

I cast a glance behind us to see if there's any chance we've been followed, but I can't see anything in the rain and darkness. Shadows shift among the trees, and I don't know if they're *our* men or others. Even Saeth has moved away at some point, and is now invisible somewhere between the wagon and the houses.

Maybe we should have waited.

I think of Francis confronting me with an ax—or scowling in the back of the wagon. *He* wouldn't have waited. If I didn't give these men a mission, they would have come up with one on their own.

The door is open, and a figure stands in the doorway, but with the light behind them, there's no way to see who it is. Light glints on a weapon near the wagon, and my heart pounds, but I realize it's Saeth, ready for trouble. The low murmur of voices carries back to us through the rain, but I can't make out much of what they're saying. Francis must be convincing, however, because eventually the door closes, and the figure follows Francis out into the weather.

When they pass Saeth, he steps out of the shadows, and Reed must sense a threat, because he tries to whirl.

My guard stops him with a hand on his shoulder. "It's Saeth. Keep walking. Head for the wagon."

The shock on Reed's face is visible in the shadows, but he keeps walking.

That shock doubles when he gets to the wagon and Thorin gives him a nod and murmurs, "Nice night, eh, Reed?"

The shock triples when I step down from the wagon to face him.

He inhales sharply, but before he can say *exactly* what I know he's going to say, which could give us all away, I point at the wheel. "Take a look. Can you fix it?"

I've made my voice an order, and he looks at the wheel automatically, but I can see him trying to work out the implications of my presence here. Thorin is close, and Francis is hopefully near the back of the wagon, providing lookout as he promised.

"Down here," I say, pointing. "It looks like a rock has broken the wheel. Crouch down for a better look."

He obeys, and I follow. Almost immediately, he turns to look at me, and I shake my head.

"Keep your eyes on the wheel," I say. "Look like you're examining it."

He nods and swallows. "Yes, Your—"

"No," I say. "No titles."

He nods again. "As you say. But there's no damage."

"I know. I need to talk to you. Thorin guessed my personal guards would be dismissed. We were worried you might be in the Hold. Are you being watched?"

"No, Your— *No*. For the first few days, I think we were. But there must be too many of us. They still come every morning to question whether we've seen you. They ask the neighbors, too."

I glance under the wagon at the other houses. A curtain shifts in the window of one, and a shadow moves in the window of another. We need to be quick here.

"What else?" I ask him.

"They've promised a thousand silvers to the first guard to report your whereabouts."

I let out a breath. That's quite a sum. Far more than I would have guessed. A far larger reward than I ever would have offered, for anyone.

The consuls must be desperate to find me. I wonder if it's proving harder to paint the king as a criminal if they don't have me in a cell. A tiny flicker of hope burns in my heart.

"Is anyone tempted?" says Thorin.

"At first we all scoffed," Reed says. "But—but much has happened. They've frozen our pay and our accounts. They've implied we were assisting the king, so a lot of the merchants won't sell to us. Food has grown scarce. I've been scraping by, but it's been more than a week. A few of the families aren't doing well."

I have to fight to keep my eyes on the wheel instead of looking at Saeth, but I know he heard that.

We'll fetch your family, I think. *I promise.*

"We're being watched from the houses," says Thorin, and there's an urgency in his tone that I cannot ignore. I glance back under the wagon just as another curtain shifts.

I look back at Reed. He's young, and I haven't known him as long as many of my other guards. It's hard to put loyalty up against a thousand silvers if they're being starved out of their homes. Right now he's tense, biting back a shiver as rain threads his hair, his eyes fixed on the wheel.

My chest is tight, because he could refuse to join us, and there'd be absolutely nothing I could do about it—aside from kill him to keep our presence a secret.

"I didn't do the things they've said," I say to him. "I haven't poisoned the people. This is another attempt to take the throne."

He nods. "I know." He glances at me before looking back at the wheel. "But Captain Huxley stripped our weapons on the first day you were gone. Some suspected—"

"Someone is coming out," says Saeth.

"Advise me later," I say to Reed in a rush. "We're planning to retake the Royal Sector, but I need more people from inside the palace. Would you be willing to join us?"

His head snaps around. "Yes. Yes, of course."

"You're turning down a thousand silvers?"

He looks at me like I'm crazy. "I swore not to take bribes against the king. How is this any different?"

The relief that swells in my chest is so potent that I nearly can't contain it. I clap him on the shoulder. "You have my gratitude, Reed."

"We have to go," says Thorin.

"Meet us in two hours," I say to Reed. "There's a small abandoned mill at the crossroads between Steel City and Artis. Can you get there?"

He nods briskly. "Yes."

I keep my voice low. "Good. The wagon will slow, but not stop. Climb onto the back. Bring whatever weapons you have." A man and woman have approached from one of the houses, so I don't wait for an answer to any of this, I just raise my voice. "Thank you! We were worried we wouldn't be able to make it back tonight, and there'd be hell to pay from the foreman."

Reed looks back at me and nods. "I'm . . . glad I could help."

Thorin and Saeth climb onto the wagon, and I follow, and Thorin says to the woman, "You're lucky to have such a kind neighbor."

The man grunts and says, "Not so lucky. He's one of the ones who was working for that crooked king."

"They're going to hang him when they catch him," says the woman. "As well they should, for what he did."

"Poisoning us all," says the man. He spits at Reed's feet.

My hands have already formed fists, but Thorin cracks the whip, and we're off.

CHAPTER SIXTEEN

Harristan

Sommer lives a short distance away, but we can't risk villagers telling two stories of a broken wagon wheel, so this time, Saeth is going to drive the horses while Thorin slips off the wagon and tries to deliver a message. It feels like both a larger risk and a smaller one, all at the same time.

With Thorin off the wagon, Francis shifts forward to sit behind me again.

"That boy is going to tell those people who you were, and there's going to be an army waiting for us at the crossroads," he says.

"That *boy* is a man from my personal guard," I say, "and I trust that his word is good."

He grunts. "For a thousand silvers a man might think about slipping a dagger between your ribs right now."

"And I could slit your throat in half the time," Saeth says sharply. "Move back."

"I didn't say I was going to!"

Saeth hooks the reins around the rail and turns on the bench, and it's a second later that I realize he has a weapon in his hand. Francis swears and scrambles back so quickly that he stumbles and nearly falls over some of the hay bales.

I put a hand on Saeth's arm. "Enough. It *is* a lot of money. You heard Reed. It's going to make anyone waver in their convictions." I look back at Francis. "Though anyone who believes they'd actually receive such a ransom is a fool. The consuls have conspired to steal my throne. They've connived a web of lies thick enough to convince half of Kandala that I'm poisoning them. You think they'll honestly pay a thousand silvers?"

"If they're just going to lie," says Francis, "they should've offered more. I don't think any of your guards would stay loyal for *ten* thousand."

Saeth scoffs. "No one would believe a ransom of that size."

"But that's exactly why," I say. "No one would believe it. A thousand is enough to turn heads yet still be believable."

"Or maybe it's just a ransom set for a king," says Francis. "And they're ready to pay every cent."

Thunder cracks overhead, making me jump. Darkness fully cloaks the road now, assisted by the clouds that obscure the moon. I wish we had a lantern, but surely that would be foolhardy.

I keep thinking about Reed's neighbor, at the vitriol in his tone.

It's impossible to know how far rumors have spread and if the public sentiment is like this everywhere.

I need more guards. I need at least one of the consuls to respond to my letters.

Instead, I'm on a wagon in the dark with a massive bounty on my head. When I was a boy, there were times when I was tempted to slip into the darkness and stay gone, to forget the palace and the

Crown and all my obligations. Even as the Fox, I had a few moments where the idea crossed my mind—right up until the last night when I met Maxon, a young man who flirted with me for a moment, then took my hand and tried to help me escape the night patrol.

They shot him in the chest right in front of me.

My breath quickens at the memory. I only knew him for a few hours, but the final moments were terrible. I don't want to consider that the measures Corrick put in place to protect the people from smugglers have started to have the opposite effect—that the night patrol is taking matters into their own hands. That they're being cruel because we've created the illusion that we approve of cruelty.

I need to think of something else.

For some reason, my brain summons Quint and the way he recast my doubts about everything. The way he flipped pages in that little book, reminding me of our days in the palace, how I forced the consuls to put the people first.

The way he made that puzzling list of dates that he refuses to explain.

I scowl and peer into the darkness. This line of thinking isn't much better. Surely Thorin is taking too long.

Just as I have the thought, my guard leaps onto the wagon, and I jump a mile. Thorin settles onto a bale behind us. "Forgive me," he says, his voice low. "Sommer will find us by the mill."

I try to calm my pounding heart, and I have to breathe shallowly to keep from erupting into coughs again. "Does he—does he—" My throat threatens to close up, and I wheeze a breath. I clench my fists, even though I know anger and tension never make this better. "Does he—seem earnest?"

Thorin frowns. "Honestly, he seems like he's starving. I wish I'd brought food. He was begging for it. I wanted to bring him with me right now. If I weren't worried we were being watched, I would have."

My chest clenches. I hate what the consuls are doing to my people. I don't even know Sommer very well. Will he join us out of desperation? Right now, there are just so many variables. I consider the rebels peeling off the wagon, determined to follow us in case there was trouble—but that was before I knew about the ransom. Now I'm worried that they're all waiting for a chance to take us down. We only brought six of them. Could Thorin and Saeth hold off six men? Would they want to?

I need to stop thinking like this. My *own* convictions are wavering.

Besides, we have one more house to visit: Saeth's family. Our plan is to pick them up under the guise of traveling to see a sick grandparent who's near death. It's the most dangerous one, because Saeth's family is the most likely to be watched—though the rebels have followed, ready to send up the alarm so we can flee if necessary. We're lucky enough to have the full cloak of night now, and the rain is helping. If we're successful, we can loop back through the woods to the crossroads to pick up Reed and Sommer.

At my side, Saeth's own tension is almost palpable. I've been feeling it for the entire drive. It might have been eagerness when we set off, but it's different now, a worry punctuated by what we learned from Reed.

I'm surprised he's not driving the horses into a gallop.

Maybe Thorin can sense it too, because he shifts closer. "You should let me go."

Thunder rolls overhead again, followed by a flash of lightning. Saeth's jaw is set. "No."

"We don't know if she's being watched. If she reacts in *any* way—"

"She won't."

"Your children will. They—"

"I said *no*."

But Saeth doesn't look at me. He keeps driving the horses.

He expects me to agree with Thorin. I can tell.

"I don't know your wife," I say quietly. "Will she react? Will the children give us away?"

Saeth thinks about this for a long moment. When he speaks, his voice is low and rough. "I didn't know they'd frozen the accounts. And now it's been more than a week without word." He hesitates. "I heard that man at Reed's. I don't even know what she might believe."

I can hear every worry he's not voicing. They echo in my thoughts along with my own. I feel like I keep asking people to make impossible choices.

I turn my head. "Thorin. Move to the back. Make a plan with Francis for when we reach the mill."

Once he does, I look at Saeth and keep my voice very low. "Do you have a way to slip into the house unseen?"

He frowns, but nods. "Yes, but—"

"Could you get them to the mill by the time we're meeting Reed and Sommer?"

"That isn't part of our—"

"Answer the question."

He inhales deeply, running a hand over the back of his neck, considering. "On foot from here, it would be tight."

And even more difficult with children in the rain, but he doesn't say that. He doesn't need to.

"If you can't make it by then, we'll do our best to make a second pass," I say. "Half an hour later."

"Your Majesty—"

"Listen to me. When we draw close, hand me the reins. I won't slow the wagon. Slip off in the shadows. Sneak into your house. *See your family.* Let your wife react, then bring them to the mill."

He stares at me for so long that I want to warn him to look back at the road.

Eventually, he says, "I can't leave you with no one but Thorin."

"You forget. I have Francis, too."

Saeth gives me a look, and I smile.

But he doesn't say anything else. He's practically vibrating with the battle between duty and obligation.

So I end the war. "I'm ordering you," I say.

He nods, then looks off into the darkness, his jaw set again. Ahead, at the crest of the hill, another cluster of homes sits between two tiny farms. Candlelight flickers in the windows of each one. Saeth swallows, and I know.

"Up there?" I say to him anyway.

"Yes."

"You should slip off soon, before we're too close."

He hesitates, then moves to hand me the reins. An order is an order.

"Adam." I put a hand on his arm before he can go.

He looks up in surprise. I never touch my guards. I never touch anyone.

"Thank you for what you've done," I say. "Please make sure your wife knows I'm grateful for your family's sacrifice."

He frowns a little. "It's not a sacrifice."

"It is." I pause. "I'm saying this now, because I want you to know that if you reunite with your family and choose not to come to the mill, I would understand."

"I will be at the mill. I swear it."

I shrug, then give a little laugh, though there's no humor to it. "If I've learned anything from being king, Saeth, it's that there are choices we *want* to make and choices others *force* us to make. Truly. If your family forces you to choose another path, I won't hold it against you."

He stares at me again, and it's too dark to make out the expression in his eyes.

"Go!" I say. "Before we're into the light."

"You have my gratitude as well," he says. "But with all due respect, Your Majesty, if I've learned anything from being a *father*, our choices are still our own."

Then he presses the reins into my hand, says farewell to a startled Thorin, and leaps into the darkness.

—◆—

I keep hoping the rain will let up, but instead, it pours down, soaking us through by the time we reach the crossroads. I'm shivering under my cloak, and it's making me cough. Two of the men who've been following on foot have rejoined us in the wagon, claiming there's been no sign of anyone on our tail. It should be a relief, but everyone feels so new, so untested. There are others who are still on foot, but we've had no sign of them yet. All part of our plan, but now I worry that they've been overtaken, that we'll be attacked when we least expect it. I sent Saeth away, and now I have one guard at my side. Thorin didn't say a word about it, but I can sense his disapproval. A dark part of my thoughts wonders if he wishes he could leave, too, and I have to shove those worries down.

For a while, the men in the back were chattering with Francis while I sat up front with my last remaining guard, but now that we're nearing the most questionable part of our mission, everyone is silent.

Thorin looks over his shoulder at the men. "Can any of you drive the wagon?"

I look at him sharply. "Thorin."

He looks right back at me. "We don't know who or what might be waiting at the crossroads."

He's not challenging me. Not directly. But he's right: there are too many variables with what we've learned about Reed and Sommer and the rest of the guards, and I hear the unspoken question all the same.

Do you want my protection or do you want me to control the horses?

One of the men has shifted forward anyway. The rain is pouring down, and he has to shove a sodden cloak hood back from his face. His name is Bert, and he says, "I sometimes drive mules for supply runs from the shipyards."

Thorin nods. "Close enough." He moves over to create more room. "We're going to draw to a walk at the crossroads, and I want you to keep the wagon straight and true. Don't stop, even if something happens. Straight and true, all the way back to the Wilds. Yes?"

Bert stares back at him. "But what if—"

"*Don't stop*," Thorin says. "No matter what. It's an open wagon. If we're attacked and you stop, the king is dead."

Bert's mouth is hanging open. But he nods.

I think *my* mouth is in danger of hanging open. I clench it shut.

Thorin looks at me. "Let's move to the back. You should sit between the bales, with your back against the planks."

Another one of the rebels has moved closer to hear what we're talking about. It's Nook, the young man whose father is still following somewhere in the rain. He looks from me to Thorin as we climb over the rail.

"That's so the king doesn't take an arrow in the back, right?" says Nook.

Thorin glances up in surprise, then offers a brief nod. "Exactly right."

Nook glances around. "Should we move more bales? What's going to stop an arrow from the front?"

Thorin pulls a crossbow from where he stashed one against the floorboards. "Me." But he looks at Nook again. "Moving bales is a good idea, though."

They start tugging. I help, and I try not to think about the fact that my sole remaining guard and this boy are putting themselves in harm's way to protect me. I hope the choices I've made so far are worth it.

I keep thinking about Quint saying how Corrick has an edge that I lack.

I try to imagine my brother hiding behind hay bales, and I fail. I tug at the hay, then have to put an arm against my mouth to muffle my sudden coughing.

Thorin eyes me, then looks out at the darkness. The rain against the trees is deafening.

I'm not completely useless, though. "Do you have another crossbow?" I say to Thorin when I can breathe again. "I can shoot."

For half a second, he doesn't answer, and I'm sure he's going to tell me there aren't any weapons left. I harden my gaze, ready to demand one. I might not be able to breathe through a sword fight or run very far, but I *do* know how to hit a target.

But Thorin nods and digs a few more out from under another hay bale. "Stay low," he says to me.

I nod.

A shadow bursts out of the trees, and Thorin snaps up his own weapon. He draws a dagger with his other hand. A cloaked figure leaps over the side of the wagon, but before we can see anything, Francis tackles it. He and the shadowy figure go sprawling into the hay-covered floor of the wagon, rolling, fighting for purchase in the rain. Someone lands a punch, and then Francis cries out. There's a *thump* against the wood as the stranger slams him to the floor. Nook inhales sharply, and I realize he's got a blade from somewhere, too.

"What?" cries out Bert from the driver's bench. "What's happening?"

"Keep driving!" Thorin grabs hold of the stranger's cloak and puts the crossbow into his back. I don't think he's going to shoot, but Nook looks like he's about to leap forward with that dagger.

"Hold!" I snap. I keep my own crossbow pointed. My heartbeat is a roar in my ears, matched by the pounding rain. "Who is it?"

The stranger lifts his hands in surrender. "It's Reed!" he says, his voice strangled from the grip Thorin has on his collar. "I was advised to climb into the wagon."

Thorin lowers his weapon, and Reed turns around. He jerks his cloak straight, but he meets my eyes and chases the agitation off his face. "Forgive me." He gives a peeved glance over his shoulder at Francis. "I didn't expect to be attacked."

"We haven't reached the crossroads yet," Francis says.

"The roads are flooded from the storm," says Reed. "I had to walk out a bit. There are trees down across the path, too."

My heart is still pounding, refusing to settle. "Can the wagon get through?"

"It was too dark to tell on foot. I didn't want to risk a lantern."

"What about Sommer?" says Thorin. "Or Saeth?"

Reed glances around as if realizing Saeth is no longer with us. "I haven't seen anyone else. How many others are joining us?"

"You and Sommer," says Thorin. "Saeth went to fetch his family. You haven't seen anyone?"

Reed shakes his head.

Thunder rolls overhead, and the rain continues to pour down, rattling against the wood of the wagon, punctuating the silence between us. The horses begin to splash on the path, and I wonder how deep the flooding is.

I told Saeth we'd give him extra time, but now I'm worried about getting trapped by this storm.

The wagon rolls on. My breath keeps rattling into my chest. Maybe the weather is delaying them all.

Somewhere in the distance, a shout breaks through the sound of the storm. My eyes lock on Thorin's to see if he heard it.

He did. "Stay low," he says to me. He looks at Reed. "We had four men in the woods, trailing the wagon, watching for trouble. You didn't see them?"

"No."

Thorin's eyes skip over the other guard's form. "Were you watched? You didn't bring weapons."

"I tried to tell you. Much has happened. Huxley searched our homes and confiscated our weapons. No one knows who to believe."

Thorin swears and hand Reed the last remaining crossbow.

Thunder cracks again, and we all jump—including the horses. They shy left, causing the wagon to shift and rattle. Up front, Bert shouts, "Whoa!" and the wagon tips dangerously before righting itself. Wood cracks, hooves splash, and I realize we've driven right into the flood. Another cry sounds in the distance, closer this time.

Followed by the clear snap of a crossbow.

Nook cries out, then slaps a hand over his shoulder. "It hit me. It hit—"

Reed shoves him back into the bales, pressing a hand over his mouth. "Don't give them a loud target, kid. Stay down. Are you all right?"

Nook huffs a breath, then nods fiercely.

"Could it be the night patrol?" hisses Francis.

"The night patrol would announce themselves," I say.

"It could be thieves," says Nook, but even he doesn't sound like he believes it.

It's not thieves. That means someone betrayed us. One of the rebels who was following? Sommer?

Or even someone from the Wilds who knew we were going? A thousand silvers is so much money.

I think of the desperation in Francis's eyes when he thought that woman had Moonflower.

Then a worse thought occurs to me. *Saeth.*

I have no idea what he would have found when he approached his wife and children. Our final words to each other were about choices. Could his family have been in such dire straits that he would've taken the reward to save them? I thought the worst outcome would be Saeth not returning.

But he knew where to find us. He knew exactly what time we would be here and how much—how *little*—defense we have.

"You said we had men in the woods." Reed looks between me and Thorin. "Other guards?" he says hopefully. "Or soldiers?"

I shake my head. "Neither. Rebels from the Wilds."

Reed turns dismayed eyes back toward Thorin, who shrugs. "It's been a long week," he says.

Another crossbow snaps, and we all press low. I don't know where it lands.

Bert, driving the wagon, makes a choked sound, then jerks sideways, ducking down onto the floorboards under the seat. I can hear his breathing from here. "I can't see them," he calls back to us. His voice is shaking.

"That means they can barely see us," says Thorin. "Keep driving."

"I'm trying!" the man calls back. "The water is deep! There must be mud!"

And there must be. The wagon keeps shuddering, and I can hear the horses struggling against the footing.

"Is there *any* chance you were followed?" I say to Reed.

He shakes his head fiercely. "I saw no one."

"There can't be many of them," says Francis from the back. "They would've attacked the wagon by now."

Nook is looking between all of us, his eyes wide, his hand still pressed over his shoulder. "Is that true?"

"Maybe," I say, though it's more likely they're testing us, waiting to see what kind of resistance we have—which isn't much. Our weapons are limited, and we don't have more than twelve bolts for the crossbows. But there's no point in scaring him.

Francis crawls low, through the hay, to get closer to us. He takes a look at Nook's bleeding arm, then offers me a censorious glare. "Did we go through all this to trade one guard for another?"

Reed moves like he's going to shove him back. "You are speaking to the—"

Then wood cracks underneath us, and the wagon shudders to a stop. At the front, Bert snaps the whip, and the horses surge forward, but we don't move. More wood cracks.

An arrow hits the wagon, then another. An unfamiliar voice yells from the woods. "They're stuck!"

"Get us moving!" Thorin shouts at Bert.

"The wheels have caught!"

My guards exchange a glance. I've seen that look before, so I'm already a step ahead of them, uncurling from the hay, tightening my grip on the crossbow.

If we're attacked and you stop, the king is dead.

We need to get out of the wagon. My breathing has already gone tight and thready. "Which way?"

"They're shooting from the north," says Thorin. He points. "Head south. Reed, take point."

"You're *running*?" says Francis.

"You are too." I grab hold of Nook's sleeve and tug. "Come on. We need to take cover."

The water is deeper than I imagined, swelling almost to my knees when we leap out of the wagon, mud grabbing my boots underneath and making it nearly impossible to walk. It's no wonder the horses couldn't pull the wagon. Reed is in front of me, Francis to my left, Nook to my right. That dagger is still clutched in his hand, and I wonder if he has any idea how to use it. Thorin is at my back, and I hear Bert splash through the water a moment later.

But then he cries out, and I begin to turn.

Thorin puts a hand against my shoulder, propelling me forward, and we finally move slightly uphill, out of the water and into the cloaking darkness of the trees. The mud is still deep, and I'm gasping from the effort of getting this far. I still have an arrow wound on my leg from the last time I was chased through the Wilds, and it's barely healed.

I cough hard. I'm not going to be able to run. I'm not.

Then we break past a copse of trees and find ourselves facing a line of four heavily armed men, and I realize it's not going to matter if I can run at all.

CHAPTER SEVENTEEN

Harristan

The men are in heavy hooded cloaks, and combined with the dark and the rain, I don't recognize them.

Their crossbows are plain as day, though.

There are only four of them, but they're all well armed, and we aren't. At my side, Nook is still clutching that dagger, but he's holding it up in front of him, as if it's going to stop the bolt of a crossbow. Bert must have grabbed an ax from the floor of the wagon, because he has one clutched in both hands. Reed has me half blocked, and I can sense more than feel Thorin still behind me.

One of the cloaked men gestures with his crossbow. "Lay down your weapons. We'll take the king, and the rest of you can go unharmed."

I recognize his voice, but I don't place it until Thorin says, "Lennard, I wouldn't expect you to turn on the king for silver."

"I've seen the proof of what the king was doing. So have you, Reed."

Proof. I need to know what "proof" they have—because I've never poisoned anyone. I have no idea what the consuls are telling the people that could have swayed opinion this quickly.

I'll probably find out from a cell in the Hold.

Hopefully not while I'm hanging from a rope in the middle of the Royal Sector.

"Any proof they have is *false*," I say. "You were sworn to *me*. This is an act of treason. You will lay down *your* weapons."

One of the other men draws back his hood, and I recognize Wadestrom, another one of my guards. His crossbow is steady, but he doesn't meet my eyes. Instead, he looks at the rebels standing beside us. "You three have nothing to do with this. Lay down the weapons and get out of here."

Beside me, Nook is shaking, but he doesn't move. Neither does Francis.

Bert is the one who looks like he's wavering. His breathing is shuddering.

"If you lay down that ax, he'll shoot you in the back," says Thorin. He's glaring at Wadestrom, and he sounds disgusted.

The third cloaked man says, "Our word is good. We only came for the king."

I recognize *his* voice, I think. Jarrett. Another guardsman.

Bert whimpers.

"Don't do it," says Reed.

"My wife is waiting for me," Bert whispers.

"Don't put down that ax!" Thorin snaps.

"They likely killed our reinforcements," I say.

"We let them go," says Wadestrom. "Because they had the sense to lay down their weapons."

Bert throws his ax to the ground, then turns to run.

Wadestrom shoots him. Bert makes a small sound, and his body crumples in the rain. It sets off a chain reaction of activity, because Nook cries out and tries to run next, but Wadestrom shifts to shoot him, too. Thorin tackles him around the waist, and the shot fires wildly, just as Francis gives a shout of pain from somewhere to my right. Another cloaked guard aims for me, but Reed shoots first, shoving me out of the way before I can even lift my crossbow. I slam into the mud and go skidding into the midst of the melee. My weapon bounces into the darkness as men shout and other bodies drop, and I lose track of what guards and attackers still have a bolt left.

But then I realize Nook has slipped, scrambling in the mud, and Lennard has his crossbow aimed at the boy.

"*Hold*," I say sharply—then I aim a kick right for Lennard's ankle.

The guard hesitates, then stumbles when my foot cracks into his leg. It earns Nook a fraction of a second—enough time to get his feet underneath him. He splashes into the flooded part of the path, hopefully cloaked by darkness.

But Nook isn't the real quarry here, and I'm in the mud with no weapons. Lennard lets him go, turning to level that crossbow at my throat.

Behind him, Reed and Francis are lying motionless in the mud. So is Jarrett, who has landed crookedly, his cloak falling across half his face. A short distance away, Wadestrom and Thorin are wrestling for control of a crossbow.

The fourth cloaked man is still standing at a bit of a distance. I can't see his face at all. It's too dark, the rain too heavy. Like all my guards, he's tall and carries himself like a soldier, so there's no clue to be found there.

He's the only one who hasn't said a word, and he raises his crossbow to aim at me, too.

I sit up, glaring at them both. I should be afraid, but I am simply filled with so much fury, so much *resentment.* "I will not surrender to you."

Lennard looks at the nameless guard, then over to where Thorin is still struggling with Wadestrom. "Kill Thorin. And Reed, if he's not already dead."

I'm so shocked by this that I almost can't comprehend the words. "No," I say. "*No.*"

To my surprise, the cloaked guard is shaking his head, too. "No. I said we could take the king. That's all."

And then I recognize his voice. The cloak slips back a little, and I see the edge of his jaw, a bit of his blond hair. This is Sommer.

He *is* young, probably the same age as Corrick, probably one of the youngest of my personal guard.

Honestly, he seems like he's starving.

I should have paid closer attention when Reed said that the consuls had stopped their pay and frozen their accounts. I should have considered how that would affect my guards.

"They were *with* him," says Lennard. "They're not going to let us take him."

Sommer swallows so hard I can see it. He looks from Reed's motionless body to Thorin to me, but he doesn't move.

I consider that he didn't move before.

He didn't shoot—and he could have.

"This is treason," I say. "You *know* this is treason, Sommer. They'll turn on you, too."

"Kill them!" Lennard snaps. "You want a part of the reward, you'd better earn it."

Thorin is struggling underneath Wadestrom, but he must hear what's going on, because he calls, "Don't listen to him, Sommer. We came to you because you were *loyal—*"

"Shut up!" Wadestrom snaps, and he tries to punch Thorin. They scuffle in the mud.

"Lennard will kill *you* as well, Wadestrom," I say. I keep my eyes on Lennard, because it's clear now who orchestrated this, even if I don't know all the maneuvers yet. "Though I rather doubt any of you are getting silver out of Sallister or whoever is promising it. They'll say we were working together and throw you right in the Hold with me."

"Fine," says Lennard. "I just need to bring back your body." He looks down the line of the crossbow.

I suck in a breath. Time stops. I hear the snap, then the whistle.

I wait for the impact, the pain, but none comes. Instead, Lennard cries out and falls to the ground. A crossbow bolt is buried in his stomach.

Another snap and whistle, and a second bolt appears in the side of Wadestrom's rib cage. The man collapses, sliding off Thorin.

My head whips around, and when I turn, there's Saeth. He has a crossbow in one hand and a dagger in the other. A little girl is strapped to his back, soaking wet and shivering, her hands pressed tight to her eyes. Nook is behind them both, half soaked in mud.

"Can I look yet, Da?" the little girl says, her voice bright and innocent.

"Not yet." Saeth snaps another bolt into his crossbow, and then his aim shifts to the last remaining guardsman. "Put it down. Now."

But Sommer doesn't lower the weapon. He's breathing fast, and he looks from Lennard to Wadestrom and back to me. His face is so pale beneath the hood, his expression a bit stricken.

I put my hands in the mud and push myself to my feet. My heart is pounding, making it hard to breathe. I thought the revolution was the worst part. The consuls working against me. But I was wrong.

It's this.

"For nothing but silver?" I say, and my voice is rough. "Really?"

"No—no, Your Majesty. It wasn't—" His voice breaks, just a little.

"Don't be such a baby," Lennard growls from the ground. He's curled around the bolt, and his voice is strained. "Just shoot him. He left us like this. He's going to *kill* you—"

Thorin has made it to my side, and he kicks him in the shoulder. Lennard cries out, then coughs blood onto the ground.

The girl gives a little yip.

"Not yet, Ruby," Saeth says, his voice as calm as if we're not surrounded by bleeding bodies and traitorous guards. "Just put your head down."

The first time I spoke with Tessa, she kept challenging me about the state of my people. She kept insisting that I couldn't judge people for doing what they had to do to survive. I stare at the men surrounding me, all of whom swore an oath to me once, and I still don't know if that's true.

He left us like this.

Do they feel like I abandoned them? Like I was poisoning my subjects, then abandoned the most loyal ones to starve?

This isn't at all what I expected to find. I want to reverse time and begin this night again.

No, if I had that power, I'd reverse time and begin my entire *reign* again.

Sommer has gone a shade paler, maybe at the sight of the blood, at the realization that he's the only one still standing.

"Forgive me." He throws down his crossbow and runs.

Saeth raises his arm to shoot, and I grab hold of his sleeve. "*No*," I cry, aghast.

He looks at me. "Your Majesty. He'll find others."

My stomach rolls. I feel like I'm going to be sick. Over his shoulder, the little girl is peeking through her fingers at me.

I wish I had my brother.

Corrick has an edge that you lack.

I want to press my hands into my own eyes.

Thorin sees my hesitation. "I'll bring him down," he says, and without waiting for an answer, he sprints into the darkness.

I inhale to issue an order to *hold*—but I can't. They're right. My stomach gives a violent clench, and for a terrifying moment, I'm worried I'm going to be sick right there in the muddy clearing. But Saeth has already turned to Nook, who's staring at everything with wide eyes, and he's giving the boy clear orders.

"See if Francis is breathing," he's saying. "Get him on his back. I'll check Reed." He looks toward the trees and whistles, then raises his voice. "Leah!" he calls. "You can come out."

A moment later, a woman in sodden skirts comes through the trees. Her blond hair is in a long braid, and she has a baby strapped to her chest. She's got a crossbow in her hands, too, and her eyes are fierce. Her gaze skips across the bodies on the ground before landing on me. She swallows, then looks at the trees.

"Adam," she says. "Are you sure there aren't more?"

"No," says Saeth, which isn't encouraging. He drops to a knee beside Reed for a moment.

"Is he all right, Da?" says little Ruby.

"Just sleeping. Put your head down." He only kneels there for a moment before he stands, and I meet his eyes.

He shakes his head, then says, "Two to the chest."

This was supposed to be easy. Simple. I want to be sick again.

"Francis is breathing," says Nook. "I think a rib is broken, though."

"They're going to find you," Lennard says to me. He winces, bracing a hand against the arrow in his gut. "They're going to find you, and they're going to make you regret what you've done to your people."

"I haven't done anything to my people," I say.

"The instant they found proof, you ran! You *hid*."

His words hit me like a fist. It's not just the words, though; it's the betrayal in his tone. Is this what everyone thinks? Is that how the consuls have spun this?

The last night I was in the palace was the same night Arella Cherry and Captain Huxley tried to speak to the people about how I was poisoning them. The night patrol chased me through the woods, and I ended up in Violet's barn, where Quint found me with Thorin and Saeth. We've been hiding ever since.

Maybe the consuls didn't have to spin anything. It's *exactly* how this looks.

"Your Majesty," Saeth says quietly. "We shouldn't remain here."

I hear what he's saying. He's urging me to make a decision.

I don't want to make it.

At my side, Saeth is still pointing that crossbow. His voice is grim. "On your order."

My breathing is tight and shallow. I've never done this part. This has always been Corrick's role. I don't want to be a part of it. It doesn't feel brave. It doesn't feel cowardly either. It feels horrific. My stomach clenches again.

Lennard's eyes shift to Saeth. "We were *friends*. We were friends, and now you're going to shoot me."

"You're a traitor."

"In front of your daughter? Do you know what they did to her?" His voice darkens. "Do you know what they did to your *wife*?"

"Da?" Ruby squeals, her tiny voice breathless.

"Head *down*," Saeth snaps.

"Adam!" Leah cries from across the small clearing.

Everyone thought my father was such a great king, but he was never forced to make choices like this one.

Maybe that's my own fault.

Our choices are our own.

The little girl is crying against Saeth's shoulder now, and her hands are wrapped around his neck, but he hasn't moved. His jaw is tight, but he's still waiting for my order.

I don't deserve this kind of loyalty.

I put out a hand. "Give me the crossbow."

Saeth jerks his head around in surprise, but he obeys. The wood and steel of the weapon slip into my hand.

"Go," I say. "Stand with your wife."

I don't wait to see if he moves. If I wait, I won't be able to do this at all.

"I didn't leave you," I say to Lennard. "I was coming to get you. I'm sorry I wasn't sooner."

He spits at my boots and swears at me. "I hope they hang you."

I pull the trigger. The snap is loud and seems to echo. The bolt goes right through his chest, and his body jerks.

It seems like he glares at me forever before the life burns out of his eyes.

I don't realize I'm on my knees beside him until the cold mud is soaking through my trousers. He didn't deserve this. None of them did.

"Forgive me," I say, and the words are thin and barely audible. My voice breaks, and I realize I'm crying. Not just for my guards, but for Bert, for Reed, for all of them. Everyone I've failed. My muddy fingers press into my eyes. "Please. Forgive me."

The rain strikes my hands like icy needles, shrouding me in silence.

"Your Majesty." Saeth's voice, just behind me. "Thorin is back. I've sent Nook to assess the wagon."

I have no idea how long I knelt there, but I jerk my hands down, grateful for the rain for the first time. Lennard's body is sprawled on the ground in front of me, his eyes wide and dead. I've seen every horrific thing Corrick has ordered, but this is the first time I've done something *myself*. My stomach rolls again, and I catch myself before I can gag too badly, then force my legs to stand.

Francis is on his feet, too, staring at me. He's got a hand clutching his side. I can't read his expression, and I don't want to. I can't decide which is the most humiliating: knowing he watched me kill someone, watched me cry over it, or watched me nearly vomit on the body.

I want to ask if he still feels like his people are ready for action.

This was only a handful of guards, and he wanted to take on the entire Royal Sector.

Between last night's coughing fit and tonight's failed mission, I rather doubt any of them will follow me anywhere at all.

A flicker of motion to my left makes me look over, and I realize Thorin hasn't just returned, he's also forcing a bound Sommer to walk in front of him. My heart nearly stops.

I'll bring him down.

I didn't expect him to bring the guard back alive.

But of course he did. I didn't give an order to kill him yet.

I take a breath and see stars. I can't do this twice. I can't.

As soon as I have the thought, I realize that my brother did it more than twice. He did it over and over again, for *years*.

I remember Tessa's rage on the night I found them both in the Wilds, when I had no idea what my brother had been doing as Weston Lark.

He's trying so hard to protect you, but you have to know it's destroying him.

I didn't know it was like this. I watched it time and time again, but I didn't know.

I should have known.

When they draw close, Sommer takes one look at Lennard, then at me, and his face goes white. His feet stop so suddenly that he almost skids, and he drops to his knees. "Please," he begs. "*Please.*" His voice breaks. "Your Majesty. Please."

Corrick must have listened to pleas like this for years.

I stoop and pick up the crossbow from the mud, then snap another bolt into place. The click of wood against steel is loud in the rain.

Sommer chokes on a sob. "Please. I didn't want to. I just needed the silver. I was out of food, and no one—no one—" His voice breaks again.

My chest is so tight that it's hard to breathe. My guards didn't deserve this. I hate that Allisander and the other treasonous consuls have put them in this position.

I stop in front of him. "Who else did you tell?"

He shakes his head fiercely. "No one. No one, Your Majesty."

Even if he's telling the truth, the others might have spread the word before coming here. Saeth is right; we can't remain. It's probably already been too long.

The crossbow is slick in my palm. I can barely think over the pounding of my heart. We came to fetch more guards, and now we're going home with fewer people than we started with.

I force my racing thoughts to organize. I wish we hadn't come. I wish I had Quint and his little book because he'd surely have an idea for a way to talk me out of this.

But maybe that's exactly the solution I need. We wanted information from inside the Royal Sector. Maybe I can get it another way.

Is this cowardly? I don't know. I don't care. I can't do this again. I can't.

When Corrick orders an execution, sometimes I don't think I can watch, and I have to think of my parents, the betrayal they faced. It helps me chase the emotion out of my chest. It helps now.

Regardless of Sommer's situation, he still made the choices that led him here. People are still dead because he betrayed me, too.

I lift the crossbow until the point touches his neck, and he cowers back into Thorin's legs, slipping a little in the mud.

I don't yield. "If I leave you alive, you will answer every question

I have about everything that has happened since the instant I disappeared from the palace."

"Yes," he gasps. "Yes, Your Majesty."

"If you try to escape, if you spend one moment fighting my people, if I suspect *one single lie*, you'll wish I made your death quick and painless right here. Is that clear?"

He nods, then winces as the point of the arrow presses against his throat. "Yes," he whispers. "Yes, I swear it."

I look at Francis. "If we bring him back, do you have men we can trust to keep him under guard? A place we can keep him secure?"

The man's eyes go wide. "I think so?"

"I need to be sure, Francis. If he escapes, he'll bring down the whole army on top of us."

He nods. "Yes. I'm sure." He swallows hard. "I'll guard him myself if I have to."

"Good."

Nook is climbing up the hill, a little breathless. "I led the horses out of the water. The wagon lost a panel from the side, but the axles are solid."

I lower the crossbow from Sommer's neck, then look at Thorin. "Gag him. Bind his feet once you're in the wagon. We'll need to keep him low in case we run across the night patrol." Then I look to Saeth, standing with his young family. His wife still hasn't met my eyes, and I honestly can't blame her. "Recover whatever weapons we can salvage," I say, "as quickly as you can."

Little Ruby still has her face pressed into her father's shoulder. "Is it time to open my eyes yet?" she calls, her voice like music in the rain.

There are still bodies scattered on the ground. We haven't won a battle. The looming war feels impossible.

Never, I think. But that sounds bleak and fatalistic, which are horrible qualities in a king. I've already failed in enough ways tonight. I turn away to head for the wagon myself. "Hopefully soon, Ruby," I say, filling my voice with a conviction that I hardly feel. "Hopefully soon."

—+—

After a while, the rain eventually lets up, clouds beginning to clear from the sky. The moon beams down on us, which isn't a blessing, because it makes everything more visible. I keep waiting for another arrow to strike the wagon. Every muscle in my body is tense, and I'm simultaneously desperate to be back in the Wilds yet also dreading it. We thought we'd be bringing back a minor victory, and all we're carrying are stories of death and failure. I think of the way Quint used to spin news from the palace, but there's no way to spin any of this.

We've learned that there was a fifth guard in the woods, the one who was first shooting at us. Saeth and his wife stumbled upon him almost by accident. Then they found Nook as he was running down the hill.

It might be the only reason any of us survived.

This was all too close.

The wagon rattles loudly in the night air. Everyone is silent, even the children, as if they can feel the weight of it all. Thorin drives, and I'm right behind him, against the wall again, bracketed by hay bales. It all seems silly now. Saeth tried to sit in front of me once he unstrapped his daughter from his back, but I waved him

off and told him to sit with his family. Now Leah is tucked against his side, nursing the baby to keep him from crying. She has one hand clutching that crossbow, and she still hasn't met my eyes. I keep thinking about what Lennard said before he died. *Do you know what they did to your wife?*

The gravity of those words weigh down on them both. On all of us. There will be a time for Saeth to know, and likely a time for me to know—but it's not right now.

Little Ruby leans against her father's legs, fiddling with the laces of his boots while we rattle along. She's glanced my way several times, and I try not to think about the fact that she very likely watched everything we did, including the way I collapsed in the mud, my hands pressed into my eyes while I cried. I have to look away.

Sommer sits bound and gagged in the corner of the wagon. We put a cloak over his shoulders, the hood up, so his features are in shadow. If anyone sees us, no one will notice unless they get close. He seemed genuinely terrified in the clearing, but Lennard looked determined. So was Wadestrom. I need to know who's been talking to the guards, what's been said, what's been threatened.

But right now, there's just . . . too much.

Francis is keeping his word, and he's watching Sommer like a hawk. Nook is on my other side, his arms wrapped around his belly like he's trying not to shiver. Or maybe like he's trying not to cry. I think his father was among the men who didn't make it back onto the wagon, and I'm afraid to ask. I wouldn't know what to say. Everything I *could* say would sound too hollow. I know from experience.

Maybe all the silence is too much to bear, because the little girl

eventually abandons her father's boot laces and begins to edge through the straw toward me. Saeth immediately notices and says, "Ruby. Stay with me."

She frowns, but I say, "It's all right."

Emboldened by this, she shifts forward until she's sitting on her heels in front of me. Until these last few weeks in the Wilds, I haven't had much exposure to children since I was one myself. Aside from the fact that she's not a baby and she's not a teenager, I'm a bit startled to realize that I truly have no idea how old she might be. Three? Five?

However old she is, her blue eyes are surprisingly cool and assessing as she regards me. I suddenly feel like I'm being confronted by one of the consuls. "You made Mama cross," she says.

Leah gasps. "*Ruby.*"

Saeth swears under his breath. He's already rolling onto his knees to snatch her back. "Ah—Your Majesty—"

"Your daughter may speak her mind." I glance from the little girl to the woman who's finally looking at me with guarded eyes. I don't know what they've been through before tonight, but I know they didn't deserve any of it.

My eyes flick back to Ruby. "I'll do my best to make it up to your mother. And to you."

"And baby William," she adds solemnly.

"And baby William. I swear it."

"And my da." She points. "His name is Adam."

"*Ruby,*" Saeth says.

But I nod, because she's being so earnest. "Your entire family. You have my word." I look to the others on the wagon and take a slow breath. "Truly, I swear to all of you."

Ruby scoots closer and peers up at me. I wonder what I look

like. My clothes are filthy, and I can see mud caked in my knuckles. My face is surely a mess.

"I saw you crying," she whispers. "Are you very sad?"

She's so young, and the words shouldn't pierce me like an arrow, but they do.

Yes, I want to say. *Yes, I am.* My breath catches—once, then twice. It's a miracle I don't start crying again this very moment.

At my side, Nook puts his face down against his knees, and a small sob breaks from his throat. It's clear I'm not the only one.

"All right," says Saeth. "That's enough." He scoops Ruby into his arms, and she squeals in protest, but he kisses her on the forehead and says something quietly.

She wraps her arms around his neck and nods, then looks at me over his shoulder. "Thank you, Your Majesty."

"You're welcome, Ruby." I look at Saeth, and I have to hesitate. My chest tightens again, and my voice feels dangerously close to breaking. I have to wait to make sure it's steady. "Adam, I truly will do my best to make it up to you."

He shakes his head, then settles back into the straw beside his family. "You already did."

But Leah's eyes flick up, finding mine in the moonlight. She says nothing, but the message is clear.

It might be true for her husband, but it's not true for her.

CHAPTER EIGHTEEN

Harristan

Our return to the Wilds is in the dead of night, which is a bit of a relief. We're only welcomed with silence. No one is out and about to stare, to shout, to publicly chastise me for every single failure.

That will happen tomorrow, I'm sure.

I'm relieved to find Quint unharmed and waiting for us, again sitting on the porch of the house beside a lantern, writing in his little book. He stares at the wagon as we roll back into sight, and I can read in his expression that he senses how much has gone wrong. He's always good at creating distractions in the face of a crisis, however, so I'm not surprised when he snaps his book shut, and instead of asking questions, he begins telling the guards which homes are now ours.

All of *his* duties in our absence were successful, of course.

I shouldn't feel bitter and resentful about that, but it only serves to highlight everything I've done wrong. Since we were expecting to bring back more guards, he's been able to secure and outfit two houses near the one we've been using—far more space than we really need.

But at least I can finally have some privacy. After tonight, I'm desperate for it.

"Saeth's family can have a house to themselves," I say. "Quint and Thorin can share the other. I'll stay where we were."

Francis is awkwardly dragging Sommer off the wagon, wincing as he does it. Nook is hovering near him, looking lost.

"You swear you can keep him confined, Francis?" I say.

He nods. "I'll see if I can get some shackles from Marcus Orthrop and put him in my cellar for tonight." He jerks his head at the boy. "Nook will help me. Then I'll find someone to stitch up his arm."

Nook looks surprised by this, but he nods quickly, then moves forward to join Francis. Maybe he needed a task.

"Take a crossbow," I say. "If he tries to escape, shoot him."

Nook blanches at that. So does Sommer. He's still bound and gagged, but he shakes his head vigorously.

I have to look away. There's still too much emotion in the air, and I just want to be behind the closed door of the house so I don't have to face any of this anymore.

But I'm the king, and I don't have that luxury. There's no King's Justice. There's no one else.

"We'll question you at daybreak, Sommer," I say. "Then we'll decide what to do with you."

He swallows, then nods.

I turn for the steps and grab hold of the door. But before I cross the threshold, I remember something else, and I look back at Francis. "Make sure you give him a meal. He did this because he was starving."

Then I close myself inside before I have to face anything—any*one*—else.

The house is quiet and warm, a relief since I've been shivering in my wet clothes for the last hour. The nights aren't cold, but a fire has been laid in the hearth anyway—surely Quint again, prepared for the weather—and there's a hot kettle on the stove, too. Only one lantern is lit, and I know we should conserve the candles and oil, but I'm tense and rattled and I've had enough darkness. I light a few others.

I hang my cloak on a hook by the fire to dry, then add my sodden tunic beside it. I should bend to untie my boots next, but I catch sight of my hands in the light, and I realize it's not just dirt in the creases of my knuckles. There are flecks of blood as well. I move to the washbasin in the corner and pump water from the well to scrub them clean.

As I watch the dirt and blood swirl free, all of Lennard's accusations slam into my thoughts at once.

The instant they found proof, you ran.

They're wrong. I know they are. I've never poisoned anyone. I've never turned on my people.

Maybe I'm a fool. I don't know what proof they could have, but maybe they do have something. Maybe these traitors have worked against me so effectively that my own ignorance will be my downfall. Without information, there's no way to know.

Not long ago, Arella was in the Wilds, telling the people that Prince Corrick's ship was a farce, that it would never make it to Ostriary. I didn't believe that either, but maybe it's true.

Maybe all of this is futile.

I abandon the basin, then drop into a chair and press my hands into my eyes again.

Now it's little Ruby's voice in my thoughts. *I saw you crying. Are you very sad?*

I didn't cry when my parents died. Then, I felt like I couldn't dare. Honestly, I shouldn't dare *now*. Everything was terrible. Everything *is* terrible.

But when our parents died, I had Corrick. Now, I have no one.

I miss my brother so much that it aches.

The door creaks open, and I jerk my arms down.

Quint.

My thoughts freeze.

He takes one look at me, sitting half dressed in the chair, still filthy with mud and blood and who knows what else, and he inhales to speak.

I point at the door. "Out."

He closes his mouth, but his eyes narrow. He walks past me toward the stove, fetches an earthenware mug and a scoop of tea, then pours from the kettle.

"I said *out*."

"I heard you." He adds honey, too, then carries the mug to me.

I don't touch it. "I want to be alone, Quint."

"No, you don't. You must be freezing. Why haven't you—"

"Don't presume to tell me how I feel."

"It's not a presumption. You're soaking wet and filthy." He gestures at my bare arms. "Gooseflesh all over. You'll catch your death of—"

"That's not what I meant and you know it!"

He blinks in surprise, and I realize I've snapped, which I almost *never* do. I run a hand across my face. "Forgive me." Then I sigh. All I'm doing lately is asking forgiveness, which I probably don't deserve from anyone. "Please, Quint." My chest tightens dangerously, and I glance at the door, then fix my eyes on the table. "Leave."

A moment passes, but he lets out a breath and moves away. I'm surprised by the sudden pang in my heart when I realize he's yielded.

But he *doesn't* leave. He walks past the door to pick up the thin quilt from the end of the bed, and he returns to drop it over my shoulders.

Then he drops himself into the chair across from me. "No."

I stare at him. I just faced outright rebellion in the forest, and I dealt with a revolution in the Royal Sector, but I don't think anyone on my staff has ever sat down in front of me and said *no*. It's so jarring that it chases the waiting emotion away from my eyes and a bit of the tightness out of my chest.

"I could have Thorin drag you out of here," I say.

"As you like." He nudges the mug toward me. "Drink, Your Majesty. You truly must be freezing."

I want to throw it in his face. I hate that he challenges me like this, because it makes all my options seem petty. I could call Thorin in here, but for what? For giving me a blanket and telling me to drink a cup of tea? I really am cold. These soaked boots have turned my feet into blocks of ice.

I draw the blanket against me with one hand, then take a sip from the mug with the other.

"Stop looking so satisfied," I say petulantly.

But he doesn't, really. He's just looking at me. His voice isn't even patronizing. Simply kind.

I have to look away and take another sip.

The honey is very sweet, and the tea warms me from within, and I wholly resent that it does make me feel better.

"Thorin and Saeth gave me a brief accounting of what happened," he says gravely. "Do you want to talk about it?"

Memories of the guards facing us in the clearing flash in my brain, and I shudder, then shake my head. "No."

I expect him to argue about this too, but he doesn't. His voice quiets further. "Are you hungry? There were rolls left from dinner earlier. Some honey and cheese as well."

"You should give them to the guards."

"I've already seen to the guards."

Of course he has. I say nothing and stare into my mug.

Quint *tsks* and rises from the table, then fetches a basket with the food, returning to sit across from me again.

"You're treating me like a child," I say sharply.

"I'm not."

Well, I'm tempted to act like one and throw this mug right into his lap. I fix him with a glare. "I really will call for Thorin, Quint."

"Oh, for goodness' sake. You will not." He fixes me with a glare right back. "And I'm not treating you like a child. I'm treating you like a man who's been through hell and could do with a bit of gentle care."

Well then.

I huff a breath—then let it out in a rush. I have no idea what to say to that. No one talks to me like this. No one *says* things like this. My heart is tripping over itself as if it's not sure what the right rhythm is.

"Did you argue with Cory this way?" I say. "I cannot imagine him putting up with it."

"With Prince Corrick? Never." Quint smiles, and there's true fondness to it. His eyes glint with unshared memories. "I sometimes think the basis of our friendship was the fact that I was the sole person in the palace who never argued with him about anything at all."

If we talk about my brother, it's going to summon my emotion, and I've spent enough time crying tonight. "Then why on *earth* do you think it's appropriate to argue with me?"

"If we were still in the palace, I probably wouldn't dare." The firelight bounces off his features, tracing gold along the red of his hair. "But last night, you grabbed my book, and you looked quite disappointed when I didn't grab it back."

Against my will, a flush crawls up my cheeks. Quint notices too much. I always forget that.

"I shouldn't have done that," I say, and my voice is a little rough and worn.

Quint says nothing, instead choosing to unwrap the cloth covering the food. He withdraws a thick slice of bread and a knife, spreading cheese and drizzling honey in a way that shouldn't be mesmerizing, but somehow *is*. I find myself transfixed by the movement of his hands, and if I weren't so certain he would argue about it, I'd order him to leave again.

I force myself to speak. "Why wouldn't you tell me the reason for the dates in your book?"

"I did tell you the reason." He holds out the bread. "Eat, Your Majesty."

There are no plates, so I have to take it from his hand. His fingers brush mine, and like last night, I feel a jolt right to my core, and the flush on my cheeks goes nowhere. My breath almost catches. I set down the tea and tug the blanket tighter because redness has probably spread down to my chest. I can't meet his eyes.

I simply do not understand how he can be so infuriating in one moment, then leave me longing for the tiniest touch in the next.

If anyone wanted to shoot me right now, I'd be an easy target.

I fight for words again. "You didn't *really* tell me the reason."

"It's nothing. Simple recordkeeping."

That pricks at me, and I frown. "Please, Quint," I say quietly. "Don't lie to me."

He holds my gaze steadily, and I'm ready for him to contradict me, but he sighs. "Well now. You genuinely mean *that*." He pauses. "It truly is simple recordkeeping. But the meaning is . . . very personal. And rather dear to me." Now *his* cheeks have grown red, and his eyes skip away. "I'd prefer to keep it to myself. For now. If it pleases you, Your Majesty."

It doesn't. Not at all. But how can I refuse *that*?

I make a frustrated sound. "You are *so vexing*," I say, then eat the bread.

His eyebrows go up. "Am I?"

My heart is stuttering again, my eyes lingering on the way the light dances across his features. But now my fingers are sticky from the honey and cheese, combining with the dirt that still clings to my arms. Grateful for an excuse to leave the table, I thrust myself out of the chair and move to the washbasin again.

I plunge my hands under the water when it runs, then splash some over my face. It's ice cold against the warmth on my cheeks, but I don't care.

When I straighten, he's right there, holding out a towel.

Lord. He's so infuriating. So kind. Both! I snatch the fabric right out of his hands and drag it across my face.

Then I snap it at him.

He catches it and holds fast, which takes me by surprise. This time, we do tussle, just for a second, and the blanket falls off my shoulders. I try to jerk the towel free, but Quint must not be prepared for the sharp motion. He stumbles right into me.

When his hands land on my bare chest, it's more than a jolt. It's a lit match. A bonfire. An inferno. His eyes are full of stars, and his hands are so warm, and even though there are a million feelings I should keep buried, a million things I should be *doing*, I've simply run out of strength to care.

I seize the lapels of his jacket, and I press my mouth to his.

If he's surprised, it doesn't show. *I'm* the one who's surprised, because I was ready for there to be an edge to his response, a belligerence, but instead there's a . . . a gentleness. A contentment, like this moment was a foregone conclusion.

His hands slide along the bare skin of my chest, one finding its way behind my neck, the other shifting to take hold of my waist. No one has ever *held* me, and my entire body is responding in a manner I'm not ready for, easing against him, my breath deepening. His lips part just as his fingers slip along the bare skin of my lower back, and when I feel the brush of his tongue against my own, my whole body jumps. I give a little gasp and draw back.

He lets me go at once.

My pulse is racing. I need to slow my breathing or I'm going to start coughing. I run a hand over the back of my neck and shudder. His hair is turning gold and his eyes won't stop sparkling, and every part of my body wants to feel him against me again.

"*So* vexing," I whisper. I feel like I can't gain control of my thoughts. "Quint, I . . ." I have no idea what to say. I have to press my hands together in front of my face. "I don't . . . I just . . . It's . . . it's been years since I've done that."

He looks at me like I've said the sky is blue. "Yes, Your Majesty," he says quietly. "Obviously."

I suck in a sharp breath, and I suddenly want to pull back farther. "*Obviously?*" I demand.

He startles. "What? Oh! No. Not obvious in that way. But if I may say, it's rather charming that you would think I could *tell—*"

"Quint." I run a hand down my face. He's truly going to be the death of me. "*What* was obvious?"

"That it simply *must* have been years, because if you were slipping paramours into your chambers, you never would have been able to keep it a secret in the palace."

He's right about that. "I've never snuck anyone *into* the palace."

"I must say, half the staff would likely be surprised to discover that you've ever fancied romance at all, because— Wait, did you say 'never *into* the palace'?" His eyebrows go up. "Well, now my curiosity is piqued."

I blush against my will. "It was a long time ago."

He studies me for a moment. "How long?" he says. "Or is that question too bold?"

I cut him a narrow glance. "Oh, so *now* you're worried about boldness."

"Just now?" he says. "Perhaps a bit."

There's no real teasing in his voice, no flirtation, but this reminds me of when we were sitting on the porch last night. Debating semantics. The way I snatched his book, how I *was* disappointed when he didn't grab it back. We're standing very close, and I can feel his warmth. My eyes flick to his mouth, the curve of his lip. There's a part of me that longs to touch him again, and I don't think it would be unwelcome—but I'm not entirely certain. It's rare that I ever touch anyone at all, and certainly not like . . . *this.*

So I keep my hands to myself, my heart tripping again. "I used to sneak out," I say. "Years ago. Before I was king."

Quint must sense my reticence, because he draws back a little, giving me space. Firelight finds his eyes again.

"It really wasn't obvious?" I say, and immediately regret it. I have to glance away.

"No, Your Majesty." He doesn't laugh, which is a mercy. "Not obvious at all."

"You said the staff would be surprised to discover I fancied romance." I hesitate. "But not you?"

"I wondered at first." He shrugs. "You were so stoic. So reserved. There's never been any mention of courtship—official or otherwise. No dalliances. No companionship whatsoever. *Nothing.* Prince Corrick is a gentleman, and devoted to Tessa, but even he has *eyes.* But you . . . you never seemed to look, never made a passing comment, never lingered. Not with anyone. Which is fine, of course."

"What changed?" I prompt, because now I'm curious.

"Delegate Plum visited from Mosswell with his husband," Quint says. "Two years ago. They were sitting in the gardens while the porters unloaded their carriage. You paused to watch them. It was only for a moment, but it was the first time I've ever seen you look . . . longing."

I frown. I remember that. Their visit had taken me by surprise, because we hadn't been informed that the consul had chosen a new delegate. And there they were, just sitting in the garden in the sunlight, holding hands.

"After that," Quint says, "I started to pay attention. You might not comment or linger, but sometimes men would pass. You would notice."

"Even *I* have eyes," I say.

He smiles—but I don't.

"I didn't mean to upset you," Quint says.

"You haven't." But I move away to sit on the edge of the bed, and I tug at the laces of my boots. I've never talked about any of this with anyone, so it's weird to reveal any of it now. At the same time, it almost feels as if Quint knows—as if he's figured most of this out on his own. "When I was a boy," I say, "I was very sick. There was a time when my parents were worried I wouldn't survive to adulthood."

"Corrick has told me those years were very difficult."

I shrug a little, then pull my boots free. "Once I made it into adolescence, I still fell ill often, though not as badly as when I was a child, so my parents would tell me that I should marry young. Create an heir as soon as possible." I give Quint a knowing look. "But by then, I was already aware that there was going to be a minor problem with that."

He stares back at me. "You didn't tell them."

I shake my head. "No. They had no idea. And I'm not going to swindle a girl into a false marriage."

"It's not uncommon."

"It's still a spectacle. I won't do it."

"You think they would've objected to your intentions?"

I frown. It's something I've always wondered, and they died before I found the courage to discuss it. "I don't know. My illness was disappointing enough. I could hear it in every whisper. No one wants a weak king. It was a constant worry. I wasn't sure how they'd react to the news that I had no desire to create an heir either." I pause. "I also wasn't sure how Corrick would feel, knowing that the pressures of the Crown, the duty of continuing the line of succession—it would eventually fall to him. He was already looking for ways to escape the palace, and this is just another trap."

Quint's eyebrows go up. "So he has no idea either?"

"He's never asked, and I've certainly never told him. You might know better than I would."

"Prince Corrick all but idolizes you. I've only ever heard him say that you have no patience for casual flirtation. Honestly, I believe he thinks you're guarding your heart—and so he guards his. It's very likely the reason he's never courted anyone himself until now."

I never really considered that.

Quint watches me, but he hasn't moved from where we were by the washbasin. The distance between us now feels like a mile. I've said far too much. He knows more than anyone. And even though it's all rather useless information, I feel bare. Vulnerable. Exposed.

On a night when I already felt vulnerable and exposed.

The worst part is that I regret this distance. I regret that I moved away. I'm already replaying the slow movement of his fingers across my skin, and I'm worried it's a memory I'm going to have to hold for another few years before anything like it ever happens again.

Because what he said was true: I do guard my heart along with everything else. I'm the king, and my entire night was just ruined because of an act of betrayal. My entire *life* has been one long string of betrayals chased by pity. The poor king who can barely hold his kingdom together. I have no idea how to trust that anything is genuine.

Quint is studying me. "I *have* upset you," he says.

"No," I say. But that's a lie, and gooseflesh has sprung up across my arms again. The heady emotion from a few minutes ago is a distant memory, and too many worries are crowding back into my thoughts.

"You pity me," I say.

"No, Your Majesty."

But he does. I think of everything he's said since he came into the house, his comment about a man needing gentle care, and on the tail of everything else that's happened, it suddenly all feels patronizing. My shoulders tighten, and I fold my arms against my abdomen. "That kiss was a mistake. I did not—I *do not*—need tending in *this* way, Quint."

He stiffens, then sighs and runs a hand across his jaw. "Honestly," he mutters. "And you say *I* am vexing."

"What?"

"*You* kissed *me*!"

I glance at the door and then back at him. "And I will thank you to keep your voice down," I growl.

He makes a frustrated sound that's not unlike the one I made earlier. "Do you somehow believe I accepted your romantic overture as if it were part of my role as Palace Master? Is that what is happening here?"

I glare at him. We're back where we started. "Enough."

"Should I have been engaging these services for every passing diplomat? Perhaps I was not informed of the full scope of my duties."

"Stop it."

"*You* stop it," he snaps. "You don't even realize the harms you're causing."

I've never heard Quint snap before, and most definitely not at me. I draw myself up, rising to my feet. "Just who do you think you are speaking to?"

"I know very well who I'm speaking to. I know *exactly* who I'm speaking to, because I might be the only person who knows you better than your own brother." He doesn't back down, and I realize he's well and truly angry. His cheeks are flushed, his eyes narrowed. "Because much like Prince Corrick, you seem determined to hide everything you want and everything you need, because you're terrified of showing one shred of vulnerability to anyone, when really, it doesn't matter. You suffer *needlessly.* Every one of us still hurts the same, still loves the same, still bleeds the same. Every one of us still *dies* the same. So you spend years of your life alone—*years,* Your Majesty, *obviously*—relying on the smallest moments of connection to survive, until tonight, when you finally relent and allow yourself a moment of happiness for one second." His eyes are so fierce they could cut steel. "And then you cheapen it by calling it an act of pity, you insult me by treating me like a whore, and then you hurt me by calling it a mistake."

All the breath has left my lungs. I'm staring at him. His words are wrapped up in anger and fury—but worse, they're full of pain, too.

Right this instant, I *am* the one causing a betrayal.

"Forgive me for not leaving when you asked," he says. He turns and goes for the door.

I'm away from the bed in a heartbeat, and I catch his arm just before he pulls the latch.

"Stop," I say, and my voice is quiet, my grip gentle. This isn't an order or a demand. "Please."

His eyes are locked on the wood, but he stops. "Yes, Your Majesty."

I cannot believe my night has gone so wrong in so many directions. "Quint. Please. Forgive me. I . . ." I hesitate. "I did not mean to offend you."

"You did not *offend* me."

The ice in his voice makes me flinch. "I did not mean to *hurt* you."

He goes still.

"I'm sorry," I say, and I am. "I'm *sorry.*"

I feel like I should touch him, should soften this in some way, but a lifetime of burying emotion has my free hand fixed and rigid at my side. I don't even know if he'd want me to. "I apologize. Truly. My intent was not to cause harm. And *certainly* not to treat you like—" I'm blushing again, because I can't quite believe he said this last part. "To treat you like a *whore.*"

He's looking at me now, but his expression is still cool, and I don't know if I've been forgiven. I have no idea how to undo this, and maybe I shouldn't want to. Maybe this is better. This night could be forgotten, locked away like so many other memories.

But I think of the way he fetched the quilt. Or made the tea. The way he's been at my side for a million little moments.

The way I was broken and hurting and I tried to send him away—but he sat down and said *no.*

The way his hands felt against my skin.

I have to close my eyes and run a hand across my face. My voice is very soft. "Ah, but you *are* vexing," I say. "Because I *wanted* to kiss you. I want to kiss you *again.*" My cheeks are surely on fire, and I have to keep my eyes closed, or I'll never be able to say all this. "But, Quint, you must understand. I have seen you at court. You know everyone in the Royal Sector. You're very pleasing to look at, and I doubt you have *any* shortage of suitors. My words—my words were more because I do not want you to feel . . . to feel *obligated* to me. To yield simply because I am your king. Just as I won't bind a woman into some kind of marriage of convenience, I have no illusions that a man might not accept a romantic advance just because I wear a—"

"Oh, *hush*," says Quint, and then he steps forward to kiss *me*.

My fingers automatically curl into his jacket, because his hands have landed on my face and I simply can't bear the thought of him letting go. But my thoughts are my enemy, and as soon as I feel the brush of his tongue again, I pull away. "But—there is still the matter of pity—"

"Honestly," he says. "Do you hear yourself? Shall I find you a mirror? I simply cannot decide if this is arrogance or stupidity, because you cannot in one breath claim to be afraid of someone yielding to your crown, and in the next worry that I'm only kissing you because I *pity* you."

"I believe we've crossed far beyond the point where you've grown too bold."

"I *must* be repaying some kind of penance, because I've been lusting after you for two years, yet on the day you finally kiss me, I am forced to have a ten-minute discussion each time we share breath."

"*Quint.*" I stare at him in wonder. "You have not been *lusting* after me for two years."

"You're right." He leans against the wall, conceding. "*Lusting* has been far longer than that. *Falling for you* has been the shorter time, but as I said, there was no indication my affections would be returned." He straightens, affecting a stern disposition. "So. Very. Stoic."

"Are you *mocking* me?" I feel like I've completely lost any sort of control of this conversation.

"Just a little." He gestures toward the door. "Shall we call for Thorin?"

In spite of everything, that makes me smile.

Quint presses his hands over his heart. "*That!*" he says. "That smile is what I've been longing for." His gaze turns a bit wicked. "Lusting after. Falling for."

"I don't believe you."

He goes still. For an instant, I think I've wounded him again, and I regret it. But then he heaves an impressive sigh and says, "Oh, dear lord, *fine*, I will tell you. I can prove it. The dates? The dates in my book that you're so curious about?"

I frown. "What do the dates have to do with any—"

He puts a hand over my mouth, and I'm shocked at the audacity until he traces a thumb along my lip, and it sends a pulse of warmth right to my core. "The *first* date," he says, "was so long ago that it isn't even in this book. I'd been working in my role for three months, and you were so stern, so severe—"

"So *stoic*," I intone behind his hand.

"Well—yes. In truth, I was a bit afraid of you. When the former Palace Master retired, I was shocked when I was promoted from apprentice."

I gently pull his hand down. "You have Corrick to thank for that."

"I know that *now*. But *then*, it was so unexpected, and I was desperate to impress the king. You were so imposingly regal, so resplendent at court, so very magnificent on the throne—"

I flick my eyes skyward. "All right, that's quite enough."

"Oh, but you are!" he declares. "But you always seemed so angry. So cold. You never smiled, never laughed. I thought perhaps I'd be miserable in my duties. The first time I saw you smile, I thought, 'I should write down the date because *this* will likely never happen again.' So I did. Then it *did* happen again, a month later, and I wrote that down, too. And then again, six weeks after that. It became a . . . a habit. An offhand preoccupation. But because I was paying such close attention, I discovered that you weren't angry and cold, but sad. You care about the people of Kandala so much. You miss your parents so very much. You love your brother so very, *very* much." He presses his hand to the center of my chest. "Every time you smile, it's a reminder of how much of that you lock away. And that's what I was falling for."

I put a hand over his and hold it there.

"No more talking," I say roughly, because as usual, he's spun me past irritation and captured me with devotion. If he keeps going, there's a chance I'll reveal any secret, swear to any oath, and offer him the entire kingdom.

I take hold of his lapel and pull him forward. His hands settle on my chest, and his eyes spark with light, but our mouths barely meet before I stop him again.

"I need to be clear about something else," I whisper against his lips.

"Oh, I *knew* it," he cries. "My penance, for certain."

I burst out laughing. "Forgive me." I draw back, suddenly shy again. "It's unimportant."

He smiles, but his eyes hold mine. "I'm teasing. Tell me." His voice is more patient. "Please."

"It really has been years," I say. "And even then, that was all . . . ah, mostly boyish fumbling. Part of my reticence has always been that people have certain . . . certain *expectations* of their king. If . . . if you expect me to be well versed in . . . in . . . well, in *anything*—" I break off, my breath stuttering. One of his hands has settled on my waist, but the other is drifting along my skin again, tracing a line down the center of my chest. His eyes are so intent on mine, and his tongue slips out to wet his lips.

I have to choke out words. "*Well.* You spoke of arrogance, but I'm *not*, truly. Or . . . I don't mean to be."

"Yes, Your Majesty." He moves in closer, then leans in to press a kiss to my neck. That hand at my waist tightens its grip. His other hand slips lower, his fingers tracing a slow circle around my navel.

My breathing turns rough. "I should be clear that my experience is— Ah, I don't want you to find me lacking—"

His hand strokes firmly over the front of my trousers, pulling a gasp from my throat.

"Do I seem concerned?" he whispers, his breath warm against my ear.

He's completely stolen my ability to speak. I shake my head fiercely.

"Good." His fingers slip to the cord keeping my trousers knotted in place, and he gives it a tug. "As I said half an hour ago, these are filthy and damp, and you must be freezing." His teeth graze the skin of my neck. "So let's have them off."

CHAPTER NINETEEN

Harristan

I've never been an early riser, but this morning I'm awake when the first beams of sunlight strike the shutters. The fire has gone to embers, and the room is cool, silence pressing in from outside. Quint's body is a warm weight against mine, his breath soft against my arm. The world outside this tiny house is full of living nightmares, and I have so many obligations waiting for me. I'm dreading every single one of them. I'd rather spend my morning memorizing the lines of his face.

I was worried that dawn would come and I would feel awkward. Uncertain. That I would want to slip out of bed, grateful for an excuse to leave.

Instead, all my emotions are just the opposite. Quint has been a part of my life for years, so there's a strange sort of comfort here. Like the moment I kissed him, what's truly startling about this is that it's somehow . . . not startling at all.

And now that I've let down my walls, my carefully constructed barriers, the fortress I've built around my emotions, I'm having a hard time remembering how to put them back up. This is terrifying. Exhilarating. Last night, I couldn't stop touching him. I'm longing to touch him *now*.

He was writing down the dates when I *smiled*. Good lord. It's the most insane thing I've ever heard. If I'd ever found out, he wouldn't have lasted one more second in the palace.

But then he gave me that whole speech about my brother and my parents and the whole of Kandala and—oh, I simply cannot take it.

Wake up, I think. *Wake up and drive me crazy.*

He doesn't. His breath keeps tickling my arm, his chest rising and falling slowly. I watch for far too long, mesmerized.

I run a hand across my face. I should get dressed. There's work to be done. Francis has Sommer bound somewhere, and I need to question him this morning. Saeth will give me a report on whatever his wife knows. There's a chance that the closest consuls will be receiving their letters by now, too. The entire country is at stake, and I'm in bed.

But Quint's hair is tousled from sleep, his jaw dusted in red from the start of a beard he hasn't shaved since we moved to the Wilds. I remember the feel of it against my face, against my neck, against my chest, against . . . other places. I thought it would be rough, but it's not at all.

Without thinking, I stroke a thumb across the velvet softness of his cheek, and he stirs, inhaling deeply.

"Do you need me to make more tea?" he says, barely awake. He made a pot sometime in the dead of night when I woke with a coughing fit. I tried to muffle the sound with a pillow, but he heard anyway.

"No," I murmur. "Go back to sleep."

His eyes crack open the tiniest bit, and when he sees that I'm not coughing, he stretches, then rises up enough to kiss me lazily.

I could drown in the taste of his mouth, but he withdraws, sliding away. I think he's going back to sleep, but he shifts closer, dropping a kiss onto my shoulder, then my chest.

A fire lights in my belly, and I press a hand to his cheek. "Quint—"

His hand slips beneath the blankets, finding my knee. "Good morning, Your Majesty."

"I didn't mean to wake you—" I choke on a yelp as he sucks my nipple between his teeth.

"Too late. I'm up." Then his hand slides up my thigh, and for a while, I forget how to speak altogether.

Later, when my heart eventually settles again, the sunlight is more fully against the shutters. We've barely dressed beyond undergarments, and the quilts are a tangled mess. It's my face against Quint's arm now, and I'm dozing while he sits against the wall and flips pages in his little book.

"If you keep track of the dates we do *this*," I say, "I will have to kill you."

He grins. "I'm drafting a ledger this very moment."

"You are not."

"No." The smile slips off his face as he focuses on the page. "I'm reading over notes from previous consul meetings. I was doing this last night, too, but now I'm hoping I'll have something we'll find useful before you question Sommer, but thus far, nothing. I still haven't been able to figure why Arella would have been speaking to the rebels with Laurel Pepperleaf, of all people. She has never aligned herself with Allisander's sector."

Oh, he's working. Now I feel guilty.

But I think of what we faced in the woods last night, and I can't quite force myself out of bed.

He flips another page. "I'd kill for access to the palace right now. I have *mountains* of notes in my chambers. Or I *did*. Who knows what anyone's done with it since we've been gone." He sighs.

That statement makes my thoughts trip and stall. He really does take notes everywhere he goes. It's part of what makes him so good at his job. "Do you write down everything I say when I'm speaking to the consuls?"

He doesn't look up. "If I'm present, I write down everything you say to anyone at all. Prince Corrick as well."

That's true. I remember how he was writing down an accounting of my conversation with Annabeth, making notes about what Saeth reported, too. I press my hands into the mattress and shift until I'm sitting against the headboard beside him. "Do you think there's any chance Allisander and Arella could have found something compromising in your notes that would provide the *proof* they claim to have?"

"That you're *poisoning* the people?" He closes his book and looks at me in surprise. "Of course not. What could it be? I've never heard you make anything close to such a claim."

He's right, of course. I frown.

Quint scoffs. "If anything, my notes would prove the very opposite. I have *years* of records detailing your desire to protect the people of Kandala."

I sigh. "Well, I can't take the rebels to attack the palace and retrieve your records. We barely survived against four traitorous guards."

"But you did. You killed the traitors—and returned with an

informed prisoner to interrogate." He flips open the book again, returning to his reading. "Quite the victory, I'd say."

I stare at him. It's a complete mystery to me how he can make our failed mission sound like a success. It's honestly a complete mystery how he can be reading at all. My world has been thrown off its axis, and he's sitting here shirtless, running a finger down the page like we need to prepare for a consul meeting in an hour. But he *is*, and I'm transfixed again. His hair was gold in the firelight, but it's so red this morning, and a bit of a wild mess. Freckles everywhere, too, splashed across the curves of muscle in his chest and arms. I want to count them all.

He clears his throat. "I'm hesitant to criticize the king—"

"Are you?" I say. "Are you truly *hesitant*?"

"—but all this staring is rather distracting."

"*You* are rather distracting." I snatch the book out of his hands.

He *dives* for it, which completely takes me by surprise. I try to keep it out of reach, but he's stronger than I expect and suddenly relentless. We grapple for it until Quint rolls me into the headboard and we send the side table rattling into the wall. He wins more by virtue of my shock than anything else. He ends up straddling my waist, the book trapped between his fingers.

I have to push the hair back from my face, and I'm breathless, glaring up at him sternly. "We were set upon by traitors last night! What if one of the guards stormed in here and thought you were fighting with the king?"

"So charming." Quint leans down and kisses me on the forehead, then returns to sit against the headboard with his book. "If Benjamin Thorin or Adam Saeth are outside that door, do you genuinely believe there's any chance they think we've been *fighting*?"

Lord. I pinch the bridge of my nose. I really need to get out of this bed.

I still don't move. I don't want to face anything outside.

I consider what Quint said about the consuls, about his notes. As always, I wish we had a way into the palace. Regardless of what he said, the guards *were* a failure. Sommer might have information, but he's a traitor. It's still a dead end in so many ways.

Quint has gone back to turning pages, so I shift to sit beside him again, reading alongside when he pauses. So many meetings, so many notes, for months and months and months. So many memories preserved in his handwriting. As Quint said last night, Corrick and I destroyed ourselves to hold Kandala together. Meanwhile, the consuls were plotting against us so carefully.

And just like our parents, we never saw it coming.

Eventually a question occurs to me. "Did you ever tell Corrick?" I say. "About your feelings?"

I've been quiet for a long time, and Quint is in the middle of a page of dry notes from a meeting where the consuls were bickering about shipping levies. His finger stops on a line, and he glances over. "My feelings?"

"For me," I say softly.

He closes the book around his finger and regards me. "You're asking if I ever told my *dearest friend* that I imagined doing wicked things to his brother, the king? Yes, of course, Your Majesty, we talked about it all the time."

I hit him with a pillow.

But then I say, "Truly. Did he know?"

"No. I never said a word."

"Why?"

"I considered it many times. *Many* times. Far too complicated.

For as much as I love Corrick as a friend, he would ultimately feel an obligation to tell you—and I don't believe it would have been received well." He pauses, his eyes holding mine. "Am I wrong?"

I look back at him, and I'm not sure what to say.

He's not wrong.

Shame heats my cheeks. I feel like a boor, and I have to look away. "Forgive me, Quint."

He touches my chin, dragging my gaze back. "Every action you take is subject to scrutiny and judgment, and regardless of any longing I might have noticed, I knew this was something you didn't share with anyone. As I said, I considered it at great length. It would have done no good. Telling Corrick would have compromised my position as Palace Master, my friendship with him, and possibly even his relationship with you. You would've felt cornered and exposed, and I would've been out of a job."

All very likely true. I study him. "So you would have kept this to yourself . . . forever?"

"Until you kissed me like it would save your life? Yes. I would've taken it right to the grave."

There's something a bit sad about that. But maybe that was the point to all his lectures last night. How much time I've wasted. How I've been keeping the same kind of secrets, to the detriment of myself. I swallow heavily.

"Oh, it wasn't *that* bad," Quint says. He takes hold of my hand and weaves our fingers together. "I was by your side all the same."

He says this offhandedly, but emotion punches me right in the chest, and I grip tight to his fingers.

He lifts our joined hands and holds mine against his face. "You said *you* never told Prince Corrick either."

"No." I hesitate. "Last night, when I said *never into the palace,* you asked about it. I used to sneak out with Corrick when I was a teenager."

Quint nods. "He once told me that's what gave him the means to sneak out as Weston Lark. He said you knew all the old spy tunnels and access points—" He breaks off and gasps, then turns to face me, his eyes gleaming with intrigue. "Do you mean you used to sneak out without him? You had a secret paramour?"

"Your eagerness for gossip is concerning."

He all but bounces on his knees. "Your lack of it is boring. Tell me!"

"Well, I *always* took Corrick with me. If I left him behind, he never would've forgiven me." I smile fondly, remembering it. We used to sprint through the palace gardens, racing for the entrance to the tunnels until I thought my lungs were going to give out. "But sometimes . . . sometimes I would encourage him to explore, or join a lively card game, or some other distraction that might buy me an hour to myself. Because there was a boy I'd met, a night watchman at a stable on the edge of the Wilds . . ."

My voice trails off, but I'm certain my meaning is clear.

"And Corrick was unaware?"

"I certainly wasn't going to tell my thirteen-year-old brother that he could find me hiding behind a barn, unlacing the trousers of a stable boy."

I expect that to make him laugh, but instead, Quint looks a little sad. He's not bouncing on his knees now, and he leans forward to kiss me.

"What's that for?" I say.

"For as close as you two are, the number of secrets you keep from each other is maddening. All this time, I thought he was the one hiding his torment from you."

I frown, considering that. "I never thought of myself as tormented. It was all very fleeting, never serious. I knew it could never go anywhere, as the boy had no idea who I was. But I used to imagine escaping the palace, remaining in the Wilds forever, living as a stable boy myself. I'd lie awake at night and dream of it, what it would be like to be surrounded by horses and fresh air instead of angry consuls and endless meetings. I think I was more in love with the idea of *that* than anything else."

Quint is studying me. "*Escaping*, Your Majesty."

Fine. Maybe I was tormented.

I heave another sigh. I've lingered long enough, and if I keep chasing this emotion, I'll end up nowhere good. I kiss Quint's hand and let go. "It's grown late. I need to dress. Since we *don't* have your books or my records or any of the consuls in front of us, I will question Sommer and make a determination of what to do with him. I also need to find out what Saeth's wife knows. I'll start there."

"I'll make an accounting of what they both say so you can compare for inaccuracies, in the event Sommer is lying—or Leah is."

It's a good idea, but I consider the way the woman was glaring at me in the thunderstorm, the way she was clutching her husband's hand.

Whatever happened, she won't want a room full of people. She might not even be willing to talk to me at all, but I have to try.

I pull a tunic over my head, then look at Quint. "You can join me when I speak with Sommer, but I'll need to talk to Leah and Adam alone."

"Yes, Your Majesty." He nods, then pauses in lacing his trousers to write that down.

I don't know what about that requires recording, but I'm transfixed again.

Before I even realize I'm staring, he finishes writing, then looks up.

My cheeks grow warm, and I hastily look for some wool socks, then drop into one of the chairs. "And, Quint . . ." I hesitate, trying to make my voice light, to take any weight out of what I'm going to say. "Surely we've moved beyond formality. You can call me Harristan."

His hands go still on the laces of his trousers again, but he says nothing.

The heat on my cheeks deepens, and I have to reach for my boots. "I'm surprised you didn't do it on your own. You haven't been shy about anything *else.*"

He *still* says nothing, and he's just staring at me now.

I tug one boot on and reach for the other. "Is this truly all it would have taken to render you speechless? If so, I would have made the offer *ages* ago."

"No one addresses you by your given name." His voice is a little hushed. "No one but Prince Corrick."

"Well, you can."

He considers this for a little while, pulling his own tunic over his head, tugging his own boots onto his feet. It might be the longest silence I've ever experienced in his presence.

Eventually, he stands and says, "Forgive me, Your Majesty. I couldn't possibly."

His response is so unexpected that I almost burst out laughing. "You couldn't possibly address me by *name*?"

He shakes his head. "No. I couldn't."

I rise from the chair and pull on my jacket, then stop in front of him. We're nearly even for height, though I might have him by an inch or two. "I could order you to do it," I whisper.

A light sparks in his eye. "If you want to *order* me to do things, I can personally assure you there are better options."

My heart stutters a little, and I give him a tiny shove. He bats at my hand, and we tussle again, just for a second, which makes me smile. But then he catches my arm, almost pulling me into an embrace. I remember the moment last night when I fell against him, when I longed to be held.

That forces me still, and I stare into his eyes. What he said earlier is true: every action I take *is* subject to scrutiny and judgment. That's been my life since I first drew breath. Corrick and I have been so wary of revealing any hint of vulnerability that I can't even think of the last moment I gave my brother a hug.

And here's Quint offering simple human contact like it's nothing. I want to grab hold and keep on holding.

But I have to let go. I have to remember that there's a reason Corrick and I are so distant and so cold. I have to remember what happened to our parents and what vulnerability can lead to. The fact that my personal guards turned traitor is proof enough of that.

And as soon as I have the thought, it's like a bucket of icy water. I have to stop hiding in this house.

"Perhaps you're right," I say. "The night is over. I have to be the king again."

I don't mean for that to sound so final, but the words fall between us like a wall. Quint steps back. "Of course, Your Majesty." The spark in his eye burns out, and the blush on his cheeks fades. "You've always been the king."

I don't know what to say, but suddenly we're back to where we were a day ago.

I hate it.

If I stand here for one more second, I'm going to do anything I can to unravel the last minute of time, and that's not prudent. So I tug my jacket straight, run a hand through my hair, and turn away.

When I step through the door, it's still somewhat early, and there aren't many people about. To my surprise, Thorin is still on the porch. Despite what Quint said, if my guard heard anything at all, he takes one look at my expression and snaps to attention.

"Your Majesty." His eyes are shadowed with exhaustion, bruises and scrapes crawling across his jaw and up the side of his face from the battle in the clearing.

A stark reminder of everything I've spent the morning avoiding.

"Thorin," I say. "You were on duty last night, too. Have you slept?"

He shakes his head. "Saeth offered to relieve me at dawn, but I told him I could manage a few more hours."

I study his tired eyes and wonder how true that is. I've had guards outside my door since the day I was born, and I've never felt a moment of shame or guilt or a need to explain myself, but this morning, I do.

"I wasn't . . . *alone* last night, Thorin," I say, and I'm not sure what reaction I expect, but I don't get one at all. A bit of warmth finds my cheeks anyway, and I wish I could will it away. "Forgive me. I should have ordered you to take leave."

Thorin frowns, then shakes his head. "I wouldn't have taken it."

My eyebrows go up, and he quickly adds, "One of us had to keep watch. We were ambushed. We could have been followed."

I suppose that's true, but it doesn't lessen the tug of guilt in my chest.

"Saeth just got his family back," he continues. "I wasn't going to ask him to leave Leah any sooner than he needs to." His eyes flick toward Quint for the barest second, and then his voice quiets similarly to my own. "I don't mind taking watch."

There's a kindness in the way he says that. A generosity. Not just toward Saeth, but toward me, too.

Some of the tightness in my chest loosens. "Thank you, Ben."

He nods. "Yes, Your Majesty."

I wouldn't normally offer parting words to Quint, because he'd busy himself with his own tasks—but just now, I can feel him behind me. It's taking everything inside me to keep from turning around, from offering an apology, from grabbing his hand and dragging him with me because I simply don't want to leave him here.

But I don't. I have to be the king, and that means touching no one and trusting no one. A king who was tormented, desperate for escape—exactly the way I was in the palace.

So I don't offer parting words. I don't even look back. I scowl and walk. But my skin is buzzing with *want* and *need*, and I can feel his eyes on my back.

He made me tea. He brought me a blanket. He said *no* and sat at my side when I was broken and hurting and lost.

Just like Thorin stayed awake all night so Saeth could be with his family. So I could be safe.

Ah, this is terrible. Was Quint right? Is this torment needless? Does it matter?

I run a hand down my face. What good is being the king if I can't do what I *want*?

I sigh. "Hold, Thorin."

My guard stops and waits.

I turn around and walk back to the house, then stride right up the steps.

Quint watches me approach. His voice is tight and formal. "Your Majesty. How may I—"

"Stop talking." I take hold of his jacket and kiss him.

His reaction to *this* is almost better than the way he went speechless over my offer to call me by name. He all but falls against the door, and when I draw back, his eyes are wide, his breathing quick.

"Forgive me," I say softly. "I won't turn away like that again. You have my word."

His eyes search mine. "Yes, Your Majesty."

"Harristan," I whisper.

He hesitates, holding his breath, then shakes his head.

Despite everything, that makes me smile. "*Still* no?"

He flushes. "Ah. Well."

But then he says nothing else.

It's rare I have the opportunity to see Quint flustered, so I let go of his jacket and run one last finger along his jaw. "So charming," I tease. "Very well. I'll return as soon as I can, Palace Master."

He sucks in a breath, but I'm already turning, losing the smile, ready to be the king.

CHAPTER TWENTY

Harristan

The house Quint secured for Saeth's family is tiny, set well apart from any others. It looks more like a remote hunting cabin than a building to serve any other purpose. From what I remember, it's a fraction of the size of the house they had in Mosswell, with no pens for livestock or even much of a yard, but there's a wide porch with a swing. The shutters are all drawn tight, but lantern light flickers through the cracks. I don't hear anything from within, but a fire must be set in the hearth because smoke curls from the chimney, too.

"That one?" I say to Thorin.

He nods. "I'll wait outside."

"No," I say. "Go sleep. You should have let Saeth relieve you earlier."

"I can remain with you for the morning.

"If you fall asleep on your feet, it won't do any of us much good, Thorin."

He gives a humorless laugh. "I haven't done much good lately anyway."

That draws me up short. "What?"

He looks over. "I suggested Reed and Sommer."

"And I agreed."

He sets his jaw and looks away.

I speak into his silence. "Saeth agreed as well. And Master Quint, for that matter. Reed *was* loyal. He died proving it. Thorin—this was not your fault. Sommer was desperate and *starving*."

He says nothing to that either.

"We should have gone for them earlier," I say. "I was worried they were locked in the Hold. I had no idea they'd be banished from the sector and left to starve. *I* failed. And not just the mission. I failed *them*. They deserved better. And now, because of it, I'm failing both of you."

Thorin is so quiet that I think he agrees, and the weight of this knowledge sits heavy in my heart. But then he says, "I've known Jack Wadestrom all my life. I don't know if you knew that. Our mothers have been close since before I was born, so he's practically family. We even made it into the palace guard around the same time. Two weeks ago I was buying him a drink when we got off duty—and now he's dead."

I let out a breath.

"He was loyal," Thorin says quietly. "They were *all* loyal. If you'd asked me to name anyone I'd expect to turn on you, Jack wouldn't have made the list. And he didn't just turn on you. He turned on *me*."

I think of the horrible battle in the clearing, the way the rain poured down. Thorin and Wadestrom were grappling in the mud, and I thought all was lost—until Saeth showed up.

"How did it change so fast?" Thorin says, and there's a desperate note to his voice. "What have they been telling them?"

"I don't know," I say. "But nothing that happened last night was a failing on your part. *Nothing.*"

His eyes seem to darken a bit, and he hesitates as if he's going to contradict me, but then he says, "None of it was a failing on your part either."

I look at the small house, all locked up tight. I consider Leah Saeth, and the mystery of whatever she endured. I consider Sommer waiting to be questioned, with answers that might be damning in ways I can't even fathom. "That remains to be seen."

—+—

Saeth's wife answers the door when I knock, and when she sees me alone on the threshold, her eyes flare wide, and she gasps. The surprise doesn't last long before it's replaced with the same icy regard from last night. She grabs hold of her skirts and offers me a brief curtsy. "Your Majesty. I thought it would be Ben, coming to summon us."

"To . . . summon you?" I echo.

"Adam said you would have questions." She lifts her chin boldly. "I presumed we would be brought before the king."

Saeth speaks from somewhere behind her. "*Leah.*" Then he appears at her side to face me. The baby is asleep in his arms, drooling onto his tunic. Little Ruby has trailed him to the door, and she's clinging to his trousers, looking up at me with big eyes.

"Your Majesty. Forgive me." He gives his wife a look. "*Us.*"

Leah scowls.

"I do have questions," I say carefully. "If you're willing to answer." I pause. "I don't mean for it to be an interrogation."

"Oh, I've been through plenty of interrogations," Leah says darkly, and I remember one of the guards saying, *Do you know what they did to your wife?* Her eyes hold mine, full of anger. "What's one more?"

Saeth inhales sharply, but I lift a hand. "You can speak openly," I say. "I'd like to hear about the others."

"Then come in, Your Majesty." She takes a step back and extends a hand toward a small table near the hearth. "I never dreamed the king would deign to visit me personally."

The sarcasm in her voice is thick. Saeth's jaw is tight, but I stopped him once, so he says nothing. Ruby's eyes flick between us all.

I step across the threshold and follow her to the table. "Your husband has stayed by my side through countless attacks, and regardless of what you've endured, you've joined him here. That's no small sacrifice. If we survive to stand against the consuls and reclaim my kingdom, the king will visit you every week, Mistress Saeth."

That burns out some of her fire—but not all of it. She eases into a chair across from me, and when she speaks, her voice has lost the edge. "Last night, Adam told me you said he could leave."

"I did. And I meant it." I glance at my guardsman, then at the baby in his arms, and finally at the little girl, who's the only one who hasn't taken a seat at the table. She's standing between her parents, peering across at me. "I still mean it," I add. "None of you are trapped here."

Leah regards me levelly. "Do you know how much money Consul Sallister is offering for information about your whereabouts?"

I wonder if that's meant to be a threat, or if it's just a question. "I heard it was a thousand silvers," I say. "Do you know how little I trust that he'd actually pay it?"

"Oh, I think he would. You know how I know?"

"Tell me."

Her eyes don't leave mine, and her voice is cool and even. "Because he paid soldiers to stand guard at my door. He paid my neighbors to report on everything I did. Captain Huxley himself showed up to question me every day for a week. He'd have guards search the house every time. At first I didn't know the king was missing—they just said Adam was wanted for treason, and if I didn't help them find him, they would hang my children in front of me."

My eyes flick to Ruby, wondering if she should be elsewhere for this conversation, but she doesn't flinch.

Leah watches my gaze shift, and she says, "Oh, they said far worse to her, Your Majesty."

Her husband reaches out and puts a hand over hers.

"When I had no answers to give, their questions changed. Gossip began to spread that no one had seen the king. Then announcements were made that the king had fled the palace after proof was found that he was poisoning the people. They said that you had a select group of guards assisting you, and Adam was one of them. No matter what I said, they didn't believe me. They thought Adam would eventually return home—or that we had a secret way of signaling him. That this had been planned, and all they had to do was wait us out."

She abruptly falls silent and looks away, and I realize Saeth's jaw is tight. But he lifts her hand and brushes a kiss across her knuckles.

"Forgive me," he whispers. "I had no idea."

She looks back at him and says nothing. But she pulls his hand to her cheek and closes her eyes.

Ruby looks between her parents, then back at me. When she speaks, her voice is so small. "The soldiers took all our food."

Leah opens her eyes again and takes a breath. "And our money. We had nothing. And the neighbors had been warned that if they helped us, they would be guilty of treason as well. They claim you've been poisoning the people, and using Moonflower profits to line your own pockets. Consul Sallister absolutely would pay this money, Your Majesty. All this and more."

The weight of their emotion is weighing on my heart—but my thoughts are churning, too. Because I *didn't* plan any of this, and they all well know it.

Right?

Could there be any chance that the other consuls do believe I'm poisoning the populace, that they really are protecting Kandala by working with Allisander?

That's too complicated to figure out, and I doubt Leah knows the answer.

I glance between her and the children again. "The soldiers took your money and food," I say quietly. "How did you survive?"

She's quiet for a long minute, and the weight of the silence presses down on us all. Eventually Saeth leans in and says, "Do you want me to—"

"No," she says, and her voice is softer. "I'll do it." She pauses. "We were left under heavy guard. They wouldn't leave us alone. Not to dress, not to wash, not to . . ." She shudders and looks away, pulling her shawl more tightly against herself. "Not to do anything. But *they* had to eat. Ruby would beg for their scraps. Most of them would mock her. But sometimes they would give them to her. And sometimes she would sneak them to me."

She's ashamed by this; I can tell. The baby fusses in Saeth's arms, but he bounces the infant a little and the child settles.

I look at my guardsman. "Were they still under guard when you arrived at your home?"

"Yes, Your Majesty."

"How many?"

"Four."

I look at him steadily, and he looks right back at me. I know we're both remembering our final conversation in the wagon, before he left to fetch his family. We were worried his wife and children were being watched like the others—but not to this extent.

And I sent him off to face four armed guards alone.

"As soon as I saw them, I knew it was worse than we expected," Saeth says, and there's a dark tone to his words. "I had a choice to make. So I made it."

He killed them. Saeth doesn't need to say it. I can hear it in his voice.

I wonder if those men did more to his wife and family than what they've said. I consider the heavy tension in this house, the drawn shutters, the way his wife drew that shawl around herself.

I probably don't need to wonder.

Corrick ordered a lot of terrible things as King's Justice, but there's a difference between execution and torture. A difference between justice and torment.

Baby William fusses again, so the guardsman taps him on the nose, then blows the wispy baby hair off his forehead. The infant startles and waves an arm, but then his face breaks out in a wide smile. Saeth smiles back at him.

I can understand now why Thorin didn't accept his offer of relief this morning.

"Were you able to learn anything?" I say.

Saeth looks back at me. "No. But I knew if they were willing to put that many guards on my family, there was a greater chance that you and Thorin would encounter an ambush on the road."

As we did.

And despite everything they'd been through, his starving wife and children followed him into the rain to come help us.

I lean in against the table and wish I had more to offer than words. My chest is tight. "Truly," I say. "I am grateful for your sacrifice."

Leah looks across the table at me. "I knew Adam wasn't a traitor to Kandala. I'm still not sure about you."

"I'm not poisoning my people, Mistress Saeth. I swear to you. This *is* treason and sedition, but it's not from my side."

"Who is it, then?"

"I don't know for sure." I glance at my guardsman, and I hate that I'm going to have to ask him to leave his family. But Thorin truly does need to rest, and I don't want to do this next part alone. "I have one other man to question," I say, "so I intend to find out."

––+––

More people are out and about when we stride through the Wilds to fetch Quint before we question Sommer. Stares and whispers follow me, a stark reminder of everyone we lost last night—but no one approaches.

Saeth is quiet at my side, which isn't unusual, but the silence feels too heavy. Nothing I can say to him seems adequate, however. There's nothing I can offer. It's not just everything he and his wife revealed. It's the weight of our failures pressing down, with no promise of relief. The day before we were attacked, he ran for miles, leading a pack of the night patrol out of the Wilds away from me. There's a chance he'll have to do it again. I wonder if I'll be looking at an exhausted Saeth tonight, begging him to take leave, replacing him with a barely refreshed Thorin—a revolving cycle of guarding and fighting and sleeping with no end in sight.

"I'm sorry I made you leave your family," I finally say.

He blinks and looks at me like I apologized for there being air to breathe. "You didn't make me leave them. Thorin needed to rest. I offered to relieve him twice, and he refused both times."

I frown. "I didn't know it was twice."

Saeth nods. "He's so angry that they've turned on us." His voice takes on an edge. "I want to hear what Sommer says, too."

"I hope he actually has information." A short distance away, a man stops splitting wood to watch us pass, and I scowl. I lower my voice and glance at Saeth. "Everyone keeps staring and whispering. I'm worried news of the bounty has spread and they're readying to turn us in. Or perhaps they're looking to retaliate after our failures." I glance around again, thinking of those men who showed up on the porch with Francis, armed with farm tools. "Should we prepare to move? Advise."

His eyebrows go up. "No, Your Majesty. That's not what they're whispering about."

"Then . . . why?"

"Because that ambush killed off most of our traveling party, and you retaliated. That boy Nook has been telling everyone that you called a guard off him so he could escape. You stood with the people in the Wilds against men who were once loyal to you." His voice turns solemn. "Everyone who was there saw how much it cost you."

I stare at him. I want to say that it's not at all what happened—but it *is*.

He hesitates, then runs a hand over the back of his neck. "At the risk of being too bold—"

"Trust me, Saeth, I'm growing immune to boldness."

"Well, you even tugged at Leah's heartstrings, because the whole walk through the rain she kept telling me she was going to shoot you herself when we met up with the wagon—and then the first thing she said when we were alone was that she understood why I stayed."

I swallow and run a hand across my jaw. That's very different from the woman who just sat in front of me and challenged me at every turn—but I believe him.

Saeth nods at my reaction. "Nook knocked on my door at daybreak to ask if Thorin and I would be training today." He scoffs. "Leah loved *that*, let me tell you."

That makes my chest clench. "No matter how much training you give them, they're not an army, Saeth. A few guards almost killed them all."

"I know."

"Then why on earth don't you sound more bleak about all this?"

"Because you've won them over." He nods at the man splitting wood, and the man looks startled at the acknowledgment, then nods back. "None of these people are turning us in *now*. We're safer than we ever were. I wouldn't leave Leah and the kids alone if I were worried."

As if to prove his words, the man sets down his ax, then drops to one knee and puts a hand over his heart.

It's the first time anyone has done *that* in the Wilds, and I almost stop short.

"It's not just that," Saeth is saying.

"What else?" I say, because I'm not sure my heart can take much more.

"If you threw yourself in front of a guard to protect a boy—as the story goes—then no one here is ever going to be convinced you were poisoning the people. No matter what the consuls say, you've won over the Wilds."

I've won over the Wilds. My heart pounds.

Now I just need to win over the sectors.

———+———

By the time we find Francis, Quint has joined us. They did keep Sommer locked in the cellar, and when Saeth tells some of the men to bring him out, they all but throw him at my feet. He's more crouching than kneeling, and he looks like a gust of wind might knock him over. The cloak is gone, but he's still in the sodden, mud-soaked clothes he was wearing last night, and his hands are bound with twine behind his back. It's a warm morning, but it must have been cold in the cellar, because he's shivering, blinking in the sunlight. He's pale, with blood crusted in his blond hair and down the side of his face, along with impressive bruising that would rival Thorin's.

He definitely didn't have that last night.

I look at Francis sharply. "What happened? Did he give you trouble?"

Sommer looks up at that, and he shakes his head violently. "No. No, Your Majesty."

Another man coughs. "We might have had a little fun before we put him down there."

There are a few low snickers from the others. I notice Nook is among them, and he looks a little uncertain, but one of the men claps him on the shoulder, and he smiles. I wonder if they let him "help" with whatever fun they were having.

My chest clenches at the thought. Much like last night, I hate this.

The worst part is that I understand why they did it, the same way I understood the dark note in Saeth's voice when he said he had a choice to make. But it's the first time I've felt pulled in both directions like this. Sommer might have betrayed us—but he was still one of my guards. And he wouldn't have done this if he hadn't been driven to it.

"What did you feed him?" I say, and I keep my tone level, without censure.

"I threw some hay down there," says another man.

A woman nearby offers a dark laugh. "I offered some of my chicken feed."

"Did you peck for some food, soldier?" taunts the first. There are flecks of grain stuck to the blood on Sommer's face, which make me think that he did.

One of the other men makes clucking noises, and they all laugh.

"*Enough*," I snap.

They're all jolted into silence.

I look at Francis. "I asked you to feed him a meal."

He glares right back at me. "Yeah, well *he* killed half our people."

"No. The others may have, but he didn't. He was trying to cap-ture *me*. He was desperate for *food*, just as you were all desperate for medicine. We will not stoop to these means." I look at the man who made the mocking chicken sounds. "You will fetch him a proper meal. Now."

He's an older man with an impressive beard and an even more impressive glower, and he doesn't move. If he thinks he can intimi-date me, he's wrong. I stand my ground, and after a moment, he gives me a half-hearted nod and mumbles, "Yes, Your Majesty," then turns away.

I glance at Saeth. "Cut his hands free."

When he does, Sommer makes a small sound, and I see that the twine sliced into his skin in several places. He must have been bound all night because he moves gingerly, rubbing at his wrists, wincing. His eyes are fixed on my boots, his breathing still hitching a bit.

I've never really questioned anyone. That was always my broth-er's purview. If I had occasion to speak with a prisoner, it was rare.

Honestly, the last time I faced a prisoner, it was Corrick himself, bruised and bleeding and starving, just like this.

I force thoughts of my brother out of my head. They won't help me now.

The bearded man has returned with a basket of food and a water skin, and he practically thrusts them at me, but Saeth takes them. There must be cinnamon bread fresh from someone's oven, because I can smell it. Quint has asked someone else to bring me a chair, so I sit.

Sommer's head has lifted a bit, and there's a new tightness to his shoulders, as if he wants to lunge for the food, but he doesn't dare risk it. His throat jerks as he swallows.

"Sit," I say. "You can eat."

He looks up, his eyes meeting mine for the first time this morning, but he doesn't move. I wonder if he expects me to trick him, just like the others did.

"We may not have a long history together," I say to him, "but you spent enough time in my personal guard to know I'm rarely anything other than forthright." I take the basket from Saeth and set it in front of him. "Eat or not, Sommer. The choice is yours."

After a moment's hesitation, he sits back on his heels and tugs at the cloth wrapping the food. His voice is low and rough. "Thank you, Your Majesty." Then he takes a swig from the water skin, barely setting it down before he shoves a slice of cinnamon bread into his mouth.

The men and women of the Wilds are still nearby, surrounding us, and while I want to send them away, I keep thinking about what Saeth said, how I've finally won them over. They lost people, too. Their curiosity is valid. And unlike what happened to Saeth's family, Sommer has no expectation of privacy here.

So I ignore their looming and focus on the guard in front of me. Unlike Thorin and Saeth, whom I've known since before I was crowned king, I don't know Sommer well. I remember choosing him, and I remember hearing his oath. Until last night, he never gave me a reason to doubt it.

It's terrifying to consider how fragile loyalty is. My father taught me so many things about being a king, but never *this*.

"Start at the beginning," I say to him, and I realize Quint has taken a seat nearby, his book and pencil ready. "Tell me what happened on the day I disappeared from the palace."

Sommer hesitates, then nods. He keeps his eyes on the food. "I didn't come on duty until midday. By then, it was already known that you were missing. Master Quint was gone, and so were Thorin and Saeth. The rumors were outrageous, because everyone had a different story. Someone said a girl had sung ridiculous songs on the palace steps all night, trying to convince a footman to find Master Quint."

He says this like it makes no sense at all, but it's probably the truest of all the rumors. I'd been desperate, and I'd given Violet my signet ring so she could convince the footman to summon Quint—but he didn't believe her. So she started doing anything she could think of to annoy him into acquiescence.

Sommer tears another piece of bread free and continues. "The consuls were the ones saying you'd fled the palace, and because it was coming from *them*, a lot of the staff began to believe it. But those of us in your personal guard suspected a kidnapping plot of some sort." He swallows. "We knew you didn't trust Sallister after what happened with the Benefactors—so we didn't either. Wadestrom and Granger started talking about a search party. We thought something had happened to you, and we'd begun to close ranks against Captain Huxley anyway." He falters, then glances at Saeth, then at me. "I . . . I don't know if you know that—"

"I know it now," I say. "Continue."

He nods. "Sallister was ahead of us, though. Or maybe the captain was. Huxley told the palace staff and the general guard that there were several among us who were assisting you to deceive the people. He and Sallister offered payment for anyone who would report a guard for acting outside orders. I still don't know if someone actually reported Granger or if they just needed someone to take the fall, but he was hung in the courtyard the next morning."

I inhale sharply. At my back, Saeth swears.

Sommer looks up at him and nods. "It sent a message, and

quick. No one knew who'd turned him in, so we all became suspicious of each other. When days passed without word from any of you, we all began to think maybe the consuls were telling the truth—especially when they cut our pay and froze our accounts."

"So you thought I was poisoning people," I say flatly. "Despite *never* hearing me make such a claim."

"They said you'd been conspiring with Ostriary to do it. That it was the true reason for Captain Blakemore's visit." Sommer glances at Saeth again, then back at me. "Rocco and Saeth were both with you on the day he arrived, so it fed suspicion. Especially since you sent Rocco away—and allowed Rocco to choose the team who sailed. Captain Huxley said you deliberately went around him for the guard placement, too. It was obvious you were working in collusion. It all began to raise a few eyebrows."

A note of challenge has entered his voice. It's subtle, but it's there, reminding me of the way Lennard spat vitriol at me in the rain last night. There's a part of him that believes these claims that Huxley and the consuls were making. I want to knock the food right out of his hands and have the men throw him back in the cellar.

But he also watched his friends die, just like Saeth and Thorin. He spent the night bound and shivering and starving, after being beaten by men who likely presumed I would approve of their treatment.

He might be a prisoner, but I need to convince him, too.

"I *did* send Rocco, and I *did* go around Captain Huxley," I say. "But there was no collusion. Rocco came to me and offered to sail with Prince Corrick because he has experience on board a ship. Rocco was *also* suspicious of Huxley—as he is the one who first told me about how you all were 'closing ranks.' I let him choose his team because he'd earned the right to do so. I may not always suc-ceed, but I do my best to treat my people fairly, Sommer." I glance at the bread in his hands. "Perhaps you should consider the food you're eating if you need a reminder."

Sommer considers that, then frowns and looks at my boots.

But he doesn't take another bite.

"What else?" I say. "Who was truly pushing this narrative that I was *colluding* with my guards and *conspiring* with Ostriary? Was it Huxley or the consuls?"

Sommer thinks for a moment, then shakes his head. "It's all getting muddled now. Consul Sallister kept saying that Blakemore was threatening to reveal your methods for poisoning the people if you didn't share a greater portion of your profits with him."

"Profits! Profits from *what*?"

"Profits from the sale of Moonflower petals."

"I don't profit from the sale of Moonflower petals!" I cry, smacking my chest. "*Sallister* does!"

Sommer draws back. "Yes, Your Majesty."

Everyone around us is absolutely silent, listening.

I make an exasperated sound and grit my teeth. I absolutely cannot believe I once called Allisander Sallister a *friend*.

"A question, if I may," says Quint.

"*Please*," I say.

"How was Consul Sallister able to convince the other consuls of this? They know the king doesn't profit from the sale of Moon-flower any more than they do."

Sommer hesitates, looking uncertain now. "Well, they know the Crown takes a cut of all sales and shipments—"

"Lord," I say, and I have to run a hand down my face. "Not the taxes and shipping levies *again*. As much as they like to ignore it, they must realize it costs silver to *run* the kingdom, surely. Where exactly do you think your own pay comes from, Sommer?"

He blanches a little at that, so I lean in and add, "And now that you're not getting it, where do you think it's going? I'm clearly not stockpiling silver *here*."

He swallows thickly.

At my back, Saeth says, "Maybe it's paying these bounties you're all so eager to claim. They stopped paying your salary and instead paid you to turn traitor."

Sommer clenches his jaw and looks away.

Quint clears his throat. "Not to divert from the point you're making, Your Majesty, but I'm still trying to understand how the consuls would *all* believe him. Some of them, yes. But Arella Cherry, for instance, was always highly critical of Allisander—"

"Oh, she was," says Sommer. "But that was before she and Consul Pelham found the proof that Kandala *was* working with Ostriary. And that bolstered Sallister's claims."

"Proof?" I say.

"Yes. She had shipping logs that dated back for decades, showing years of secret dealings with another kingdom, including letters that indicate a means to poison the people. She actually may have been the first consul to know that the mission to Ostriary was a farce, because rumor says that she brought her proof to Baron Pepperleaf's daughter. The baron himself is the one who sent the armed brigantines."

None of this makes sense. I remember Arella and Roydan searching through shipping logs, but there's no proof of poisoning—and if there was, why wouldn't they bring it to *me*?

But I'm stuck on the last part of what Sommer said. "What armed brigantines?"

"The ones sent after Prince Corrick and Captain Blakemore. To stop them from reaching Ostriary."

I'm frozen in place at these words. The world seems to go still.

The night I left the palace snaps back into my memory with crystal clear focus. It was the night when everything went wrong, when I snuck into the Wilds as the Fox to see what I could learn. Arella Cherry and Laurel Pepperleaf had stood in front of the people along with Captain Huxley from the palace guard. I had no idea what they were doing there.

They said I was poisoning the people. It was so clearly a false claim that I disregarded it.

Then they announced that Captain Blakemore's ship would never reach Ostriary. That also had to be a false claim, so I disregarded it as well. How on earth would they know?

Armed brigantines. They sent warships after my brother.

I'm not breathing. I'm not even sure my heart is beating.

A strong hand grips my shoulder, and I almost jump. Quint has risen from his seat, and the edge of his hand is warm against the skin of my neck.

He'd never touch me like this in the palace.

Right now I don't want him to let go.

As if he realizes I can't speak, he says, "What happened to these brigantines?" he says, and his voice is as hollow as I feel. "Did they return?"

Sommer looks between me and the Palace Master, and he seems to recoil into himself, as if he wishes he could un-share this particular bit of information. "Forgive me, Your Majesty. I thought you knew. They said—they said that's why you fled. That you knew you'd been found out when you heard about the brigantines—"

"You didn't answer," I choke out, and my voice sounds like it's coming from a distance. "*What happened to the brigantines?*"

"Were they successful in stopping Prince Corrick?" says Quint. "What happened to the *Dawn Chaser*?"

"No one knows." Sommer shakes his head. "They never returned."

CHAPTER TWENTY-ONE

Corrick

Lochlan and I sleep till late afternoon. Well, I do. He's still snoring away, so he might keep going until nightfall, for all I know. It doesn't matter. We have nowhere to be until tomorrow at midnight, when we're due to exchange another message with Ford Cheeke.

We're back in the boarding house for now, but we have more silver from Oren, so we've got a bigger space, with two beds and even a sitting room. We arrived so late last night that Lochlan was sure they wouldn't even open the door, but I told him that a little silver usually takes away anyone's sour spirits. He didn't like that, but I was right. They welcomed us in. A basket of pastries has been left outside the door for our breakfast, too, along with a pot of tea that has long since gone cold, a pitcher of water, and a small bowl of cut fruit that has a fly or two buzzing around it. The house is quiet, but it's obvious the food has been here for a while.

I don't remember ever sleeping this late in my *life*, but this might be the first good night's rest I've had since leaving Kandala. I rub at my eyes and carry the food inside.

The sitting room has a larger table than the last, along with a secretary's kit, filled with paper and pencils and even two fountain pens. I consider what Ford said about passing letters to Rian and wonder if I could send something to Tessa. I've been thinking about it since last night. There's so much I want to say—but none of it needs to be read by Rian's eyes.

The cynical part of my brain wonders if he'd share my thoughts with her at all.

I take a piece of paper anyway and write without thinking.

Dear Tessa,
I'm coming, my love.

The words look too sentimental, and I want to crumple the paper up at once.

I also want to fold it into a tiny square and carry it close to my heart.

But writing the words gives them a weird sense of permanence, like a promise. Like an oath.

I think of Harristan, and my chest tightens. Below those words, I add more.

Dear Harristan,
I'll find a way home, brother.

"What are you doing?" says Lochlan from the bedroom.

I look up to find him sitting up in bed, running his hand down his face, blinking in the afternoon sunlight.

"Nothing." My voice sounds rough, and I clear my throat. "There's food if you're hungry."

He nods and says nothing, then disappears into the washroom.

I stare at my words on the page. My promises that I have no way to keep.

But we're closer than we were before.

Lochlan comes out of the washroom a few minutes later, so I do fold up the note and put it in my pocket. He watches the movement, and his eyes narrow.

I go tense, waiting for him to ask me about it, but he doesn't. He just sits down and reaches for the basket of food.

And then we sit in silence.

I keep thinking of the moment he pinned me in that alcove. The way he convinced me to act. *The King's Justice wouldn't hesitate.*

Or the moment not long before that, when he kept me from falling to my death.

Or the way I asked for his advice, and he gave it.

We're both trying to get out of here, so we're motivated to work together, but I don't really *hate* him anymore.

Perhaps that's just a good night's sleep talking.

"Quit staring at me," he says.

"I'm not." But maybe I was. I give him a look, then very deliberately shift my chair one inch to the right so I'm at a slightly different angle.

"Why did you fold up the paper?" he says peevishly. "You know I can't read it."

I inhale to fire back at him, but I remember again how the little notes I wrote to Tessa during our palace meeting probably needled him, like we were whispering behind his back. I wonder if it feels like I'm hiding something from him now.

I sigh, then withdraw the paper from my pocket and unfold it.

"You'll mock me," I say, "but I was writing a note to Tessa. And to my brother." I hesitate. "I wasn't going to send it. Obviously. I was just—" I break off and frown. He's staring at *me* now. My voice is a little rough again, but I've gone this far.

I keep my eyes on the paper and grit my teeth, bracing myself. "It only says—"

He reaches out and folds it over my fingers. "Keep it to yourself, Cory."

I'm frozen in place, because this is an unexpected kindness wrapped up in aggravation. I really do want to stab him with the fountain pen for continuing to call me that. I fold up the paper and put it back in my pocket, and we sit in silence again while he eats an orange. The scent of citrus fills the air.

If we have to spend the next twenty-four hours like this, I'm going to hand myself over to Oren Crane.

I turn my chair back to the table and reach for another piece of paper. "Do you know your letters?" I say.

"What?"

"Your letters. The alphabet. A-B-C. Did you have any education at all?"

He stops with a slice of orange halfway to his mouth. He looks like he's trying to figure out if this is the prelude to mockery, but I kept any rancor out of my voice because my question was genuine.

He eventually sets down the orange slice. "It was a long time ago, but I learned my letters. At the forge they used our initials to track our hours on the wall."

I nod and write an *L* on the left side of the paper.

Then I raise my eyebrows at him, prompting.

He eats the orange slice and gives me a look. "What are you doing?"

I tap the paper like a patient teacher. "What's that?"

"An L." He narrows his eyes at me. "What are you *doing*?"

I complete the rest of his name in capital letters.

LOCHLAN

Then I look back at him. "Do you know what it says?"

His eyes flick between the paper and me, but he hesitates. I wonder how often he's seen his name written. I'm sure it's not often enough for him to be certain, but he clearly wants to guess. He's worried I'm trying to trick him, though. I can tell.

"I'm not trying to trap you, Lochlan. It's your name."

I have no idea what kind of response I expect, but I don't get any at all. He's just looking at the paper, eating the orange. I wonder if he thinks I'm mocking him, even though that wasn't my intent. My cheeks suddenly feel warm, and I wonder if I should just crumple the paper up and leave him alone.

But then he says, "Do Karri."

I write her name below his, and he stares at that for a moment. Then, "Tessa?"

I nod and write. Before I'm even done, he says, "Do yours."

I do, and then we have a list of names below his own.

LOCHLAN
KARRI
TESSA
CORRICK

He studies this for a little while, his eyes tracing over the letters, but then he takes a small biscuit from the basket and sits back. A little frown line has appeared between his eyebrows, and he looks away.

I can't tell if he's ashamed at his lack of knowledge or if he's bored with this altogether.

He eventually scowls and says, "I know the letters, but they don't mean anything."

"Oh," I say. "So each letter makes a different sound. Once you learn what the sounds are, you can read."

His scowl deepens.

"No, look," I say, before he can get frustrated. "I'll show you with your own name. There's the L, and when it's at the beginning of a word, it sounds like *luh*. Then the O, which can sound like *oh* or *ah*. Then the C, which . . ." I frown at the *ch* and run a hand back through my hair. I don't remember how I learned all this. "Wait, that one's kind of unusual because it's with the *H—*"

"All right, I'm done." He starts to shove back from the table.

"What?" I demand. "Where are you going?"

"Teach someone else, Your Highness. I'm not your trick pony."

"I know." I slam down the pencil and match his scowl. "It's a real pity, too. A trick pony would've been a lot more fun at every turn."

He startles, then runs his hands over his face and sighs. He drops back into his seat heavily and glares at the paper, his jaw set.

So maybe we are going to have to sit here without speaking.

But he eventually runs his finger over Karri's name. "I haven't told her."

"That you can't read?"

He nods and pushes the paper away. We sit in silence again, but this time it's different, and I'm not entirely sure how. He's not confiding in me, not really.

But almost.

"Do you think she would care?" I finally say.

"Maybe she wouldn't have. But now it's been so long that it feels like a lie."

I go still at those words. "I can understand that." He scoffs, and I raise my eyebrows. "You don't think I felt that way about Tessa and *Weston Lark*?"

He considers that for a while, and I can see him wanting to reject it. But he can't, because it's really no different. I'm remembering the early days, the shame I felt for the way the night patrol had killed her parents, all the different ways I tried to figure out a new path to make things better—and failed.

"She's so smart," Lochlan says, musing. "She can do better."

"Undoubtedly," I say.

"You're such an ass," he says, and he kicks my chair.

"Oh, were you talking about Karri? I was talking about Tessa." I give him a wicked look. "Though I'm not sure my response would change."

"Maybe we're meant to be stuck here. Sparing them both. A stupid forge worker who can't read, and the spoiled prince that everyone hates."

Ouch. He doesn't say it with rancor, but the words sting more than they should.

"A lucky turn for Kandala then," I say, "seeing as there's currently a dire shortage of the latter."

Lochlan gives a sharp bark of laughter like I've truly surprised him, but then his eyes narrow and he gives me a rueful glance. "I didn't expect you to ask for his help," he says.

"Hmm?"

"Ford Cheeke."

"Ah. Tessa once told me that I turn everyone I meet into an adversary, so I'm trying to change that."

"Well, your 'plan' is full of holes."

Lord. I don't need him to tell me that. I look away.

He's still studying me. "I can't believe you convinced Crane that you were *pretending* to be Prince Corrick."

"Should I have told him *you* were Prince Corrick?"

"No, I just wish you'd given me some warning. It's no wonder you were able to run in the Wilds as an outlaw for so long. You've got some balls, man."

This time I'm the one startled into laughter, and he grins.

But it's like we both realize we're smiling at the same time, because we sober immediately.

Lochlan says, "There's no way to be sure Rian will get us back. He could still trap you and hold you for ransom."

I scrub my hands over my face. "And Oren could still kill me. The fever sickness could still decimate Kandala. Rebels could still swarm the Royal Sector and kill my brother while I'm gone. Shall we list *everything* that could go wrong?"

"All this food could be poisoned." He shoves the basket in my direction. "Have a pastry."

I sigh and take one.

Lochlan does, too, then pours himself a glass of water. To my complete and utter surprise, he fills my glass as well.

"Don't get used to it," he says when he sees my look.

"I guarantee I will not." What a weird truce we've formed. I consider what he said about Karri, turning his words around in my head. "And you're not stupid. Your judgments have been sound at every turn."

He sets the glass on the table, then sighs. "Not *every* turn, Cory."

I scowl at the use of my nickname again. Of course he's going to ruin it.

He smiles a little deviously. "Sorry. I've been calling you that for so long it's not even on purpose anymore. Not every turn, *Your Highness*."

I roll my eyes. "I'm not sure your disdain is better."

"Do you really hate *Cory* that much?"

"No. Of course not. It's just—" I break off, digging my fingernail into the wood of the table.

It's just what my brother calls me.

That sounds so juvenile. But he's studying me curiously, so I quit squirming like a schoolboy and look at him. "No one ever calls me that but Harristan."

"No one?"

"My parents. When I was a boy. But not often. And *never* publicly." I pause. "And Tessa, too, sometimes. But that's . . . that's not the same." I feel a hint of warmth crawl up my neck at the memory of her quiet voice in those intimate moments. "Even still, it's quite rare."

Lochlan says nothing else. His eyes are picking me apart. I feel like a prisoner in the Hold, tense under his scrutiny, and it makes me keep talking.

"For what it's worth," I say evenly, "I know how you must envision the life of the 'spoiled prince who everyone hates,' and certainly some of it may be correct. But my role as King's Justice hasn't exactly inspired close friends and fond nicknames."

As soon as the words are out of my mouth, I expect him to mock me, because it sounds a little too pitiful, a little too self-indulgent, even for me.

But he doesn't mock me. Instead he simply says, "I can tell."

Somehow that's worse, and I frown—especially since he didn't say it cruelly.

"But not *everyone* hates you," he continues. He looks at the hearth as if this conversation is making him equally uncomfortable. "And you're not even all that spoiled. I expected you to be a huge pain in the ass on the ship, but you weren't. I thought you'd be ranting day and night about the food, or the beds, or the coarse talk from the sailors—"

"Oh, please. I spend hours in the Hold. The sailors can't come *close* to the language hurled at me on a daily basis. You had a few choice phrases yourself."

"I remember."

"I'm certain you do."

Our voices have gone a bit sharp, and our gazes match. The reminder of the way we met has shifted the conversation again, and I wish I hadn't mentioned it.

"That day you broke my arm," he says, "I thought you'd have the guards kill me right there. That consul was telling you to."

I remember that.

I want him dead, Allisander was saying.

He will be, I said. *But I can't kill him twice.*

"It was his mistake to get so close," I say. "I only broke your arm to get you to stop."

That's true, but his eyes are piercing like he doesn't fully believe me. Our conversation has twisted and turned in a way that keeps making me want to squirm. The air between us goes so silent for so long that I can hear people out on the street, vendors calling their wares.

When Lochlan finally speaks, his voice is very quiet. "You want to know what I think? On the day we escaped your execution, I think you wanted it to happen. I think you were relieved."

It's not at all what I expected him to say, and my heart thumps. "No."

He leans in. "You're *lying*."

I wonder if he wants me to be lying. I hold his eyes, and I keep my voice even. "I'm not."

"I saw you with Ford. *I saw you*. You don't want to do any of this." He shifts closer. "When we captured you and Tessa in the Wilds, you kept telling me all the times you *wished* you had killed me. But every single time, you didn't do it."

My mood darkens at the reminder. Lochlan kept jabbing me with a crossbow, threatening her life every time he threatened mine. "Oh, I wanted to then, I promise you."

"But you didn't kill me. You were relieved that we got away. You wanted us to escape. You *traitor*."

"Can I kill you right now?"

"Admit it!"

"I can't, because it's untrue."

He slaps the table. "You were! You wanted us to escape so you wouldn't have to do your job! Admit it."

"No! Because you're wrong!" I shout. "Where's the relief, Lochlan? Where? You think Sallister was bad after you punched him in the face? You should have heard him *after* you escaped. You should have heard *all* of them! I'm the King's Justice. Your escape wasn't a relief at all! It meant I was going to have to hunt you down. It meant I was going to have to order your death *again*." This time I slap the table. "After your calls for revolution, they wanted me to make it *worse*."

He jerks back like I've hit him.

"You know it, too," I growl. "Or was there some *other* spoiled prince you were going to execute on the night you captured me?"

His eyes are dark and haunted in the afternoon shadows.

"You think I didn't want to release every single prisoner in the Hold? I *couldn't*. There's never any relief for me," I snap. "Not ever."

"There's never any relief for us either!"

"I know!" I cry. "You don't think I know? Why do you think I was Weston Lark at *all*?"

His chest is rising and falling rapidly. So is mine.

I force my hands to unclench, and when I can speak again, my voice is deadly quiet. "I truly care about the people of Kandala. I try to be as fair as I can. I try to be *just*. You were already sentenced to death for smuggling. That's why I didn't retaliate for what you did to Sallister. That's why I don't care if people swear at me in the Hold. The cruelty is an illusion. Because you're right: I don't want to do any of it." I pause. "But who else is there?"

It's a rhetorical question, but he runs a hand across his jaw and seems to consider it anyway. There's no good answer, though, and he seems to come to the same realization. We fall into silence again, but any amicability between us seems to have evaporated. Maybe it can never really exist for very long. We'll tolerate each other until we manage to get out of here, and then that will be it.

But he drains his glass and sits back in his chair. When he speaks, his voice is very low, quiet and rough. "My little brother used to call me Lolly."

I look over. "You have a brother?"

"I used to."

Oh. I clamp my mouth shut.

"When we were little, he couldn't say *Lochlan*, so he started with La-La, which quickly turned into Lolly. He never stopped, even when it would make me crazy. Even when we were *way* too old for it. It sounds like a name you'd give a dog." Lochlan rolls his eyes, but there's fondness in his voice. He shrugs a little. "He died a year ago. He was nineteen. He and Da got the fever sickness, and they managed for a few days, until they just couldn't breathe any-more." He pauses. "I was working in the southern part of Steel City then. My mother sent word, but I didn't make it home in time. When Ma caught it, she went like that." He snaps his fingers. "Maybe that was a mercy. I don't know."

I've heard hundreds of stories like this all over Kandala. Maybe thousands.

I inhale to say that I'm sorry for his loss, but Lochlan's eyes flash to mine.

"*Don't* say you're sorry," he says sharply.

"I won't say it." I pause, and the weight of loss is thick in the air. "But I am. I lost my parents, too. A quick death might be a mercy on the dying, but it's usually not for anyone else."

He's quiet for a moment after that, and he looks into the hearth. "They probably would have gone a lot quicker, but I heard they might have been getting extra medicine from some outlaws who'd make the rounds through the Wilds."

My head snaps around.

Lochlan puts up a hand. "Don't. I don't know if it was you. I don't know if I *want* to know if it was you."

I swallow. "Fine."

"I only told you because . . . because I didn't know that. About Cory. I'll stop."

As soon as he says it, I feel a jolt in my heart, and I'm not sure what's causing it. Maybe it's about us both missing our brothers. Our families. Or maybe it's the way Lochlan said *I can tell* when I told him I don't have a close circle of friends.

Maybe it's the thought that I might have been helping his family as Weston Lark—only to lock him up for execution as Prince Corrick.

Maybe it's all of it.

Before I can help myself, I say, "You don't have to stop. I've gotten used to it, too."

Then I look at the table and dig my fingernail into the wood again because I don't want to meet his eyes. Everything inside me feels jangled up and uncertain, but I've already been too vulnerable. I need to lock these emotions away, but we've gone in too many directions, and I'm not sure how anymore.

The air between us is so heavy, and Lochlan must also feel the need to focus on something else, because he reaches for the piece of paper with the names on it. He slides it back in front of himself, then runs a finger over Karri's name again. He's frowning at the letters as if he's trying to read through sheer force of will.

"If the letters all make different sounds," he says cautiously, "then . . . then why do *Karri* and *Corrick* start differently?"

He's really not stupid at all. "Sometimes they make the same sounds." I clear my throat, glad for a new task. "Here, we should start with shorter words."

I shift my chair forward and pick up the fountain pen again. My heart is still thumping, but on a new piece of paper, I write *CAT*.

As if he can see through me, Lochlan says, "I know you're still worried about Rian. You might give him Oren Crane, but he could turn on you anyway. He could use you against your brother."

Those words force me still, because aside from losing Tessa, this is truly my greatest fear. Harristan would give him anything he asked for.

Lochlan is quiet for a moment. "I don't trust him either. We might hate each other, but I've got your back."

I don't hate you anymore, I think—but I can't say it.

Instead, I say, "Rian could have an army."

He shrugs a little. "Well, I've faced an army before." He holds out a hand. "Still breathing, Cory."

I give him a nod. "Still breathing."

Then I reach out and clasp his hand.

CHAPTER TWENTY-TWO

Tessa

The morning after we return from Rian's palace, Erik doesn't wake at sunrise, which takes me by surprise. Now that we have animals, there are chores to be done, so I occupy myself with feeding them and cleaning out the pens and stalls, then sweeping the small barn free of cobwebs. Once the animals are taken care of, Erik is still sleeping, so I set a hay bale against the wall of the barn and practice with a new dagger the way he showed me. I remember the way Rian grabbed my arm, and I swing hard each time, trying to keep my aim straight, my movement swift.

By the time I'm done, my shoulder aches, so I slip back into the house to start sorting through everything Rian provided, using one of the spare bedrooms to organize my apothecary supplies. I lay out bottles and instruments and my books and any herbs I have from the ship, then grind and pour and measure anything that might be useful when we head into town tomorrow. Within a few hours, I have a rather comprehensive kit assembled, but now it's midday and there's still been no sign of Erik.

I remember him wincing in the wagon last night and wonder if his wound was worse than he was telling me.

Men. Worry might be twisting in my gut, but I scowl anyway. I wash up from my work, then peek into his sleeping quarters, where he's snoring in the sunlight.

Well, at least I know he's still breathing.

I don't want to disturb him, but he hasn't slept this late since we arrived, and it doesn't seem typical. We were gone quite a long time yesterday, and I creep into the room, studying him, trying to determine if his coloring looks off, or whether his skin looks clammy.

No and no.

But still. He could have developed an infection. A fever could make him sleep like this. He's shirtless, but his blankets cover his waist, so I can't tell if his wound has started seeping or if the bandages are still in place. I move closer, wondering if I can touch him without waking him.

Someone bangs at the front door to the house, and I jump and give a little yip—but that's nothing compared to the way Erik startles, throwing blankets aside and pulling a dagger from under his pillow.

"Erik!" I cry, stumbling back. "It's just me!"

He blinks at me, freezing in place.

Someone pounds at the door again, but it's abruptly cut off.

Erik straightens. "Then who's that?"

A woman's muffled voice is audible from outside. "Ellmo!" she's saying sharply. "Stop pounding on the door like that. They could be out on the water."

The boy's little voice comes back at once. "Do you think we could take the honey if they're not here?"

"We're here!" I yell. "I'll be right out."

Erik gives me a withering glance, then sighs. "Allow me a few minutes to get dressed, Miss Tessa." But then he frowns. "Why were you in here?"

I'm already by the door to his quarters, and I can feel heat in my cheeks. "I was worried about you. It's late."

He looks at the sunlight streaming through the window and grimaces. "Forgive me. The animals need to be fed—"

"I took care of it. You needed the sleep. I was worried you had a fever."

He shakes his head. "I'm all right. Just tired."

Ellmo shouts, "Are you sure you're in there, Miss Tessa?" before Olive hushes him.

Erik glares, but he rubs a hand over his face. "I'll be out in a moment. Tell that little demon I'll soak him in honey if he bangs on the door like that again."

"I'm pretty sure you'll tell him yourself."

When I get to the door, I'm surprised to find Olive with a basket, and Ellmo peering in the windows. I invite them both inside.

"You don't need to peek," I tell him. "You were already inside last night."

"But it was dark!" he says. "I didn't even get the toys you promised."

"They're in one of the bedrooms. You can go look. But don't bother Erik. He's getting dressed, and he was ready to soak you in honey for waking him up."

He scampers off. It looks like Olive has a new bandage on her arm, so I say, "Was your wound bothering you?"

"Not at all. I checked it this morning and wanted to put a fresh bandage over it." She gives me a smile, then sets the basket on the table in the kitchen and begins unwrapping. "I know you got plenty of food from our *king*"—that disdainful tone again—"but I needed to make bread today, so I made an extra two loaves for you." Her cheeks turn a little pink. "A bit of an apology for shooting at you yesterday."

"You didn't have to do that! You already helped us unload."

"Well." She smiles. "I did." She hesitates. "I was also going to ask if you still planned to take the wagon back into the city."

I glance at the hallway. "Erik and I were going to go back to see about getting a goat," I say. "But I don't know if he feels rested enough for that."

I tried not to let any worry into my voice, but she frowns anyway. "Is he unwell?"

"He was injured on the journey here. He's been trying to hide it, but I know it pains him."

Olive nods. "I thought he was moving stiffly last night." Her voice drops. "A bad injury? You sound worried."

Her brown eyes stare into mine, and I study her across the table. We've only just met her, and despite how things turned out, she *was* shooting at us in the woods. But I keep thinking about the way she warned me about Rian. The way she keeps saying *our king*.

I don't know how much Erik would want me to say, but I sense that any admission of his injury would make him unhappy.

"It could have been a lot worse," I finally say, and I can read in her eyes that she knows I'm hedging. Between us, the loaves have been unwrapped, and they smell heavenly. "I'll get a knife. I'm sure he'll be hungry."

Ellmo's little voice comes from the next room. "I know I'm hungry, Mama!"

I laugh under my breath. "So we're feeding both the boys."

"We can all eat if you like," says Olive. She unwraps the rest of the cloth and pulls out a roll of cheese. "I brought cheese, too."

While I start to slice the loaves, she looks around the small kitchen, and her eyes light up a little. "Do you have matches for the stove? We could toast the bread." Her eyebrows go up. "And are those fresh tomatoes? *Our king* certainly does want your favor."

I find the small box of matches and light the stove, setting a cast-iron pan above the flame. "Well, he's not getting it."

She smiles. "I like you."

I like her, too. She has an easy manner that's hard to ignore.

Or maybe I just like that Rian seems to irritate her as much as he irritates me.

Erik's voice rumbles from the hallway. "That puzzle is far too hard for a five-year-old."

"I'm seven!" Ellmo cries.

Olive rolls her eyes and reaches for the small jar of lard on the counter. "Don't hold it against me, but I haven't decided about your husband yet."

I nearly knock the pan right off the stove. "My *what*?"

She looks at me in surprise. "Oh. I'm sorry. I assumed you were married."

"No! We're—we're—"

I have no idea how to finish that. *Friends* would be true, but still feels awkward.

Olive gives me a look. "But you're a couple, yes? You're sharing a house." She raises an eyebrow. "It sounded like you were in the bedroom together."

My cheeks surge with heat. "What? No! I—it's—"

Erik chooses that moment to walk into the kitchen in nothing but his trousers, with his tunic in one hand. He must have shaved, because his face is a little damp, a few droplets still clinging to his chest. We've been sharing the house, and I've changed his bandage several times now, so it's not like I haven't caught a glimpse of him without a shirt, but I'm suddenly aware of . . . of what this looks like. Not to mention the cords of muscle down his arms. The sheer breadth of his shoulders.

"Why are you both staring at me?" he says.

I jerk my eyes away and turn back toward the stove—but Olive jerks *her* gaze in the opposite direction and nearly walks right into me with the knife in her hand. I all but fall into the stove. The pan rattles heavily.

Erik clears his throat. "As flattering as this is, please don't kill yourselves because I walked in here without a shirt on. Miss Tessa, I do think the poultice needs changing."

That steals any heat from my cheeks, and I look back at him. The bandage is stained, like his wound seeped during the night. The skin surrounding the bandage has reddened. My earlier concern returns.

Olive bumps my shoulder. "Go see to your not-husband," she murmurs, and I realize *her* cheeks are still pink. "I'll make lunch."

"He's not my anything!" I whisper back. "He calls me Miss Tessa!"

"Oh, I thought that was a Kandalan thing. I found it endearing."

Erik says, "You two know I can hear you, right?"

I heave a sigh. "I'll get my supplies." I cut a glance at Erik. "But he's more like an annoying big brother than anything else."

While she cooks, I have Erik sit in one of the chairs. When I pull the bandage free, he hisses, as it brings blood and a thin layer of pus with it. The surrounding skin is swollen and inflamed.

He must read my face before I can say anything. "Not good?"

I put a hand against his forehead. I thought his face was damp from shaving, but now that I'm sitting this close to him, I wonder if he's sweating—but it's also a warm day. "I'm worried it's infected. Do you feel like you have a fever?"

"No."

I give him a look, but he looks right back at me, adding flatly, "I can be more annoying about it if I need to be."

"Look," I say. "Olive thought you were my *husband*."

"I'm ten years older than you!" he exclaims.

The pan on the stove sizzles as Olive adds some buttered bread. "It's not *that* dramatic a difference. My father and mother were *fifteen* years apart."

I'm not really listening to them. I'm peering at his abdomen again. The stab wound isn't healing well at all. Puncture wounds are always so tricky. I remember tracing Corrick's scars in the lantern-lit darkness on the ship, hearing him tell me about the smugglers who'd attacked him. He had a stab wound similar to this, too.

I thought that one was going to do me in, he said. *Took ages to heal.*

"It's bad, isn't it?"

Erik's voice calls me back, and I blink, then look up. He's not teasing me anymore, and his eyes hold mine.

"It's not great," I say. "Spending half the day walking and then unloading a wagon probably didn't help." I chew at my lip, thinking of the way he was pulling dusty tarps off the rowboats, too. I'm better with elixirs and creams and poultices. Easing pain. Providing remedies for fevers and coughs. I don't have much experience with long-term injuries like this, and I'm going to have to go back through my books to see what my father's old notes say. I'm worried we might need to cut the infection away, but I don't know if it's gone that far yet.

"I can make another poultice, but if I can trust you to lie down for a while"—I fix him with a glare—"I think you should leave it to the air and let the infection dry out a bit. I'm worried it's beginning to spread."

"Do you have spirits?" Olive says, adding cheese to the bread. "Whiskey? Anything stronger? It might be better to cut out the infection and rinse it with that first."

Erik stares at her. "And then what? Set myself on fire?"

Ellmo appears in the doorway, and he gasps, but not with horror. "Can I watch?"

Olive doesn't turn away from the stove. "It's what the surgeons had to do after the war." She pauses. "There were a lot of wounds like that."

Erik meets my eyes, and he looks like he's expecting me to find her suggestion insane—but when I obviously don't, he swallows.

"What do you think?" he says to me, his voice low.

"I think you're on the edge of infection spreading, if it hasn't already." I hesitate. "I don't know what kind of healers they have left here. You saw the citadel. If the infection spreads quickly, you could be dead in days."

He runs a hand across his face and swears. "Well, *damn*, Miss Tessa."

Ellmo lights up and repeats it immediately. Erik looks like he's going to growl at the boy, but Olive turns from the stove.

"Ellmo," she says. "I need exactly one hundred white shells from the beach to clean the pan after lunch. If you bring me too many, I'll make you go fetch them again. Go now, or your food will be cold."

He scurries out so quickly that the door slams behind him. Olive takes the pan off the heat, then turns to us. "He'll be gone for a while. He gets a bit mixed up once he gets past the sixties."

"You need shells to clean the pan?" I say.

"No, but he needed a task." She dries her hands on a towel, then busies herself with arranging the food on some plates.

Erik is still looking at me. "Have you done it?" he says.

I hesitate, then bite my lip. "No?"

His eyes just about bug out of his head, so I rush on, "I'm an apothecary, not a surgeon! I watched my father do it a few times in the Wilds, though. And I've stitched up plenty of wounds. I can be quick."

"And I can help," says Olive. "I've watched a lot more than a few times."

He swears again. "Fine. There's plenty of liquor in the chests from the ship. Get two bottles."

"Two?"

"Yeah," he says roughly. "One is for me."

—◆—

Despite my promise, I'm not quick.

The stab wound is far deeper than I thought, and it seems I cut pus and inflamed skin away forever. In the beginning, Erik is stoic and nearly silent, but as time wears on, he's cursing Rian and his crew, cursing Prince Corrick, cursing me and Olive—especially every time I flush the wound with alcohol. He sweats through his clothes twice over, and a few times I've worried we should tie him down, but Olive always draws him back, wiping away sweat or telling him a story or being sharp when he needs a distraction from the pain. She also pours a good dose of liquor down his throat when he needs it. When Ellmo returned with a hundred shells, Olive told him to take his lunch to "keep watch" by the docks.

She's quick thinking and kind, despite her brusqueness, and I really like her. Working with her is as easy as working with Karri, and it's odd that I only met her a day ago. I feel as though I've known her for far longer.

Eventually, Erik's blood runs bright red, and there's no sign of pus or mottled skin. His eyes have gone heavy-lidded, and Olive drags a cloth across his forehead.

Erik shakes his head. "No . . . no more," he says, and his words slur together. "No more, Misssss Tesssssa."

"No more," I agree, packing clean muslin around the wound and binding it in place. "You can rest now."

"It looks much better," Olive says to me quietly. "You did a good job."

"I'm glad you were here," I say, then hesitate. "I really don't think he could've gone much longer."

"Probably not. But he'll be no good for the rest of the day." Olive pats him on the cheek and begins to move away. "Be a good soldier and don't wet the bed."

"I'm not a soldier." He reaches out and catches her hand loosely. "Why don't you be a good nurse and stay awhile?"

Olive giggles and we exchange a glance. "Well now," she says. "I suppose he's *not* your husband."

"I'm not anyone's husband," he slurs, sounding aggrieved. He doesn't let go of her hand. "But you're very pretty. Maybe one day I could be *your*—"

"That's *enough*, Erik," I say, taking hold of his hand and pulling him free. "You can say anything you want when you've got your wits about you." I set his hand back on the bed, and his eyes flicker closed.

But just as I'm about to shut the door, his voice calls me back. "Stay close, Miss Tessa."

I pause with my hand on the frame. "I will."

"I promised him I would keep you safe, too. I have to keep one promise."

For a breath of time, I can't move. I swallow past the tightness in my throat. "You will," I say. "I'll be right here."

Back in the kitchen, Olive unwraps the cheese sandwiches, which are still a bit warm, while I rinse my hands in the basin. Then she lights a fire under the kettle and finds the small sack of coffee that Rian gave me yesterday. Again, there's a weird comfort to her presence. We're both quiet, and I know she heard what he said. Despite what we just did, and despite the ease we had in working together, I *don't* know her very well at all, and I don't know how much to say about it.

The silence is too much to bear, though, especially while I'm rinsing Erik's blood and sweat off my skin. "Thank you," I say. "I really don't think I would've been able to do that alone."

"You don't have to thank me." She lifts her bandaged arm. "I owed you."

"That was nowhere near the same."

"Still. I didn't mind." She hesitates. "He seems like a decent man."

It's the first time she hasn't groused about him riling Ellmo, so I smile. "He is. He's one of the king's personal guards. Back in Kandala."

"Maybe that's why I thought he was your husband. He's very protective."

The end of that sentence feels like there's more to be said, and I wait for her to say it . . . but she doesn't. I stare at my food, and she stares at hers, and eventually the kettle whistles. Olive sets to making coffee, and I'm glad, because I've only seen Rian do it on the ship.

But while she does it, my throat tightens as I think of what Erik said.

I promised him I would keep you safe.

I don't know if he meant Corrick or Harristan. Maybe it doesn't matter.

Maybe it wasn't even a real promise. Maybe it's just one he made in his heart.

I have to press a hand over my own to ease the ache. It doesn't help.

"You don't have to tell me," Olive says quietly. She pours powdered milk into the coffee and adds a twist of the honey that Ellmo envies, then slides a cup in front of me. "I know you just met me. But I know your guard isn't the only one with a deep wound."

The pain in my chest goes nowhere. I have to close my eyes. I don't even know if I can speak.

Oh, Corrick.

Maybe she can sense my agony, because instead of waiting for me to answer, Olive keeps talking. "*My* husband died in the war," she says. "Three years ago."

That's enough to startle my eyes open. "You had a husband?"

She nods and gives me half a smile. "Ellmo didn't get here himself, you know." The smile slips off her face, and she continues, "I didn't want him to fight, but of course everyone had to fight. I begged Rian not to send Wyatt out on the water, and he swore it wasn't his choice, but . . ." She shrugs. "Maybe he was telling the truth, but I doubt it. Wyatt was a strong sailor. A good leader. And Rian does what he has to do." She runs a finger around the rim of her cup and shrugs. "He always has."

I'm staring at her now. Remembering how she said she didn't trust Rian either, how he might *mean well*—but he doesn't care who gets hurt. "You've known him for a long time?"

"I've known him since he was born." Her face twists. "Rian and I share a father." She scowls and takes a sip of her coffee. "And a horrific uncle. *Faithfulness* and *honor* don't seem to be qualities that run very clearly through the family tree."

My hand is frozen on my own cup. I can't stop staring. Corrick and I sat at dinner with the king while Rian talked about the battles for the throne in Ostriary, how their king had dozens of siblings and illegitimate children all squabbling over who should rule after the king's death.

Olive runs a finger around her cup again. "I'm surprised Rian didn't tell you." She shrugs. "Then again, maybe he's forgotten I'm out here. That wouldn't surprise me either. He knows I've got nothing left to say to him."

"You're . . . you're a *princess*," I say.

She laughs a little. "Well. I suppose. Does it matter?"

"Rian told us everyone fought over the throne."

"Not everyone." She shrugs. "I didn't want it. Wyatt was happy to help defend Fairde—and when Rian was trying to save people, I was happy to help patch them up, just like I helped you. But when he started grappling for power . . ." She grimaces again. "I didn't like it. Everyone thinks he's a good man. And in a lot of ways, he is. But sometimes he uses that trust. That belief. That loyalty. He *hides* behind it. And I don't think many people see it."

I swallow thickly. "I saw it," I whisper. "Not at first—but eventually."

She smiles, but it's a sad smile. "That's always how it is, with him."

And maybe she's struck the core of the reason I feel this level of kinship with Olive, even when I shouldn't trust anyone at all. Maybe it's the understanding that someone else was fooled by Rian, even though he doesn't seem to be *trying* to fool anyone at all.

"I know," she says. "I heard it in your voice when you told me why you weren't in the palace at Tarrumor." She pauses. "When you said there were . . . *complications*."

My throat tightens again, and my eyes fill.

Complications.

Olive puts her hand over mine, and I blink, surprised to see that her eyes are full as well.

"You can tell me," she says again. "I'll listen."

"Corrick wasn't my husband," I say, and my voice breaks. "But I loved him." The tears spill over. "I loved him so much."

She comes around to me and wraps me up in her arms. Corrick and Erik would probably be warning me away, telling me to be on the lookout for a trap. But there's too much emotion in the air, and I can't look at every single person with so much cynicism. I just can't. Her arms tighten on my back, and I press my eyes into her shoulder, and I sob until I lose track of time.

At some point I run out of tears, and I lift my head. I feel wrung out.

On the counter beside me is a pile of grass and wildflowers, most of them with roots and dirt still clinging to them. I frown.

"From Ellmo," says Olive. "He came in and saw you crying."

My heart melts. "That is very sweet."

"He has his moments." She reaches for a kitchen cloth and blots at my face. "I'm *sure* you couldn't do that to the drunken lout who's probably going to need new bedding later. Do you feel better?"

I remember the way Erik seemed so uncomfortable with my tears in the rowboat. "I do, actually."

"Good." She hesitates. "Is it bad that I'm dying to hear about everything Rian did wrong?"

That makes me laugh through the last of my tears, and for the first time, my heart seems to settle, just the tiniest bit. I trust Erik, but this is a different kind of comfort, to share grief with someone who can understand it so acutely. "No. I'll tell you everything."

And I do.

CHAPTER TWENTY-THREE

Corrick

Now that *everyone* believes I'm Prince Corrick—whether in truth or playing a role—keeping track of my identity gets a lot easier. Lochlan and I have spent a day learning the streets of Silvesse, but at midnight, I'm able to walk right up to the door of the Harbor Station at nightfall and request an audience with Mr. Cheeke.

While we're waiting to be admitted, Lochlan leans close. "Lina and Mouse are in the alley."

I sigh. "Making sure we do as we're told, I'm sure."

Once we're inside, Ford Cheeke spares no time. He drops a piece of parchment on the table in front of me.

"Our king has responded," he says.

I pick up the paper.

Prince Corrick of Kandala is dead. Oren Crane is attempting to trick you to gain access to me.

My heart stalls in my chest. Maybe I really am an idiot, because this is not an outcome I envisioned.

Lochlan is staring at me rather desperately, and I realize he doesn't want to admit he can't read it.

"So Rian thinks I'm dead," I say to Ford, giving Lochlan the information he needs. "Your king is *wrong*. I proved my identity to you."

He spreads his hands. "We might be at an impasse. Short of delivering you to him directly, I'm unsure how to convince him otherwise."

I'm unsure, too. I stand there thinking, desperate for a new way.

I can't walk out of here a failure. I have no doubt Lina and Mouse are waiting to drown us in the harbor if Ford doesn't give us good news.

"What about Tessa?" Lochlan says quietly, and I look at him.

"Tessa?"

"What were you writing to her earlier? Could you convince *her*?"

I look back at Ford. "I need paper and a pen. I'm going to give you a message to send back."

He gives me the supplies, and I spend less than a minute writing. I fold the paper in half and hand it to him. "Send him that. Then he'll believe it's me."

He unfolds it and reads it, and his body gives a sharp jolt. His eyes flash to mine, and his cheeks flush. "I absolutely will not send this."

"Do you want me to kill you instead? Lina and Mouse are waiting in the alley."

He huffs a breath. "*Fine.* But you will have to return at nightfall, three days hence. I don't have a ship leaving for Fairde again until daybreak tomorrow."

Three days. My jaw twitches. We're so close that I can feel it.

But there's nothing I can do about the delay.

"Fine." I look at Lochlan. "We're done here."

Once we're outside again, he all but pokes me in the arm. "What on earth did you write that made him so angry?" he demands.

"I said, 'It's me, you arrogant prick.'"

"Nice opening."

"Thank you. Then I said, 'Tell Tessa I'm alive. Tell her I said, "Mind your mettle." Ask her if it's really me. You'll have your answer.'"

Lochlan glances at me. "You think that will work?"

As usual, I have a glimmer of hope that's matched by a wash of fear, because Rian could crumple this up and not tell Tessa anything at all. But I'm banking on his altruistic desire to help his people. At the end of the day, he still *needs* Kandala.

And I don't need to feed more worries to Lochlan.

So I give him a nod. "I know it will."

CHAPTER TWENTY-FOUR

Tessa

Erik sleeps all the way through to the next morning. I've checked on him twice, but his breathing is slower, and there's no sign of fever whatsoever. When I come back in from feeding the animals and practicing with the dagger, he's standing in the kitchen barefoot, blinking in the morning sunlight. He's shirtless again, but I'm gratified to see that there's no redness surrounding the bandage today, no sweat on his brow.

"You're awake!" I say in surprise.

He winces and rubs at his eyes. "Oh. Oh, that's loud."

His voice is so rough, and I bite my lip. "A bit hungover?" I whisper.

"Hmm. How much did I drink?"

"Olive was the one pouring it down your throat, but I think it was most of the bottle."

"The *whole* bottle?" he exclaims, but then he winces again.

"It was either that or tie you down."

He frowns. "Did I hurt you?"

"Not at all. You've got *quite* the vocabulary, though." I light the stove under the kettle and pull what's left of the loaf of bread from the basket on the counter. "I learned a few new phrases I'll be trying on Rian later. How do you feel? You look better."

He gestures to his waist. "*This* feels a lot better. The rest of me feels like I've been trampled by a horse."

"Excellent. I've already fed the animals. You can rest here today. Olive and I will head into town. She knows how to drive horses. Oh! You don't know yet. She's a princess."

He blinks at me. "Am I still drunk?" He runs a hand down his face. "What is happening."

I slice the bread, drizzle honey on it, and hand it to him. "She's one of Rian's many half siblings." I tell him everything Olive told me about her husband, how he died in the war. "She said he wasn't supposed to be in the midst of the fighting, but Rian ordered him in anyway."

Erik takes a bite of the food and processes that for a moment. "I can see that."

"Me too." I drizzle some honey for myself. "I told her we had made arrangements to be in town this morning, and she agreed to go with me if you were still recuperating. I think it's—"

"You shouldn't go alone, Miss Tessa." He's frowning now.

"I won't be alone. I just told you Olive will go with me."

"Make me another poultice. I'll ride with you."

"Absolutely not. I'm not risking another infection. Do you really want to go through that again? You need to stay here."

He sighs. Frowns.

But says nothing. His eyes are fixed on the counter now.

I reach out and put a hand over his. "If we're stuck here," I say quietly, "I need to be able to go places without a guard."

His eyes snap up, and he looks back at me steadily.

"And I really like Olive," I add.

"I know," he says. "I can tell." He pauses. "At the risk of being an annoying big brother again, it's good to see you smile."

Emotion catches in my throat and sticks there. "That's not annoying." I take a bite of the bread just to have something else to focus on.

But then I give him another smile. "I'm not the only one who likes Olive, you know."

"Oh no?"

"I'm trying to remember if you told her she was pretty before or *after* you asked her to marry you."

He chokes on his bread, and I have to pour him a glass of water.

I nod emphatically. "It was quite the proposal. You looked ready to pull her into your lap."

"Now you're being an annoying little sister." But his cheeks are reddening.

My eyebrows go up. "You *do* like her!"

He eats his bread, then licks a bit of honey off his thumb. "It's hard not to like a woman who knows how to handle a crossbow."

I smile. "To say nothing of the fact that she nearly knocked me into the stove when she saw you without a shirt on."

He grins, but his blush deepens.

"Well, well, well," I say. "How interesting. Now I'm going to feel bad that you only said she was pretty after she told *you* not to wet the bed."

The grin falls off his face. He swears under his breath.

My smile broadens. "Still want to go into town with us?"

He exhales heavily, defeated. "I'll see you when you get back."

—+—

The skies are heavy and overcast, but the heat of the day presses down anyway. I'm wearing another light dress, my hair pinned to my head, with the dagger strapped to my waist again, and even in the wagon, I'm already sweating. Olive made us coffee again before we left, and Erik didn't emerge from his bedroom *once*, which I found hilarious.

I don't realize Olive is concerned about his absence, though, until we're on the road and she asks about it.

"Was Erik still sleeping this morning? Should you have left him, do you think?"

"Oh," I say. "He's fine. He's just hiding from you."

"Hiding!"

I bite my lip and nod. "I might have told him some of the things he said when he was drunk."

"Drunk men say a *lot* of wild things. He was downright charismatic."

I giggle, but I notice that her cheeks are pink, too, so I bump her shoulder and say, "He's a good man."

Ellmo pops up in the wagon behind us. "Erik said he would take me out on the rowboats when he heals. Do you think that will be tomorrow?"

"When did he say that?" Olive says.

"When you were getting the horses ready."

"It'll be a bit longer than *tomorrow*," I say. "Maybe a few weeks."

But as soon as I say the words, the length of time drives home that we really are stuck here. That Corrick is dead. My breath catches.

Olive reaches out and squeezes my hand.

I look over in surprise.

She's looking at the road, but she gives me a nod. "I remember," she says quietly. "The loss hits you over and over again, and always when you least expect it."

That helps me sniff back the tears before they can form. "Yes," I say.

She squeezes my hand one more time, then takes up the reins again.

"I'm really glad I met you," I say.

She smiles. "Even though I was shooting at you?"

"That might be my favorite part." I give her a sly glance. "Erik's too. He said it's hard not to like a woman who can handle a crossbow."

"Did he!"

I nod.

She smiles, and she's still blushing. But then she frowns. "Well, it's nice to be fancied, but he'll be wanting to return to Kandala. He's duty bound to your king, I'm sure."

"Well, *your* king is in no hurry to make that happen."

"You might think that, but Rian will do whatever he can to get access to steel, so he'll find a way back before long. I'm in no hurry to have my heart broken by a guardsman sworn to another country."

There's a note of finality to *that*, so I let it go.

She glances at the crates in the wagon. "You brought a lot of supplies. Do you expect a lot of people?"

It's my turn to blush. "I really don't know *what* to expect. I told that boy Henry to have people come if they needed an apothecary, but I know that a lot of people here don't trust Kandala. So maybe we won't need it all. I just . . . I need to do *something.* Maybe that's silly."

"It's not silly." Olive hesitates, and she keeps her eyes on the road again. "It makes me feel guilty."

"Guilty! Why?"

She shrugs a little. "After the war . . . after Wyatt . . . I was so resentful of Rian, of Oren, of all the fighting, really. I just wanted to be . . . away. I haven't left my house much. I haven't done anything for the people. And you aren't even from here, and you're already trying to help."

"Well, we'll see," I say. "Maybe I won't be helping anyone at all. I might have packed all these crates for nothing."

Olive clucks to the horses to pick up the pace. "If so, we'll go back to the house and make more cheese sandwiches."

Ellmo's ears perk up. "Can we do that now?"

But then we crest the hill, and the little village Erik and I found the other day comes into view. Dozens of people have gathered near the little food stand where we met Henry. No, *hundreds* of people. They're everywhere. Some are on crutches, some have arms bound in a sling. There are a lot of people in the shade, leaning against trees or buildings, while other people tend to them. When they spot the wagon, many of them send up a cheer.

I stare. "I . . . don't think I brought too much."

Olive shakes her head. "I don't think you brought enough."

———◆———

We work for hours, sweating in the sun. I barely find a spare moment to eat or drink, because it seems that the line of people is neverending. I hear stories of the war, of hunger, of desperation. Some people are simply ill, while others have more serious, lingering injuries. I'm glad I got practice on Erik's infection, because similar wounds are common, and my dress is stained with blood and tears before long. I wish *I* had a bottle of whiskey to drink.

Olive is right—I didn't bring enough supplies to treat everyone, and when I run out, I begin making a list of names and ailments so I know what else I need to make so I can return with it tomorrow.

I am surprised to discover that almost everyone knows Olive. After the way she talked about hiding herself away after her husband died, I expected them to treat her like a stranger, too, but everyone knows her by name.

As I'm wrapping gauze around an old woman's forearm from a burn, she says, "It's so good to see Livvy helping you. She's been cooped up for far too long. Such a shame about her poor Wyatt."

I nod. "She's becoming a good friend."

"He wanted her to take the throne, you know. We would have supported her all the way. But she was so sad after her husband was gone."

My hands go still on the gauze. "Rian wanted her to take the throne?"

"What? No. Wyatt. He was a good man for her." She winces a little when I tie off the bandage. "Redstone is a fighter, and he's kept us safe. But we didn't want to fight. I'm glad it's over."

I stare at her. This is the first time someone other than Olive has described Rian in this way, without the usual adoration. I want to ask her more, but she glances to her left and says, "I've kept you too long. There are so many more people." She touches her fingers to her heart, then kisses them. "You have my thanks, dear. A lot of us were worried this was a trap, because we remember what Kandala did, but when we saw you with Livvy, we knew it was all right."

Before I can say anything to that, she's gone, and I'm on to the next person.

By the time night falls, I want to sleep in the wagon. Olive looks the same.

"Maybe Ellmo should drive us back," I say to her.

I expect him to give me a saucy response, but then I realize he's sound asleep in the back, curled up on the rolls of muslin beside my empty crates.

Olive and I lean on each other on the way back to the house, and I think about the day, about missing my friend Karri, about my longing for Corrick and the hole in my heart that aches with every beat. But Erik was right—I needed to move. I'm glad that I did.

When we finally arrive at the house, though, Erik is sitting in front of the barn, a lit lantern on the bench beside him. As soon as he sees us, he's on his feet. The lantern lights up his face, and I can tell he's unhappy.

"What's wrong?" I say. "Are you unwell? What happened?"

"What's wrong?" he demands. "What's *wrong*? You've been gone for more than twelve hours. I was ready to saddle one of the horses, and this injury be damned."

Olive and I exchange a glance, then climb down from the wagon.

Erik isn't done. "It's well past nightfall. How could the two of you even see on the road? What if you'd encountered thieves? I *knew* I should have gone with—"

He stops short as Olive steps in front of him and takes hold of his shirt. She rises up on her toes and kisses him on the cheek. "Thank you for your concern. We won't worry you again."

Then she pats him on the arm and moves away.

Erik just stands there, holding the lantern. The edge falls out of his voice. "I . . . well . . ." He runs a hand over the back of his neck and clears his throat.

"Come on, Ellmo," says Olive, pulling her sleepy son out of the wagon. "Time to go home."

"Thank you for your help today," I call.

She smiles broadly. "I can't wait to do it again tomorrow. I'll come at sunrise to help you prepare your tinctures."

Then she disappears into the shadows.

I stop beside Erik, who's staring after her. "Close your mouth," I whisper.

He clamps it shut. The look he gives me is aggrieved.

I smile. "She'll be back in the morning."

That chases the dark look out of his eyes. He grins. "I heard."

I cluck to the horses, to lead them into the barn so I can remove their harnesses. But then I remember what she said, so I stop and look back at him. She's already well away into the trees now, but I keep my voice low so there's no danger of her hearing me.

"She doesn't want her heart broken by a man whose only goal is to leave."

He nods, sobering. "Noted, Miss Tessa." He pauses. "I told you before. I don't give anyone a reason to cry."

His voice is gentle when he says it, but there's still something sad about it, and I remember the way he described his life before. Sworn to the king, so he kept his heart tightly tethered. Everyone in Kandala hid so much: what they wanted, what they felt, who they really were.

It makes me regret saying anything at all.

CHAPTER TWENTY-FIVE

Tessa

Our days fall into a busy rhythm. Olive and Ellmo arrive at dawn, and we eat and prepare our medicines and supplies for the day. Then we head out in the wagon as early as we can, trying to beat the heat of the day. By the third day, Ellmo begs to stay behind, and to my absolute shock, Erik tells him he can remain at the house with him—so Olive and I head out on our own.

We go farther west today, and I can see more of the damaged bridge from here.

"I see why Rian is so desperate for steel," I say.

Olive nods. "There used to be a lot of active trade between the islands, but it's harder now, because everything needs to be transported by ship—and a lot of ships were damaged in the war. Oren has six or seven ships docked offshore in Silvesse, but he keeps them well manned, and of course he won't put them to the good of the people. We're rebuilding as quickly as we can, but it all takes time."

"Can we take a boat to the other islands?" I say. "I don't mind helping other people if they need it."

Olive hesitates. "For that, you might want to talk to Rian. I don't know how active Oren has been in these waters. You said you were attacked between Silvesse and Fairde?"

My heart stutters. *Of course.*

"Right," I say. "I wasn't thinking. I don't know where it was." I fight to remember the name of where we were when Oren Crane's ships attacked, but it's been too long, and too many things were going on.

Olive sighs. "I still can't quite believe Rian took his daughter. I know he's made promises for steel, but . . ." Her jaw tightens. "I'm surprised Oren doesn't have his head on a stake already."

"It's the *last* thing we expected to find on that ship. Corrick thought he might have been smuggling weapons or something of the sort."

She laughs a little humorlessly. "No, Rian will do whatever he needs to do, and then he'll convince you it was all for the good of mankind."

That sounds about right.

I study her, though. "You think Oren Crane will attack Rian?" I ask quietly.

She looks right back at me. "For taking his daughter? I think Oren will tear him apart in whatever fashion causes the most pain."

A shiver rolls through me. We've been working together for days, but we haven't talked about anything like . . . like *this*.

And I'm struck by the fact that it reminds me of the way I used to talk to Weston Lark about King Harristan and Prince Corrick, before I knew who Wes really was. I'm reminded of my conversation with Erik, about how our minds can change as we gain new information. Everyone here seems to love Rian, and I know he's working to rebuild Ostriary. His people told stories on the ship of how he risked himself to save them. Their loyalty was genuine.

Everyone seems to hate Oren, and maybe he really is vicious.

But Rian took his daughter—and now she's dead. Corrick and Lochlan and Kilbourne are dead, too.

Oren will tear him apart.

"Do you think Rian deserves it?" I say, and my voice sounds hollow.

As soon as I say the words, I remember a conversation with Wes, not long before I learned the truth about him.

Do you think they deserve it? I said. I was talking about the prisoners sentenced to die.

I think that very few people truly deserve what they get, he said. *For good or for bad.*

You only deserve good things, I told him—before I knew he was the prince I hated.

Before I knew he was only doing those things because he had a kingdom to protect.

I swallow.

Olive straightens her back and cracks the reins. "I can never decide."

Then we crest another hill, and we face another line of people who need our help.

—+—

The sun is beginning to set again when the crowd finally begins to dwindle. My dress clings to me, and tendrils of hair have escaped to stick to my face. After the first day, I cut the sleeves off my dresses, and my hours in the sun have brought up an even deeper tan to my skin than what I had on the ship, and I've discovered some blond streaks in my hair. In Kandala, Karri used to talk about how much she missed the warmth of Sunkeep, but I'm missing the cooler temperatures of the Royal Sector and the Wilds. A sheen of sweat gleams on my arms. I'm grateful when a middle-aged woman brings us both a bottle of some sugared tea. I've hardly had a chance to eat all day.

"Was it like this in Kandala?" Olive asks me. "Did you see so many people?"

"No," I say, thinking of my days working for Mistress Solomon. But then I reconsider, remembering my secret rounds with Wes. "Well, yes, but it was different. Not all at once. I had to treat them in secret."

"Secret!" she says in surprise.

I flush. "It's hard to explain."

Hoofbeats pound in the distance, and we snap our heads up. So do many of the people who still remain. There's an air of alarm, and I see hands grip tight to tools, a few mothers shooing their children back into houses. Even Olive takes a sharp breath and a quick look for Ellmo before remembering he's safe at the house with Erik.

Yes, the scars of war are still here, hidden behind the healing and rebuilding efforts.

A dozen horses crest the hill, and I'm shocked to discover that it's Rian and his people. The remaining crowd settles.

My pounding heart does not.

I recognize Gwyn and Sablo, but the other men with Rian seem to be guards. Rian's eyes find me at once, but he still has a hundred feet of ground to cover, and his entrance has generated a lot of attention. As they draw closer, people don't hesitate to approach him, offering greetings, patting his gleaming horse, smiling up at him. Someone laughs and hands him a giggling child, and Rian sets the little boy on the animal's withers in front of him.

"There now," I hear him say as they walk. "You hold the reins. Be gentle."

The people of Kandala would never be like this with the king. The guards would never allow it anyway. I try to imagine King Harristan walking among the people, and I can't even picture it.

But here, it's obvious that they really do love Rian—and the worst part is that it's obvious that he loves them back. He's just as genial in response, just as kind, listening to their stories and greetings and genuinely returning their affection.

I hate that he makes it so hard to . . . to simply *hate* him. I have to turn away and busy myself with putting away my things.

At my side, I realize Olive is doing the same thing.

We both look at each other in surprise.

"I can't watch the fawning," she whispers, and for the first time, I think I hear *her* voice crack. "It makes me remember Wyatt. Maybe that makes me weak."

I reach out and squeeze her hand. "I can't watch it either. Maybe we can *both* throw up on him today."

That startles a giggle out of her, and we share a more devious glance this time.

Eventually, the hoofbeats stop behind us, and a man clears his throat, and we have to turn around.

On horseback, Rian seems ten feet tall, especially backed by guards. They all block the sun and throw shadows over us both.

He must have given the boy back to his parents because he's alone on the horse now.

"Oh, hello," I say. "I couldn't see you past your admirers."

"Hello, Miss Cade. I've been all over the island looking for you." He doesn't smile. His eyes flick to Olive. "Livvy. You've finally decided to leave your house?"

"I finally had a reason to," she says. Her voice is as cool as mine—and his.

"I was surprised to find my nephew with the guardsman from Kandala."

"Oh, he's your nephew now?" she says. She presses a finger to her lips. "I'm not sure Ellmo even remembers who you are."

"That's not my fault," he says.

I realize this is going to dissolve into family drama, and he didn't tell me why he was looking for me. "Why have you been all over the island?" I say.

That snaps his attention back. "Because you weren't at home."

"I told you what I was going to do with the supplies you gave me."

He hesitates, and a little frown line appears between his eyebrows. In that flicker of time, I realize he didn't really expect me to help anyone at all.

Before he says anything, I fold my arms. "You like to think you're better than Corrick," I hiss, "but deep down, you're so much worse."

That hits him like a dagger, because thunderclouds roll through his eyes. "Do you really think so?"

"Calculating? Cynical? Manipulative?" I look at Olive. "Have I forgotten anything?"

She snorts. "Hypocritical?"

His eyes narrow. "Maybe I shouldn't have bothered coming to find you at all." He glances past us at the supplies we've obviously been using, at the people who are still dispersing. Some of the tension slips out of his expression. "But I am grateful for what you're doing. I don't mean to be cynical. You surprised me, that's all. I know how much you hate me." He hesitates, his eyes flicking to Olive. "Both of you."

Olive sighs and turns back to what she was doing. "What I think about you doesn't affect how I feel about the people of Ostriary."

"I know," he says, and he sounds genuine. "Which is why I'm grateful."

Those words hang in the air for a little while, until she finally turns and looks at him.

There is nothing friendly in her expression.

I want to reach out and squeeze her hand again, but it might be too much. I peer up at Rian. "You still haven't said *why* you were looking for me."

"I've received an interesting series of letters from the harbormaster in Silvesse." He hesitates. "It indicates that my uncle still believes his daughter is alive and I'm holding her prisoner. He's planning a rescue. If we could trick him into thinking we're holding her away from the palace, it could be an opportunity to trap him for good."

His uncle.

Oren Crane.

My heart pounds again. "Why are you telling me this?" I say. "What does it have to do with me?"

He looks back at me steadily, and he pulls a folded piece of parchment from his saddlebag. His hand grips it tight.

But then he says nothing.

Olive takes a step closer to him. "If you need her house, Rian, just say so."

I whip my head around. "What?"

"It's obvious that's why he's here. We're on the outcropping, and it's easily defensible. It keeps most of the island out of the line of cannon fire, too. If he stages this 'prison' at your house, they could surround Oren's ship in the cove and trap him without a problem."

Behind Rian, Sablo taps his chest, then nods. Gwyn says, "Plenty of trees for hiding, too."

Rian looks between all of them, then lets out a breath. He looks down at the parchment he was holding, then carefully folds it up and slips it back into his saddlebag.

"Yes," he says slowly, letting out a breath. "I want your house." He looks at Olive, and his voice drips with sarcasm. "And I'll need a decoy. Interested, Livvy?"

"Why don't you get one of your sycophants." She raises her eyebrows at the people behind him. "Are you busy, Gwyn?"

"I'll be busy taking care of Oren."

My heart trips and stumbles in my chest. "I'll do it," I say.

"Tessa!" says Olive.

Rian startles, too. "What? No."

"Why not?" I demand. "I'm the right age. I can't fight, but I can sit and look like a prisoner."

"Absolutely not."

Olive grabs my hand. Her eyes are piercing. "Tessa. You don't know what he's like. What he's done."

I look right back at her. "I do know what he's done." I turn my head and look at Sablo, who's missing a tongue. My eyes flick to Gwyn, whose little Anya was tortured. "I've heard a lot of stories about what he's done."

"This isn't why I came," Rian snaps.

"We don't need a decoy for Oren," says Gwyn. "We just need a location so we can lay a trap."

"You don't?" I demand. "You think he won't send a scout to make sure you really have a prisoner? You have *one* chance to get him, and you're not going to lay the most perfect trap you can?"

Rian is glaring at me, but that gets him. A muscle twitches in his jaw. "I don't need you. I have my own people."

"Why risk one of your own people?" I demand. "If I die, you lose nothing."

"And if I succeed?" he says. "You clearly want something."

"Yes," I say. "I want passage back to Kandala. If Oren is out of the way, there's nothing stopping you."

He considers this for a minute. Then he nods. "Done. I'll arrange it. Miss Cade, we'll see you in two days at dawn. Be ready."

CHAPTER TWENTY-SIX

Harristan

It's nightfall again, and I have more questions than I started the day with. I should be focusing on all the lies about colluding with Ostriary, but instead I'm fixated on the fact that consuls watched me send my brother off on a ship to fetch more medicine—and then they sent warships after him.

"You need to eat," Quint says quietly. He's sitting at the table with me, just like last night, and once again, loss and worry and heady emotion are filling the air.

Alice delivered stew half an hour ago, but I haven't touched it.

I stare into the bowl, at the congealing mass of beef and vegetables that have long since stopped steaming. I don't want to touch any of it. I push the bowl away.

Quint pushes it right back. "You haven't eaten since this morning," he presses.

Every muscle in my body is taut, and every breath I inhale feels like a battle. Forget eating. Forget *everything*. They tried to kill my brother. I long to find a horse and a crossbow and ride into the Royal Sector and shoot every consul I can find.

I'd be dead—or captured—before I made it through the gates.

"Sommer said the brigantines didn't return," Quint says. "Our sailors have never been able to navigate the rough seas southwest of Sunkeep, so there's no reason to assume they would suddenly be able to now. Captain Blakemore surely would have spotted brigantines long before they were a threat. Prince Corrick would know that *you* wouldn't send warships after him. I have to believe Captain Blakemore would be able to use his nautical skills to evade them in unfamiliar waters—and those ships were destroyed in the rough seas just like so many others."

I've had these thoughts, too. They feed me a few crumbs of hope.

But I want more than crumbs. I want more than the hope that warships simply sank.

"Is this more of your perpetual optimism?" I ask, and as soon as I say it, I see the tiniest flinch in his eyes.

I frown. "That's not condemnation. I envy it."

He's quiet for a minute. "If the consuls believed those warships were successful, they would have been bragging about their victory right along with the claims they've already made. There's a reason this hasn't been made public. They don't want to advertise failure."

Also true.

It still does little to ease the burn of anger and worry in my heart.

Is this my fate? To have everyone I love taken away from me?

"You said yesterday that you must be serving some kind of penance." I draw a heavy breath so my voice doesn't break. "Is this mine?"

"For what?"

"For everything." My fingers press into the table. "For everything I've done wrong."

He shifts closer, and his hand brushes over mine. "You've done nothing wrong."

I sent Corrick away. I swallow, and my throat is tight.

"Do you think he's dead?" I say.

It's the first time I've spoken these words, and they fall like a stone into a pond. The silence that follows is deafening, accented by the crack of the fire in the hearth.

The fact that he doesn't answer immediately makes me assume the worst. I look up and find Quint studying me in the candlelight.

My chest clenches. "You do," I whisper.

"No. I was debating whether to share a story. I thought it may provide some . . . hope."

I frown. "Then why were you debating?"

"Because it doesn't have a happy ending. It might not offer any hope at all."

My heart gives a lurch, and I want to refuse. But he hasn't left my side all day, and I keep thinking of the way his hand fell on my shoulder when we were questioning Sommer. He misses Corrick, too. I run a damp hand over the back of my neck and say, "Does it give *you* hope?"

"I won't know until you hear it."

I draw a long breath. "Very well. Go ahead."

"When my grandmother was young, she had a sister who disappeared in the woods when they were picking flowers. She said she was quite distraught, because she and her sister had been very close. Couldn't be consoled, really. Her mother, too. Her brother and her father had half the town come out to help look for the sister, and everyone kept reassuring them that they would find her. So many people were looking."

I study him. He already told me the story didn't have a happy ending. "They didn't find her?"

"They found her body. She'd been killed by a wild animal."

"Why on *earth* would this story give me any shred of hope?" I demand.

"Because my grandmother used to say she *knew*. She always said she could feel the loss in her heart. That's why she couldn't be consoled. She knew they wouldn't find her sister alive."

I stare at him, my breathing quick. Quint reaches out and touches the center of my chest, and it's so new that the warmth of his hand against my shirt takes me by surprise.

"Do you feel it?" he says, and his voice is so quiet, forcing me still. "You've known loss. In your heart, do you think he's gone?"

His eyes flicker with firelight and stare back at me, unflinching now. In this moment, I realize he's begging for the same kind of hope that I am.

I put a hand over his, holding his palm against my chest. My breath hitches, and I think of my brother. My brave brother, daring and reckless and downright incorrigible.

Cory.

I'd give anything for him to be here right now. I wish I'd never let him get on that ship. The thought feels selfish in so many ways.

As always, he'd be so much better at all of this.

But even though he's absent, I don't feel like he's *gone*.

As soon as I realize it, a certainty seems to fill my chest, so cool and sure that it chases the waiting tears away and settles my pounding heart. I can breathe for the first time in hours.

"No," I say steadily. "I don't."

Quint nods fiercely in agreement. "I don't either."

Maybe it's ridiculous, because this is the most nebulous hope, but it gives me the greatest relief. I take a deep breath.

"Thank you." I take his hand off my chest and clasp it between mine. Emotion is swelling in my heart. "Thank you." I draw his hand to my face and press it to my cheek, then kiss his palm. "*Thank you.*"

His hand softens against my jaw, his thumb stroking over my skin. "Yes, Your Majesty."

I go still. "Harristan," I whisper.

He shakes his head.

"*Still* a refusal?" I say. "Even now?"

That almost gets him. But then he sighs and draws back. "Well, you see, every time I consider it, I remember yet another moment and determine I simply could not possibly."

I turn those words around in my head and determine they're complete nonsense. "What does *that* mean?"

"I'll remember you facing down one of the consuls, or standing in front of the rebels in the sector while they threw fire at you, or negotiating with Tessa when you wanted to reclaim the palace. Censure me if you must, but I cannot call a man like that something as simple as his *name*."

He really is going to drive me insane. I have to run a hand over my jaw.

"Just this afternoon!" he exclaims. "You squared up to that brutish man with the beard who was refusing to bring food to Sommer. He was twice your size—"

I give him a withering look. "That's quite impossible."

"Please don't ruin my memory. He was possibly *three* times your size, and you—"

"That's enough, Palace Master."

My use of his title draws him up short again. "Ah. Is that how it will be now?" He pushes the bowl toward me again. "Very well. *Eat.*"

I still don't want to, but this time, I obey. The food has gone cold, but I consider how Leah Saeth spoke of her daughter begging for scraps while guards tormented them, and I don't complain. I think of Reed, who was probably hungry, too, and died proving his loyalty. And despite myself, I think of a bound Sommer trying to forage for chicken feed in the cold cellar. I shouldn't have any empathy for treasonous guards, but I do. I can't help it.

But I eat my cold stew. Quint sits with me the whole time.

He ate an hour ago, so he really doesn't need to. His little book sits on the table, but there isn't much light, so he's not flipping through notes either. He's quiet, watchful, not quite watching me, but not . . . *not* either. It shouldn't be different from the thousand other times we've sat at a table beside each other, but it is. Earlier, there were no walls between us, no barriers, but now an entire day has passed and I don't know how to proceed again. The idea of courtship is something I put so far from my mind that I never considered the mechanics of it.

Of all the reasons I wish for my brother's presence, this is an area where I could desperately use his counsel.

But he's not here, and I can't sit here in silence. Now that I'm not panicking over warships, it leaves too much room for new worries to crowd into my head.

"Has there been no word from Karri or the runners yet?" I say.

"No."

I frown. Jonas Beeching, the consul of Artis, was the closest, and also the likeliest ally. The fact that we haven't heard from *him* is concerning.

I try to shake it off, but thinking about Artis makes me think about the last time I saw my brother at the docks. "If Corrick survived the warships, he would suspect *something* is amiss in Kandala. He'd attempt to return quickly, don't you think?"

Quint nods. "If he returns with Captain Blakemore, they're walking right into a hornet's nest."

I mentally play that out in my head. We originally had no warning that Captain Blakemore's ship was arriving at port, because the *Dawn Chaser* had a Kandalan flag. Would Corrick sail under the same? That might give him an advantage—though the Ostrian king would no longer feel the need to send a spy.

Then again, if they were trailed by warships, I rather doubt the Ostrian king was happy about it. The man might send back his whole navy to attack Kandala. I remember what Captain Blakemore said about Kandala's history with Ostriary.

For one shining second, I want to leave it all to Consul Sallister and the others.

Go ahead, I think. *Enjoy ruling while the country is at war.*

But no. I could never do that to my people. Sallister would hand over the keys to the kingdom if it meant he got to hold on to his silver.

As always, there are too many variables, and there's simply no way to know when—or *if*, I think grimly, despite whatever I feel in my heart—Corrick will return.

But still, we should be cautious. I look at Quint. "If we don't have word from any of the runners within the next few days, we'll need to station people at the docks to listen for gossip. We need to hear if any unfamiliar ships are coming to port, if any brigantines set sail, if there's any talk at all of sailors from Ostriary. Let's talk to Violet. Maybe she can take some of the children for walks along the water."

Quint reaches for his book. "Yes, Your Majesty."

I watch him write that down, the firelight turning his hair gold. I think of the way he kept pushing the food in front of me, when he knew I hadn't eaten.

I think of the little flinch in his eyes when I spoke too sharply. How there must have been a thousand such moments between us that I never noticed—yet he stayed by my side through every single one.

My chest clenches. I wish I could undo them all.

His eyes flick up. I'm staring again.

I clear my throat and glance away. "I'm sure word has spread about the guards we killed. The consuls will use this to strengthen their claims. We need to undo the harms they're causing. I need my people back."

He nods. "Do you have a course of action?"

Little Ruby kept staring at me, her eyes so big. "Food," I say. "They're starving. We need to find a way to feed them." I hesitate, wondering if the men who wouldn't feed Sommer would be willing to risk their lives to feed guards who might be just as willing to kill them to get at me. "I'll need to talk to the people in the morning to convince them."

"You will. I have no doubt." He says this so offhandedly while he writes.

I watch, entranced. I simply cannot comprehend how he manages to be so kind and so vexing and so determined—and so optimistic.

He's the impressive one, truly.

"If I may," I begin, and his eyes flick up again, the pencil going still. My tongue stalls when his eyes meet mine, and the silence hangs between us for a moment.

"You may," he prompts.

It makes me blush and smile in spite of myself, and I try not to stumble over my words. "*Why* do you write everything down?" I say. "Your predecessors didn't." I frown a little, trying to remember. "At least . . . I don't think they did."

He closes the book and sets it on the table. "They may not have, but I find it suits my needs."

I study him, because he's said this in much the same way he brushed aside my questions about the list of dates in the front of the book. He's not lying, but he's not giving me the whole truth either.

I study him, curious now. "I sense I'm going to have to pry secrets from you, Palace Master."

He stares at me, implacable. I stare back.

He breaks in less than a minute, tossing down the pencil. "Very well." He sighs. "I'll deny you nothing, so I don't know why I bother trying. I'll have you know, it's not a flattering story. When I was young, I was quite the burden on my family. Couldn't stop talking, couldn't finish my chores, couldn't be trusted to do anything, really." He hesitates, then offers a little shrug. "Downright useless."

I frown. "No."

"Oh, but I was. My mother would send me to fetch a sack of flour, and I'd spend an hour arranging stones in the creek. My father would tell me to feed the chickens, and he'd find me weaving straw under the rabbit hutch, telling stories to random travelers. I had a sister who was perfect, worked right alongside my mother in the kitchen and never forgot a thing, so I always felt like a complete fool—which really only made things worse. My father grew so sick of it that they sent me to live with my aunt and uncle in Mosswell for a while, because *they* thought it was a matter of discipline—and so I endured a long, miserable year that made absolutely no difference. But the following summer, my father brought me home and said he'd hired me out to a miller down the lane who'd gone blind. He needed someone to read notices and bills and draft any new ones for customers. I'm sure my father expected I would do a poor job, but that the man wouldn't have any way to know the difference. Honestly, I was just glad to be out of my family's reach, so I went."

None of this story has gone anywhere I thought it would, and I'm not sure what to say.

Part of me wants to find his parents so I can lock them in the Hold. The darkest part of me wants to do worse.

But now I'm remembering that moment we sat on the porch, when I asked Quint if he had a family, if there was anyone he was missing.

How he said *no*.

"The man was older," Quint is saying, "and so kind, and when I saw all the papers and notices that he had waiting for me, I told him that I was unsuitable. No matter how badly I wanted to be away from my family, I wasn't going to swindle someone. His name was Pascal, and he asked if I could read and write, and I said I could. Despite everything else, I'd always had rather good pen-manship. But then he asked if I was honest and trustworthy, and I said I was, which was why I'd be unsuitable. I explained about the stones in the creek or forgetting the sack of flour. I told him about my aunt and uncle who'd make me sleep out in the cold or tie a rope around my mouth whenever I'd talk too much."

I draw a frustrated breath. "I hope you know I want to kill almost everyone in this story."

"It was a very long time ago, Your Majesty."

"How long?"

"Ten years? I was fourteen or fifteen or so. Pascal said as long as I was honest and could read and write, I would do, because the last person who'd tried to help him kept sneaking his coins, and he was worried he'd lose the mill. He said he didn't care how much I talked, because he couldn't see anymore, so listening to me gave him something to do. He gave me a ledger and a jar of pencils, and he told me to write down everything. No matter how big or small, everything. Every task, every duty, every single thought in my head if I wanted. He said I could read it back to him later and we would figure out what was most important. If people came to the mill, I was to write down the person's name, anything they said— *everything*, Your Majesty. Sometimes I would write down what they wore."

"This all sounds rather hellish."

He smiles. "Do you think so? I found it a bit freeing. Pascal said that this way it didn't matter if I forgot anything, because I could read it all back to him later. I wasn't perfect, especially not at first, because I'd write down that I saw a butterfly, or that the sun was very hot that day. But as I said, he was very kind, and very patient— and I did write down the things that mattered, too. We got on well. When the afternoons were quiet, he'd ask me to read off my notes, and I began to realize that writing things down actually helped me remember a great deal—instead of allowing me to forget. I found myself telling him everything that happened without needing to resort to my notebooks at all. Then the mill grew busier, and he hired a girl to help him tend the shop and the house. I was a bit frightened then, remembering my sister's perfection, thinking he was going to have me discharged. Instead, he told the girl to come to me for her duties. He said, 'Quint always knows every detail. You'll do whatever he tells you needs doing.'"

He pauses, and I can hear the weight in his voice, the importance of that moment. How much it meant to him, to finally feel valued. Before I can acknowledge it, he blinks and looks up. "Within a few years he wanted to retire, because he'd grown too old to work. By then he'd hired half a dozen more people. He was selling the mill, and I was worried I might end up with a boorish new employer, but Pascal's brother worked for the mill that supplied the Royal Sector. He'd heard that the Palace Master was aging and that King Lucas was urging him to take on some apprentices. Pascal encouraged me to apply, and his brother knew I'd done good work, so he provided a reference. I never thought I'd be considered, but here I am." He taps the book. "Writing things down."

"And here you are." I narrow my eyes. "With your boorish new employer."

Quint laughs, and it makes his eyes sparkle.

"Does Corrick know that story?" I say.

"He knows I worked in the mill before I came to the palace. But I've never shared the rest of it." He grimaces and looks away. "Not with anyone, really. As I said, it's not a flattering story."

"I disagree," I say. "Your determination and tenacity are rather inspiring."

"Well now." He blushes, though he seems pleased. "I shall add that to my treasure trove along with the knowledge that I am 'very pleasing to look at.'"

I grimace, then run a hand down my face. "I did say that, didn't I?"

He nods, then opens his book, lifting his pencil. "I should write this down." He speaks slowly, drawing out each syllable as he writes. "Tenacious . . . determined . . . very pleasing to—"

I snatch the book right out from under his pencil. This time, when he comes after it, I don't let him tussle. I let go of the book, take hold of his shirt, and kiss him. He yields immediately, his mouth softening under mine. No tension, no uncertainty. Just simple *ease*, simple comfort. There's something so gratifying to that.

"Ah, Quint," I whisper when I draw back.

He smiles when I say his name. "I knew you'd break first."

I brush a thumb along his lip and don't smile back. There's so much I want to say, but I've spent too many years trapping every sentiment behind a thousand walls in my head.

You're so much more than pleasing to look at. You're brilliant. You're flawless. You're exquisite. Have you not noticed the effort it takes to summon words when I look at you?

But the words stall on my tongue, proving exactly that.

"I wish I could have met you when I was escaping the palace as Sullivan," I say instead.

His eyes flare in surprise, but then he smiles mischievously. "Instead of your stable boy?"

That makes me blush. "*Well.*"

But I say nothing more, because I'm imagining it now: meeting Quint years ago, finding him toiling over books and records in some mill somewhere. He would've been chattering endlessly to everyone, I'm sure, somehow managing to preserve his core of kindness despite the way his family treated him. Red hair and sparkling eyes and just enough wild defiance to drive me crazy.

I remember what I was like before my parents were killed, before I was forced to rule a kingdom that seemed determined to tear itself apart. I very likely would have fallen for him on the spot.

I don't know what he sees in my face, but the mischief slips out of his eyes. "Why do you wish you could have met me as Sullivan?"

Because if I'd met you then, I don't think I ever would've gone back.

I can't say the words. It would've meant leaving the palace. Leaving my brother. And nothing would've changed. My parents would still be dead. Kandala still would've fallen to the fevers. The consuls would still be running roughshod over the people.

And it would all be my fault anyway, just in a different way.

The impact of it strikes me harder than I expect, tightening my throat before I'm ready, and I can't even answer.

Quint must see a flicker of my distress, because he rescues me—as usual. "Wait. Let's imagine it together. I presume with your love for horses that *you* would've played the role of the stable boy. What reason could you have had for visiting the mill?" He taps at his lip, thinking.

He truly is the kindest man I've ever met. I cannot believe any-one ever made him feel useless. I stare into his eyes. "I spied the captivating young man writing ledgers, and I was transfixed."

"Captivating! I really must write these down. And then what would you have done?"

I slip my hands to his waist and pull him against me. I'm pleased to earn a gasp from his throat when my fingers find his skin.

I lean close, speaking low. "Here. Let me show you."

CHAPTER TWENTY-SEVEN

Harristan

Quint sleeps, but I don't. I toss and turn fitfully for hours, eventually giving up sometime long after midnight, when I slip out of bed. I pull on my trousers and a tunic in silence, freezing in place when he stirs and rolls over—but then he goes back to sleep.

I grab my boots from near the hearth and carry them to the door. I'll lace them up outside so I don't risk waking him further. I don't really know what I'm doing or where I'm going, but I can't lie in bed and worry any longer, and it seems unfair to keep anyone *else* from sleep.

But when I draw close to the door, I hear voices outside, speaking very low. I stop, straining to hear, but the voices are too quiet to make out what they're saying. I can't even tell if one of the voices belongs to Thorin or Saeth.

Nothing about the tone seems to indicate danger, but I'm frozen in place again. The memory of the traitorous guards is still too fresh. My heart pulses hard against my rib cage, urging me to make a decision.

Maybe I *should* wake Quint.

No, this is so foolish. If someone meant me harm, they'd be breaking down the door. I put my hand on the latch and draw the door open.

Thorin was sitting on the top step, his back against the post, a crossbow on the boards beside him. He springs to his feet when he sees me. "Your Majesty."

Alice, the young woman who brings us food, was sitting against the other post, and she scrambles to her feet as well. Her eyes are wide, her cheeks bright pink in the moonlight, and she skitters back a few steps. An array of playing cards were laid out on the boards between them, but they've scattered into the darkness from the flurry of movement. Alice always looks a bit terrified of us all, but just now, she looks prepared to bolt.

"Forgive me—" Thorin begins.

I lift a finger to my lips and shake my head, then pull the door shut as silently as I'm able. "Master Quint is still sleeping," I say quietly.

"Yes, Your Majesty." My guard is very deliberately not looking at the young lady waiting in the shadows. It's possible his cheeks are turning pink, too, and I don't think I have ever in my life seen Thorin blush. I glance from him to the cards, and then to Alice.

I might not know how to navigate my *own* courtship, but I'm not a complete and total fool.

"Forgive *me*," I say to Alice. "I've ruined your game."

"Oh! No. We were just about finished." She pulls back another step, and her eyes flick to Thorin rather desperately, but he doesn't move. Her blush seems to deepen, and she tucks a lock of hair behind her ear. "I—I should go home. It's very late."

"It *is* very late," I agree. "Should Thorin accompany you?"

Thorin's eyes snap to mine. "Your Majesty," he hisses, "I cannot—"

"No!" Alice says quickly. "No, I'm fine." She darts into the darkness.

"Go after her," I whisper to Thorin.

He looks at me like I've lost my mind.

Her voice calls back to us musically. "I'll try to bring you an extra apple biscuit at breakfast."

"Do you think she's talking to me or to you?" I say to him.

He sets his jaw and stares back at me.

"At the very least say *thank you*," I add.

"Thank you!" he calls back in a shouted whisper.

"You're welcome!" her musical voice calls back. "Good night, Wolf."

My eyebrows go up. "*Wolf?*"

Thorin gives a ragged sigh and stoops to pick up the fallen cards—but he doesn't explain.

I tug my boots onto my feet, but I skip lacing them and move to help. Thorin glances up in surprise.

"What were you playing?" I say, holding out the cards I've gathered. "I'll join you."

He takes the cards, straightening them in his hands, looking at me like this is a trap.

I sigh and run a hand over the back of my neck. "Lord, I really am a boorish employer."

He frowns like he couldn't possibly have heard me correctly. "What was that?"

"Nothing. Sit." Without waiting for him, I drop to sit against the post.

After a moment, he does the same. He slides the cards together between his hands and stares out at the night. He hasn't answered my question about the game, and now I sense I've made him truly uncomfortable, so I don't ask again. I'm beginning to regret coming out here, ruining his diversion. He's not riding the edge of exhaustion like he was the last time we spoke, but I still remember the desperation and shame in his voice. *I haven't done much good lately anyway.*

I wonder if he feels like this is a failure, too. Like I've caught him slacking in his duties.

With a start, I wonder if my gentle ribbing felt like something entirely different. Like mockery. Like reproach.

"I truly did not mean to interrupt your game," I say.

"I swear to you, I was keeping watch the entire time—"

"Thorin, I know. I'm glad you had some company. I didn't mean to replace her." I look up at the stars, inhaling the cool night air, wondering if my lungs will catch and I'll start coughing.

I don't.

He's studying me somewhat dubiously, so I glance over. "Deal your cards, Ben."

"I don't think I know any courtly games."

"We're not at court."

He still looks doubtful, but he shuffles the cards between his fingers. "Would you know Red Sevens?"

"I would."

His eyes flare in surprise, probably because it's a tavern game, usually accompanied by plenty of drinking and gambling, but he doesn't comment. I watch as he deals, flipping the cards down on the boards. Maybe the earlier conversation with Quint has stuck in my thoughts, but something about it is reminding me of my time as Sullivan, as if this is just another night that I've snuck out of the palace with my brother in tow.

I remember playing Red Sevens in the Wilds, laying silver on a table to bet while Cory chewed on his lip next to me, watching with rapt attention. I always knew how to tell if someone was lying—I'd learned early from watching consuls and advisers lie to my father. I could read the motion of their eyes or the set of their jaw. When I'd play cards in the Wilds, it was no different when men and women would try to cheat me in a tavern or across a table in the firelight. I always let the lying and cheating happen, and then later I'd ask Corrick which people were honest and who'd stolen my money. He always thought it was a lesson. A game for our walk back to the palace.

He never knew that I let the cheating happen because I had no guards at my back. I couldn't risk a fight. We risked enough just sneaking out of the palace at *all*.

Thorin finishes dealing, then lays out the requisite four cards between us, and takes up his own hand.

As dealer, he should go first, but he hesitates. He studies his cards and then surreptitiously glances at mine.

I immediately see the problem. "You're not to let me win," I warn.

A smile finally breaks through. "Yes, Your Majesty. But you can go first."

Fine. I lay down a six of spades. "I honestly thought Alice was afraid of you both," I say.

He hesitates. "Well, she . . . *was*."

My eyebrows go up, and Thorin glances away, abashed.

"When she brought dinner," he says, "I told her she doesn't need to keep running from me like she's tossing food to a wolf."

"And how did she respond?"

A light sparks in his eye, and he lays down a five of hearts. "She said, 'Maybe I like wolves.' "

"Aha. Now I understand why she called you Wolf." I lay down a queen of diamonds. "I suppose *Fox* was taken."

He laughs outright, but then cuts himself short, glancing at the door, mindful of Quint. "She came back an hour later, clinging to that tree there." He nods at the darkness. "I asked if she was here for the king, but no. She said she was here for me, but she didn't have any food to toss, so . . ."

His voice trails off. He's blushing again.

Now I'm genuinely curious. "What?"

"So I asked how she felt about wolves who were good at cards." His blush goes nowhere. "She sat down and told me to prove it."

Maybe I should be out here asking *him* for advice on courtship. "Did you?"

"Oh no, I was definitely letting *her* win." He grins, but it fades quickly, and he scrubs a hand through his hair. He peers at me as if he's only just realized that he's having this conversation with *me*. "Forgive me, Your Majesty. It's very late. May I . . . may I be of service?"

I shake my head. "I couldn't sleep." I gesture down at the cards that are still tucked in his hand. "Play your card, Wolf."

But just as he lays down a king of spades, we notice movement along the tree line at the same time.

Thorin drops his cards and has his crossbow in hand before I'm even aware that the figure is moving toward us. He's on his feet a second before I am, and again, the cards go spinning.

"Hold," I say sharply, just as a woman gives a short burst of scream.

She's cringing in the shadows, expecting to be shot by a crossbow, but I recognize her. Annabeth, the woman who haltingly told me about sneaking into the palace to lay explosives before the rebellion in the Royal Sector.

"It's all right," I say. "Thorin won't hurt you."

She's frozen in place, eyes flicking between the two of us like a hare that's been spotted by a predator.

I glance at Thorin. "Put down the crossbow," I whisper.

He lowers it to his side, but he doesn't put it down entirely.

"Did you come back to talk?" I call softly.

She nods. Without me saying a word, Thorin moves to the side of the porch.

He still doesn't set down the crossbow, though. Annabeth doesn't move any closer.

I'll never make any progress like this. I step off the porch and stride through the darkness to join her. A whisper of sound tells me Thorin is about to follow, but I hold up a hand and he stops.

"Anyone could be in the trees," he calls.

That gives my heart a kick it didn't need, but I nod and keep walking. When I reach Annabeth, she's tucking a shawl around herself, even though it's not very cold.

"My guard won't harm you," I say.

"I had to sneak away again. My husband didn't like what I did before." She frowns and tucks graying hair behind her ear.

"With the explosives?"

She shakes her head. "No. Coming to see you."

My mouth forms a line. Maybe I haven't won over *everyone* in the Wilds.

She looks at me. "But I've seen that family you brought back. Nook has been telling us what they did. How they helped." She pauses, her eyes searching my face. "He's been telling us what your traitorous guards did, too. What they must have done to that little girl." She swallows. "And everyone's heard what that blond one from down the cellar said."

Sommer.

I nod. "The consuls are doing all they can to turn my people against me—including these lies about poison."

"A lot of us believe you." Her fingers work the stitching of her shawl. "That you weren't poisoning anyone."

"I wasn't. Truly."

"But if you weren't . . . a lot of us are wondering why no one is getting sick anymore."

I stare at her.

The words seem to swell in my thoughts like they don't make sense, but of course they *do*.

"No one is getting sick?" I say.

She shakes her head. "There are still some fevers and coughs here and there, but nothing like it used to be. And no one has died in . . . in *days*."

I try to think of the last time I heard of a death, and she's right—it's been days. Now that I'm paying attention to it, I can't remember the last time I heard someone cough other than myself.

Even that hasn't been as bad as it was.

Incredible. I can't believe I haven't noticed.

I turn and look back at the porch and call to Thorin. "Wake Master Quint."

Annabeth's voice pulls me back. "If . . . if you weren't poisoning the people, who was?"

"I don't know," I say. "But very likely whichever consul is sitting in the palace, making up lies about *me*. Whichever consul is orchestrating this whole thing."

I grit my teeth. *Allisander.*

"If this is true across Kandala," I say sharply, "I have no doubt that he's already beginning to spread word that the sole reason the fever sickness has lessened is because I've been removed from power."

Her face twists. "I—I told you we made uniforms so we could set the explosives for when the rebels took the sector. We still have some."

My ears perk up. We have weapons in the Wilds, but *nothing* compared to the Kandalan army. Access to explosives could give us an edge. They could allow us to plan something bigger than just minor missions to acquire guards.

"You still have explosives?" I say.

She shakes her head. "We still have the uniforms."

Oh. I try not to let my face fall. "As much as I appreciate your honesty, I'm not sure how much it will help. I lost half a dozen people attempting to get more guards. I don't have a way to get more explosives all the way from Trader's Landing."

"You don't have to go that far. The ones we set are still in the palace."

"*What?*"

She nods emphatically. "We never set them all off. Most of them are lining the walls of the passages behind the throne room. But there are more scattered through all the walls in the western wing."

Words freeze in my mouth. I can't stop staring at her.

They set explosives behind the throne room. I wonder how long they were there. I wonder how long I sat with literal bombs waiting to go off behind me. My breathing shakes a bit, and I genuinely can't tell if it's fury or fear.

Annabeth takes a step back. "So many of us were dying," she says, and her voice is so small. "We were dying, Fox."

There's a note in her voice that tugs at my heart, and I have to run a hand across my jaw. I've gone through so many emotions tonight. "I know," I say roughly. "I know." I draw a heavy breath. "But if you'd bombed the whole palace, you would've killed everyone. Not just me and the consuls. My guards, my whole staff. They had nothing to do with the fevers. You would have killed *everyone* just to retaliate against me and my brother?"

She swallows thickly. "We thought of that. Some of us have family that work in the palace. We tried to keep the explosives away from the bottom floor. So the staff could escape."

Footsteps are approaching from behind me, and it has to be Quint. Annabeth backs away another step.

"Wait," I say. "Please."

"I've been gone too long. My husband will notice."

"Then I'll come talk to him with you."

She shakes her head. "No! No. I'll try to come back." She takes another step away.

She can't run again. Every time I talk to her, I barely learn anything at all. "You still haven't told me how you managed to gain access," I say quickly. "Or why you didn't set off all the bombs in the first place."

"We were supposed to," she says, backing away farther, just as Quint appears at my side. "But some of the girls said the building would collapse. That we wouldn't be able to save anyone at all." She glances past me at Thorin. "We couldn't do it."

Then she turns and sprints between the trees.

Quint wastes no time. "What happened? What was she telling you?"

"She said she and the other women laid explosives throughout the entire palace," I say. "That they didn't set them all off, and more remain in the walls of the west wing and behind the throne room." I turn to look at him in the cloaking shadows of the trees. "Only the east wing was damaged during the first attack. No other parts of the palace. Do you think that could be true?"

He spends a moment considering. "It could be, I suppose. I'm not sure what good it does us to know of it, however."

I don't know. My thoughts won't stop spinning. I turn to head back toward Thorin.

"She also said that people are no longer getting sick," I say to both of them. "Have you noticed that?"

Thorin nods. "Alice said that no one has died in a few days."

"And I haven't heard as much coughing," I say—and immediately cough to contradict that. I scowl and add, "Well, in others. But even so, whoever *was* poisoning the people has stopped now that I'm not in power. This will be used to prove my guilt. Every time we gain a little ground, they manage to gain *more*."

We reach the house, and I drop onto the porch steps again. "We still haven't heard back from any of the consuls. We hardly have any weapons here. The rebels were only able to take the Royal Sector the first time because they had explosives—and now those are locked away in the palace, too." I look at Quint, his hair rumpled from sleep. "Even your books and records that might help me prove my innocence are *there*. Karri once said that Lochlan had an army here, and maybe there are enough people, but we certainly can't march on the sector this way."

Quint looks back at me, and I'm hoping for his usual optimism, that he's seen this from some angle I haven't. But he says, "No, Your Majesty. We can't."

I sigh and scoop Thorin's cards into my hands, setting them straight between my fingers. Again, I wish I could go back to the days when the most complicated part of my life was escaping the palace as Sullivan.

I stop short on that thought, and my hands go still.

Escaping.

Corrick and I used to escape the palace all the time, using the old spy tunnels that have long since been forgotten. Most of them are collapsed or caved in—near impassable in many spots, really.

Aside from Quint, no one knew Corrick was doing it.

No one knew *I* was doing it.

"What?" says Quint. "What have you thought of?"

"You definitely have notes in your rooms that would help prove my innocence?" I say. "And maybe more?"

"I believe so. Why?"

I wet my lips. "I've been planning this like a battle. Like a *war.*" I pause. "I've been thinking of everything like a king."

"As you should."

I shake my head. An idea is forming, and it might be crazy— but it might also be brilliant.

I also don't know anyone else who might be able to accomplish it.

Quint's eyes narrow. "What are you thinking?" he asks more carefully.

"I need to sneak into the palace," I say. "To fetch the explosives, because we desperately need an advantage. And your records, too."

Thorin's eyes flare wide. "You want to *sneak* into the palace? Alone? Your Majesty, this is simply—"

"No," I say. "Not alone." I look between them both. "Quint, do you know how to climb a rope?"

CHAPTER TWENTY-EIGHT

Corrick

By the time that ship returns from Fairde with an answer from Rian, I'm going to be ready to throw caution to the wind and swim there myself. I've spent days in Silvesse now, and while I no longer hate Lochlan, I've been forced to spend time with Oren Crane's people, and they're so much worse than he could *ever* be.

Honestly, they're so much worse than *I* could ever be.

It's obvious why Crane has such a stronghold on this island, why people whisper about him but don't do anything to stand against him. Anywhere there's a murmur of dissent, he sends his henchmen to take care of it. Now that Lochlan and I are relegated to waiting for a response, Crane keeps sending us along to watch.

I understand why. It's not just so he can keep an eye on us.

It's a lesson. A warning.

Cross me, and this is what I'll do to you.

When I watch Lina goad Mouse into breaking a man's fingers,

one by one while he screams, I'm reminded of the time I stood outside a cell and told Rocco to do the exact same thing to Consul Sallister.

It was different.

But it also wasn't.

I can feel the undercurrent of tension among the people, though. It's so similar to Kandala, where everyone wanted things to be better, but solutions seemed impossible. It's clear that many people have heard a rumor that I'm from Kandala, that I'm a sign that help isn't far off, because I catch a few secret glances, people who kiss their fingers and touch a hand to their heart when Lina and Mouse aren't looking. But others scowl at me when it becomes clear I'm with Oren Crane's people. Like when Mouse is slamming someone into a wall while Lina and the others egg him on, and I stand to the side, powerless. I wonder how it makes me look. I wonder how it makes *Kandala* look.

On the night we're finally due to return to the harbormaster, my nerves are on edge again. I have no idea how Tessa will respond to my words. Would she write a letter back? I should have said more—but I know the message would have gone through Rian, so I wasn't going to pour my heart out through *that* man's lips.

I could have at least told her I loved her.

Mind your mettle. I'm such a fool.

"You look like you're going to come out of your skin," Lochlan says. "Calm down."

I'm pacing the floor of our shared room, and I glance at him. He's sitting at the table, studying a paper by candlelight, trying to puzzle out the sentence I've written. He's been a quick study over the last few days, and he's easily learned a hundred words on sight already. We had to spend silver to buy more paper. Now he has quite the stack, both from practicing his own penmanship and from reading words that I write for him.

It's very weird to go from watching someone scream while an ear is ripped off their head to going back to the boarding house and teaching a man to read. It's no wonder my nerves are shot.

"Never mind about me," I say. "This is your first full sentence. See if you can read it."

He sighs and looks at the paper while I resume pacing. "I . . . w-w-wiss . . ." He blows out a frustrated breath. "*Wish?*"

"Yes," I say. "Very clever."

"Shut up. 'I wish I were as—' "

"You don't like the praise? You're learning this all so very quickly." I truly mean it—but I'm enjoying that he thinks I'm entirely mocking him.

"*Shut up!* 'I wish I were as . . .' " He hesitates, whispering under his breath, because he must not be willing to stumble over pronunciations out loud now. He looks up at me. "As strong?" Another glance at the paper, and he frowns. "And . . . bravy? Brave!"

"Yes! Go on. From the beginning. You'll have it all now."

He takes a breath and begins slowly, but more confidently. "I wish I were as strong and brave as Corr—" He stops short, realizing what he's reading. He flings the pencil at me, but there's no real vitriol to it. "You ass."

I duck and snatch it out of the air, then resume my pacing. "And with that, the trick pony learned to read."

He goes still, as if struck by that. He stares at the page again, then sets it on the table. Candlelight flickers across his features as his eyes trace over the letters.

"Thank you," he says, and his voice is a bit hollow. "Your Highness."

After days of *Cory*, it gets my attention, especially since he says it without a lick of disdain. I stop between the bed and the window to look at him, but I keep my voice light. "So formal all of a sudden, Master Cresswell?"

He's not looking at me now, but he shrugs a little, abashed. "You're the king's brother. I sort of . . . forgot." He gives a soft, humorless laugh, then nods at the paper. "I know we're stuck here, but you . . . you didn't have to do that."

I stare at him. I'm not sure what to say.

Maybe he's not either, because he glances at the window. "It's almost midnight."

As if on cue, there's a knock at the door, and Lochlan shoves all the papers into a box, then drops a blanket on top.

I'm the one who draws the door open, and I'm not surprised to find Lina there, waiting with Mouse. "It's time to go, *Your Highness.*"

The way she says it is completely at odds with the way Lochlan said it.

"Or am I still calling you Weston?" she says. "I can't keep track."

"I can't either, honestly," I say.

"He's Weston," says Mouse. He looks at me. "You're Weston."

Lina scowls. "We *know,* you idiot." She elbows him in the stomach.

He frowns and rubs at his gut, drawing back. His eyes are wounded.

Despite the fact that I watched him crush a man's ribs earlier, he has my sympathy. Our roles are very different, but he clearly doesn't want to do any of this any more than I wanted to be the King's Justice. The saddest part is that I don't think he has the full capacity to understand that he could resist them. He could crush

Lina one-handed and walk right out of here if he wanted to, but the longer I spend with them, the more I realize that whatever Lina did to him seems to have left him with the mind of a boy. A boy who's been beaten down so severely that he doesn't even try.

I look him in the eyes, because none of them seem to. "Thank you, Mouse. I do appreciate the reminder."

He gives me a nod. "You're welcome."

I take an apple from the basket on the table and offer it to him, because I've seen the others steal his food, poking his arms and saying he could stand to miss a meal. "Here," I say. "We had some left."

His eyes light up a bit, but before he can take it, Lina swipes it from my palm and bites right into it. "Thank you."

I glare at her, wishing I could order him to pull *her* teeth out of her mouth.

She glares right back at me, and she knows it, too.

Lochlan swears under his breath, and he pushes past me. "Let's go."

Lina takes one more bite of the apple and turns to follow him.

When her back is turned, I reach into the basket and grab a muffin from the bottom. It's from this morning, so it's a little dry and crumbly, but I take Mouse's wrist and press it into his hand.

He looks down as if he can't fathom what I've just put against his palm, but then he sees the muffin.

He inhales sharply, and I tap a finger over my lips, glancing at Lina. She doesn't hear him, but Lochlan does, and he looks back.

"Our secret," I whisper to Mouse, as Lina stomps down the hallway.

Mouse worriedly follows my gaze, then looks back at me and Lochlan. For half a second, I'm worried I've made a misstep, that he's going to turn on me for offering him food behind her back, even something that's just a simple kindness.

But then he tucks the muffin into one of his massive pockets, and for the first time since I've met him, Mouse smiles.

—+—

When we head deeper into Silvesse, Lina doesn't lead us south, toward the harbor. Instead, we head back toward the cove where Oren Crane's ship is docked.

"Where are we going?" I ask. "We're due to meet with Ford Cheeke."

"Not anymore," she says. "He's already given his messages to Oren."

My heart thumps in my chest. That wasn't part of the plan at all. "What? When?"

She looks back at me. "At dawn, when the ships docked."

My thoughts are spinning. Ford Cheeke wouldn't have given messages to Oren Crane. Oren shouldn't have been able to reach him. Ford was terrified of him.

Did Lina and Mouse hurt the man and his daughter?

Lochlan glances over his shoulder and meets my eyes. I don't know what to make of it either, and I don't know if I can ask.

Like the first morning we went out to Oren's ship, we have to row and climb up to his boat. I've grown more used to the rowing, and Lina says, "You're turning into a bit of a sailor, aren't you, *Weston*?"

I don't know why she's saying the name like that, and I don't like it. It rolls around in my head with the way she came to the door, like the way she questioned which name was real.

When we climb onto the deck, torches are lit, and the sails are open and billowing in the wind. Small fires flicker farther out on the water, too, and I realize there are other ships in the moonlight, waiting just beyond this one.

And in front of us is Oren Crane, standing with Ford Cheeke.

"This can't be good," Lochlan mutters.

He's right about that. I try to ignore the pounding in my chest, because I have no idea what this could mean. "I wouldn't expect to find the two of you together," I say.

Ford is glaring at me. "It was nice of you to show his people how to access my offices, Your Highness."

"You knew how we got in. You should have put guards on that alley." I glance between the two of them and let my gaze stop on Oren. "I hope you got what information you wanted, because I rather doubt he'll send any messages for me now."

"I think I did," says Oren. "Lina kept telling me that your story was too easy. That there was no possible way that you could've convinced someone that you were a prince of Kandala, simply fallen from a ship, right here on Silvesse. If you were, why wouldn't you try to bargain with *me*?" His eyes are almost black in the moonlight, and the sails snap in the wind. "Because *I* have ships. *I* could've gotten you back to Kandala. *I* could've used a bargain for steel in exchange for medicine, if that's what you so badly need."

He's also a tyrant, and I wouldn't bargain with him if my life depended on it.

Which it might, in a second.

My spine is absolutely rigid, but I keep my voice easy. "So you fetched the harbormaster yourself? Of course he told you I'm the prince. That's what I told *him*."

"He also told me about all the ways Kandala tried to trick Ostriary in the past. I don't know why my nephew ever thought he could trust any of you. I was a boy when your people set our ships ablaze, but I still remember."

"No matter who you think I am," I say, "I don't know anything about that. I wasn't even *born* yet."

"You're lucky you were born at all," says Ford bitterly.

I frown. "What?"

"Enough of that," says Oren. He pulls folded parchment out of his jacket, and he holds it out to me. "It doesn't matter if you're a prince or not. It doesn't matter if you're tricking me or not. My sweet little nephew has set the trap you told him to lay."

I take the paper and unfold it. My palms feel damp.

We'll have Bella under guard in the old Mason house on the north point. I'll have people in the woods, too. The water will be clear.

It's not as incriminating as it could be—but it's pretty damning.

I snap my head up. "I didn't tell anyone to lay a trap."

Oren shrugs. "It doesn't matter if you did or not." He looks to one of the deck hands. "Pull the anchor."

"Where are we going?" says Lochlan.

"We're going to rescue my girl," says Oren. He gestures at the paper. "You see yourself. The water will be clear."

I frown. "You just said Rian is laying a trap."

"Oh, I'm not the one getting off the ship to get her, Your Highness." He smiles viciously. "You are."

CHAPTER TWENTY-NINE

Tessa

Erik hates literally everything about this plan.

I know this because he's told me at least a thousand times a day since I first announced it.

"If I do this and we succeed, Rian will take us home," I keep telling him.

"If you do this and we *fail*, you could be dead," he keeps responding. Then he'll grip his waist and try not to wince, because I know he's still in pain.

"Well, if I'm dead, then it won't matter at all!" I've started snapping, just because I'm as nervous as he is.

Olive and Ellmo have begun to exchange glances when we start this up. She usually drags her son out of the house while he keeps hanging back, wanting to watch the fight.

But now it's nightfall, and Ellmo is at the palace with Anya and some of the others, because Olive won't risk her son getting anywhere near Oren Crane.

I honestly didn't expect her to risk herself, but she's here at the house with me, waiting while Rian's people are outside, checking the coastline, preparing the house to look like it's holding a prisoner.

I expected dozens of armed men, but there aren't.

"Do you think I made a poor choice?" I whisper to Olive.

She passes me a cup of coffee with milk and honey and says nothing for a long moment. "I think my uncle terrorized these islands for a long time. I think Rian sees a chance to finally *win*, and he's going to take it."

I accept the coffee, but I don't take a sip. "That doesn't answer my question."

She looks at me. "You shouldn't have to risk yourself, Tessa. You aren't a part of this war." She pauses. "This war shouldn't be happening at all anymore. It was over."

I swallow, thinking of the revolution in Kandala. The way Harristan and Corrick tried to keep the peace. "Was it really over, or was your uncle biding his time, waiting for another chance to take over?"

She doesn't say anything to that.

"Was he gone from *this* island," I say carefully, "while he was terrorizing another one?"

Her eyes flick up. "The bridges are down. Communication is slow. I don't know."

"Rian took Oren's daughter prisoner. Now he's going to take *Oren* prisoner."

She sighs heavily.

So do I.

Erik appears in the doorway of my bedroom. He's wearing the utilitarian parts of his guard uniform, and he clicks a bolt into a crossbow. "Maybe we can get them in the room together and I can shoot them both," he says sourly.

"We need Rian to get us *home*," I say.

He grunts. "I still don't trust him."

"He made a bargain," I said. "I'm going to hold him to it."

But a little voice inside me whispers that I'm doing this while tricking someone else, the same way Rian tricked me and Corrick.

Oren is someone who did horrible things. And I'm doing this with good reason.

But is it justified? Were Corrick's actions justified? Were Rian's?

Ugh. Everything is all tangled up, and I'm still not sure about any of it.

"Do you still have your dagger?" Erik says.

I pat my hip, because I do, but Rian appears in the doorway. "She's a prisoner. She wouldn't have a *dagger*."

Erik steps between him and me. "No one should get close enough to know the difference."

"You're wrong," Rian says. "Someone *might*. I'm not risking this on a technicality. I wouldn't have a hundred soldiers guarding one girl, especially if she's supposedly *hidden*. I'd barely have more than *one*. Oren won't come close if he's spooked, and it'll ruin this whole plan."

Now I understand why there aren't dozens of soldiers outside.

"So you didn't bring . . . *anyone*?" I whisper.

He blinks, then gives me a wounded look. "Of course I brought my people," he says. "I have a hundred men waiting in the road. But we need to draw him off the water. You don't understand why he's always been so hard to catch. Oren has always been behind his cannons. He has a dozen henchmen doing his bidding. I wouldn't be surprised if he sends someone to make sure you're really *here* first."

"So she's *bait*," Olive snaps. "Not a decoy."

Gwyn Tagas pokes her head in the room. "Rian. A lookout spotted a ship on the water."

My heart gives a lurch. None of this is what I expected at all. "I don't look anything like Bella," I say. "They'll know I'm not her if they get close."

"We'll tie you up and put that over your head. I'll guard you myself." Rian tosses a cloth sack in my lap.

The cloth falls over my fingers, and I stare down at it in shock.

I'm remembering the last time I had a cloth sack tied over my head.

He drops to a crouch in front of me. "Tessa," he says quietly. "I know you hate me. But I never lied about the most important parts. I care about my people just as much as you care about yours—and I know you see that." He pauses. "I didn't force you to do this. You volunteered—just like you volunteered to help people in the villages." His gray eyes seek mine, and I remember what they looked like when we were clinging to the rigging, thirty feet above the ocean. "You can help them again."

I swallow, thinking of everyone in Kandala waiting for us to return. "I said I'd do it, and I will."

He lets out a breath, and relief blooms in his eyes. "Thank you." He presses a palm to my cheek. "I swear to you, I'll be right here the whole—"

"No." I straighten, pulling away. "Rocco will be my guard."

Rian stares back at me. "Tessa—"

"That's my requirement," I say. "If you still want me to do this, I want Rocco." I hold his eyes. "Not you."

Rian stands. He looks at Erik. "You're still injured."

"I only need my hand to shoot a crossbow."

Rian scowls. "I will not—"

"How far away was the ship?" Olive says. "Do you have other people to move into position?"

Rian swears. "Fine." He tosses a length of rope at my feet, then glares at Erik. "Make sure she's really bound. If this fails because of you, nothing she says will save you."

Then he's through the door before any of us can respond.

Erik gingerly bends to fetch the rope.

"I'm sorry," I whisper. "Are you sure you can—"

"Of course I can, Miss Tessa. I wouldn't have left you with him regardless."

"No matter what happens, I won't let him harm you."

Erik's eyes meet mine. "I'm not afraid of him." He looks up, past me, at Olive. "Do you have a safe place to hide?"

She nods. "I'm going into the barn."

"And Ellmo is safe?"

Her face softens. "Yes. He's soaking himself in sugar and cocoa in the palace. He hasn't seen Anya in ages. I think they're baking something sweet."

"Good." He uncoils the rope. "Give me your hands, Miss Tessa."

When I hold them out, he looks up at Olive again while he loops the rope around my wrists. "Do you have a weapon?" he says to her.

"I stashed my crossbow," she says.

"Livvy!" Rian calls from somewhere outside. "You need to get out of there."

Olive doesn't move.

Erik doesn't tie my wrists tightly at *all*, then reaches for my ankles next. "What about a dagger?" he says to Olive.

"I have a blade hidden under my skirts." Her voice is serious, but she gives him a wink. "You really are a big brother, aren't you?"

"In truth, I'm the youngest." He tugs the knot at my ankles—again, too loose—and stands.

"Livvy!" Rian calls again, and Olive scowls.

"Go," I say to her, and I hate that my voice is breathy. "Be safe."

"*You* be safe," she says.

I swallow and nod briskly.

She still doesn't leave. Instead, she smacks Erik on the arm. "And *you* keep her safe. I haven't had a friend in *ages*, so you'd better not let anything happen to her. Do you hear me, you big—"

He takes hold of her waist and kisses her.

It's not a little kiss either. I gasp out loud. I think my cheeks are turning pink.

Hers definitely are. A small sound escapes her throat.

Erik lets her go. "Trust me."

She's staring up at him. "I do."

His eyes flick at the doorway. "Go, before he comes in here to get you, and I have to shoot him in the face."

Her flush deepens, but she nods quickly, and then, without another word, she's gone.

Erik turns back to me. "Don't you say a word."

"Can I say I appreciate the distraction?"

That makes him smile. He drops to one knee again, and I don't miss the slight sound of pain on his exhale.

"You're still hurting," I say.

"Eh. Not like before." He shrugs it off and draws his dagger. "I'm going to slip this under your thigh," he says, and his voice is very low, like he's worried he'll be overheard. "If someone gets close to you, if anyone *touches* you, I want you to use it. Point down, just like I showed you."

I think about the times I've practiced in the barn, which just now feels completely inadequate. "I won't be able to see—"

"I don't care. Anyone on our side won't be sneaking up on you. Move your leg. I'm sure Rian is going to look in soon, and I don't want him to see."

I inhale sharply and obey. He slips the dagger under my thigh, the hilt pressing against the skin behind my knee. I can feel the danger of it, like a promise. His brown eyes look into mine.

"It's all right to fight for what you believe in," he says.

I frown. "Am I fighting for what *I* believe in, or am I fighting for what Rian believes in?"

Erik goes still for a moment, considering that. "I've heard enough about Oren Crane to know he shouldn't be ruling a country."

"Should Rian?" I say, thinking of the steps Rian has taken to get to this point. But my words are lost, because another shout comes from outside.

"Douse that lantern! The ship is drawing closer."

Erik disappears from my side. The room goes dark.

Then he's back in a heartbeat, and the cloth of the hood brushes against my hair. I remember another night in the dark just like this, when my hands were bound, and I was left in the dark to wait for my fate.

"I'll be out of sight, Miss Tessa. But I'll be here." Erik ties the hood, and then he's gone.

I shiver at his sudden absence. I have to close my eyes and pretend the darkness is intentional. The dagger under my leg presses into my thigh. I'm remembering a carriage ride. Blue eyes daring mine. Corrick offering me his dagger, when I was terrified of everything I'd learned. Offering me *escape*.

Oh, Corrick. My love.

I miss him so much that my heart aches. I can hear his voice, smell his scent, feel his touch. I'd give anything for him to be here now.

But I stop the sob before it can form. He's not here. I am. And maybe Rian has made mistakes, but so did Harristan. So did Corrick. So have I. We're all just doing our best with the information we have.

So I shift my weight against that dagger, and I tug my wrists to see how loose the rope is.

When Oren Crane comes, I'm ready.

CHAPTER THIRTY

Corrick

Fairde isn't far.

Or maybe it's that the journey doesn't seem to take too long because my heart won't stop pounding in my chest, and I just want to go back and regroup.

"She won't trust me," I've tried protesting. "What makes you think your daughter is going to come with *me*? She knows I was on the ship with Rian."

Oren shrugged. "Then you're going to have to do your best, aren't you?"

"What if we refuse?" Lochlan asked.

"If you're not going to do your part, I'll drop you both in the ocean right now."

That made us both shut up.

We're sitting against the main mast when lights from the island become visible in the distance. Ford Cheeke is sitting a short distance away, leaning against the ship's railing. He's been glaring at me for the duration of the journey, and we've hardly exchanged words, because Oren has been on the main deck. But now Oren is at the bow, talking to one of his officers, and we're alone with Cheeke.

I still can't quite figure out if he's an ally or an enemy.

He clearly doesn't have the best opinion of Kandala.

"What did you mean that I shouldn't have been born?" I say to him.

He snorts. "Don't play stupid with me. I knew you were just as corrupt as your father when you wrote that note to our king."

I stare at him. "I truly am puzzled."

"Our countries have been at each other's throats for generations. I warned Rian that he wouldn't be able to effect a trade agreement for steel. Just look at what's transpired." His voice wavers. "And now Penny is at risk again, with Edward no better . . ."

"What did they do to Penny?" says Lochlan.

"As if you care," he seethes.

"I care," I say. "I didn't do this to you. And I genuinely do not know my father's history with Ostriary."

"You wrote that vicious note to our king—"

"Because he *is* an arrogant prick!" I hiss. "He came to *us* in poor faith. He lied about his identity and hid a prisoner on board his ship. He chastised me for the way my brother ruled Kandala, when he himself could barely hold a kingdom together. We exchanged words at least a dozen times that were easily twice as vicious. On his side as well as mine. I wrote that because I knew he'd *believe* it. Fawning platitudes would have been the lie."

Ford blanches. "Oh." He pauses. "Well, you certainly could've said so."

I scowl. "I'm having a hard time believing that our countries have been at each other's throats, as you say, when I don't know anything about it. Neither does my brother."

"That's because we didn't realize you survived the assassination attempts."

I freeze when he says this, because I'm remembering a very different conversation with Rian, while sitting on a ship in the darkness, just like this. I remember being pummeled with new information that I couldn't process then, because there was all too much.

Honestly, I can barely process it *now*.

The attempt on Harristan's life was thwarted when he was young.

Your Consul Montague tried to poison him to force your parents into demanding a higher price on steel.

Consul Montague later tried to kill my parents. He tried to kill *us*. He died trying.

Later, we never knew who was behind the attack that ultimately left Harristan sitting on the throne.

I wonder if I'm finding out right now.

Rian told me he expected to find my father sitting on the throne when he made it to Kandala. That's why he came under our flag, using false documents. That's why he pretended to be the son of a Kandalan spy who'd been sent away six years before. It was a good story, and I didn't really question it.

But now that I think about it more carefully, my father definitely would've known who he was sending to Ostriary. He would've *known* the original Captain Blakemore's son, even if Harristan and I didn't. Rian and Harristan are close to the same age, so the six years between twenty-three and seventeen wouldn't change someone's appearance very much. I know Rian didn't expect to find Harristan, but he certainly couldn't have expected to fool my father.

Which means he didn't expect to find him on the throne either.

I wonder who he expected to find.

I grit my teeth. "Rian really *is* an arrogant prick," I mutter.

Ford Cheeke and his daughter had all those books and records, but I was so focused on finding Tessa and getting a way home. I didn't consider asking about what they might know about Kandala. But before I can ask him anything else, Oren is heading back toward us.

"We're close enough," he says.

"She's *your* daughter," I say. "Why would you trust me to rescue her?"

"I don't trust you at all, which is why I'm not walking into a trap. Want to prove yourself? Go get Bella. Now get off the ship. The rowboat is waiting."

My mouth is dry. I have no cards left to play.

We *are* walking right into a trap. A trap *I* set.

I'm handing myself to Rian—if he doesn't just kill me outright, thinking I'm Oren Crane.

As I climb down the rope ladder with Lochlan, my brain is spinning, trying to find a solution, but there's nothing. We ease into the rowboat, and my hands find the oars.

I half thought Lina and Mouse might follow us, but they don't.

I frown at Lochlan. "He's sending us alone?"

He looks back at me, then looks at the dark shore that's much farther off than I expected. "I don't like this. We're about to end up dead either way."

My breathing is quick and shallow. "All right. New plan. Rian has to have a decoy, right? We'll just get her and take her back to the ship."

"You don't think he's going to figure out that it's not his daughter?"

"I'm counting on Rian's people to try to stop us, and they can battle it out with Oren then."

"So we just have to rescue someone who doesn't want to be rescued."

"Yes."

"Someone who's probably a soldier in a dress, waiting for Oren so they can stab him a thousand times."

I hadn't thought of that. I clench my jaw. "*Yes.*"

Lochlan sighs. "I can't believe I agreed to get on that ship. All right, Cory." He digs in with the oars and pulls hard, and the rowboat surges forward. "Still breathing."

CHAPTER THIRTY-ONE

Tessa

For an eternity, I hear nothing. It's so quiet in the house that I begin to piece together sounds from the night: the distant waves lapping at the shore, the insects in the trees outside. It's warm, and a drip of sweat has worked its way down my spine. Erik put this sack over my head, but he didn't tie it around my neck. It still reminds me of the night I was bound in the palace, waiting to face the King's Justice.

Corrick would want me to fight. He'd want me to plunge this dagger into Oren Crane, too.

It was one of the first things I said to Erik after Corrick died: *I want you to teach me to fight.*

But I'm not a killer. Not really. Even the night I snuck into the palace to kill Harristan and Corrick, I couldn't do it.

Just now, the memory makes me feel immeasurably weak.

I keep thinking of the way Bella came exploding out of that room on the ship, sweating and sick because Rian had been poisoning her. Am I fighting on Rian's side because he's *right*, or am I fighting on his side because he got to me first?

But I trust Olive. I trust her opinion of Oren. That helps steel my resolve.

I wish I knew where Erik went. I don't even know if he's still in the room with me. I don't think so. Earlier, he whispered that he'd be checking the other windows periodically because he didn't want us to be taken unawares—and he still doesn't trust Rian.

The silence goes on for so long that time seems to stretch into infinity—and when sound finally comes, I nearly jolt out of the chair.

It's a grunt and a scuffle in the hallway somewhere behind me, then the clear sound of a punch being thrown. Glass breaks somewhere, and a man utters a muffled curse. My heart leaps into a gallop, and I jerk at my loose bindings automatically.

Then a hand brushes my arm, and I cry out. I hear a sharp, indrawn breath, but I'm already scrabbling for the dagger. My hand closes around the steel hilt, and I pull it free with a ragged cry.

Suddenly, my thoughts don't matter. My reasonings don't matter. I'm being attacked, and I fight back. Just like I've practiced, I swing that dagger down with all my strength.

I strike nothing, and instead, I'm wrenched out of the chair sideways, landing on the floor on my back. It nearly knocks the wind out of me, but I kick hard, relieved when I make contact. I try again, but his weight lands on top of me, grabbing my wrist and smacking my hand against the floorboards until I let go of the blade. I don't know if this is Oren Crane or one of his attackers, but I'm pinned to the floor underneath his body, and my fingers scrabble desperately, seeking the dagger.

"No," I say, because tears are already burning my eyes. I struggle against his grip, wishing I could see. "No—please—Erik—help—"

My assailant goes still. Completely frozen.

I take advantage of his stillness to redouble my struggles, my fingernails clawing at the floor. Steel brushes my knuckles, and I twist my wrist, grabbing hold of the dagger.

His grip loosens the tiniest fraction. I squeal in rage and lift my arm to drive the blade into whatever I can reach.

But he catches my wrist again. There's no violence to it, just a secure grip.

The man is breathing so hard I can feel it against my chest.

Then he says, "Tessa?"

My heart stops. I can't breathe. The dagger falls out of my hand and clatters to the floor.

It's impossible.

Without warning, the sack is yanked off my head. Cool air rushes in to soothe my tear-stained cheeks.

But there he is, right in front of me. Blue eyes and a smattering of freckles and those sharp features that I'd recognize no matter how many shadows cloak the room.

"Oh, Corrick," I whisper, and my breath hitches.

He's staring down at me in wonder, as if I'm the one who's been dead all this time. My thoughts refuse to believe that he's here, that this is real, that this is possible.

"Am I dead?" I say, and my voice breaks.

"No, my love." He takes my hand, and he brings it to his face. He kisses my fingertips, then presses my palm to his cheek. "Very much alive, I promise you."

I blink, and his face goes blurry before clearing. A tear rolls down my cheek. I'm afraid to move, I'm afraid to *breathe*, like this is a dream. Like I'll touch him and the illusion will shatter.

His heart is beating against mine, though, and I can still feel each breath he inhales. I finally let my fingers move, running my thumb along his lower lip. My vision goes blurry again, and my breathing shudders so hard that I can't catch myself, but I don't want to blink the tears away this time.

"I don't want you to disappear," I say, and then I realize I'm crying in earnest.

"I won't," he says. "Never again. I swear it." He leans down to kiss me. "I swear to you. Never again."

And then I'm glad that *he* is the one who moved, because *this* feels real, the brush of his lips against mine, the way he kisses the tears off my cheeks, the scent of his skin, the rasp of his voice in my ear. "We really do have to stop meeting like this."

It makes me huff a laugh through my sobs, and I grab him around the neck, clutching him fiercely. "And to think I almost killed you."

"That was a good strike," he murmurs against my neck.

"I've been practicing," I say, and my breath refuses to stop hitching.

"I can tell. I'm *very* glad you were blindfolded."

I know I need to find out what happened in the hallway, or where Erik went, or *why* Corrick is a part of this—but I can't stop clutching at him. Inhaling his breath. *Feeling* him.

But then he sits up, pulling me with him, tugging me into his lap. Before I can ask him anything at all, his hands find my cheeks, and his mouth lands on mine. Every emotion pours through his kiss, and *this* is what finally convinces me he's real. I can feel his longing. His loss. His worry. His fear.

His love. His hope.

For the first time since arriving in Ostriary, I feel settled, like my world has been righted. I have Corrick back, and I can face any challenge.

Then he breaks free, his blue eyes filling mine. His hand presses to my cheek, his thumb brushing along my lip. "Don't fight him. I've told you before what people will do with me."

A jolt goes through me. "What?"

But he's looking up, past me. "Are you still going by Captain Blakemore? Or should I address you as Your Majesty? I have a hard enough time keeping track of my own identities, honestly, so you're going to need to help me with yours."

I scramble out of Corrick's lap to see that Rian is in the doorway of my bedroom, a crossbow leveled. Sablo is beside him, an identical weapon in hand.

"Call me whatever you want," says Rian.

Corrick climbs to his feet more slowly than I did. "I rather doubt you want me to do *that*."

"Do it anyway," a strained male voice calls from the hallway, and I'm shocked to realize that the male voice I heard earlier was *Lochlan*. "It'll make you feel better."

"Was this a trap for me the whole time?" says Corrick.

Rian shrugs. "Only since I knew it was really you."

A cold wind blows through me at those words. "What?" I whisper again.

"So you double-crossed me?" says Corrick. "I shouldn't be surprised."

"I'm not sure you're in a position to be pointing fingers. I've heard a dozen reports that you've been torturing people for Oren Crane."

"You've heard wrong," says Corrick. "Any torture has been by his own hand. I specifically *spared* the man he told me to execute."

A muscle twitches in Rian's jaw. "I know who you are. I know what you've done in Kandala. I don't believe that for a minute."

I'm not even listening to him. "Did you know?" I demand. "Did you know he was alive?"

Corrick looks to me. "He knew. I specifically asked him to tell you, to verify my words."

I think back to the day we met Rian on the road. He pulled that parchment out of his pocket—but he never showed it to me.

I don't even need to ask what it said. I know exactly what Corrick would have written to prove it was him. "So I really *was* bait," I finish.

"You volunteered," says Rian.

Corrick looks at me in surprise. "You *volunteered*?"

I lift my chin. "In exchange for passage back to Kandala. Someone needs to warn your brother about the Moonflower poison."

Corrick glares at Rian. "He was never going to give us passage back to Kandala. He's going to use me against Harristan." He pauses. "I admit to being a bit surprised that you didn't take the opportunity to grab Crane while you could. You wanted me that badly?"

Rian swears. "No, you jackass. I want *steel* that badly. I want to help my people. So I told my uncle that if he sent you here, I'd deliver his daughter to him. He could keep Silvesse."

"I've seen what he's doing to the people of Silvesse," Corrick says. "You sacrificed an island just to get me? That doesn't exactly sound like you're caring for your people." He pauses. "And what are you going to do when you have no daughter to deliver?"

"It doesn't matter. I already have you. He only has one island. I have the other five. I've bought myself *time*."

Outside the house, some commotion has gone up, but I can't make sense of it. Maybe Rian's soldiers have drawn closer now that Corrick has been caught.

Rian takes a step toward Corrick. His eyes are so angry. "You thought you would trap *me*, and you failed."

"No," Corrick says. "I offered you exactly what you wanted. Again, you rule like a despot, with double dealings and empty promises and *lies*. I offered you a solution to the crimes ravaging your country, in exchange for a return to my own. If you wanted steel so badly, you could've worked *with* me, trapped Oren Crane, and again, I would have been willing to negotiate with my brother on your behalf." He takes hold of my hand. "Now, I will not."

"I know what Kandala has done," Rian snaps. "Your own consuls have been working against the people for *years*. No one here *trusts* you."

"You're wrong about the people of Ostriary," says Corrick. "Many people on Silvesse were desperate for Kandala's help. You're just too angry to see it."

"Many people *here*, too," I say.

"Say what you want," Rian replies "I have plenty of detail from Ford Cheeke about what you've been doing in Silvesse."

"Is that the same Ford Cheeke who was kidnapped by Oren Crane before I was dragged here?" says Corrick.

Rian looks like he's been hit by a fist. "Oren got to Ford?"

"Maybe you're not the only one capable of double-crossing."

Outside, a woman gives a ragged scream, and it chills my spine.

From the hallway, Erik says, "Olive." Then I hear the clear sounds of a scuffle again.

"What's going on?" Rian calls.

Olive comes pushing through the people to get into the room.

Her face is streaked with tears. "What have you done?" she screams at Rian. She shoves him in the chest, hard. "*What have you done?*"

"What?" he whispers. "What happened?"

A soldier has followed her, breathless and sweat-streaked. There's soot in his hair. "I rode here as fast as I could," he says. "It's the palace at Tarrumor. You need to return at once. Oren Crane is attacking."

CHAPTER THIRTY-TWO

Harristan

For tonight's mission, I don't have any rebels. Just Quint and my guards. I didn't even want that many people, but Thorin and Saeth insisted.

Actually, it was mostly Saeth. Thorin must have fetched him while we were getting ready to leave, because they were both on the porch when we stepped out of the house. When Saeth saw me laced into my boots with a dagger at my waist, his eyes just about bugged out of his head.

He set his jaw and blocked our path off the porch. "Your Majesty. You *cannot* go into the palace alone."

"So you're ordering *me* now?" I said.

He inhaled sharply, frustrated—but then let out that breath. "On this? Yes."

Thorin punched him in the arm. "*Saeth.*"

"What's he going to do? Have us discharged? Cut our pay? This is insane and you know it."

Thorin looked back at him, then set his own jaw and moved to block us, too.

I inhaled a breath of fire, ready to tell them both to clear a path, but then Quint put a hand on my arm. "They're not stopping you. They're protecting you."

I sighed. "It's a wonder I'm the king of anything anymore. Fine. Come along."

We slip silently through the forest until we come to one of the tunnels Corrick and I used to access the back gardens of the palace. The entrance is well hidden, and the lock completely false. I enjoy Saeth's surprise as we step inside.

"Who else knows that these still work?" he whispers in the near darkness.

"Hardly anyone," I say, and I don't whisper, because now that we're in the tunnel, no one will be able to hear us. Our feet splash in the water that always lingers along the floor of this tunnel. "Most of them really have collapsed, especially the paths that run longer distances under the sector."

"How did you ever discover them?" says Quint, and it's too dark to see him, but I hear the note of intrigue in his voice. "All of the palace historical records indicate that they've been sealed shut or destroyed."

"When I was young and relegated to convalesce in bed so often, I was left with piles of books. I *read* all those historical records." I smile a little. "When I grew old enough to slip away, I decided to try to find out if any of the tunnels still worked. To my surprise, they did."

I can remember my shock the first time I came out the other end of *this* one, and I found myself in the Wilds. I ducked back inside at once.

And then went right back out.

"I simply cannot believe you and Corrick were able to slip out of the palace for so many years without anyone knowing," says Quint.

"We had quite the list of excuses for where we'd been," I say. "No one ever knew."

Somewhere in the darkness, Saeth makes a sound that's either disbelief or incredulity, but without seeing his face, it's impossible to determine.

"You already strong-armed your way along for this journey," I say without any rancor, "so you might as well speak your mind."

He's quiet for a moment. "I wouldn't say *no one* ever knew."

I almost stop short—which is dangerous in these tunnels because they really are so dark. I have to force myself to keep walking. "What?"

"I was only a hall guard at the time, Your Majesty. But it was *definitely* known among the guards that the crown prince and his brother had developed quite a talent for slipping out of sight and escaping the palace."

"Impossible," I say. "We never would've been allowed to continue."

Saeth says nothing. Thorin says nothing. The weight of their silence speaks *volumes*, however. Our feet continue to splash through the tunnel. In a moment we'll be at the other end and we'll have to be silent again.

"Truly," says Quint, "the suspense here is a torment." Though he doesn't sound tormented at all. He sounds *delighted*.

"Indeed," I say. "Explain yourselves."

The silence stretches on for another moment, but it's Thorin who finally yields. "Admittedly, we didn't *always* know. I'm still rather shocked that you were going out a window, to be honest—"

"Out a *window*!" Saeth exclaims.

"Not every time," I say.

"Exactly," says Thorin. "Forgive me, Your Majesty—but of course you were allowed to continue. Who in the palace guard was going to admit to King Lucas that we couldn't keep track of his sons?"

"Not me," says Saeth, and there's a dark note to his voice that I can't quite unravel.

"Fascinating," I say, in spite of myself.

"Understandable," Quint says. "King Lucas was rather severe when it came to moments of disappointment."

That takes me by surprise, and I frown. "My father was never severe."

Now they're *all* silent.

"Talk," I say. "We're nearly at the end." I pause, softening my tone, making it less of an order. "Please. I want to understand."

"King Lucas was well loved by the people," Quint says, "and well loved by *you*. But much as Corrick handles anyone relegated to the Hold during your reign, Micah Clarke handled anything punitive for your father. There may not have been smugglers to interrogate, but your father had no tolerance for failure or dissent within the palace."

Micah Clarke was the King's Justice when my father sat on the throne. He was killed when my parents were assassinated.

I knew crimes were committed and that Micah Clarke . . . *handled* things, of course, but much like discovering that the guards were turning a blind eye to my teenage antics, this is a completely new angle I've never imagined.

Suddenly Quint and the guards come into dim view as the first threads of moonlight reach into the tunnel from the end.

I stop and look at them. My heart is beating hard, and I don't want to ask this question, but I rather desperately want to know the answer.

"Was he horrible?" I say quietly. "My father?"

Thorin and Saeth exchange a glance—and say nothing.

Lord, I think, and I have to run a hand across my face. I'm remembering a conversation I once had with Corrick, where I told him that what something *looks like* was all that mattered. I wonder if I've fallen victim to the same exact thing. I wonder if my parents were well liked by the people because they gave the impression of a loving, joyous family—while behind closed doors my father had people in his employ who allowed him to secretly be callous and cruel.

But as I think about it, other moments click into place. Like the time my father forced me to publicly humiliate Allisander for daring to ask a question. It ruined our friendship—and ultimately led to his role in the revolution.

I consider the fact that I was desperate to escape the palace at all. The way I took my brother with me every time.

Maybe I knew my loving family was an illusion we presented all along, but I just didn't want to accept it.

No wonder the consuls had no problem conspiring against me and Corrick. They probably spent my father's entire reign doing the same thing to him.

Captain Blakemore and his first lieutenant sat with me in the palace on the day of their arrival, talking about how Kandala was seen as an aggressor in Ostriary. I thought it was ridiculous at the time.

All of a sudden, I'm not so sure.

I look up at Quint and my guards. They still haven't answered my question. I don't have the courage to ask if *I* was horrible, so I don't.

But then I consider the way Saeth and Thorin blocked me from leaving the porch—from risking my *life*—when they weren't willing to stop me from leaving the palace years ago.

My chest feels tight. There are too many things to say, and dwelling on any of this won't help me tonight.

I don't force them to answer. With a start, I realize I don't *need* them to answer. They've been answering for weeks now.

I turn back for the opening. "Stay low," I say, and my voice has gone a bit rough.

When we emerge into the night air, I'm struck by the sense that something is vastly different, and at first I think I've come through a different tunnel than I originally planned. But of course that's ridiculous, because I know each access point, each wall of the palace, each guard placement, each door and window that will allow me to slip back inside without being discovered.

I inhale deeply, my eyes sweeping the vast grounds, and then I realize what's wrong.

"Stonehammer's Arch," I say, staring toward where the lit archway of torches usually stretches over a pond behind the palace. It's been burning for my entire life, kept alight by a complex system that provides lantern fuel to all of the different branches. Corrick and I used to dare each other to climb across when we were boys. "It's gone dark."

I don't know why, but the lack of fire stretching across the pond seems to drive home the treachery from the consuls more clearly than anything that the rebels ever did. The glow from the fire was supposed to defy the night eternally, a symbol of love built by my great-grandfather for his wife.

I shake off the loss. "It doesn't matter. Come."

When we reach the wall of the palace, I'm gratified to see that no guards are stationed out here, just as before. They're still stationed on the outer wall. My heart settles a bit to know *some* things are the same. I look up at the window that used to be mine, not far from my brother's. It's after midnight, so almost all the windows are dark. Only a few lights are lit, and most of them are farther down the wall.

"Should we head for the servant quarters?" says Thorin.

"No," I say. "I'll throw down a rope." Then I grab hold of a brick, boost myself up, and Saeth swears.

But they let me go.

He was right earlier. This really is insane. But it feels good to finally feel as though I'm *doing* something. The palace wall isn't meant to be scaled, but it's full of tiny footholds and narrow ledges, and I know them all by heart. I reach my old window in less than a minute, taking hold of the wrought iron railing that surrounds my balcony. The window is opaque with darkness, but I hook a leg and hang there, holding my breath, listening, watching for any sign of movement.

Nothing.

I finish climbing the railing, then slide my hands along the window, feeling for the latch that's just a bit loose. It gives with a light *snap.*

And then I'm back in the palace.

It's so surreal that I freeze there for a long moment, taking in the familiar shadows, the scent of vanilla and oranges from the oil the cleaners use, the way the moonlight strikes the walls. I could close my eyes and imagine it's a month ago and my brother is down the hall.

But a month ago, nothing was better. Not really.

I spur myself into motion. I have a length of rope at the bottom of my chest at the foot of my bed, and I head right for it.

Something scrapes against the wall behind me, and I whip around, my heart in my throat.

It's Saeth. He's a little breathless, and he gives me a look. "I don't think I would have believed that if I didn't see it myself," he says a bit ruefully. "But one of us had to follow you."

I nod and dig the rope free. "Toss this to Thorin and Quint."

Once he does and we're all in my room, we barely speak. Quint's quarters aren't far from my own, and they're our first goal, and then if we're successful in making it that far, we'll attempt to reach the throne room to see if we can secure some of the explosives that are supposedly hidden in the walls. It's very late, so no servants should be in the hallways, but we have no idea what guards will be.

For the first time, I'm glad we brought Thorin and Saeth. They each have a crossbow strapped to their back, but they unstrap them now. They head into the hallway first, with us tucked tightly behind.

To my complete and utter shock, there are no guards at *all*.

But then I realize how completely foolish I've been. Of course there are no guards. There's no one here *to* guard. I'm gone. Corrick is gone. Quint is gone. Even Tessa is gone. With the king absent, there are no high-ranking political guests, no dignitaries, no one to impress.

"Do you think the whole floor is empty?" I whisper to Quint.

"It certainly seems so," he breathes. "I didn't expect quite this level of . . . emptiness."

He's right. It does seem empty.

And so do his quarters, when we reach them.

Quint stops in the doorway and stares. His entire room is completely bare, like an unused suite. I rarely had occasion to visit his quarters, but I do remember they were always in a bit of disarray: books and papers always haphazardly stacked on his desk, an odd jacket thrown over the back of a chair, pens and pencils *everywhere*. He had bookcases lining the walls, and I do know he had dozens of shelves bearing the books he was always filling with the notes he took. Now there's nothing. Just a wall.

For an instant, he's silent. I don't even think he's breathing.

Then he draws a shuddering breath.

It's my turn to put a hand on his shoulder.

He shifts to look at me. "They took everything."

Likely *destroyed* everything, but I don't say that. He probably doesn't need me to. This room wouldn't have been emptied otherwise.

This is another dead end.

His breath gives another tremor. "We have—this is—" His voice hardens with frustration. "The consuls are *lying*. They're lying about everything. Without my records, you have no way to prove the truth."

My heart gives a tug. I move close and speak right to his ear. "*We* know the truth, Quint."

His eyes stare back into mine—and he nods. But his eyes are still full of sorrow.

I press a hand to his cheek. "This isn't a failure."

"It wasn't worth the risk."

"There are still explosives to recover," I say.

At my back, Thorin gives a humorless laugh. "Maybe we'll get lucky and the rest of the palace is equally deserted."

"I'm not counting on it," says Saeth.

I'm not either.

—◄+►—

The throne room isn't empty at all. It's *full*.

We hear voices from the stairwell thirty feet down the hallway, and we cling to the shadows long before we dare to emerge. Light shines into the hallway from the chandelier, and at first there are so many voices that it takes me a few minutes just to make sense of who's in attendance. Captain Huxley of the palace guard. Arella Cherry, who I always thought was an ally, and someone who stood for the people. Allisander Sallister, who must be behind this whole thing. Jasper Gold, who always just wanted silver and gold to line his pockets. Laurel Pepperleaf, her high-pitched voice only backing down when her father overrides her.

Quint and I exchange a glance when we realize *he* is here.

I keep thinking about those battleships he sent after my brother, and I want to take one of the guards' crossbows and go shoot him right now.

Roydan Pelham, the consul of the Sorrowlands, says, "The king's letter claims his innocence. Are we *certain* he knew of the poison?"

"Of *course* he's going to claim innocence!" Allisander blusters. "What's he going to say? 'I've been poisoning the people for years, help me keep it a secret, friends!'"

"Roydan." Arella sighs. "You've seen the shipping logs from Trader's Landing. This is exactly what we've been suspecting for months."

What? I want to scream. *What have you been suspecting?*

"Why don't you share with the rest of us?" says Jasper, sounding exasperated. "Because I also received a letter, and I must say that it's very convincing, Allisander. It's a bit concerning that you haven't been able to recover the king yet. The people don't seem willing to turn him in, despite all these claims of *poison* that you keep making."

"You must see the proof in your own sector," says Allisander. "No one is getting very sick anymore. It's *clear* that without the king on the throne, the poisoning has stopped."

Something smacks against a table, like the sound of papers being thrown down. "Here," says Arella. "Over the last year, Roydan and I have been monitoring the shipments in and out of Trader's Landing. When we began to see some anomalies, we had to go through the shipping logs, and we discovered some erratic records going back for *decades*. It seems that King Lucas began the poisonings with the intent to sell a 'cure' and share the profits with Ostriary." She gives a heavy sigh. "Consul Montague may have been trying to put a stop to it, because you saw what happened to him. Then King Harristan encouraged the Moonflower production to continue, knowing the root growth in the northern sectors would continue to aid in spreading the poison. It's no wonder he named his brother as King's Justice. It's no wonder the penalties for smuggling were so high. They *had* to be so brutal to keep this kind of scheme in place for so long."

There are gasps throughout the room.

My back is pressed against the wall so hard that my spine might crack. I have a fist pressed against my teeth so I don't cry out and give us away.

My father might have put all of this in place, but I had no idea. I had *no idea*.

"Can you believe it?" Allisander crows. "Can you believe it? He was forcing me to grow it as *medicine*, knowing I was actually committing his crimes."

As soon as I hear his voice, my blood turns to ice.

Because then, *right then*, I realize: I might not have had any idea about the poison, but Allisander absolutely did. He would've had to. Because his father owned the land the Moonflower was planted on. His father would have had to be in on the plot before Allisander was ever named as consul.

His father, who wanted a bigger parcel of land so he wouldn't have to split his *profits* with Lissa Marpetta.

It's no wonder they cleared out Quint's room. He was right—it's quite possibly the only detailed proof I might've had that any of this is false. That I truly never knew.

I take a long, slow breath so I don't explode.

Then the worst thing in the world happens.

I start coughing.

I slap a hand over my own mouth a second before Saeth grabs me, his own hand clamping over mine, drawing me farther back into the stairwell. My lungs are burning with the need to cough, and I'm involuntarily fighting his grip.

But then he draws me to a stop, and I'm able to regain some composure. I'm wheezing from the strain of trying not to cough again, but Saeth and Thorin cling to the archway, listening.

Male voices carry from the hallway. "I heard it, too. Check it out."

Quint grabs my hand and tugs me upward, back toward my quarters, but I pull him in another direction—down.

"No," I say. "This way."

Thorin meets my eyes, ready to protest, but I leave no room for argument. There's no *time* for argument. Shouts have picked up in

the hallway. I don't know if it's palace guards or the consuls themselves, but either way, they'll have armed people with them—and
they'll be on us in a heartbeat.

We run down the stairs, and Quint's hand is still closed on
mine. I don't let go. When we reach the bottom, I tug him left,
pulling toward the darkest, coldest parts of the palace: the wine
cellars and the butchers' kitchens. All rooms with no exit.

Quint balks, and Saeth whispers a warning, but I shake my
head fiercely.

"Trust me," I say.

We run. Footsteps beat against the stairs now.

The hallway is dim, because the staff has gone home—if they
haven't been mostly discharged. I haven't used this exit in years,
and there's a part of me that's terrified that it's been found and
sealed over. If so, we'll be out of options. But if we'd gone out my
window, we would've been an open target in the gardens. I remember the night we fled the rebels, and we barely made it out alive.

My heart is pounding so hard that I nearly miss the butchers'
rooms. The coppery scent of dried blood tangs the air, but I grip
tight to Quint's hand and drag him inside, the guards right
behind us.

Saeth and Thorin look at the four brick walls of the room, all
lined with drying slabs of beef, then look at me like I've lost my mind.

I move to the back wall, where a wooden ledge runs the length
of the room. It looks like a bench for tools, and perhaps it is, but I
know it's false. I pull at the wood slats, expecting them to give
immediately.

They don't.

Panic flares in my chest. Quint joins me, pulling by my side,
but they've been nailed down.

"Under here," I say, breathless from the run. My voice is weak and thin. "We need to pry the wood up."

Saeth and Thorin have already started pulling at the wood, and for a single agonizing moment, nothing moves. I watch them exchange a desperate glance.

But then the wood gives all at once. Dust explodes upward. Bits of wood crack and fall, giving the impression of a deep well below.

A man shouts from the hallway. "I heard something break! It sounds like they went down this way!"

"Is there a ladder?" says Quint in a panicked rush.

"No." There's no time to explain more than that. I simply take a deep breath, then leap.

CHAPTER THIRTY-THREE

Harristan

I can't remember how far the drop goes, and the fall seems eternal. I haven't used *this* particular escape route since I was seventeen years old. As the wind rushes by my cheeks, I'm met by a horrific stench, and I realize the palace butchers could have been using this gap under the bench for disposal of some rather unsavory substances.

My feet land with a *squelch*, and I really don't want to think about that too long.

Quint lands with a stagger and a gasp, and I grab hold of him before he can fall into ... whatever we're standing in. It's nearly pitch-black down here, with only a bare strip of light from the gap above. I'm trying to get my bearings.

"We have to run," I say, as the guards land beside us. "It'll take them no time at all to follow."

"Go," says Saeth. "I'll hold them off."

"*You* go," says Thorin, giving him a shove. He pulls the crossbow over his head. "I'm not telling Leah why you didn't come back."

There's no time to argue, and I have to lead. We run.

I keep my hands out in front of me because the darkness truly is absolute, and I can't remember how many steps until the turn. Even still, I slam into a wall, and then Quint slams into me.

"Left here," I breathe, feeling like I'm speaking through water, tugging at his hand even though everything feels disjointed and lost now.

Somewhere behind us, shouts erupt.

Then the snaps of a crossbow.

"*Run*," Saeth urges.

We run.

We hit another wall, and for an instant, I can't remember which way to turn. There are a lot of false tunnels down here, deliberate mistakes so anyone without a real reason to be here couldn't sneak into the palace. I close my eyes and think back to my teenage years. Waiting for my mother to finish yet another game of chess. Waiting for my father to set aside his bottle of brandy and retire for the evening. Counting the minutes until Cory would tap on my wall, waiting for my signal that the coast was clear and we could slip into the servants' passageways.

Back then, if we were using the passage out of the butchers' kitchens, I always whispered just a little too loudly around the guards that I was sneaking down to the wine cellar for a bottle.

I'm still reeling from the knowledge that they knew I was actually sneaking out of the palace, and they didn't care.

Or they were too afraid of my father to care.

"Your Majesty," Quint urges, and I realize I'm still at the wall, deliberating.

These memories help. *Left*, I think, and I tug his hand.

I'm glad it's dark, and the sounds of battle have faded behind us. There's nothing but silence now, and once we're out, no one will be able to follow us.

But that includes Thorin, too. My steps slow, and I come to a stop. My breathing is loud in the narrow tunnel, my heartbeat rocketing in my ears. I strain to listen for anyone. Anything.

Nothing.

"How much farther?" says Saeth.

"We'll be out of the tunnel soon, and I'm not leaving Thorin."

"We don't know how many they—"

"I'm not leaving him," I say. "You heard what Sommer said. If they catch him, they'll *hang* him."

But in my heart, I know they'll do worse. They'll torture him to try to find *me*.

The tunnels remain silent.

Please, I think.

"We need to move," Saeth says.

I plant my feet. "Not yet."

I count to ten.

To twenty.

To a hundred.

And then I hear a breath.

Saeth shoves me aside, lifting his crossbow.

"It's me," says Thorin, and his voice is rough, coming closer. "You need—you need—"

Then I have no warning because he grunts and nearly runs right into us. Saeth catches most of his weight and swears. I don't realize the problem until he says, "Shit. Where did they get you? Ben, *talk*. Where?"

"Arrow. Ribs. I'm all right. You need—"

"Grab on to me. We'll get you out. Your Majesty, how much farther?"

"This way," I say.

But Thorin keeps gasping as we walk. "I can walk. You need— you need to leave me. They're going—"

"We're not leaving you."

"You have to *run*." He makes a pain-filled sound. "You have to warn—" He breaks off on a grunt.

"What happened?" says Saeth. "How did you get away?"

"They left me for dead," says Thorin. "I thought they'd follow—" Another pain-filled gasp. "And I could've shot them from behind. But they didn't. They turned back."

"They turned back?" Quint says in surprise.

"Yes. But they said they can't wait. They're going to attack the Wilds for sheltering the king."

———+———

I can run fast, but never far. Never for long. My lungs always scream for air until I'm more in danger of passing out than collapsing from exhaustion. But maybe the rumors of the poison being stopped are true, because tonight it's not as hard as it usually is. Maybe it's Thorin's wheezing breath as he tries to keep up with us all. There's a dangerous amount of blood along the side of his tunic, but he refuses to stop. Quint sprints along beside me, though Saeth is well ahead. He kept circling back until I told him to just *run*.

The woods are eerily silent, but I know why. It's the middle of the night. It takes time to call up soldiers, to saddle horses, to ready weapons and equipment.

I remember from the night I had to do the same thing to send the army after Corrick and Tessa.

Then, the time felt eternal.

Right now, I know it's not going to be very long at *all*.

The worst part is that I don't know what to do. If the army attacks the Wilds in the middle of the night, a lot of people will die. This is exactly why we haven't attacked the Royal Sector. The rebels don't have the weapons—or the manpower, honestly—to stand up to that kind of attack.

We can warn the people, but it might not do any good. There's a chance we'll get back in time to tell them they're about to die.

"We can't fight the army," I gasp to Thorin and Quint. "The rebels will need to flee."

"But *where*?" says Thorin.

"There are hundreds of them," Quint agrees. "*Thousands.* They can't get into the Royal Sector. Steel City no longer has a consul—the army would run them down without any resistance at all."

"Trader's Landing doesn't have a consul either," says Thorin, gasping between phrases. "And Mosswell's border would take hours on foot. They wouldn't be able to run that far. Not in the middle of the night—if they'd even find refuge there. It leaves Artis."

"I didn't hear Consul Beeching in the palace," says Quint.

Neither did I—but that doesn't mean he wasn't there.

I remember Jonas Beeching at one of the last consul meetings I ever held. He wanted funding to build a new bridge over the Queen's River. Corrick rejected his proposal because he was asking for too much, and Jonas seemed so dismayed about it. He said there was a miscalculation, and Corrick practically accused him of trying to trick us out of more silver, but he's also never been greedy like some of the others.

If I led the rebels into Artis, Consul Beeching could stop the army. With me missing, there still isn't anyone who can order military action within his sector. So he *could* offer sanctuary and buy us time.

If he was willing.

I just don't know if he would be. The rebels held him prisoner on the dais in the middle of the Royal Sector on the night they tried to take the palace. They killed someone close to him. He could just as easily tell the entire army to kill everyone in retribution. If he believes these claims of poison, he could do it to get to *me*. He could hang me right in the town square.

He could create a very public execution, just like my brother always did.

But still. It's the only close sector with a consul who has the authority to stop the army. If the rebels try to run anywhere else, we might as well just surrender.

They can't simply march into Artis and expect Consul Beeching to take action, however. I'm going to have to get to him first.

As usual, nothing is easy.

"Artis it is," I say.

—◆—

We aren't subtle when we reach the Wilds. We bang on doors, we shout, we throw rocks at walls. As people wake to discover the commotion, they help. Quint goes for the houses to the north while I head toward the south. I lose Saeth for a bit, and I know he's gone to wake his family—but he's back within minutes.

"Leah has them," he calls to me before moving on to another house. "She's running."

My breathing is thin and reedy, because I've run way too far, but it's Thorin who looks worse. I'm relieved when I see Alice wake, coming out of a house, taking hold of his arm.

"Stay with him!" I yell to her, and then I, too, move on.

All the while, my heart is surging in my chest. We're not going to be fast enough. The army will have horses, while these people are on foot. I need to get to the stables myself if I'm going to have any hope to reach Beeching. He needs his people to be ready at the border.

In the back of my thoughts, I keep considering everything I realized about my parents, how perhaps they weren't well loved at all.

How Consul Beeching might not care.

How he might stand on the steps of his manor and watch all of these people die, and gladly.

I swallow these worries away and head for the stables, hoping to find Quint along the way.

I don't, but to my surprise, Saeth meets me there, and he begins saddling a horse beside me.

"No," I say. "I need you to help *them*."

His jaw is set, and he keeps buckling. "My duty is to—"

"Your duty is to follow orders." I turn away from my horse and take hold of his arm. "I might not fight like a soldier, and I might not be able to run. But damn it, Adam, I *am* the king, and if there's one thing I can do, and *well*, it's ride."

He looks back at me for a long moment. If he truly insists on following me out of here, there's not much I can do about it. I'm not going to waste time arguing.

"*Please,*" I say to him. "You're strong and you're armed and there are so many of them. We've almost lost. Right now, they need you more than I do."

He gives a sharp nod. "Yes, Your Majesty. But take my crossbow. Keep your hood up. Watch the footing near the streams."

Then he shoves the weapon into my hands, gives my horse a clap on the neck, and he's gone.

I tighten two buckles, strap the crossbow to my back, and then I am, too.

Dozens of people are already running when we trot out of the barn. I take care not to trample them. I look for Quint among them, but he's nowhere to be seen. I don't have time to look either.

A shout goes up somewhere in the distance. "The army!" a man calls. "The army is coming!"

It's even faster than I expected.

Please, Quint, I think. *Please be safe.*

"Run!" I shout. "Run toward Artis! Claim sanctuary from Consul Beeching!"

Then a path opens up in front of me, and the horse leaps forward.

——+——

It's been a long time since I've ridden a full-out gallop like this, with the wind in my hair, burning my eyes. I'm crouched low to the horse's neck, my fingers soft on the reins, trying to let the horse find the best path in the dark. Artis isn't a wealthy sector, and it's not even a gated one, what with the way the Queen's River slices it in half. The horse tears down quiet streets toward the consul's manor home, and I keep thinking that I could be making this ride for no reason other than to be leading everyone right to their death.

I keep expecting to find obstacles, but no one stops me. No one challenges me. Like the halls in the palace, there are few people even out and about. It's eerily quiet.

When I reach the consul's manor, the cobblestone path that leads to his home is gated, with a small guard station and one man attending. He's smoking a pipe, and he sets it in a little dish on a table when he sees me.

My horse practically skids to a stop, breathing hard and dripping sweat, but the animal paws at the cobblestones, ready to run again if necessary.

Any other time I've been here, I've had heralds and guards and advisers, and my visit has entirely been planned. I've never ridden right up to the gate alone, in the middle of the night. I'm not sure what to say to gain access.

"I need to see the consul," I say breathlessly, keeping a tight grip on the reins. "It is a matter of great urgency."

The man doesn't even get off his chair, and he looks me up and down, then scoffs. "Just who do you think *you* are? It's the middle of the night."

"King Harristan. Open the gate."

He snorts and lifts the pipe. "All right, Your Majesty. A pleasure to meet you. Why don't you come back in—"

"Now." I draw the crossbow off my back and point it at him, then shoot the pipe right out of his hand. "*Open. The. Gate.*"

He swears and scrambles out of the chair while I load a new bolt. "Now!"

He opens the gate.

I gallop through. He's shouting behind me, likely calling for reinforcements, but I don't care. We're going to need them.

When I make it to the manor, I'm startled to find that lights glow in most of the windows despite the late hour. I practically throw myself off the horse and sprint up the steps to the main door, then pound heavily with the butt of the crossbow.

I keep banging until a latch is thrown, and the door swings open.

Consul Beeching's guards face me, their faces lit with surprise.

"I need to see the consul," I say. "I am King Harristan, and it is a matter of great urgency."

They stare at me, then look at each other. They're both better prepared than the man at the gate was, and I watch their hands go to their weapons.

"*Please*," I say desperately. "I need—"

"That's enough," says a man from behind them. "Let him through."

The guards step aside. Just behind them stands Jonas Beeching, and his eyes widen when they fall on me. A dozen people are behind him, either seated in chairs or standing along the walls, but I don't have eyes for any of them. He's the only one of importance right now.

"Your Majesty," he gasps. He looks like he's seen a ghost.

My chest is heaving like the horse's. "I haven't poisoned the people, Consul. I know what they're saying, but I haven't." I have to pause to take a breath, and I push sweat-soaked hair back from my eyes. "I had no idea what my father was doing. Maybe—maybe I should have. But any treachery he plotted with Sallister and with Ostriary was kept from me. I swear it."

He says nothing.

"I've been hiding among the people in the Wilds," I say. "But Sallister is sending the army to kill them. They're coming to Artis for sanctuary. You have to stop the army at the border."

He still says nothing. His eyes are fixed on mine, and he stares like he can't believe I'm daring to ask him for anything at all.

"You must!" I cry. "Jonas, you must! I know they attacked the Royal Sector. I know what they did to you. But they didn't deserve to die of the fever, and they don't deserve to die now."

My breath catches, and I think of all of the people who've already lost so much, and who will lose even more, just because they hid me away. Just because they *believed* in me. I might not be able to do anything else, but I can at least return the favor.

"I will surrender to you if you demand it," I say. "You can hand me to Sallister yourself. Hang me in your courtyard. But please! Please, Jonas. You can stop this. Send your own soldiers to stop them at the border. Allow the rebels sanctuary in Artis."

He draws a breath, then gestures to a woman near the wall. "Pour His Majesty a glass of water."

I'm frozen in place, because that doesn't mean *anything.*

But Jonas immediately looks to his guards. "Send word to the border at once. Let's remind Sallister that he doesn't control the king's army *yet.* Wake my medical team. I'm certain there will be injuries."

The breath eases out of my lungs, and I cough. Once, then twice. I run a hand across the back of my neck and find it damp.

Jonas pulls a chair toward me. "Please, Your Majesty. Sit."

I sit. The woman sets the glass of water beside me.

I drain the whole thing. I feel everyone's eyes on me the whole time.

He pulls another chair toward me. "May I join you?"

As if I care about *manners* at a time like this. "Yes," I say.

He eases into the chair. "About the matter of your . . . ah, *surrender,*" he says.

My eyes flick up, and my chest goes tight at once. All of a sudden, I'm worried he's going to have someone shoot me right here, or Sallister will, the instant he arrives and discovers part of his plan has been thwarted. My entire body goes cold, and I feel like I need to say everything at once. "If I may—please spare my guards. Thorin and Saeth. They should not be punished for their loyalty. Quint as well. Could I possibly write a letter to my—"

Jonas *tsks* and lifts a hand. "I don't *want* it."

I go still. "What?"

He looks up, past me, then lifts a hand in a gesture. I follow his gaze to discover a girl Tessa's age rising from a chair. She looks as tired and haggard and travel-worn as I feel.

"Karri," I say in shock.

"It took me so long to deliver each letter," she says in a rush. "The other consuls kept saying there was too much proof, and they sent the night patrol after us. They killed my escorts. No one would listen until I got here."

Now I'm staring at *her* the same way Jonas was staring at me.

The consul clears his throat. "I was *supposed* to be at the palace tonight. But as fate would have it, Your Majesty, you actually aren't the first person to arrive at my gates with a wild story of people in need." He pulls my folded letter from his jacket pocket, the one I wrote with desperate hope that one of the consuls might listen.

"As I said, I don't want your surrender." Jonas looks between us both, then taps the letter. "This girl has spent the last few hours convincing me to be your *ally*."

CHAPTER THIRTY-FOUR

Corrick

For as hard as Rian fought to conspire against me, he's remarkably quick to let me go when his country is under attack. Within minutes of learning that Oren Crane has abandoned me and Lochlan here in favor of attacking the palace at Tarrumor, Rian and his people have departed, taking soldiers and horses with them. It leaves me free in the house with Tessa, as well as Lochlan and Rocco, which would seem ideal—until I realize there's a woman with dark spiral curls pulling desperately at Rocco's arms.

"Let me go," she's saying. "Let me go, Erik. I need to get him."

"I'll go with you," he says. "I'll *help* you. Let me saddle a horse—"

"We can take the wagon," says Tessa briskly. "We'll go after them."

"It's too *slow*," the woman wails. She slips free of his grip and bolts from the house, the door slamming open behind her.

Rocco doesn't even glance at me. He makes a sound of pain, presses a hand to his waist, and runs after her.

"Corrick." Tessa takes hold of my hand and squeezes tight. Her eyes are gleaming in the moonlight. I can't believe I'm here. I can't believe she's with me. I want to take hold of more than her hand. I want to inhale her breath until the end of time. I want to make sure no one ever takes her away from me again.

But she says, "We have to go. We have to help Olive."

"We just got free," says Lochlan. "You want us to ride *into* their war to help some girl we just met?"

"Yes," she says, but she's not looking at him. She only has eyes for me. Every emotion I'm feeling, I see echoed in her gaze. Love. Desire. Need. Relief. Hope.

But there's also a plea there.

I remember the very first night she looked up at me in the Wilds, the very first time she needed my help—how badly I wanted to give it, no matter the risk. I think of all the nights since that she's begged me for action, for revolution, for change.

I have no idea who Olive is, or why any of this is so important to Tessa. I just know it *is*, and I'm done failing her.

I bring her hand to my mouth and kiss her knuckles. My mind is already making plans. I know Tessa can't ride well, and I rather doubt Lochlan can. "You said there's a wagon? Do you have any weapons?"

Lochlan's mouth drops open. "You *can't* be serious."

"As you said, you've faced an army before. This probably won't be *much* worse."

"We have everything the guards brought on the ship, so there's armor and supplies, too," Tessa announces. "Come on. We have to hurry."

I move to follow her, but Lochlan is staring at me as we pass.

I look right back at him. "You don't owe him anything. You don't have to fight *this* battle."

"You're right," he says. "I don't owe *him* anything at all."

Then he falls in step beside me.

—••—

Tessa talks while I drive the wagon. The horses run hard, the wood rattling and bouncing over cobblestones. Lochlan clings to the railings in the back. I learn everything that's happened while she's been on Fairde, from their walk to Rian's palace to the poison that she assumes is spreading through the water. I don't have *all* the pieces of what happened in Kandala yet, but I have a lot of them. I learn about Olive and her son, Ellmo, and the medicines they've been distributing, and the way everyone here reveres Rian.

In turn, we tell her about Oren Crane, about Lina and Mouse and the rest of his henchmen, about the way he seems to have a stranglehold on Silvesse that he maintains through fear. She hears about how Lochlan and I have been forced to work together, but he doesn't mention the reading lessons, so I don't either.

"Why was Olive so panicked?" says Lochlan. "You said she and Rian don't get along."

"They don't," Tessa says. "But the children were in the palace." She pauses. "To keep them safe while Oren was 'rescuing' me."

I glance at her. "The children?"

"Little Anya, too," she says.

I remember the little girl from Rian's ship who played jacks— well, *knucklebones*—with me. She had bright eyes and a lively laugh and scarred arms from whatever Oren Crane did to *her*.

I grit my teeth. As much as I hate Rian, Anya is a child. I think about Lina and Mouse and what I've seen them do, and I crack the whip, driving the horses faster.

The glow of fire lights the sky before long, and Tessa gasps.

Smoke begins to obscure the moon. We hear the sounds of battle before we see it, because the boom and roar of cannon fire followed by screams are unmistakable.

"We're close," Tessa says, and there's horror in her voice. "The palace is just over this hill."

Then we crest another hill. Tessa gasps again.

"The palace," she says.

"What palace?" says Lochlan, and he's right.

There's no palace at all. There's nothing but fire.

—+—

We tether the horses and take a spot at high ground to try to assess the situation. We're armed and ready for battle from what we gathered from the guards' trunks, but I know Tessa isn't a soldier—and from the look of things down below, the three of us aren't going to make much of a difference.

Oren Crane's ship has pulled into the harbor, and he appears to be firing on what's left of the palace. Without Rian and his best people *here*, there was no one left to defend anything. It seems that a lot of Oren's men have already claimed the ground below. What's left of it, anyway.

Tessa pulls a spyglass from our supplies and peers down at the harbor. "This is horrific. I don't see Olive or Erik. Not Rian either. I don't know Oren's people, though." She hands the spyglass to me. "What do you see?"

I look through the lens. "Oren is still on his ship." I frown. "With Lina and Mouse."

Lochlan swears. "They're horrible."

"She is," I agree. "Mouse wouldn't be." I shift the spyglass and find a crumpled body leaning against the railing. Ford Cheeke.

He's bleeding from his temple, and there's more blood in a pool under his body. I don't know if he's dead or not, but it doesn't look good.

I swallow heavily. I didn't do it, but I feel as though I was a part of the cause.

"I'm sorry," I whisper.

Another cannon fires. The sound cracks through the night, and we all jump. Fewer screams erupt down below.

Because Oren's people are winning.

My heart keeps pounding. I don't know how to help here. I tried to do the right thing, and it didn't work. I tried to be the King's Justice, and it didn't work.

I look at Tessa and Lochlan. This isn't even my battle, but they're both staring at me expectantly. They're looking at me to *lead*. Somehow it reminds me of that day in the clothier's shop, when I needed to be the one to provide hope. Just like when I had to handle things for my brother, success—or failure—has become my responsibility.

I steel my spine and look through the spyglass again. Oren is on the ship. Untouchable from the shore. He's sending people down to fight on the ground, but he's safe on the water, as usual. He used *my* plan to get Rian and his people away so they'd have an advantage.

He used Rian's desire for revenge, or for *me*—or both—to get them away.

The numbers down below are dwindling. I don't have an army. I don't know the people here to rally townspeople. It's not like Lochlan's rebels in Kandala. We don't know anyone at all. My chest tightens dangerously.

Tessa puts a hand on mine. "You don't have to win this war alone."

The weight of her hand presses into mine, and again, I can't believe she's here, that I've found her, that we're together. I can't help it. I pull her to me.

"Forgive me," I say. "I don't know if I can win this war at all."

Lochlan picks up the spyglass and looks himself. "Do you remember what you said about the treble hook when we were on Silvesse? Do you think you could still do that?"

I frown. "That I could scale the wall to break in?"

"Yes." He glances back at the wagon. "We have some treble hooks in the guard gear."

I look at him sideways, because I can't figure out his angle. "Ah . . . if only we had a building to break into?"

He hands me the spyglass. "There's half a dozen rowboats sitting in the harbor. No one's touching them because they're useless against a brigantine. Half of them might be on fire. But we could try."

"Try what?" says Tessa.

"You don't need to scale a *wall*," says Lochlan. "How about a ship?"

———

Tessa is going with me first, because I wouldn't have it any other way. Our treble hooks whistle up through the night and latch against the hull with a *clink*, and we wait to see if anyone hears. The sounds of the battle and the slap of the water against the hull must be too loud, because no one comes to investigate. I wait anyway. I've been double-crossed too many times now.

But then we're climbing.

"If only we had masks, it would be like old times," she says, a little breathless from the effort.

I look at the faint tracing of her profile in the moonlight. "I like it better this way."

"I hope you know I plan to sob all over you properly later."

"I hope that's not *all* you plan to do all over me later."

She gasps, then grins, her smile bright in the darkness.

"Not for nothing, but I am *right here*," Lochlan says from below us.

But then the ship fires again, and we clutch tight to the ropes as they shudder with the force of the cannon fire.

"I'm rather shocked to see the two of you getting along so well," she says once we're climbing again.

"We've come to an understanding, I think," I say.

"Karri will be so relieved."

If we can get back, I think, but I don't say that.

I tap my finger over my lips, and she nods, because we're nearing the rail. The three of us climb over silently. This part of the deck is pitch-black, which is why we boarded here. But there aren't dozens of people on board anymore—most of Oren's sailors are on land, or down below, firing the cannons. We're going to have to be strategic to take out Oren, but we don't need to sneak past a ship full of sailors. Even still, I tell Lochlan to stay at the back, to make sure no one can come up from behind us. Then Tessa and I slip along the railing, staying in the shadows.

Oren's attention is focused ahead, on the battle on the ground, so we have an advantage.

He's standing with his back to the main mast, though, so I can't just shoot him and be done with it.

I grit my teeth. Lina is off to the side, closest to us, but she looks bored. I suppose the death and destruction of hundreds of people doesn't excite her. I don't know where Mouse is now. Maybe they've sent him ashore, too.

But there's Oren, right there, against the mast. Watching Rian's city fall. The fires are so hot that I can feel them from here.

Tessa's hand brushes mine, and I give it a quick squeeze. We cling to the shadows and wait for him to move.

He doesn't.

The ship fires again, another cannonball rocketing toward shore. The floorboards underneath us give a shudder, and I expect that to be the moment that Oren steps away from the mast, but it's not. He's clinging to that spot like it'll save his life—and it very much is.

Sweat forms in the small of my back. We can't stay here forever. Someone will eventually look this way. More sailors will eventually come up on deck. I look from Oren to Lina and wonder if we should shoot her first—but there are enough people on the deck that I worry they'd retaliate before we could get to Oren.

I consider my brother praising Rian's crew, their devotion to him. I don't get the sense that Oren has that. There's a reason he spends so much time on this ship, protecting himself. Torture and fear breed something, but it isn't loyalty.

We have to take him out first.

He needs to move away from the mast.

As if he knows it, he's stock-still, braced against the wooden beam. In any other situation, his refusal to move would almost be comical. The few sailors on board have changed position. Even Lina has moved. But Oren doesn't.

And then, suddenly, he does.

I lift my crossbow, but I don't have a good shot. I have to slip out onto the deck, just a bit. And *there*, he's turning.

A board creaks, or maybe light shifts, but Lina sees me. She gives a shout of warning. That might be what saves Oren's life, or maybe he just has fate on his side. Because I pull the trigger just as a swell of water hits the ship, throwing us both off-balance.

My bolt goes shooting past him. And I'm visible on the deck.

Oren's eyes flare wide, and I scrabble to get another bolt from my belt, but it's not going to be quick. I'm not going to be fast enough. I can't get it loaded, and Oren is surging toward me; he has a blade—

Another crossbow snaps, just beside me. A bolt appears in his chest, and he crumples.

Tessa is breathing hard. "I'm not watching you die *again*," she says.

Lina screams in rage, and I lift my newly loaded weapon to fire just as Tessa is wrenched away from me. Lina's body jerks as my bolt goes through her shoulder, but I don't kill her.

She smiles anyway, and I look to my side.

"Good job, Mouse," says Lina. "Break her neck."

CHAPTER THIRTY-FIVE

Tessa

Arms have come around me from behind, and it's like being grabbed by a mountain. I suddenly can't breathe. My ribs might already be cracking. I remember Olive telling me about Lina and Mouse, and Corrick just told me about how horrific they are, but now I understand.

A woman's voice is telling him to do it, too. "Crush her, Mouse," she says, and her voice is undercut by pain. I wonder if Corrick shot her. I don't know how many bolts he has left, but I wonder if he's going to shoot the man crushing me against his chest.

"Smash her bones," the woman says, and I want to whimper, but I don't even have the breath for that. I'm beginning to see stars.

"Please don't," says Corrick, and I'm surprised by the even calmness of his tone. "Oren is dead, Mouse. Lina is about to be. You don't have to listen to her anymore. Tessa never hurt you. Tessa never hurts anyone."

The man's arm's don't loosen. "She killed Oren."

"Because he was killing all those people." Corrick pauses. "I love her, Mouse. She's very precious. Please give her back."

For a moment I hear nothing but crackling flames and water slapping the boat. But then his arms loosen, and I slip to the ground, my lungs heaving for air.

Corrick pulls me to him, and I stare up at the largest man I've ever seen.

I expect him to shoot Mouse, as if perhaps I'd been in the way and it wasn't safe, but he gives the other man a nod. "Thank you," he says.

"You're welcome, Weston. Thank you for the muffin."

My breath shudders, and I look up at Corrick. "The—the muffin?"

"I'll tell you later. Mouse is a good man. He's just been forced to do bad things."

Lina gets her legs under her, and she's spitting with rage. "He's *not* a good man! He's a *fool*. An *idiot*. And I'm going to rip every single bone from his—"

Mouse steps forward and grabs her. Her rant turns into outraged shrieks, and she starts smacking at his arms. He lifts her in the air, and I suck in a breath, worried he's going to snap her neck.

But then he tosses her over the side.

I give a sharp little yip and cling to Corrick. I can feel his heartbeat under my hand. A second later, we hear the splash, and then Lina's distant outraged cursing continues.

"I thought he was going to kill her," I whisper.

"She would have deserved it," Corrick says.

Mouse leans over the side to peer down at the darkness. "I didn't kill her." He looks back at me. "Lina can swim."

I nod swiftly. "You did the right thing."

My relief is short-lived, however, because there are still sailors on deck, and other men have begun to come up from below, hearing the screams and coming to help. Corrick lifts his weapon, but Mouse steps in front of him.

"No!" he shouts. "Weston Lark is our captain now. You will surrender to him or I'll throw you over the side."

They skid to a stop, exchanging glances. They take in Oren's body, and Lina's yowling from down below. I wait for a mutiny, for them to surge toward us anyway, but they don't.

They lay down their weapons.

I look up at Corrick. "*Captain* Lark?"

He smiles. "I don't hate it." He loses the smile and looks at Mouse, then at the others. "Signal a cease-fire to the men on the ground. Tether the cannons."

They exchange glances again, and then one of the men must decide to take charge. "Boone, see to the cannons! I'll raise the flag for parlay. Mouse! You'll need to shout."

From behind us, Lochlan says, "You did it. You ended their war."

Corrick looks out at the fires that are burning, at the battles still being fought on land. I can't see anyone I recognize. No Olive. No Erik. No Rian, even.

Corrick's expression is grim. "Not yet," he says.

It takes hours before the sounds of battle go silent, and the first threads of dawn begin to appear on the horizon. Mouse has been shouting at the shore for parlay, to cease fire, but we haven't had a response. A man who was bleeding on the deck is discovered to be alive, and Corrick tells me his name is Ford Cheeke, and he was the one who helped bring this plan together. We're able to get him sitting up, but I don't have any of my treatments, so I can't help him much more than that.

I want to leave the ship, to look for Olive and Erik, but Corrick is worried that Oren's men might try to take control again, so we don't. As his men return, they learn that the ship is under our control, and they lay down their arms, too.

We stay vigilant and wait.

Eventually, a small rowboat leaves the dock, heading for our ship. Corrick takes a spyglass, then hands it to me. "They're in cloaks," he says. "It's too dark to tell who it is. It could be a trap."

"I could club them when they come over the side," Mouse offers.

"No," says Corrick. "But thank you." Then he seems to reconsider. "If it's Rian and he tries to kill me, I wouldn't mind the protection."

Mouse nods, and I swallow, because I'm wondering if Corrick should have given more qualifications. But then the rowboat draws near, and I see that it *is* Rian . . . and Olive and Erik as well.

I lean over the side, heedless of danger.

"You survived!" I cry. "I've been worried all night!"

Olive looks up at me as she climbs, and her smile is bright. "I've been worried about *you* all night."

Her smile tells me that her little boy must be safe, but I have to hear it anyway. "Where's Ellmo?"

"It took us forever to find him," she says. "Because he and the other children hid in the palace—and then Oren's cannons kept blasting through the walls."

"He's a smart little devil," Erik says behind her. He looks pale, and I'd bet he's reopened his entire wound. "He got *everyone* safe."

Then they're climbing over the railing, and they're on the deck. And Rian still hasn't said a word.

He's glaring at Corrick, however. The emotion seems mutual.

Especially when Erik gives Olive's hand a squeeze, then leaves her side to come stand at Corrick's side.

I suddenly feel like new battle lines have been drawn.

"You're *welcome*," Corrick finally says.

Rian scowls. "You helped him enact a plan that killed more of my people."

"No. *You* did that. I never intended to double-cross you. From the very instant I got on your ship, my motives were to work with the king of Ostriary to barter for Moonflower in exchange for steel."

"I will never trust anyone from Kandala," Rian says. "I know what you've done to your people."

Corrick is glaring back at him. "I'm going to have a rather hard time trusting anyone from Ostriary. I've learned enough about *you* to know that any deal I make would be subject to trickery and deceit."

"Kandala is the one guilty of trickery and deceit," says a groggy voice near the railing, and I look over to see the older man has spoken. "As I've said before, Your Highness, your country is not known for fair dealings."

Rian crosses his arms and regards Corrick. "I told you there was a reason I wasn't forthright with you when I came."

Corrick looks between the two of them. "I can't answer for the actions of my father or my grandfather when I don't have any proof of what they've supposedly done."

"I have plenty of proof," says Ford Cheeke. "My records go back for decades. Your country reneged on deals trading lumber for steel, and when we tried to make a claim, you sent ships to kill our people."

"Exactly," says Rian. "And you can't even deny it. Your own consuls have tried to assassinate the royal family on more than one occasion."

I gasp out loud and look at Corrick. "More than one?"

He shakes his head, but his expression is locked down now, revealing nothing.

Rian hasn't looked away from him. "You know I'm not lying about this. You know your country is overrun by sedition and sabotage."

A muscle twitches in Corrick's jaw, but he doesn't say a word to deny it. He can't.

The sad thing is that I can't either.

"I still won't negotiate with you," Corrick says to him. "And Harristan certainly won't, once he learns of what you've done."

Rian smirks. "Good luck getting back to Kandala then."

Olive huffs and smacks him in the arm. "Ugh, *honestly*. This is why I've been on the point for so long. If Oren is out of the way, I'll sail you back to Kandala myself, Tessa."

I stare at her. "Wait. You can do that?"

"Of course I can do that. Ellmo would honestly love it. We're an entire family of sailors. You think Rian is the only one who knows how to raise a sail?" She scoffs. "I used to watch our da smack his knuckles because he could never get his knots right."

Rian glares at her. "When I was *five*." He takes a step forward to face Corrick. "And no one said I was letting you go."

Corrick's eyebrows go up. "Letting me?" he echoes. "I rather think you're outnumbered, Your Majesty."

Rian inhales a furious breath, and for an instant, he looks like he really is going to throw a punch or draw a dagger or shove Corrick right over the railing—but Erik takes a step forward, forming a bit of a barrier between Rian and Corrick. To my surprise, so does Lochlan. Mouse moves close enough that Rian glances at him warily, then back at Corrick.

Suddenly, a lot of the sailors surrounding us look more alert. I hear the click of more than one crossbow, and I don't have to look to know they're aimed at Rian.

He goes very still. His mouth clamps shut.

"Should we put him over the side, Captain?" one of the men calls.

Corrick's gaze darkens further. His voice is low and dangerous when he says, "They're talking to me, you know."

"Corrick," I whisper, because I know this dark look in his eye. I know what he's capable of when he's cornered. I know what he's willing to do when he sees no other options.

At first, I don't think he'll respond to me, that he's too far lost to this battle of wills or fury or revenge against Rian. But he turns those cool blue eyes toward me. "Tessa."

"He's not doing it the right way," I say softly, "but he really *does* want the best for the people of Ostriary."

"I know," he says. "Believe it or not, so do I."

I stare up at him in surprise, and he nods. "I do, Tessa. I can't speak to any past conflict with Kandala, but I've seen the effects of this war. I saw what Oren Crane was doing, and the harm caused."

But then he looks back at Rian, and his voice is cold and resigned. "I got on board the *Dawn Chaser* in the hopes that our countries could help each other. I acted in good faith. But you never have. Even now, you're only willing to offer threats and violence. If you could be trusted to negotiate honestly, perhaps we could come to terms and Kandala could provide assistance, but as it stands, I don't see a way forward."

Those words are piercing.

Because I don't see a way either.

By the way Rian is glaring, it's clear he feels the same.

Corrick looks to Erik and Lochlan. "Stand down. He's free to leave." He glances up at Mouse. "Let him go, Mouse. Don't harm him." He looks to Olive. "If your offer to Tessa was genuine, we will gladly accept. I will ensure you're compensated for any expenses."

But Rian doesn't move. His chest is rising and falling rapidly, his eyes a little desperate. He looks to Olive.

"Livvy," he says softly. "Do something."

"I think you've already done enough," she says, and I realize her voice is broken and breathy, too. When I look up, I realize she was just as hopeful as everyone else on the islands. The emotion in her voice tugs at my heart.

I think back to the beginning, how Rian sat at the table and spoke to the king. How earnestly he talked about the need for steel. How badly I wanted to believe he was fighting for everything *right*. I remember all the people I helped who were so desperate for Kandala to finally be on their side. How much *they* all trusted Rian—because he'd given them reason to. Good reason! He really has helped so many people.

But I also remember everything Rian did wrong. The people he hurt. The people who died. The way he nearly destroyed so many lives.

I can see why Corrick won't negotiate with him.

But I also don't know how we can leave here, knowing that

Kandala has a thriving supply of what they need. I don't know how we can sail away on a ship with Olive, knowing that she's returning us to a country that's turning its back on hers.

And just like that, I realize the solution.

Olive is moving away, dabbing at her eyes now, and Erik is reaching for her hand. I grab it first, pulling her around to face me. She sniffs hard in surprise, blinking away tears.

"It's all right," she begins. "I wouldn't trust him either—"

"No," I say. "I have an idea." I reach out and take hold of Corrick's hand, too. "Your Highness," I say, and he raises his eyebrows.

"Yes?"

"Prince Corrick of Kandala, allow me to introduce Princess Olive of Ostriary. My newest, dearest friend."

He glances between me and her as if trying to track the course and timing of this introduction. "A pleasure," he finally says.

Olive looks from me to him. "What are you doing?"

I take a deep breath. "Olive loves her country and has been found to be trustworthy. She has offered to grant us passage home, out of the goodness of her heart. Instead of working with Rian, would you be willing to introduce *her* to King Harristan so *she* can negotiate for steel?"

"*What?*" Rian sputters.

"Tessa!" Olive gasps. "But I—I—"

I squeeze her hand tightly, then glance at Erik. "Perhaps with Rocco as her escort? For protection?" I smile sweetly. "She is a princess after all. And devoted to her people." I look back at Olive. "Right?"

Her mouth works for a moment, but no sound comes out. She looks from me to Erik to Rian, and back to me again. "Well . . . yes."

"So would you?" I say to Corrick. "Would you be willing to allow *Princess Olive* to act as liaison for negotiations with Ostriary?"

Corrick smiles. "Ah, Tessa." He takes my hand and kisses my knuckles, then gives Olive a nod. "Princess Olive, I would indeed."

Chapter Thirty-Six

Harristan

Even with Consul Beeching's intercession at the border, there are a lot of casualties. A lot of injuries. Worse, a lot of missing people. It takes days to sort through them all. Quint and Saeth's family made it safely into Artis, but there's been no sign of Thorin—or Alice, the girl who tried to help him. There's been no sign of Violet, and no sign of Nook, the boy who helped when we faced the traitorous guards.

I know some people fled into the other sectors or went into hiding. The rebels were always rather skilled at going to ground and running from the night patrol, and this is no different. Rebel camps have been built along the river in Artis, just outside Sallister's reach, and Consul Beeching's guards patrol night and day. There are occasional shouts of joy when people find their way here from where they've been hiding and families are reunited. But as days pass and Quint and Karri and I walk among them, accompanied by Beeching's guards, I know that there are many people who won't be coming back at all.

By the fourth day, I ask Jonas for guards and horses and an armed escort back into the Wilds. I don't think Sallister would be brazen enough to attack another consul's people—if the army remains at all—and I need to see what's left.

Jonas surprises me by joining us. We ride through the forest, and I'm struck by how deserted the area is. I've grown so used to the sounds of children playing, or men chopping wood, or women calling their families for dinner. Every house is deserted.

I'm dismayed to see that many of them have been torched and burned.

The soldiers were thorough.

We come to the small house that Quint and I shared for our last few days in the Wilds—surprisingly untouched—and then the one that Saeth and his family shared—burned to the ground. A tiny stuffed doll lies in the mud about twenty feet from the door, and I recognize it as one I saw Ruby clutching. Saeth isn't with us, but I climb down from my horse to pluck it from the ground, then knock the dirt from it to tuck in my saddlebag.

As we ride on, I know we're going to come to the cellar where Sommer was kept, and I've been dreading it. I don't have any idea whether anyone would have released him during the panicked flight from the Wilds—and it might have been reckless to do so. He might have helped our attackers.

But the thought that he might be lying dead in the cellar is almost too much to bear.

Quint must sense my sudden sorrow, because he reaches out and touches my hand, just the tiniest brush of his fingertips. He's grown very good at these small movements now that we're surrounded by people of grand importance again, even though I wouldn't mind larger ones. But I look up.

"Sommer," I say, and he nods.

Jonas hears the weight in my voice, and of course I've told him of the guards who tried to capture us. "Where was he held?"

I nod ahead. "This way."

"I can have my guards retrieve his body."

I start to shake my head—then think better of it and nod. "We can at least give him a burial."

I hold my breath when they pull the cellar doors open, because it *has* been several days, but instead of the stench of death, we're confronted by Nook and Violet, armed with pitchforks, blinking in the sunlight.

"Violet!" I say in surprise. I climb down from my horse. "Nook! What are you doing in the—"

But I don't get any further than that because Violet tackles me with a hug. "Fox! You're alive!"

Some of the consuls' guards move forward to remove her, but I lift a hand. "It's all right. Violet, what are you doing here?"

"We've been hiding! They keep sending the night patrol through, so we haven't been able to leave. We go out at night sometimes to scrounge for food, but no one searches the cellar, so we've been staying down there. It sure was *dark*, I tell you. But we've got candles now, and Wolf taught me all the card games he knows—"

"Wolf!" I say in shock.

And then I realize more people are coming up from the cellar, just as dusty and worn as Violet and Nook. Alice, too. Then Thorin, his chest bound up in bandages. His entire frame sags in relief when he sees me. "Your Majesty," he says.

I'm so relieved to see *him* that I nearly give him the same greeting that Violet gave me. "Wolf," I say, extending a hand, and he smiles, reaching out to clasp it.

But then another man follows him out of the cellar, and I remember the reason we came to the cellar at all: Sommer.

He's not bound anymore, and he looks from me to Thorin to the guards like he wonders if he should flee back down the steps.

Thorin grabs hold of his sleeve and drags him forward before he can. "The night we had to run, I knew *I* couldn't go far—and I knew Sommer was trapped down here anyway. I figured I'd wait it out and see what happened. Alice wouldn't leave me, so she hid down here, too. We could hear the soldiers and the fighting overhead, and I told him what was going on." He pauses, and his voice grows softer. "It became obvious when people were caught. Sommer told me to cut him loose. He said he'd help." He pauses again. "So I did. And he did."

I study them both. They look back at me, but it's Sommer who looks beseeching.

Eventually, I turn to Nook, and I remember the way the men had him participate in retaliating against Sommer for his role in what happened. His father was one of the men who was killed. He was just as affected as I was.

"Sommer is guilty of treason, Nook. Should we bring him back with us? Has he earned his freedom? Or should I leave him in the cellar?"

Nook's eyes widen, and he glances between me and Sommer. "You're leaving it up to *me*?" he says.

As soon as I hear him say it, I almost take it back. He's barely sixteen years old, if he's even that.

But then I realize Corrick was even younger when I named him as King's Justice, and he had to do a lot worse.

I nod. "Yes. I'm leaving it up to you."

Nook looks at Sommer. "He stabbed a soldier that was about to shoot me." He pauses. "And he saved Violet, too. We're even."

"*Also*," Violet says, "Chickenseed is *really* bad at cards."

I raise my eyebrows. "Chickenseed?"

Sommer heaves a sigh and looks at Nook. "Thank you for my life *and* my nickname."

Alice giggles.

Thorin looks past me, seeming to realize for the first time that Consul Beeching is by my side, and we're backed by men who aren't palace guards. "Have you reclaimed the Royal Sector?"

"Not yet," I say.

—⊷—

On our ride back, Jonas indicates that he wants to speak privately with me, so we ride ahead of the group, leaving enough distance that we won't be overheard.

"That girl adores you," he says to me. "That's part of why I agreed to help you, you know."

I look at him. Jonas is older, older than my parents were, and he was never particularly close to them—so he's never been particularly close to us either. We've never had a strained relationship, but of all the consuls, I know him the least well. He's granted me a lot of assistance. Quite a bit more than I expected. He even sent food and sundries to the homes of my guards when I asked, when I fully expected him to balk at something that would so openly defy restrictions that have been put in place by others. I've been keenly aware that his help *now* will likely have ramifications later, like a debt to be repaid. So I'm not sure what to make of that comment.

"You just met her," I say.

"It doesn't matter. I've seen the way the people from the Wilds look at you when you walk among them. I think they would *all* hug you like that if they could." He pauses. "We've all seen Arella's proof, and it's rather convincing. I do believe your parents had devised quite the plan to fleece silver from the people, and they were working with Nathaniel Sallister and Lissa Marpetta to do it." He studies me in the sunlight. "I do not, however, think that you or Prince Corrick had anything to do with it. In all honesty, I don't believe there's anything Allisander Sallister can say to convince me otherwise. Unfortunately, he and some of the others refuse to yield in *their* claims that you did. I'm worried about what that might mean for the future of Kandala."

My spine goes cold when he says that.

Because he's ultimately talking about civil war.

"Why don't *you* believe Sallister?" I say.

"Because despite your aloof demeanor, I simply don't believe you would be poisoning the people when you genuinely seem to care for them." He gestures at everyone following us. "That girl's reaction to your arrival spoke volumes. I saw you pick up that doll. I heard you consider burying your treasonous guard. And it's not just now. When you rejected my funding request for the bridge last month, it was obviously for the protection of—"

"When I rejected your request," I say flatly, "you said I was heartless."

He breaks off in surprise, then looks over, and I have no trouble holding his gaze.

"Don't try to deny it," I say. "I remember."

"Yes, Your Majesty. I did say it." He lets out a breath. "But I wasn't talking about you. Or—not entirely. I was angry. We truly *do* need a bridge, and Sallister was accusing me of trying to manipulate my proposal for my own profit, when he's the one who is always after every coin." He grimaces and looks away. "But I'm ashamed to admit that when I reviewed my proposal later, I discovered that our engineers *had* inflated the numbers. I still don't know if it was deliberate or an oversight, but you and Prince Corrick were right to reject it."

I'm not sure what to say to this. We ride on in silence for a while.

Jonas eventually looks over. "I simply don't believe their claims because if you were in on it, there'd be no reason for Sallister to stop. There would've been no reason for you to risk your life in the sector on the day the rebels attacked the palace. There would've been no reason for you to offer amnesty. You could've had the army kill the rebels. You could've had them kill us *all*. But you didn't."

"I had no idea about the poison, Jonas. I wish I did." I swallow, and my throat is tight. I think about Quint's years of notes about all the ways I've tried to protect everyone—and all the ways I've failed. My brother's years of doing horrific vicious things until he was broken and couldn't take it anymore. I think of all the loss and pain and suffering that my people endured. "I would have stopped it the very instant I took the throne."

"I know," he says. "And that's what I've been telling Arella and Roydan. They've requested to speak with you this evening."

My shoulders immediately go tense as I remember the conversation I overheard. I know Sallister is working against me, but he's doing it in poor faith. Arella and Roydan are different. They genuinely do have proof that points to the royal family, and Arella has always been openly critical of our methods to keep smuggling activity to a minimum.

They have no motivation to help me.

"What did you tell them?" I say.

"I said I would ask if you were receiving visitors."

So he allowed me the chance to refuse—and to refuse privately.

I want to. Everything, as usual, is still so precarious.

But a refusal, I know, would imply guilt. I draw a slow breath. "Please send word that I'll welcome their company."

—+—

By the time Roydan and Arella arrive, I've spun myself into knots. I've asked Jonas for the room to be mostly empty of guards, because I don't want to heighten any tensions. I have Thorin and Saeth at the wall, with Quint seated beside me, his book and pencil ready. I'm so grateful for his presence, and I realize I've *always* been grateful for his presence.

Jonas didn't bring any guards of his own to the room, but Roydan and Arella did. A servant pours wine and tea and lays out a tray of pastries, and we all sip and stir and exchange pleasantries like this is a social visit, until I'm ready to explode from the pressure of it all. But they asked for this meeting, so I wait.

"Your Majesty, I believe I should be direct," Arella finally says.

Do you really think thirty minutes of pleasantries could be considered direct? I want to say. But I don't.

"Please," I say.

"Jonas has been urging us to consider that you were unaware of the actions of your parents, specifically your father."

"I was," I say quietly. "I don't have a way to prove it to you, but I was."

"Your penalties were always very harsh," she says. "Prince Corrick's actions were never subtle. You know I have always been an outspoken advocate for change." She pauses. "It was alarming to hear rumors that the King's Justice was secretly moving among the populace as an outlaw himself."

"I've heard those rumors," I say carefully.

"Some people say he did that in an attempt to capture more of the people," she says. "To punish those who might have uncovered his wrongdoings."

I look right back at her. "I hope you know we have always heard your concerns, Arella. We may have been harsh, but I hope you believe that I have been fair. That my brother has been just." I pause. "If Prince Corrick was moving among the people as one of them, it wasn't to cause harm."

She's quiet for a moment, studying me, but I meant every word, and I don't look away. "When I discovered the shipping logs from Trader's Landing," she says, "I wasn't sure what to believe. A tremendous amount of steel had been shipped to unknown cities over the course of *decades*, and there were notes from Consul Montague about side promises with unknown cities, as well as some correspondence with King Lucas that seems to indicate some argument over who would receive the greatest share of the profits. It wasn't until we found a note about the means to infuse the poisonous roots of the Moonflower into the water supply that we began to suspect the worst."

"Of me," I say.

She nods. "Yes." She pauses. "Some of the correspondence is inconclusive, and with your parents dead, and Consul Montague dead, we may never have the full picture of it, Your Majesty. But you've been removed from the throne and the poisoning has stopped, and word has begun to spread among the sectors. It's rather damning."

"As planned," I say evenly, though my stomach has formed a knot.

"Possibly," she concedes. "Especially since some of the notes from Montague—and others—indicate some not-so-veiled threats on your life when you were a child, using this very same poison."

I've gone still, and the silence in the room is thick. Even Quint, at my side, has stopped writing.

Jonas clears his throat. "Your frequent illness as a child was never a secret," he says.

"And as much as you've tried to hide it as an adult," Arella adds, "it was still obvious to those of us in your inner circle."

She pulls a folded piece of parchment from under the table and slides it across to me.

> Look what it's done to your son. This is what you want to do to your people.
> – Barnard

I'm frozen in place. It's not proof of anything—but it also is. I think of all the times we visited Consul Montague when I was a child, or the times he'd visit the palace. I try to remember if I felt more sickly then, but it's been too long. There's no way to know.

"So you think Barnard Montague tried to assassinate them to *stop* them?" I say.

She exchanges a glance with Jonas and Roydan. "There's no way to be sure. And he wasn't without fault. He was clearly skimming profits from whatever trade deals he'd made with Ostriary for steel. Some of those records go back to your grandfather's reign. Possibly even older. It's taken us weeks to go through everything. They hid the evidence well."

"From me as well," I say. "I had no idea. Truly. I hope you believe me."

She studies me for a long time, but it's Roydan who speaks, and he leans over and pats me on the hand like I'm a child. "I do. You were dealt a rough hand. You've done your best."

I look at him in surprise. He's so old, and I've known him since . . . well, since birth. I know he occasionally dotes on Corrick, but he's never really done it to *me*.

Arella sighs. "I do, too."

I snap my head around to look at her.

"I do," she says again. "When I first discovered proof, it seemed obvious that this had been a long-running plot between you and Consul Sallister. Again, your penalties were so swift and brutal. Baron Pepperleaf's daughter seemed to be an ally of the people, because she was so interested in Tessa Cade's medicine. I shared my records with her, and she told me Captain Huxley had information on the king." She hesitates. "But as time has gone on . . . I've wondered if the opposite could be true. That Laurel Pepperleaf was interested in Miss Cade's medicine because she was worried she would discover the truth about the poison. Because it has become clear that Captain Huxley has been on Consul Sallister's payroll for *years* to feed him information about the king. Both Allisander and his father before him."

The more I learn about Sallister, the more I want to see *him* at the end of a rope. I turn my head. "Thorin, why did you and the rest of my guards close ranks against Captain Huxley?"

"Because he couldn't be trusted."

Arella's mouth forms a line.

I sit back in my chair. "You and Roydan have been quietly reviewing these shipping logs for quite some time now. When you suspected poison, you didn't consider coming to ask me directly?"

"I should have," she says. "And I wish I did. Because now Sallister has taken residence in the palace and he's practically sitting on the throne himself."

I make a disgusted sound. "I suppose I'm lucky I didn't find him sleeping in my bed."

Her eyes flare. "That *was* you!"

"Yes."

She sighs and glances between me and Jonas. "Well, as Jonas said, it has become clear that you couldn't have been poisoning the people. If you were in the palace, you surely noticed that the halls were empty. Most of the staff has resigned. Your personal guard—"

"I know what they've done to my personal guard," I say darkly.

She clears her throat. "Yes. Captain Huxley has maintained as many guards as he could, but nowhere near the number that once lined the halls. I wouldn't trust anyone who remains."

"I wouldn't either."

"Allisander may believe he has power now, but he does not have the support you once did."

My eyebrows go up. "So are you saying that you will join Consul Beeching? You will support my claim to the throne?"

"I will," Roydan says.

Arella nods. "As will I."

Despite the relief in my heart, their voices carry the weight of unspoken dread, of more to say, and I hold my breath.

"There is more you need to know," Arella continues. "Allisander still has the means to continue poisoning the people. He can spread it through the water and weaken the populace again, claiming that perhaps someone *else* is now working against Kandala— either Consul Beeching, or me, or even you yourself, as retaliation for his actions. When he heard we were coming to speak with you, he threatened to release more poison immediately. He controls access to the cure, so he could weaken our defenses while fortifying his own."

My fist is tight against the table. At my side, Quint is writing furiously.

"Allisander has also revealed that word has reached the palace that the lookouts at Port Karenin have spotted a ship in the ocean flying the Kandalan flag."

Corrick. I gasp aloud. Quint snaps his head up.

Arella nods. "I've sent word to Sunkeep to verify the reports, but the ship will arrive before my runners will."

My heart is pounding so hard in my chest. "How soon?"

"Within days. But Your Majesty, you must—"

"*Days!*" My brother is returning within days. My heart wants to explode with so many emotions. "You've known this since we sat down?" I demand.

"I have." She lifts a placating hand. "His arrival will not be simple. Consul Sallister and Baron Pepperleaf have access to armed brigantines. They're prepared to destroy the ship upon arrival unless you surrender to them at dawn tomorrow."

Every muscle in my body ices over.

"Artis has ships," says Jonas. "We can attempt to form a blockade across the Queen's River—"

"And wage a cannon battle right here at the docks," I say. "We'll kill half the people we just rescued." I run a hand across my face. "And he'll release his poison anyway."

The room goes so still. So silent. I think of Violet springing out of that cellar to throw her arms around me.

"So I am to sacrifice myself or I am to sacrifice my brother," I say quietly.

She nods.

It's no choice at all really. Cory has been sacrificing himself for me for years. I know what I have to do.

"Tell him I'll surrender," I say.

The room erupts with protests. Jonas, my guards, even Arella and Roydan.

But not Quint. His eyes are dark and fixed on mine.

Because he knows. He knows I won't be swayed from this.

He said it himself.

You love your brother so very, very much.

"Enough," I say, and they fall silent. "*Tell him.* I will arrive at the palace at dawn. I will be alone. I want assurance that no brigantines will sail the river, and Jonas, I want your sailors patrolling twenty miles north and south of the docks to be sure of it. You tell Allisander that if we spot *one single sail*, I will not appear. Those are *my* terms."

Arella nods. "Yes, Your Majesty."

I look at Jonas. "I want my brother to arrive safely, and I expect you to honor your alliance with me and continue it with him."

He stares at me, his eyes wide, but he nods as well. "I will. I swear it."

My heart won't stop pounding. I look at Arella and Roydan. "Go. I expect a report back by midnight that he accepts." My thoughts are spinning now, and I barely know what I'm saying. "Consuls, if you'll excuse me, I need to spend the evening preparing."

I don't even wait for a response to this; I simply stand and head for the door. Quint and the guards follow me, but my pulse is a thundering rush in my ears, so I have no idea if they're speaking.

Despite everything, I'm somehow still shocked when Quint follows me right into my sleeping quarters. I brace my shoulders against the wall and run my hands through my hair and try not to scream.

He catches the door before it can slam shut, then eases it closed. He stops right in front of me and takes hold of my wrists.

"Breathe," he says. "You don't have to go alone."

"I do," I say. "I *do*. He's not going to imprison me. He's going to hang me, Quint. He's going to do it as publicly as possible. He'll hang anyone who comes with me, you *know* that—"

"I do know that." His voice is so quiet, his hands so gentle against my wrists. "I'll go with you."

I stare into his eyes. I wasted so much time.

"Tell me what you need," he whispers.

"I need you to stay," I say, and my voice breaks. "I need you to stay for Corrick." Quint is shaking his head, and I add, "You told me you would deny me nothing, Quint."

He goes still. He sighs.

"Please," I say. "Please." I swallow tightly, and it hurts. "It—it would help me to know that my brother wasn't alone."

Quint stares back at me, and finally, he nods. "Yes, Your Majesty."

Out of anything he could say, *that* jars me out of my emotion for a fraction of a second. "Oh, for goodness' sake, Quint, *still*?"

He blinks, and I realize his eyes are gleaming with tears. "But this is the most regal thing you've ever done."

"Lord." I press a thumb to his cheek and brush away the first tear that dares to fall. "No tears yet. If I'm going to die at dawn, there's work to be done."

He blinks in surprise, then pulls his little book from his jacket. "All right. Go ahead."

I take the book from his hands, but gently this time, no tussling. Then I kiss him softly. "No," I say. "No book, no notes. *You* rest."

He frowns. "You know I won't sleep."

"Very well." I step away, moving toward the desk in the corner of the room, which has been stocked with a rather impressive set of fountain pens and papers and an entire array of wax seals. "Tonight, it's my turn to write."

I have so many things to say to Corrick, and my thoughts can barely contain them all. He'll be returning to a country that's still divided, on the brink of war yet again. He'll have to rule. He'll have to *lead*. I tell him everything that's transpired, but a lot of other things, too. A lot of things I wish I'd told him when he was here. A lot of things I'll never have the chance to say.

Quint sits with me and writes a few letters of his own, but I keep going, well into the night, and eventually he does rest. Despite his promise not to sleep, he drifts off, too, his breathing slow and even.

I write on.

As I near the end, I look out the window at the darkness, thinking back on every moment I spent with my brother at my side. Every moment we'll never have again.

And it gives me an idea.

CHAPTER THIRTY-SEVEN

Tessa

This journey by ship has been much more enjoyable than the last one.

It helps that Corrick doesn't hate anyone on board. Rian remained behind in Ostriary, but most of his crew is manning the ship with Olive. Mouse is traveling with us, too. I was uncertain about that at first, but Corrick was worried that in his absence, the man would still be abused by those who remained from Oren's followers. Olive expressed her worries as well, but since we shoved off, Mouse has been quiet and reserved, working with the crew and doing what he's told—though he still refers to Corrick as Weston.

At night, we all sit under the stars and play games while enjoying lively conversation. There are no barbed comments, no caustic remarks, no tricks or lies or threats. Ellmo and Anya play knucklebones on the deck in the morning, and Olive and Erik can sometimes be found embracing in shadowed corners. Lochlan's usual edge seems to be gone, and I'm reminded of the day he once said to me, *I am kind.*

When he plays games with the children or helps the sailors gut the fish or brings me a plate of food, I feel like I'm seeing it for the first time.

Or maybe I'm just . . . *allowing* myself to see it. New information, like Erik said that day in the woods.

"What's Erik going to do when Olive has to go back to Ostriary?" I murmur to Corrick one night when we're in the dim confines of our quarters. We've made the turn north up the Queen's River, and the rocking of the ship has grown stronger, but I almost don't care anymore. We're so close to home. Two or three days at most.

"Quit his job," Corrick says immediately.

I swat him on the arm. "I'm serious."

He looks back at me. "So am I. After everything we've gone through, can you truly see Rocco returning to his post among the king's personal guard?"

I study him for a moment, considering—and I'm shocked to realize he's right. "Wow."

"I wouldn't be surprised if he asks Harristan for leave the very instant we get back."

I blow out a breath. "It wasn't too long ago that he was telling me he'd give the king forty more years if he could."

"Well, I could be wrong, but based on the way he and Olive have been attached to each other, I'd expect him to moon around for all forty." Corrick smiles and tugs me against him. "Haven't you learned? Love changes things."

Before I can come up with an answer to that, his mouth falls on mine. He steals my breath until my heart is racing against him, warmth pooling in my belly.

But then he pulls away, his hands chastely on my waist.

Which is exactly what he's done every single time he's kissed me on this ship.

We're so close to home, and my cheeks are on fire, so I grab hold of his shirt and hold him against me this time.

He laughs so softly that it's almost a growl. "Tessa."

"Why do you keep pulling away?"

"I told you I would make a declaration before the king. I gave you my word." He strokes a gentle finger along the side of my face, but then a devilish glint sparks in his eye. "No matter what I want, I meant what I said."

"You mean we can't do anything until you talk to your *brother*?" I demand.

"Well—no, of course not. But I thought you—"

"*Lord*, Corrick." I press my lips to his again, thrusting the full length of my body against his. This time I pull a real growl from his throat—especially when I tug his shirt free of his trousers. I don't even hesitate: I simply pull it straight up, and he helps me by yanking it right over his head. Then my hands are on the bare skin of his chest, and he buries his fingers in my hair, and suddenly I'm drowning in the taste of his mouth.

I'm so eager that I expect him to be quick, but his hands are slow. Gentle. Patient. When he draws the lacings free on my vest, I'm so desperate for his touch that I seize his wrist and pull his palm against the bare skin of my waist. His fingers trace a line of fire all the way up my rib cage, and when he lingers on my breast, it's my turn to make a low sound of need.

I don't know when we make it to the bed, just that we've abandoned most of our clothes on the way. His arms are so strong, and his body is so warm, and I've never felt so cherished, so loved, so adored. When we come together, he's so careful, his blue eyes close and intent on mine. I press a hand to his cheek, run a thumb over his mouth. We have so many moments, so many memories, and this one etches its way right to the top.

But then he moves, and I gasp, and his fingers trace the edge of my breast, and suddenly I can't think at all for a while.

It's late and I'm tired, but neither one of us is sleeping. I'm laying across his chest, running my fingers through the new scruff of beard growth on Corrick's chin.

"Is this annoying?" I say.

"Quite a bit."

I grin. "It's very different."

"It felt *very* rebellious."

That makes my smile widen. But as I gaze down at him, I suddenly realize it's not the facial hair that looks different. It's . . . *him*. He's always been bold and unflinching as the King's Justice, but something in his bearing has changed. It's like the moment he agreed to go after Olive, or the way he stared through the spyglass and helped formulate a plan to take down Oren Crane. The way he's formed more than just a friendship with Lochlan, and how he seems to have secured something akin to true loyalty and allegiance. Even his final speech to Rian about how he *also* wanted the best for the people of Ostriary was startling. It's a new presence that he's acquired. A steadfast look in his gaze, maybe. There's a determination there. A powerful resolve.

His blue eyes fix on mine. "Do you like it?"

I stroke a thumb over his chin. "Very much," I say, and I'm not really talking about facial hair at all.

He runs a hand across his jaw, capturing my fingers within his own. "Harristan will probably insist that I have Geoffrey shave it the instant I get back to the palace." He goes still when he says that. "It feels so odd to say that after so many weeks."

He looks up, over my head, at the dark porthole on the wall, and I follow his gaze. We can see the first hint of lights somewhere in the distance, the promise of cities in the more populous sectors.

"We're almost home," he says.

"I've missed Kandala so much."

He's quiet for a moment. "Me too."

Longing fills his eyes, and when he says the words, I hear the weight in his voice. But it's not *Kandala* that he's missing so much.

It's his brother.

CHAPTER THIRTY-EIGHT

Harristan

It's not hard to sneak out of Consul Beeching's house. Or maybe my guards just allow me to do it, the way they did when I was a teenager. Maybe they think I'm running away from my duty and this is the only way they can keep me alive.

They're wrong.

Regardless, I slip onto a horse bareback and jog out of the manor stables, then canter all the way to the Wilds. My heart was in my throat last night, pounding with panic, but now I'm settled with purpose. My letters are written, my goodbyes said. I even wrote a letter to Quint, left by his side on the bed.

And now I'm here, pulling open the barrier to the spy tunnel that leads into the palace.

Walking it alone for the last time.

I stare at the wall of the palace in the moonlight, wishing Stonehammer's Arch were still lit so I could see it a final time.

Ah, but there are so many wishes that I can't make come true.

I latch my fingers into the wall and climb. Back into my quarters I go. The darkness is more absolute tonight. It's later, the moon at a different angle.

A scratch of sound echoes behind me, and I spin, ducking low.

Then, to my absolute shock, Quint steps through the window.

"Quint!" I hiss. "Are you insane?"

"I rather feel as though I'm owed the same answer, Your Majesty."

"Go back!" I say.

He holds up a piece of paper. "Tell Consul Beeching that what I am doing ensures the safety of all citizens," he reads. His eyes flick up to find mine. "You couldn't think to wake me?"

I frown and look away. "That's not *all* I wrote."

"You didn't write nearly *enough*."

"Please, Quint. I need you to go back. I need—"

"*I* need to know what you're doing." He walks right up to me and hits me in the chest.

My eyes flare in surprise. But then I see his pain, and I put a hand to his cheek. "Forgive me." I hesitate. "Sallister and Huxley will be here at dawn to wait for me. Possibly Baron Pepperleaf and any of their other allies. You know what they're doing to the people."

He frowns. "And?"

"I'm going to hide in the servants' hallway and light the explosives behind the throne room."

He stares at me, his chest rising and falling rapidly. He's clearly waiting for there to be more to my plan.

There isn't.

"You'll die," he says.

"I'm dead anyway. But I can take them with me. They won't be able to stand against Corrick."

He swallows so hard I can see his throat jerk. He nods and puts a hand over mine.

"Thank you," I say. "You must go quickly. It'll be dawn soon, and we can't risk being found out."

"I'm not leaving you."

"Quint. Corrick needs you—"

"No, Harristan." He takes my hand. "*You* need me."

Of course he would say it *now*. This time my eyes go blurry with tears, and he steps closer, his finger gentle as he brushes them away. "No time for tears. There's work to be done."

"You're right," I say, and I tug his hand.

———+———

We slip through the abandoned servants' hallways, which are silent and dark. When we find the passage behind the throne room, I'm worried that Annabeth was lying, and there will be no explosives, or that there will be a chance that they've already been discovered and moved, but we tug and pull at wall hangings and tapestries and sconces and paintings until we finally find them.

And there they are, just as she promised. Strung together with narrow bits of twine, dozens of bundles of explosives, tucked behind various paintings in hollows carved out for exactly this purpose.

"This was well planned," Quint whispers to me.

I nod. "They almost killed me then. So maybe it's fitting that their explosives will prevent him from causing more harm."

"You brought matches?" he says.

That draws me up short.

Lord. No. I forgot matches.

Quint laughs under his breath, then tugs a small box from his jacket. He taps it against my chest. "I grabbed them from the servants' closet."

"I would be lost without you."

"I know. Where shall we hide?"

I look around. "Do we have to? We'll be able to see the sunrise through those windows. We'll hear them on the other side of the wall."

"Very well. Shall we sit?"

We do, shoulder to shoulder, arm to arm, and I listen to him breathe. I lace our fingers together and feel his heartbeat.

And when the sky begins to lighten, he says, "Would Sullivan the stable boy keep visiting the mill, do you think?"

I turn and look at him. "Every day. And when the miller was retiring, the stable boy would be devastated to learn that the miller's boy was heading off to the Royal Sector to take an apprenticeship in the palace."

"Oh, the miller's boy would be a fool to do that. Work for some stoic king who rarely smiles?" He scoffs. "No, he'd take over the mill himself and hire the stable boy to fill his barn with a dozen quality steeds."

I smile and kiss him. "But why on earth would a miller need—"

The sound of a voice stops me. Then another. Allisander, for sure. I'm not certain on the other one, but I think it might be Captain Huxley. I'm frozen in place. They're on the other side of the wall, so they'll never see us, but I'm trembling anyway.

Quint's hand never leaves mine. I'm gripping so tight. So is he.

I kiss him one last time, pulling his hand to my heart.

Then I find the box of matches. My hands are shaking so hard that I nearly drop them all.

Quint reaches out and steadies me, his fingers supporting mine. "For Kandala," he says.

I nod. "For Kandala."

Then I strike the match.

CHAPTER THIRTY-NINE

Tessa

On our final morning at sea, I wake to find Corrick fully dressed and laced into his boots before the sun has fully crested the horizon.

He's also cleanshaven.

I put a hand against the warm smoothness of his cheek when he bends down to kiss me. "No more rebellion?" I tease.

"We'll have enough shocking revelations for Harristan. I'll spare him this one."

That makes me smile. I can hear the eagerness in his tone. "How soon until we reach Artis?"

"Less than two hours." He pulls my hand to his mouth and kisses my knuckles. "I'm going to go up top and discuss our plans for arrival with Olive and Rocco. The ship isn't a secret this time, so there might be a bit of fanfare at the docks when we draw near. I'll want to be on deck so everyone can see that I've returned safely." He pauses. "I'd like for you to be by my side."

Everyone. I wonder if he means his brother.

But I nod quickly. His excitement is infectious, and my own heart thumps. "I'll get ready right now."

He kisses my knuckles again. "We're almost home."

I take hold of his hand, gripping tight. "Almost."

For a long moment, his blue eyes hold mine. But then he gives me a nod, a quick caress of my cheek, and he's gone.

—◆—

I'm shocked by the number of people lining the docks when the ship sails close. I've lived in Artis all my life, and the docks have never been so crowded. I've never seen tents before either, but they stretch along the shore for a mile at least, and I can see more in the distance. Corrick mentioned fanfare, but there must be *thousands* of people waiting on our arrival. The sun is bright overhead, and I can see guards and patrol officers moving among the crowds. No palace guards, though. No hint of blue-and-purple livery anywhere.

Corrick has been by my side along the railing, but his earlier excitement has turned into something darker. "This isn't right," he says.

"What's wrong?" I say—but I can feel it, too.

"There should be palace guards here. The ship would have been spotted from Port Karenin days before we made it to the river. Word would've been sent to the palace." He turns his head toward the bow of the ship, where Erik is standing with Olive. "Rocco!"

Beside us, Lochlan is also looking out over the crowd, searching for any hint of blue and purple the way I am. "Maybe the king couldn't come?" he guesses. "Maybe something happened and he had to stay at the palace."

Erik—well, Rocco again, returned to his palace livery—has joined us by the railing. He looks out over the crowd, too, surveying the complete and total lack of guards. "His Majesty still would have sent a contingent of guards. With crowds this big, it's clear that your arrival was expected."

At my side, Corrick's expression has gone very still, very cold.

The face he used to wear when he had to do the most terrible things of all.

"Advise," he says to Rocco.

The guardsman shakes his head. "I cannot."

But then we draw closer to the dock, and I'm able to make out individual faces. Just as I recognize my best friend standing with a group of people, Lochlan sucks in a breath.

"Karri," he says, and the relief in his tone is obvious. "But who's that she's standing with?"

Corrick says nothing.

I glance up at him. His eyes are ice cold and fixed on the shore.

I reach out and take his hand. For an instant, he doesn't move, and his fingers simply tremble in mine. But then he grips tight.

"Corrick," I whisper.

He says nothing. I don't think he's breathing.

"Miss Karri stands with Consul Beeching," says Rocco, when no one answers Lochlan's question. "Along with Thorin and Saeth of the king's guard."

Thorin! My eyes jerk back to the dock, and I realize he's right. Thorin is there beside Consul Beeching, along with Saeth, who I barely know.

I can't make out their expressions from here, but neither of them are in their guard livery.

A bolt of fear pierces my chest.

Corrick's fingers are gripping my hand as if it's all that's keeping him tethered to the deck of the ship. I don't think he's taken a breath in more than a minute. His jaw is like granite, his eyes harder than I've ever seen them.

But when he speaks, his voice is so even and cool that he could be a stranger. "We need to dock immediately."

"Corrick," I say again, but he doesn't look at me. His cold eyes are fixed on that dock, on his brother's guards, on the complete lack of blue and purple anywhere at all.

It reminds me of the night that Consul Sallister forced him to execute the prisoners. This is the most distant Corrick of all.

But his hand stays tight on mine. It seems to take forever for the ship to be tethered to the moorings, for a gangway to be rolled out. Corrick is quiet and still the whole time, his eyes never ceasing the search along the shoreline. I know who he's looking for. I don't say a word, but I look for him, too. So does Lochlan.

None of us find any sign of the king. No sign of Quint. No other guards.

Then the ship is rocking against the dock, and Rocco is indicating that we can disembark. Corrick has been frozen in place for so long that I don't think he's going to be able to move, but he does. His stride is strong and sure—but his hand trembles against mine again, his fingers suddenly fluttering in my grip.

"It's all right," I whisper, but it's a lie. Nothing is all right.

"Keep breathing," says Lochlan, and Corrick's head shakes, almost imperceptibly.

Then we step onto the bridge to shore, and the people begin to applaud.

For an instant, Corrick's step falters, but Lochlan puts a hand on his shoulder. I grip his hand more tightly. The applause grows in strength, but I don't hear it. I don't feel my feet striking the narrow bridge. I only feel the weight of expectation, of fear, of dread.

As soon as our feet land on the solid ground of Artis, the people send up a cheer, and so many of them try to press close that I'm worried we're going to be overrun. The sound is deafening. But Rocco is there, and to my surprise, Mouse is at our back. Even still, there's too much noise, too much shouting, and I can't make out the words. I can't make sense of anything.

But then I realize that people are beginning to kneel, in a slow, rippling outward fashion, the way they do for King Harristan.

And then I realize what they're saying.

Long live the king.

My breath catches and freezes in my throat. Beside us, Rocco has put a hand over his heart, and he's dropped to one knee himself. So has Lochlan.

So has everyone.

I look up, and Corrick's eyes are finally on mine, and for a blazing second, he looks terrified, before the cool blue ices over and I realize I'm the only one standing.

Oh, I'm such a fool. A sob chokes free of my lips, and I begin to drop to one knee myself.

Corrick grabs hold of me before I can. He pulls me hard against him, his arms tight against my back. His breathing is quiet in my ear, but the beat of his heart is so hard against my chest. I wrap my arms around his neck.

"I'm sorry," I whisper. "I'm so very sorry."

His face presses into my neck, and it's only then that I hear his breath shudder. I stroke a hand over the back of his head, and I remember all the times we talked about appearances, and cynicism, and vulnerabilities, and I hope I'm not weakening him now.

But he's clutching at me so tightly and his breath is shaking against my neck and I don't know what else to do. He shouldn't have to learn that his brother is dead while people are cheering for his safe return.

"Corrick," I whisper again, and I realize I'm crying, too. "Oh, my love. I'm so sorry."

"Your Majesty," says a voice, and Corrick snaps his head up. The desperation on his face is so absolute. His eyes are wide and searching, as if his brother has suddenly appeared, as if this has all been a moment of grand confusion.

But Harristan is dead.

This is someone addressing Corrick.

Seeing the realization dawn in his eyes is like watching him learn the truth all over again. His gaze fractures, his shoulders nearly fall, his body jerks like he's taken a blow.

But Corrick draws himself up at once. All emotion put away, locked down.

The man who spoke is Jonas Beeching, and he's risen to his feet. "Forgive me," he says gently. "I know that this is a shock. But much has happened during your absence, and there are many matters that must be addressed—and swiftly."

Corrick goes rigid. I didn't think his eyes could go colder, but they do. His hand slips out of mine, and he turns to face the consul. I shiver at the sudden distance, and I want to grab his hand back. Not just for me, but for him, too. I wonder if it was like this for Harristan when their parents died. Were the former king and queen lying in pools of blood, while the consuls suddenly turned to Harristan, at age nineteen, and started making demands of him?

With a shock, I realize it must have been exactly like that.

And now they're going to do the same thing to Corrick.

Lochlan steps forward, and he must be realizing the exact same thing. "Look," he snaps at the consul, who blinks at his brazenness. "The man just lost his *brother*, so you can give him a few minutes—"

"I *assure* you," says Consul Beeching, "we cannot—"

"Enough," says Corrick, and for as cold as his voice is, he sounds exactly like his brother. So much so that everyone around us goes quiet. I think he even startles himself. But after a bare hesitation, he continues. "Consul Beeching, please have your people see to Princess Olive of Ostriary. This is her ship, and she graciously returned me home. We can take care of whatever needs addressing for Kandala immediately."

"Good," says the consul. "I do have a carriage waiting." He gestures ahead.

Rocco moves to clear a path, and Corrick nods, moving to follow. Consul Beeching looks to some of the people surrounding him, and I realize Karri and Thorin are back behind several guards who have followed the consul. Those same guards are now moving to separate me and Lochlan from Corrick, drawing us away, propelling us in the opposite direction.

I gasp. "Corrick!" I call, but the crowd is too loud, and I don't think he'll hear me.

"Miss Cade," says the consul, "you will go with—"

"No!" Corrick turns around at once. His eyes meet mine, and again, I see that flicker of panic, of desperation, of *need*. But only for a moment, and only for me. Then it's iced over. "Miss Cade will remain with me."

There are a few gasps around us, but I don't hear who makes them.

"Lochlan and Karri should follow us as well," Corrick says.

The guards go still. Now it's Lochlan's turn to look at him in shock.

Consul Beeching's mouth works silently for a moment, and he glances at Lochlan a little dubiously, but then he says, "Yes, of course, Your Majesty. This way."

I'm worried that we're all going to be forced to share a carriage, but there are several waiting, and I'm glad to see that Karri and King Harristan's guards Thorin and Saeth have also followed us.

"Tessa and I will share a carriage alone," Corrick declares, and that's all he says before he barely allows time for a footman to open the door to one. Once we're inside, the door slams, and the ice simply *melts* from his expression. His face falls into his hands.

Then he doesn't make a sound.

It's so silent in the carriage, but I climb onto the bench beside him and wrap my arms around him. After a moment, he picks up my hand and pulls it to his heart, the way a child would clutch a treasured doll. When the driver cracks a whip and the carriage begins to move, we remain just like that.

I have no idea how long we have, but it won't be enough time.

I brush my fingers through his hair, stroking his back, letting him breathe.

"I should never have gone," he whispers.

"You don't know what happened."

"I know I wasn't *here.*"

"If you hadn't gone, you never would have learned the truth about the poison. Kandala would have been no better off."

That seems to settle him, but just a little bit.

Then his head lifts, and he finally looks at me. His eyes glitter with unshed tears, and he says, "I loved him so very much, Tessa."

The emotion in his voice breaks my heart. I shed the tears he can't, and I nod. "I know," I say. "I know you did. And he knew, too. I swear to you, he knew."

"What am I going to do?"

I look into his desperate face, and I put a hand against the warmth of his cheek. The cheek he shaved this morning because he didn't want to disappoint his brother. I brush a thumb along the smoothness of his jaw to remind him of it. "You're going to be a great king."

CHAPTER FORTY

Corrick

My dear brother. I keep thinking of the last words you said to me when you left Kandala.

"Be here when I get back."

Cory, please forgive me. I'm so sorry I won't be.

Harristan's letter is thirty-five pages long, but it takes me forever to read beyond the first few lines. I've been trying not to cry, but by the third page, he's said so many things that I'm glad Tessa is already asleep in bed, and I'm alone. By the time I get to the end, I read the entire thing again.

Quint wrote me a letter, too, but his is short.

My dearest friend, you will make a fine king. I hope you understand why I couldn't leave him alone during his finest hour.

I read it a dozen times, wishing for more.

My brother is dead. My best friend is dead.

I haven't quite convinced myself that any of this is real, that Harristan orchestrated it to protect me and the people, that the villains died in the same terrible explosion that took out most of the palace. I have no one to punish, no vengeance to chase, no way to ease this pain.

I simply have a kingdom that's practically in shambles.

Harristan's letter has numerous passages that make me long for all the things we never got to say in person, but most of what he wrote is practical: outlining everything that happened, everything I need to do, and everything he hopes for—both for me and for Kandala. Despite his efforts, it's going to take *months* to straighten out the mess left behind. I've only spent a day trying to unwind who I can trust and who might still be secretly working against me, and I'm already exhausted. But now it's after midnight, and the manor is finally quiet. Tessa fell asleep two hours ago, but I feel like I'll never sleep again, so I'm staring into the hearth in the sitting room, alone.

I'd give anything for Quint right now. I'd give anything for . . . *anyone.*

I have a handful of consuls left, so those will need to be replaced. I don't even know if I can trust any of them—including Jonas. He's offered me anything I could need, but I haven't been gone from Kandala for *so* long. I know gifts and promises usually come with conditions and favors that are expected later.

I can't rule from here either. Not for long. I've heard that most of the palace was destroyed, so that will need to be rebuilt, which will take funding. Consul Beeching's men reported that looters were discovered trying to pick through the rubble, so his guards have been posted along the site to prevent thieving. Aside from

Thorin, Saeth, and Rocco, I don't know who among the palace guards can be trusted, so those will need to be reevaluated and rehired. I've heard statements from both Thorin and Saeth, and it's given me the barest glimpse of everything my brother went through in my absence. I was barely able to hold it together when they told me about his nights as the Fox, and how he was injured by the night patrol.

That wasn't in his letter, but he had to have started that before I'd left. I wish I'd known.

Then again, perhaps I deserve it, for all the years he never knew of my nights as the outlaw Weston Lark.

Emotion swells in my chest again.

A hand knocks softly on my door, and I pull out my pocket watch. It's well after midnight.

I immediately think of Quint, and my heart leaps for the briefest moment.

But of course it can't be Quint. He's dead.

I press the heel of my hand into my eyes and rise to answer the door, because I don't want to call for entry and risk waking Tessa in the next room. I know one of my brother's guards—well, one of *my* guards—is on the other side, and I really can't imagine who they'd allow to knock at this hour.

When I draw the door open, I'm both surprised and not at all to find Lochlan.

There are a thousand things I could say to send him away. *It's late. You should be sleeping. You don't need to be here. What are you doing?*

But his eyes are dark and intent on mine, and somehow I know he can feel the weight that's threatening to crush the air out of my lungs. Every single word stops in my throat.

Saeth is the guard standing along the wall behind him. My brother said quite a bit about Saeth and Thorin and their loyalty in his letter. I'm not sure how to address any of it yet. The guard's voice is low and somber when he says, "Master Cresswell said you would be expecting him, Your Majesty."

My body nearly flinches at the title. Every time I hear it, I expect to see Harristan—and I have to remind myself that I never will again.

I swallow and glance at Lochlan. Now my voice doesn't want to work.

His eyes hold mine for a moment, and then he says, "Yeah. He is." He puts a hand on my shoulder and gives me a not-quite-gentle shove toward the chairs in front of the hearth, then pushes past me. "I know what you need. Come on. Sit."

In the hallway, Saeth raises his eyebrows at me, just a bit, in question. The way they'd look to my brother.

That thought is almost enough to bring tears to my eyes again, but I don't want to cry in front of Harristan's guards, and I definitely don't want to do it in front of Lochlan.

"He's fine," I say, and my voice is a rasp. Saeth nods, and I let the door fall closed.

Then I just stare at it. It's late and I'm tired and my brother is dead.

Behind me, something thumps against the table. I turn to find Lochlan setting two glasses on the sideboard. He uncorks a bottle of amber liquid.

"I'm surprised you're still here," I say, and I mean it. The day has been full of tense discussions and interrogations and so many demands and gatherings that my head wants to spin. It was clear that Lochlan was overwhelmed in the first hour, and I told a servant to find him quarters and a hot meal at the first opportunity. I later sent word that he was under no obligation to stay.

"Karri didn't want to leave Tessa yet." He glances at the closed door to the bedroom. "Is she sleeping?"

"Yes."

"Karri, too. But I knew you'd be awake."

"Still breathing," I say roughly.

"Still drinking, too." He pours an inch into each glass. "This time, you can have all you want."

I don't move away from the door. "I really can't."

He lifts one of the glasses. "Come on, Cory."

Cory. The name slams into me so hard that I feel the impact. It's a fist to the gut, an arrow to the chest. I can't breathe. My heart feels like it must have stopped. My knees seem to be buckling.

Lochlan moves forward to catch me, and before I can stop myself, my breath is hitching against his shoulder.

"I know," he says, and his voice is so very quiet.

"I should have been here," I say, the words a desperate gasp.

"I know."

"I could have helped him."

"I know."

"I tried to get back as quickly as I could."

"And you did."

My breathing shudders again, but he doesn't let go. I don't know how long we stand there like that, but when I finally straighten and scrape the tears off my face, I take what feels like my first deep breath in hours. I'm wrung out and exhausted, but somehow the knots of tension and pain around my heart have loosened.

I drop into the chair in front of the hearth. It's barely more than embers now, and I shiver. I didn't even cry like that on Tessa, and despite everything we've been through, I can't quite believe I did it to Lochlan.

A hand appears in front of me, holding a glass of the liquor he poured earlier. "Drink."

I don't take it. "It's not appropriate. Harristan never would have—"

"You're not Harristan. Drink."

"I'm the king now, Lochlan." I say this flatly, without any emotion. "You can't order me to—"

"I can hold you down and force you, and we both know it. I just don't want to tangle with the man out there. Now *take it*."

I take it. I meant what I said, though. Harristan was never one for drinking much at all. He never wanted to be seen as out of control, as under the influence, as someone who could be swayed by something as simple as a splash of liquor.

You're not Harristan.

I drain the entire glass. Lochlan does the same.

He fetches the bottle and pours more immediately. Then he lifts his glass. "To brothers."

I lift mine and tap it against his, and the ring of the crystal is like a bell in the quiet of the room. "To brothers."

When he drains this one, I don't.

It's tempting. I already feel the burn from the first, and I'm longing for any kind of release from the ache in my soul. A part of me wants to tip back the whole bottle, to find oblivion at the bottom.

But I'm remembering the countless times I tried to pour more for my brother, and the equal number of times he left his glass sitting practically full.

I never wholly understood why, but now I do. I always felt the weight of responsibility as King's Justice, but this . . . this is suddenly altogether different.

I take a sip to complete Lochlan's toast, but then I set the glass down and look into the glowing hearth.

Lochlan watches this, then sets down his empty glass. He's quiet for quite some time.

"Who's on your side here?" he eventually says.

I turn my head and look at him. "What?"

He lifts a hand and gestures around the room, indicating the manor. "Everyone has been all over you all day. Who's on your side?" He pauses, and when I don't say anything, he adds, "Is there anyone?"

"Tessa, obviously." I lift a shoulder in half a shrug. "I trust Rocco, but I know he's distracted by Olive—and it's likely she'll want to return to Ostriary to report on what's happened. He might want to go with her. Harristan put his faith in Thorin and Saeth, so I'll do the same—but that doesn't mean I have that same loyalty."

He's looking at me as if he's waiting for more.

But there isn't.

"That's it?" he says.

I nod. "Consul Beeching seems earnest, but we'll see if his promises to support my reign pan out. Roydan Pelham is older, so I have his support, but his sector is smaller and he doesn't have a lot of political sway. Arella Cherry and I would often argue over my methods as King's Justice. She's already begun to make demands and may not completely support me as king. But the consuls might not even matter at this point. There's been too much corruption. The *people* may not support me as king."

He frowns. "I heard them cheering."

"You heard them cheering because I was *alive*. The laws of

succession were not at risk. There would be no war while consuls fought over the throne. Wait until it sinks in that Cruel Corrick is now King Corrick. It likely already has."

Lochlan studies me.

I study him right back. "I promise you, there are people in Kandala right this instant—possibly in this very manor—having fireside discussions just like this one, wondering who will gain my favor, and who is most at risk now that I'm in power." I sit back in my chair, then lift a hand, indicating the manor the way he just did. "And they're plotting my death, just like you once plotted my brother's."

Lochlan goes very still. After a moment, he draws a long breath, then runs a hand across his jaw. "All right. You've got one more."

"You're plotting against me?" It would almost be funny if it weren't all so serious. "Should I call for Saeth, or are you just going to pull my hair again?"

"No, you idiot. I'm on your *side*." He pauses. "I can stay. If you need me to."

My heart pounds at the offer, and I feel the need to glance away. I don't want to acknowledge how very much I want to accept. "Unfortunately, ruling a kingdom isn't like running the streets of Silvesse, Lochlan. Life at court is . . . complicated."

"You taught me to read while figuring out a way to keep us alive, then ended their war and took out Rian's biggest rival. I think ruling Kandala might be *easier*." He grimaces. "But you're going to have to help me, because I don't know who all these people are. I'm sure I'm going to use the wrong fork at dinner or start a war because I have no idea what *brocade* is."

"Your fabric knowledge is *truly* the least of my worries."

"That's a *fabric*?"

I smile in spite of myself, but then it flickers and fades. I keep thinking of the people waiting to watch me fail. Those knots around my heart feel like they've begun to tighten already. Acknowledging *want* and *need* feel too close to all the things we always used to hide. Harristan's letter warns me against it, but I've spent too many years protecting myself against any vulnerability, and I've already been too vulnerable tonight. Keeping a former rebel leader by my side could have far-reaching ramifications. I already saw Consul Beeching's look when I told him that Lochlan could follow us to the manor.

I run a finger around the edge of my glass. "This is a truly generous offer, but I can manage."

"I know you can." His eyes hold mine.

My heart pounds a little harder, but I say nothing.

He shrugs a little. "You know—it would make Karri feel better, to stay here for Tessa. So she wouldn't be alone. Especially if Olive leaves."

"For Tessa, then," I say. "And Karri."

He puts out a hand. "I suppose we'll have to put up with each other a *little* longer. For their sake."

I clasp it, gripping tight. "You're learning already."

———

The nights are interminable, but the days pass quickly. For all the people I had to talk to as King's Justice, there are somehow more who demand my attention as king. They all want something from me, and it's often far more than they're offering in return. I'm desperate to leave Artis and return to the Royal Sector, but dozens of prosperous families have already offered to host us—and I know that throwing favor to one will cause a tizzy among the others.

More than once, I stare at the ceiling of my bedroom after yet another exhausting day and say to Tessa, "I'm so grateful to Harristan for allowing me to start from *scratch*."

Lochlan has joined me for many of my meetings. Everyone is shocked at his presence, but no one questions me. When they question *him*, I'm ready to speak in his defense, but I don't need to. He's always quick to defend himself. As days pass, I'm surprised to discover that his unsophisticated manner is rather useful—or maybe I've just grown accustomed to it. But he'll ask questions that no one else would dare to voice, or say things no one else would dare to utter. I still want to hire him a governess with a switch, but I also don't mind when Baron Pepperleaf comes to pay his respects, and Lochlan tells him he should start packing for the Hold.

Tessa herself is a balm, a constant source of comfort. She wraps herself around me at night and allows me to whisper my fears. During the day, she's by my side as well, always fearless, always unhesitating in front of the people, always kind.

In my letter from Harristan, I have strict instructions for the week after my return, so exactly seven days after my arrival, I call for a carriage at dawn, and Tessa and I climb inside. I have two dozen guards now, all of whom were among the palace guard before the palace was destroyed, but I know what happened to my brother and I'm still not entirely sold on their loyalty. It's nowhere near enough, but I haven't yet put anyone in charge of hiring more. Today, at least, we have Thorin.

Tessa is watching the world pass by outside the window. "Harristan didn't say *why* we have to do this?" she says.

"No," I tell her. "Just that he made a promise, and he'd like for me to fulfill it."

We don't go far, just down near the docks, to where some narrow townhouses have been built along the water. It's not far from the line of tents that still stand, even though the attack on the people in the Wilds is long since over and it would be safe for them to return to their homes. I understand that the destruction was purposeful, and a lot of them don't have homes to return to.

When we stop, the guards take a position around the carriage, because we've already generated a fair amount of gawking.

Thorin opens the door to the carriage and stands at attention. "I'll knock for you, Your Majesty."

"No need," I say. "I'll do it." Because that was in my brother's letter, too.

"He would have come to the manor," Thorin says. "I could have sent a summons."

"No," I say. "My instructions were very clear."

When I knock, I'm very aware of the small crowd that gathers on the street. I haven't spent much time outside the consul's manor yet, and I hate how the feeling of freedom on the streets in Ostriary feels like vulnerability here. Especially when people begin to whisper.

But then the door swings open, and I'm facing Adam Saeth, in a loose tunic and trousers, with a little girl clinging to his neck. She's clutching a torn doll that's a bit filthy, but clearly well loved.

"Your Majesty," Saeth says in surprise. He glances at Tessa and the guards and carriage, and concern flickers through his expression. "What—why—?" He frowns and whispers something to the little girl, then sets her on her feet. "How may I serve?"

"I am here to call on Mistress Saeth, if she is receiving visitors," I say. "I have strict instructions from my brother to visit her, in her home, every week."

He stares at me.

"He was quite firm on this point," I add.

Saeth doesn't move.

After a moment, the little girl tugs at his tunic and whispers, "Da? Should I fetch Mama?"

"Ah . . . yes," he says.

But before the little girl can go anywhere, a voice calls out from behind him. "Adam? Adam, is it the young man from the bakery again? Tell him I simply do not *need* any more raisin bread—"

"Leah," says Saeth, a touch too sharply, and then his wife appears.

She's holding a baby against her shoulder, and she takes one look at me and goes as wide-eyed as her husband.

"Oh," she gasps.

"Our *king*," says Saeth, with gentle emphasis, "was told by his late brother to visit you every week."

Now it's her turn to stare at me. I'm uncomfortably aware of how many people have gathered in the street now.

"He didn't say *why*," I add solemnly—though, seeing their family, I believe I'm beginning to understand some of it. "But if my brother made a promise, I'll keep it."

Mistress Saeth takes a step forward, and to my surprise, her eyes glisten, just a bit. Her voice is very soft when she speaks. "Your brother was a very good man, facing a horrible time. He had to make terrible choices. I am so sorry he's gone."

Her emotion catches me before I'm ready, and my chest tightens dangerously. I could listen to people sob at my feet in the Hold and not crack, but when people talk about Harristan, I can barely keep it together.

Her eyes hold mine, and whatever she sees there makes a solitary tear spill down her cheek. She reaches toward my face, before catching herself. "I'm sorry." She casts a worried glance at her husband. "I'm sure I'm not allowed to touch you."

I'm so aware of the people, of the ache in my heart. Harristan would never let anyone touch him. I wouldn't either, honestly. There was a reason I didn't mind when people called me Cruel Corrick, that I allowed the illusion of the heartless executioner to form. Displaying vulnerability would be reckless. In moments like this, I wish I could go back to my nights of donning a mask as Weston Lark.

But Tessa reaches out and squeezes my hand, and I remember something she said to me months ago, during one of our countless talks about how I wanted to make things better for Kandala.

Corrick, you hid everything that you are.

No more hiding.

I give Mistress Saeth a nod. "You can touch me," I say.

I don't know if I expect her to put a hand on my shoulder or against my face, but she doesn't do either. She thrusts the squealing baby at her husband, then wraps her arms around me in a hug.

It's so unexpected, but the warmth and empathy in the motion is so real. To my surprise, it doesn't summon more emotion, but it helps settle something inside me. It lets me breathe, chasing back my tears instead of summoning more.

"I must have looked *truly* miserable," I say against her shoulder.

She gives a little laugh, then kisses me on the cheek before letting go.

Like the moment it happened on Silvesse, I'm struck by the motion, and I freeze.

Mistress Saeth blushes a bit. "Forgive me. I forgot myself, Your Majesty."

I shake my head. "I appreciate your compassion. And I'm very glad my brother sent me."

Her blush deepens. "You ... you don't need to come every week."

"If he promised, I will."

"No, I'm certain you're very busy." She glances at her husband, who's still staring at us, and is quite ignoring the baby who's chewing on the lacing of his shirt. "And I really don't think Adam's heart could take it."

Saeth scowls. "*Leah.*"

The little girl slips forward and holds up her arms to me, as if she wants a hug now, too. Saeth sighs and reaches for her. "Ruby—"

But I catch the little girl under the arms and pick her up, and she wraps around my neck only a *little* too tightly. There are gasps among the gathered crowd, and I'm not surprised. I don't think I was ever hugged by a child as Prince Corrick.

Tessa smiles. "You're going to end up getting hugs all over Kandala."

Saeth sighs again. "And a knife in the ribs, if this keeps up. Your Majesty—"

"Really, Captain," I say to him. "I rather doubt I'm in any danger from your daughter."

"No, but I—" Then he stops short at what I said. His wife gasps. Even Thorin snaps his head around. But he smiles.

I look at Mistress Saeth. "Would your husband's heart be able to take a promotion?"

She breathes in. Glances at her husband, and then back at me. "Yes. Yes, it would."

I turn back to Saeth. "It would likely be terrible in the beginning. There is much work to be done, still. But the hours would be better."

"It would take me out of your personal guard," he says.

"I know," I say. "But if I am to rebuild, I need to do it with people I can trust. The position is yours if you want it."

"Yes. I do. Thank you."

I glance at the few guards who've traveled with me. "Salute your new captain, gentlemen." When they do, Thorin reaches out to clap Saeth on the shoulder.

I turn my head to look at the little girl. "I'm afraid I need my neck back now."

She giggles, and a little more of the tension around my heart eases. When I set her down, I realize that more of a crowd has grown, and I look beyond them to take in all the tents and structures that have been built to hold the people who fled here from the Wilds.

Thorin has drawn open the door to the carriage. "Back to the consul's manor, Your Majesty?"

I look at the dark interior, considering everything that's waiting for me. Again, I wish for moonlit paths and the mask so I could be an outlaw instead of a king who has to lock himself away for endless meetings and arguments and interminable loneliness.

But then I realize I don't need to wish for anything at all.

I reach out and take Tessa's hand. "No," I say to Thorin. I look down at Tessa, then brush a kiss along her knuckles. "It's a beautiful morning," I say to her. "Would you care to go for a walk?"

CHAPTER FORTY-ONE

Tessa

As the weeks pass and the air turns cooler, Corrick and I walk among the people every day. We've visited every sector, spending days on the road, and at every opportunity, we leave the confines of stuffy meeting rooms, and instead choose to talk to anyone, of any status. Often we're joined by Lochlan and Karri, or Olive and Ellmo—who seem in no hurry to return to Ostriary. There are still rumors that King Harristan was conspiring with Consul Sallister to poison the people, but word has spread that the king and Palace Master sacrificed themselves to stop the poisonings and save all of Kandala, so as time passes, Harristan is viewed as a hero in most people's eyes, not a traitor.

People are less certain of Corrick, because of his reputation as King's Justice. At first, people look at our guards and keep a safe distance—but it doesn't take long for rumor to spread that their new king is at ease among the people.

A more potent rumor is that their new king was once an

outlaw who secretly helped the people because he was powerless to stop the corruption in the palace. This one seems to stick and grow. They love the mystery of it. He's confronted with it all the time.

"Is it true, Your Majesty?" someone will whisper. "Were you an outlaw?"

Sometimes he'll pretend not to hear, and he'll just give them a wink. Or he'll pull me close and say, "No more an outlaw than my beloved Tessa." When the inquiries have an edge to them, Lochlan will often scoff, "Why would a spoiled prince be an outlaw?"

But it's Olive who says one day while we're walking through the market in Steel City, "The Outlaw King! Your Majesty, I had no idea I was negotiating with a secret rebel." She gives him a bump with her shoulder.

But *the Outlaw King* sticks somehow, and we begin to hear it often. In the streets, in quiet murmurs, in messages left at the gates of the consul's manor. At first, the remaining consuls seem a bit outraged, telling Corrick that it's disrespectful and that it could lead to the elites turning against him.

"They already turned against me," he says hotly. "If the people think I'm one of them, I welcome it. The elites could do with a little humility."

And that shuts them up.

He's as brave and steadfast as I've ever seen him during the day, and I'm frequently reminded of that moment on the ship when I lay across his chest and thought of the way he'd changed, becoming more determined. More resolved. I see it in his manner with the remaining consuls, in his demeanor with the guards, even in his unlikely friendship with Lochlan.

It's at night that he shares his grief, in our quiet moments together where he doesn't have to be an outlaw *or* a king. He can simply be Corrick.

"I sometimes feel like I see them in the crowds," he murmurs late one night, when we're curled together and a late autumn draft has started to slip through the shutters. "Isn't that ridiculous?"

"No," I say. "I thought I saw my parents for *months*."

He kisses me on the temple. "I almost called out the other day. It was just a man and his son pushing a food cart. I would've made a fool of myself."

I swallow the lump in my throat, because I hear the *need* pulsing under his voice. He misses his brother so much. He misses his best friend. "You wouldn't have."

He faces challenges, too. Assassination attempts are frequent. Some are amateurish and easily stopped. But some are more nefarious, and people have breached the manor's defenses. I know Corrick is eager to return to the palace, which is more defensible. The wealthy patrons from every sector who come to call are almost worse. Everyone wants something from him. Everyone wants to pledge their "loyalty," and for the first time, I find myself turning a bit cynical. It hasn't escaped my notice that anyone with a daughter of marrying age brings her along to meet the new king, so she can pay her respects. Some of them are so obvious I half expect them to climb right into his lap.

What's amusing is that Corrick pays them so little attention that I don't think he's even aware of it, until the night we're preparing for bed and he says, "If Zora Chandliss loosened her corset any further, I'm not sure her dress would have stayed on at the dinner table."

That makes me smile. "Oh, you noticed this one, did you?"

He frowns. "I notice all of them. I was hoping you didn't."

"I notice all of them, too," I say, pulling at the laces of my own corset. The maid seems to have knotted it. "I know what they're doing."

He catches my waist, forcing me still. "Are they upsetting you?"

His eyes are so earnest, so intent. I have the sense that I could say *yes*, and he'd order every single young woman to be stopped at the gate. I shake my head.

"I know who you are," I say softly, and I press a hand to his cheek, letting my thumb drift along his lip. He leans into my hand and takes a breath.

"I could make them all go away," he says, and his hands are warm and heavy against my waist.

"Oh, Corrick, you don't have to order the guards to tell them to go away. Honestly. They're just doing what their families tell them to—"

"I meant I could ask you to marry me."

My hand freezes against his cheek.

"It would be different now," he says in a bit of a rush. "There will be demands, expectations, *risks*. It's not like when I was simply Prince Corrick—"

"Oh yes, when you were *simply* Prince Corrick. Truly the simplest time of my life."

A smile finds his face, but his eyes are still serious. "You've seen a bit of it, these past few weeks. As my companion, you can be overlooked. As my betrothed, you could not. There will be pressures, as well. There are always worries when there is not a clear heir. My life is always at risk now, and yours would be, too. Even more than it is already." He pauses. "To say nothing of future children. You know what was done to Harristan."

He's talking about the poison, the way consuls tried to manipulate his parents—though his parents certainly weren't innocent either. A little spike of fear pierces my heart, and I swallow.

"This is quite the proposal," I say roughly.

"It's not a proposal yet," he says quietly. "I didn't want you to feel obligated to say yes. I wanted to make sure you knew you could say no. That no part of *me* expected you to uphold these—"

"I love you," I say. "Of course I'm going to say yes."

His eyes are still troubled. "You don't *need* to say yes. We could remain together without—"

"Corrick." I step into him and press a soft kiss to his lips. "There could be a dozen crossbows pointed at me, and I'm not going to say no."

"Let's try to avoid that part, shall we?" He kisses me back, pulling me tightly against him. In moments like this, I can forget everything else for a breath of time, and we can just be Corrick and Tessa, together against the night, the way we always were.

But then he draws back, and I blink in the firelight of our manor bedroom, and he's the king trying to hold a country together, talking about marriage and the pressure to create an heir and poisoned children.

I'm just Tessa, a girl who fell in love with him.

All of a sudden, I'm reminded of the day I asked if Harristan was inviting someone to dinner. The way Corrick said, *Haven't you noticed? My brother never invites a companion.*

"You don't have to ask me to marry you," I say immediately. "*You* don't have to feel obligated. You don't even have to keep me here. Corrick, if this is a mistake, if you should be marrying someone who will give you more political leverage, if I'm putting you in greater danger—"

"Tessa, stop."

"I'm serious." I draw back, realizing I've been looking at all those other girls all wrong. "I'm not a political ally to you."

"Tessa, you helped me negotiate a peaceable treaty with Ostriary. You helped me see the ways I could be a better King's Justice. You've stood by my side throughout countless attacks. When you were trapped on Ostriary, you took action to help the people. Even when you believed in Rian, it was his conviction that inspired you, and seeing that inspired *me*. Truly, how could you be a *better* political ally?"

I flush. "Well, when you put it that way . . ."

He smiles. "There's no obligation. There's no better choice."

I stare up at him. "Then my answer will be yes," I whisper, and he swallows. "But don't do it because of the girls," I add quickly, "or . . . or because of the consuls or because you're under pressure or because of anything that worries you. Do it because you *want* to. Do it whenever *you're* ready."

Emotion flickers in his eyes, just for a moment before he blinks it away.

"And when you have a ring," I say lightly, trying to take some of the intensity out of the moment. "Not when you're warning me about threats against the Crown."

He presses a hand to my cheek. "Yes, my love."

That catches my heart and gives it a squeeze. I blush and turn away, tugging at the lacing of my corset again. "Now if you don't mind, the maid tied these knots something *fierce*—"

He catches my hand and turns me back around. Without hesitation, he drops to one knee.

There's a ring in his hand, and a determined look in his eye.

"Tessa Cade," he says, "I'm ready now."

⚊✛⚊

Corrick is right. Once we're engaged, it's worse. Suddenly people are asking *me* for favors, sending me requests, attempting to use me to gain his favor. One morning Corrick and Lochlan head to Steel City to meet with three barons who are volleying for who should be named consul, and I've gratefully remained behind with Karri and Olive because I simply can't take the glorified bickering much longer. We're eating lunch in my sitting room when a guard knocks to announce that I have a visitor.

When the man calls out, "Laurel Pepperleaf, Miss Cade," I choke on my food.

"Tessa!" Karri hisses.

I gulp down half a cup of tea. "I'm fine," I sputter. "I just—her father was in league with Allisander. Corrick said she was interested in my medicine because she was trying to make sure I didn't find out about the poison. I have no idea why she could be here."

Olive sits back in her chair. "Well, I'm not leaving."

I give her a look and tell the guard to send the woman in.

The last time I saw her, Laurel Pepperleaf was resplendent in a silk gown, her blond hair gleaming, the picture of perfect wealth and privilege. She hasn't lost the air of sophistication and wealth, but her eyes are shadowed, her hair pinned back, her clothing more demure.

When she enters the room, I don't say a word. I don't even stand.

Cynicism has set in, for *sure*.

She hesitates, then offers me a curtsy. "Thank you for agreeing to see me," she says. "I wanted to congratulate you on your engagement."

I don't thank her, and I don't beat around the bush. "When we met," I say, "you seemed interested in my medicine. I was eager to talk to you, especially when you were so interested in going to Ostriary. I was disappointed to learn you were simply trying to protect your father's interests in poisoning the people of Kandala."

She jerks like I've hit her. "No! That's not what I was doing. I *was* genuinely interested in your medicine." She swallows. "And I really did want to go to Ostriary."

"To make sure we didn't learn the truth?"

"No. To find more Moonflower."

I study her. "I find it hard to believe that your father was working in league with Allisander Sallister and you were attempting to work against him."

"My father is in the Hold. But I didn't know what they were doing. My family has been friends with the Sallisters for generations. My grandfather was a consul! Until the truth was revealed about Ostriary, I never had any idea they were a part of . . . all this."

I study her, remembering the maps in Rian's palace, the way one of the sectors was marked with *Pepperleaf* instead of *Sallister*.

In my silence, she takes a step closer to me. "I really *did* want to know about your medicine." Her voice almost cracks. "I begged him to come to court that night because I wanted to meet you."

Olive and Karri exchange a glance across the table, then look at me.

"I don't believe you," I say. "And I don't know what you could possibly want from me now. I can't pardon your father. I wouldn't even if I could."

Her face crumples, and she presses her hands to her eyes—and that tells me all I need to know. She came to beg for a pardon. There's a part of me that's disappointed, that it's something so simple, so easily rejected—and so inappropriate. She had to know I would refuse. What did she think, that I would let her father out of prison because she's pretty and begged?

But I haven't grown cynical enough to say something like that, and I can feel the true pain behind her tears.

"I'm sorry," I say to her more quietly. "I know he's your father. But you must be aware that deceiving the entire population of Kandala is not something worthy of a pardon."

"I know." She wipes at her face. "I don't want a pardon. You're right—he doesn't deserve a pardon." She stares at me, her eyes still glistening. "Haven't you ever trusted someone, only to find out everything you thought you knew was a lie?"

My breath almost catches. Luckily, I've been getting a lot of practice in the last few weeks at being less reactive. "More than once," I say. "If you don't want a pardon, then why are you here?"

"When my father was committed to the Hold, his fortunes reverted to me," she says. She shudders. "It feels like blood money."

"It is," I say.

"That's why I don't want it. I want you to take it, and I want you to put it to use wherever it will have the greatest effect. All of it."

I go completely still. It's Karri who gasps.

"Perhaps you could start rebuilding homes in the Wilds," Olive says. "I've seen some of the destruction."

"Or building schools!" says Karri. "Now that no one is sick, the people could learn—"

I lift a hand. "This *still* won't grant your father a pardon," I say to Laurel.

"He doesn't deserve a pardon," she says, and even though her eyes are still red, her voice is tight and firm.

We stare at each other, and I remember something Quint said to me, the night I met Laurel.

Don't let them make you *cynical, my dear.*

I press a hand to my chest, feeling a pulse of loss. It's a good reminder. A needed reminder. Because Laurel didn't *have* to do this. She could have given the money to her friends. She could have spread it among her own sector. She could have thrown it into the sea.

And I realize that I'm as guilty of judging her as other people were of *me*, when I first came to the palace. Maybe with cause, but she doesn't deserve it.

My voice gentles. "I'll discuss your offer with Corrick," I say. I hesitate, wondering if I should apologize for misjudging her, but maybe that should wait until after this is settled, and she's proven to be trustworthy.

Maybe a *little* skepticism is good.

She offers me another curtsy. "Thank you, Miss Cade."

Once she's gone, I pick up my tea to take a sip, and I realize Karri and Olive are both staring at me. Now it's Karri who has tears in her eyes.

"Don't cry yet," I say, then pick up a pastry. "We'll see if she actually makes good on that offer."

She reaches out to poke me in the arm. "That's not why I'm crying!"

"Why are you crying?" I demand.

"Because of *you!*" she says.

"Why on earth are you crying because of *me*?"

Karri looks at Olive across the table, who also looks the tiniest bit misty-eyed. But Olive simply looks back at her. "I don't think it's fully sunk in yet."

"*What?*" I demand.

"Tessa, my dear friend." Karri reaches out and puts a hand over mine. "You are going to make a great queen."

CHAPTER FORTY-TWO

Corrick

Two months after we arrive, we're given word that we are able to return to the Royal Sector. The east wing of the palace is now habitable, though the central portion and the west wing will take at least a year of repairs.

Lochlan and Karri have been staying with us in Consul Beeching's manor, but when servants begin packing to return to the Royal Sector, I'm surprised to hear from Tessa that Lochlan and Karri are planning to return to their small apartment in Artis.

I go to find Lochlan, and he's loading his own belongings into a trunk.

"The servants would have gotten to your quarters," I tell him.

He snorts. "I don't need *servants*."

"Well, they would have." I pause. "Are you really not moving to the palace?"

"I don't belong in the palace." He gestures around the room. "I really didn't belong *here*. I shouldn't have stayed this long, but I was worried these people were going to tear you apart."

"Oh, they're still going to try."

"I know." He studies me. "But you're on your feet now." He pauses. "Your Majesty."

I'm still not used to it. The title tugs at me in a way that hurts.

I wonder if it did that to Harristan after our father died. I wonder if it will ever stop.

I cross my arms and lean against the doorway. "How will you keep up your studies?"

It's a genuine question. When he determined to stay, I hired him a tutor the very next day.

Lochlan looks back at the things he's packing. "Karri will help me. You don't need to keep paying someone."

"I didn't mind."

He says nothing to that, and silence builds between us for a while.

Eventually, I break it. "Do you really want to leave?"

He scoffs. "I already told you. I don't belong there."

"That's not what I asked."

His hands go still on his belongings. "You've done enough for me. I can go back to my job in the forges and stop making a fool of myself in front of all these people."

"You're not making a fool of yourself. I rather liked it when you told Baron Vannerling to go stick his head in the watering trough if he needed to cool off."

Lochlan smiles.

"And I could give you a job in the palace," I add.

"Cleaning privies? No thank you."

I raise my eyebrows. "The role of King's Justice is open."

He stares at me.

"Rather unexpectedly," I add.

"Shut up, Cory." He goes back to packing.

"I'm making a genuine offer, Lochlan. I've been receiving increasing pressure to name someone to the role, and I need someone I can trust, but who would be willing to stand firm when we differ on matters of importance. I had considered one of my brother's guards, but I don't know that they would contradict me when necessary."

He says nothing to that.

"For example," I continue, "I'm not sure I could find another person in the kingdom who would say, 'Shut up, Cory,' directly to my face."

He grins. "I bet I could."

"*Exactly* why you're perfect for the role."

He sobers. "I wouldn't be like you."

"I don't want you to be like me. That's why I'm asking you."

"What's the pay?"

I can tell that he's teasing, but I tell him anyway. He blanches. Sits down.

I smile and turn away from his door. "Get used to servants," I call.

CHAPTER FORTY-THREE

Tessa

Six months after we return from Ostriary, life in Kandala begins to go back to normal. Once each sector had a named consul and Corrick was residing in the palace, he had an official coronation, and people traveled from all over the sectors to watch him accept his crown. He turned twenty on the day before his coronation, and there's a part of me that will always wonder if he deliberately waited, as if he didn't want to be crowned king at nineteen the way his brother was forced to be.

Like Harristan, Corrick is always busy, always in demand, always talking to someone or reading something or sitting in a meeting. I still see his grief in private, though, and I remember my talks with Olive, the way my grief over *him* would sneak up and hit me when I least expected it. But he lost his brother and his best friend all at once, and I sometimes worry that he won't recover.

Corrick was right about Erik Rocco, and the first time Olive leaves Kandala to return home, Erik is right by her side. I hug them both so tightly before they go, and I tell him he'd better be on the ship when she comes back. They've been back and forth from Ostriary three times now, always bringing lumber in exchange for steel—since we no longer need Moonflower—and I know Corrick is happy to see that she's kept Mouse among her crew, because the man refuses to call him anything but Captain Lark.

The last time Olive visited, however, I couldn't help noticing that she couldn't keep a single meal in her stomach.

"Olive!" I whisper at her when we're alone, glancing at her stomach deliberately.

"Hush!" she says. "It's early yet." She pauses. "But Erik and Mouse might be making a few runs without me in the spring, if that's all right. But I'll be back for your wedding next summer."

"Of course it's all right!"

She bites at her lip. "Rian has asked if he might visit while I'm away."

Well, that socks the joy right out of me. Rian has always looked after his people, so I know he's been taking care of Ostriary, but the last time he came here, he caused nothing but trouble. "Why?"

"I think he'd like to apologize," she says. "To start anew."

"Do you think he really means it?" I say.

Olive heaves a sigh. "I can never really tell with him."

I think about everything Rian did wrong, the way he double-crossed so many people. I remember clinging to the ropes high above the ocean, wanting to trust in his ideals. It's so tempting to tell her yes, to think that Rian might be able to come here and forge a new beginning.

But unlike Laurel Pepperleaf, I don't know if I could ever trust him.

"Tell him I'll send word when I'm ready for him to visit," I say, and she smiles.

I hug her twice as tight before she leaves that time, and I give Erik all my apothecary notes on what to do to help with morning sickness. They beg me to visit at least once, and I keep promising to go, but I don't think I will. The memories are too raw, too harsh, too painful.

Corrick has lost too much, and I'm staying right here by his side.

It's winter now, just past the solstice. We haven't had much snow yet in the Royal Sector, but the northern sectors are probably getting quite a bit in the mountains. This was always a challenging season in the Wilds, because there was never enough food, never enough firewood. But in the palace, I can curl up with Corrick in front of a roaring fire at night, and he'll draw a blanket around us both. Karri and I can drink chocolate creams and play games and read books and never go cold.

I rather like winter here.

But one morning at breakfast with Corrick, a steward brings me a letter that's been delivered to the palace. It only has my name in script on the front, and a simple seal on the back. I don't recognize the handwriting, and at first, the letter makes me frown.

Miss Tessa Cade,

Thank you for allowing us to select a well-bred horse from our stable for your riding needs. We believe we have found the perfect creature, a small black palfrey that is guaranteed to be sure-footed over the cobblestone streets of the Royal Sector. You are invited to visit at your leisure to determine whether the animal is suitable.

Yours sincerely,
Sullivan Lark

I gasp out loud and drop the letter.

Corrick stares at me. "What? What is it?"

My mouth works, but no sound comes out. I can't give him one single shred of false hope. I can't.

I look back at the letter.

A small black palfrey.

That's the exact kind of horse that Harristan and I shared on the night the rebels took the Royal Sector.

Sullivan.

This can't be a coincidence. It can't.

There's an address at the bottom of the letter. It's out in Mosswell, and several hours away in this weather.

"Tessa?"

I look back at Corrick. "We need to go see a man about a horse."

CHAPTER FORTY-FOUR

Sullivan

When I hear the carriage rattling down the lane, I know. The cottage is closed up tight against the weather, and we have a fire blazing in the hearth, but I throw a scarf around my neck and head out into the swirling snow anyway.

I half expect a full contingent of guards and soldiers to be following them, but I only see two horses pulling the carriage.

Good, I think, as I shiver in the chill. Tessa was smart. This is already risky enough. My heart settles a bit.

A second later, the door bounces open behind me, and a cloak is thrown over my shoulders. "Honestly. If you're not careful, you'll catch your death of cold and you'll miss your chance at seeing him."

I'm anxious now, so my answer is just as peevish. "I don't see how that's possible with you constantly throwing clothes and blankets on me."

Quint's eyes flash my way with feigned annoyance. I reach up to brush snowflakes out of his red hair, and the annoyance is replaced with a smile.

Miller, I think. *Not Quint.*

But I can't get used to it. Even after six months, I don't want to call him by any other name. I might be accustomed to Sullivan myself, but Quint . . . will always be Quint.

"We must be formal," I warn. "We do not know who might be in attendance, and we cannot risk giving ourselves away."

"You're cautioning me?" The annoyance is back. "I am not the one who chose to send a letter directly to the *palace.*"

"It's not as if I signed it," I snap. "No one is watching for letters from a long dead king."

We've been arguing about this for a week.

But then the carriage is drawing to a stop, the horses throwing up slush, and to my absolute amazement, the two palace guards who've driven the carriage are Thorin and Saeth.

As soon as they see us, they do a double take. Then Saeth grabs Thorin's arm. His eyes are wide.

"You're a ghost," he whispers.

"No," I say. "Just lucky."

They move to climb down from the front of the carriage, likely to do their duty and open the door, but I don't have the mettle to wait any longer. I stride right up and open it myself.

Then I find myself facing my brother, the king.

The shock in his face is so pure. The wonder. The relief. He's frozen in place as if he's afraid to move, as if he's afraid to *blink,* his hands braced on either side of the doorway. I'm frozen as well, because I haven't seen him since the moment he got on that ship to

Ostriary. He's so familiar and so different all at once, and I can't stop staring at him. Our breath fogs in the air between us.

Then I reach out to rough up his hair the way I did when he was a boy. "It's all right, Cory."

He practically falls out of the carriage to give me a hug. His arms are so tight against my back that I can feel his heartbeat. His breath shakes, just a little, but so does mine.

I grip him back just as tightly. "I missed you, too," I say. "It's been so hard to stay away. Quint—ah, *Miller*—has been after me for sending the letter in the first place. But I had to tell you."

He draws back to look at me. He says absolutely nothing, but then he hugs me again.

I hug him just as tightly. "We *can* go inside," I say. "If it pleases you, Your Majesty."

I'm partially teasing, partially not, and he pulls back again. He's holding me at arm's length, his eyes searching my face as if he still can't believe it. "There's a part of me that wants to punch you, you know."

"I do know," I say. "And I'm sorry."

Tessa moves close, and she sets a hand on his arm. "And there's a part of *him* that deserves it."

That seems to strike Corrick like an arrow, because he frowns and pulls back farther. "I do." But then he grabs Quint in a hug as well, but only for a moment. He draws back and gives him a look. "When I told you to take care of my brother, I'll have you know that this isn't quite what I had in mind."

Quint smiles, looking a bit too pleased with himself. "We were sharing a house together. I simply couldn't help it."

Corrick smiles in return, but I don't. I made mention of Quint in my letter to my brother, of course, but this is one thing that I've wondered about for the better part of a year.

"There were so many things I never discussed with you," I say to him. "Were you very surprised?"

"Surprised?" He takes a step back, regarding me. "Of course not. Quint could charm a brick wall into lively conversation."

"Brick walls are often *easier*," Quint says, and Tessa laughs softly.

For some reason, that makes me blush, just a little. "No—I meant—" I break off. "Never mind. It's cold. We should go inside."

But Corrick frowns. "You meant . . ." His eyebrows go up. "You thought I didn't know?"

I stare back at him, but the words catch in my throat and refuse to form.

They don't *need* to form, because he bursts out with, "How could I not know? You made eyes at that stable boy for *months*!"

"What?" I sputter.

"Every single time we went into the Wilds." His voice drops to a mockery of mine. "'Go find a game of cards, Cory. Doesn't that look like a lively dance, little brother? I'm going to go see some horses. Why don't you join those boys by the fire. I'll be back in an hour.'" He rolls his eyes. "I was young, but I wasn't *stupid*. Lord, Harristan. No one likes horses *that* much."

Quint bursts out laughing. Even the guards look like they're trying to hide a smile.

I look between the two of them. "Don't tell me. You knew *this*, too?"

Thorin and Saeth exchange a glance, but it's Saeth who shrugs. "There was that one footman who always seemed to make you tongue-tied. What was his name?"

"Murphy," Thorin says immediately.

Corrick's eyes light up. "That's right! You used to spill your tea every time, too!"

I simply cannot believe this.

Quint leans over to give me a kiss on the cheek. "So charming."

"All right," I snap. "Enough. Let's go inside with all of you. I'll take the crown back if this is how it's going to be."

—◦—

Quint heats some mulled wine while we sit by the fire. At first the guards moved to take a position by the wall, but I urged them to join us, too. It settled something in my heart to see them look to Corrick first, to know he's won their loyalty the way I did. Corrick gave me a sly look and said, "Of course you should sit with us. You're friends of Sullivan's."

"I'm so glad to see you both," I tell them. "Adam, are those a captain's bars on your sleeve?"

Saeth nods, then glances at Thorin. "I'm trying to make sure no one has cause to close ranks against *me*."

Thorin smiles. "Only when we play cards."

"And you, *Wolf*?" I say. "Do you still see Alice?"

His cheeks turn pink. "I do."

"They're getting married," says Saeth.

Thorin's blush deepens. "I'd invite you both to come, but I expect you'd be recognized."

"I could say the same thing about mine," says Corrick, and my eyes snap to his.

"Very likely," I say, and my voice goes a bit rough. There's a pulse of longing in my heart that I've felt ever since news about the royal engagement made its way to Mosswell. "I don't think I could go anywhere near the Royal Sector. Not for some time yet."

But I glance at Quint and wonder if I could convince him to go. We argued for a week over sending a letter, and it was worth it. Convincing him to sneak into the Royal Sector might take a month.

I glance across at Cory, and he's watching me like he knows what I'm thinking. His blue eyes are intent and daring. It reminds me of a thousand moments when we were younger, sitting across a table, waiting until dark when we could escape the trappings of the palace to race across the gardens and sprint through the tunnels into the Wilds.

Tessa looks between us, and she smiles. "I'll have an invitation sent anyway," she says. "If any of you are good at *anything*, it's sneaking."

"On that note," says Saeth, "how on earth did you escape? I saw the rubble from the explosion. Did you make it to one of the tunnels?"

"Yes—by sheer luck," I say. "After we lit the fuse, we ran. We got to the stairwell we used to escape that night, which was farther than I expected. But Annabeth was right. The palace *did* collapse into the lowest levels. We were trapped below for a time." I hesitate and meet Quint's eyes across the room. "Two days. Maybe three."

"I had a broken arm," Quint says. He gestures to me. "Sully had broken ribs. We were filthy and hurting when we were finally able to crawl out."

"But if you escaped," says Corrick, "why didn't you simply go back to Consul Beeching?"

"By that point, too much had happened," I say. "You were already home! They were calling you king! Consul Beeching had kept his promise. Rumors were saying that King Harristan had sacrificed himself to save the people from the wrongdoings of the consuls. We kept hearing it in the streets." I shrug. "Too much had gone wrong. Too many people had been hurt. The wheels had already been put in motion. I couldn't undo that."

"But you could have told *me*," Corrick says, and then I hear the pain undercutting the anger in his tone.

"No, Cory," I say evenly. "I couldn't."

He glares at me, drawing himself up, facing me in a way he never would have in the past.

In that one shift, I can see how he's grown into this role.

"You're proving my point," I say. "If you *knew*, you never would have risen to be king. You always would have known I was in the shadows, judging your choices, your movements, your ideas."

"Then why did you tell me at all?" he demands.

I reach out and ruffle his hair again. "Because I love you too much."

He catches my wrist, but then he grips my hand tight. His eyes gleam. "I'm very glad you did."

"So am I," says Tessa.

"Besides," says Quint as he fetches the kettle to pour steaming cups of mulled wine, "I rather like having a cottage in Mosswell. The village gossip is downright *vicious*, and Sully can play with his horses all day—"

"Wait. You really *do* have a stable?" Tessa says in surprise.

"Oh, yes," I say. "Farther down the lane. Twenty horses. We did quite a business in the fall. Should have some foals come spring, too."

Corrick looks between us in wonder. "*Twenty* horses? How did you make *that* happen with just the clothes off your backs?"

Quint and I exchange a glance. "Oh, escaping from the palace took quite a bit of time, and once we knew you'd arrived safely, it's rather possible we snuck back through some other tunnels because we knew how to reach the treasury—"

"The looters!" Corrick smacks me on the arm. "You *thief*!"

I smile. "You *outlaw.*"

Tessa lifts her cup. "Cheers, gentlemen. We can all drink to that."

ACKNOWLEDGMENTS

My sixteenth book! Is this real life?

As always, I am so incredibly grateful to my husband, Michael. The writing of this book took us through some of the weirdest times we've had, and I still remember that moment in the basement when I was sorting through books and *Letters to the Lost* fell open to the dedication page. It says, "For Michael. I'm so lucky to be on this crazy ride with you. (Mostly because we keep each other from jumping off.)" I still mean every word, and I am so thankful for every moment we have together. Thank you for being my best friend for all these years.

Mary Kate Castellani is my incredible editor at Bloomsbury, and we have now worked on TEN BOOKS together. A lot of authors don't have that privilege, and I'm amazed that we've been able to accomplish so much. Thank you so much for everything over the years.

Suzie Townsend is my phenomenal agent, and I am so grateful

for your day-to-day guidance, especially when things get tricky and complicated. I am so incredibly lucky to have you, along with Sophia Ramos, Olivia Coleman, and the entire team at New Leaf Literary on my side. Thank you all so much for everything.

The team at Bloomsbury is beyond compare when it comes to their dedication to every book they work on, and I am so grateful for everything. Huge thanks to Kei Nakatsuka, Lily Yengle, Erica Barmash, Faye Bi, Phoebe Dyer, Beth Eller, Kathleen Morandini, Valentina Rice, Diane Aronson, Jeannette Levy, Donna Mark, Hannah Bowe, Laura Phillips, Nicholas Church, Adrienne Vaughan, Rebecca McNally, Ellen Holgate, Pari Thomson, Emily Marples, Josephine Blaquiere, Barney Duly, and every single person at Bloomsbury who has a hand in making my books a success.

Huge thanks to the Cursebreaker Street Team! If you're a part of it, thank YOU. It means so much to me to know that there are *thousands* of you interested in my books, and I will never forget everything you've done to spread the word about my stories. Thank you all so very much.

Huge debts of gratitude go to Melody Wukitch, Sarah Rifield, Jodi Picoult, Gillian McDunn, Stephanie Garber, Isabel Ibañez, Bradley Spoon, Reba Gordon, and Amalie Howard, because I honestly don't know how I would get through the day without your support. I am so grateful to have you all in my life.

I kept this book very secret, so very few people were able to read it before publication, but I can't create something with *no* readers at all. I want to take a moment to specially thank Jodi Picoult and Reba Gordon for reading early chapters and offering insight.

Tremendous thanks to readers, bloggers, librarians, artists, and booksellers all over social media who take the time to post, review, tweet, share, and mention my books. I owe my career to people being so passionate about my characters that they can't help but talk about them. Thank you all.

And many thanks go to YOU! Yes, you. If you're holding this book in your hands, thank you. As always, I am honored that you took the time to invite my characters into your heart.

Finally, tremendous love and thanks to my sweet, talented, loving boys. A few months ago I was driving down the road and my nine-year-old started *sobbing* in the back seat. I nearly pulled over on the highway because I was so concerned. "What's wrong?!" I cried. He was apparently reading the acknowledgments for my books, because they found the ice cream promise in *Defend the Dawn* and he was looking for more promises. (Heh.) But he closed the book and he tearfully said, "I read what you wrote. You love us so much, Mom! You just love us so much!"

Yes, my sweet Zachary, I do. I love you all. I'm so lucky to be your mom.